Sow the Seed

Born in Gainsborough, Lincolnshire, Margaret Dickinson moved to the coast at the age of seven and so began her love for the sea and the Lincolnshire landscape. Her ambition to be a writer began early and she had her first novel published at the age of twenty-five. This was followed by many further titles including *Plough the Furrow*, *Sow the Seed* and *Reap the Harvest*, which make up her Lincolnshire Fleethaven trilogy. Many of her novels are set in the heart of her home county but in *Tangled Threads* and *Twisted Strands*, the stories include not only Lincolnshire but also the framework knitting and lace industries of Nottingham. Her 2012 and 2013 novels, *Jenny's War* and *The Clippie Girls*, were top-twenty bestsellers and her 2014 novel *Fairfield Hall* was a top-ten bestseller.

www.margaret-dickinson.co.uk

Also By Margaret Dickinson

Plough the Furrow

Reap the Harvest

The Miller's Daughter

Chaff upon the Wind

The Fisher Lass

The Tulip Girl

The River Folk

Tangled Threads

Twisted Strands

Red Sky in the Morning

Without Sin

Pauper's Gold

Wish Me Luck

Sing As We Go

Suffragette Girl

Sons and Daughters

Forgive and Forget

Jenny's War

The Clippie Girls

Fairfield Hall

Welcome Home

For Dennis, Mandy and Zoë

ACKNOWLEDGEMENTS

Although 'Suddaby' airfield is fictitious, I would like to acknowledge that the Lincolnshire Aviation Heritage Centre at East Kirkby, owned by Fred and Harold Panton, has been a valuable source of information. The fully restored Control Tower and the magnificent Lancaster B Mk VII NX611 were an inspiration.

My very special thanks to Cyril Barker, of Skegness, a Dunkirk veteran, who relived painful memories of that time in order to help me in my research.

I am also deeply indebted to Mrs Fiona Ryan, of Skegness, for the loan of her personal notebooks and papers written during her service as a WAAF.

My sincere gratitude to Mrs Betty Watson, of Skegness, an ex-WAAF, not only for sharing her memories with me but also for her wonderful help in reading through the final typescript.

And last – but never least – my love and thanks to all my family and friends especially those who read the novel in the early stages – my sister and her husband, Robena and Fred Hill; Pauline Griggs; Linda and Terry Allaway; and my daughter, Zoë, who again helped with the final draft.

M. D.
Skegness, 1995

Part One

Part One

One

LINCOLNSHIRE, 1926

'IF I say ya'll go away to boarding school, Missy, then go ya will.' Esther Godfrey wagged her finger in her daughter's face. 'And I'll have none of ya chelp neither! Not from a thirteen-year-old, I won't.'

Kate faced her mother, her insides churning. 'I'll be fourteen soon. I can leave school then. You know I can. Please, Mam . . .?' Her boldness was fading now, almost before it had begun. She could hardly believe that she had actually dared to argue with her mother. No one, but no one, defied Esther Godfrey when she stood like she was standing now; feet set apart, hands on hips and green eyes flashing fire.

They were so alike; long, rich auburn hair, the mother with hers piled high on her head, the curls held in place by combs with only escaping tendrils to soften the firm jawline; the girl with hers flying wild and free, her mouth clenched mutinously.

Esther Godfrey was a striking-looking woman, beautiful some might have said, with a smooth forehead and a well-shaped mouth. She had still retained her slim figure despite the recent birth of a child, though her breasts were rounded with the ripeness of a nursing mother's.

Hers was an expressive face; her smile could brighten the day like the sun appearing out of the clouds, but her anger was every bit as threatening as the gales that raged across the marshes from the sea.

3

And at this moment her face was like a menacing thunder-cloud.

In the wicker cradle in one corner of the kitchen, the baby began to whimper.

'Now see what ya've done – woken her up after I've spent the last hour settling her.'

Kate flung out her hand towards the cradle, with a last spark of defiance. 'It's 'cos of her you want to send me away, in't it? You don't love me any more – not since you got Lilian!'

As she saw the colour drain from her mother's face and watched her reach out to grasp the corner of the kitchen table to steady herself, Kate felt a stab of guilt. Strong though Esther was, she had given birth only three weeks ago.

'Oh, Kate . . .' The anger, too, was gone. Now there was reproach in Esther's tone. 'That's not true . . .'

With a sob Kate rushed from the kitchen, through the back scullery, wrenched open the back door and ran across the yard.

Ignoring her mother's voice calling her name, Kate ran on, across the lane and up the slope of the sand-dune. Reaching the top she paused a moment, her glance sweeping the flat marshland in front of her. Beyond the marsh was a second line of sand-dunes and then the beach and the sea.

Maybe Danny was on the beach.

She was running again, down the sandy slope and across the marsh, jumping the creeks, bounding over the tufts of grass until she gained the crest of the eastern dunes. Her gaze scanned the wide stretch of sand.

Then she saw him.

Head down, hands thrust into his pockets, he was following the high-water mark, searching for anything left by the ebbing tide.

'Danny,' she yelled. 'Danny!'

4

He looked up, waved and began to run towards her.

Breathless, she sank down into the sandy hollow that was their own special place. It had been their den, their boat, their desert island, and always, it was the place they met.

Danny took a flying leap into the hollow, landing with a thud and showering her with sand. He sat down beside her and held out his hand. On the flat of his palm sat a huge whelk shell.

'Just look at that, Kate.' Gently he blew the remaining grains of sand from the shell. 'Did ya ever see such a beauty? It's the biggest I've ever found.'

Kate stared at it, but when she made no response, she felt Danny looking at her more closely. 'What's up, Katie? You look funny – ya face is all red. You bin crying?'

'I've had a row with me mam.'

'Oh, heck! What about?'

'School.'

Danny looked puzzled.

'She's sending me to boarding school in Lincoln come September.'

'Boarding school!' He gaped at her. 'Whatever for? I thought ya'd be leaving school, like me.'

'I can't leave till I've passed me fourteenth birthday. And *that's* not till September!' Kate said moodily.

There was silence between them, then Danny grinned, sudden excitement in his voice. 'I say, guess what? I saw Squire Marshall yesterday and he's tekin' me on from next Monday. What about that then?'

She looked at him, this boy whom she had known all her life. His curly black hair shone in the spring sunlight and although his chin was still boyishly smooth and his voice had not yet broken, he seemed to be changing before her eyes almost. She couldn't get used to seeing him in long trousers. He wore a pair of proper braces now – men's braces

– but his thin arms stuck out like sticks from the rolled-up sleeves of his open-necked striped shirt. Suddenly, he seemed to be growing up – and growing away from her.

'That's nice. I'm glad.' She tried to sound pleased – for Danny's sake – but her own misery destroyed her delight in his news. 'I want to get a job too.' There was longing in her tone. 'I don't want to go to school any more.'

He was avoiding her gaze now. She watched as he picked up handfuls of sand and let it run through his fingers. He seemed so intent on what he was doing that Kate thought he had forgotten she was even there.

She prodded his bony shoulder. 'Don't ya care if I go away?'

He looked up quickly then. 'Of course I care. Ya know I do!' He leaned forward and bumped his nose against her cheek in a clumsy attempt at a kiss. 'I'll always care for you, Katie Hilton.'

Kate wasn't quite sure why he whispered it when there was only a lone black-headed gull soaring above them to hear. She giggled, embarrassed, but his gesture had banished her tears.

'Here, ya can have this.' He held out the whelk.

'Are ya sure?' Kate knew the huge shell would have taken pride of place in his collection.

'Yeah, go on, I want you to have it. Just – just so's . . .' A faint redness crept up the boy's neck. He thrust it into her hand and then stood up suddenly, pushing his hands into the pockets of his trousers. Embarrassed, he scuffed at the sand with the toe of his sturdy boot. 'So ya dun't forget me when – *if* – ya go away.'

She held the whelk to her ear and heard the sound of the sea. 'I'd never forget you anyway,' she said softly, slipping the shell into her pocket. 'Not as long as I live, I won't.'

He sat down again and resumed his sand-sifting. 'Why

does yar mam want to send you to boarding school anyway? T'ain't for the likes of us.'

Kate sighed. 'She says she dun't want me staying on the farm all me life – that she wants something better for me. But I reckon—' She hesitated and then plunged on. 'I reckon she – she wants me away from here. Away from Fleethaven Point altogether.'

He looked at her hard now. 'Why?' came the blunt question.

She smoothed her white pinafore over her knees drawn up under her chin. 'Ever since the baby came, she dun't – want me any more.' Her mouth trembled dangerously again.

'Don't be daft, Katie, 'course she does.'

'Well, it dun't feel like it.' She paused, then with a note of belligerence added, 'How would you know anyway, Danny Eland? *You've* no brothers or sisters.' She tossed her long auburn hair which fell in shining waves down her back to below her waist.

'No,' he mumbled in reply. 'But I wish I had.'

'Ya can have our squealing Lilian then – and welcome!'

They sat in silence for several moments while Danny sifted sand into little heaps and then flattened them with the palm of his hand, only to begin the process over again. 'Does . . .?' he began and then stopped.

'What?'

'Does Mester Godfrey want you to go?'

'Me dad?'

'He's yar *step*dad,' Danny reminded her pointedly.

'I know, but he's like a proper dad.'

Danny looked up. 'But ya remember yar real dad, dun't ya?'

Kate wrinkled her smooth forehead. 'Sort of. In – bits.'

They sat in silence, each trying to remember Kate's father.

But their memories were fragmented, like a jigsaw with pieces missing.

'I can just remember him coming back from the war,' Danny said. 'He was in a terrible state, wasn't he?'

'Can't remember that. But I do remember him tekin' us to town in his motor car to buy a big Christmas tree off the market.'

Danny was laughing. 'Oh, yes – we could hardly get it in your back door. I'd forgotten.'

There was another silence before Danny said softly, 'I remember his funeral though – after he drowned.'

'You held my hand when we stood at the side of the hole.' She shuddered. 'I remember that all right. Wish I could forget it, sometimes.' She frowned. 'We threw something on top of the coffin, didn't we? What was it – flowers?'

Danny shook his head. 'Just earth.'

Another silence.

Kate hugged her knees. 'Then Mr Godfrey came and married me mam and we all lived happily ever after.' She pulled a wry face. 'At least, till Lilian was born.'

'Came back, ya mean,' Danny muttered.

'Who came back? Me dad?'

'Mr Godfrey – yeah.'

'What d'ya mean – came *back*?'

'It was just – summat I heard me dad say once.'

'What?'

Danny said nothing.

'Come on, Danny, *tell* me,' Kate insisted. She scrambled up and grasped his shoulders, shaking him. 'Tell me or I'll . . .'

He caught hold of her arms and they struggled with each other like a pair of playful puppies, just as they always had throughout their childhood. Kate shrieked with laughter, her anguish forgotten for the moment as they rolled over and over, her petticoat flying, her black stockings wrinkling around her ankles. Danny was on top of her, pinning her arms back against the sand. They stared into each other's eyes, panting hard, their breath mingling.

Faintly, borne on the wind, there came the sound of a whistle. Immediately, Kate began to struggle. 'Let me up, Danny. That's me grandad coming. I'll go and meet him. He'll not let me mam send me away. He'll tell her!'

Danny released her and stood up. He held out his hands to pull her up from the sand, but before he had regained his breath, she was up and out of the sheltered sandy hollow racing down the slope of the eastern dunes. Across the flat marsh she ran, jumping the winding creeks, squelching through the mud, her long hair flying free.

'Katie – Katie, wait for me,' she heard him calling behind her. But as always she was darting ahead of him. He was still splashing through the streams as she was climbing the line of sand-dunes which ran parallel to the road leading from the town of Lynthorpe to Fleethaven Point. Then she was beneath the elder trees, slithering down into the lane.

'Grandad – Grandad!'

The rattling wheels of Will Benson's carrier's cart came to a halt. 'Why, Katie, me little lass, what are you doin' at home? Ah thought you'd be in school.'

He leaned down from his high seat on the front of the cart above the broad backs of his two horses and held out his hand to her. 'Up you come then, me lass.'

'It's still the Easter holidays, Grandad.' Kate settled herself on the narrow seat at his side and smiled up at him, tossing back the strands of hair which fluttered across her face.

'O' course it is. Ah'd forgotten. Why, here's Danny an' all,' Will said, as the boy came crashing down the wooded slope of the dunes and into the lane. 'Come on, lad, climb up. There's no room on the seat, but you can stand on the shaft. Hang on, mind.'

Danny grinned up at the carrier, caught hold of the side of the cart and pulled himself up. 'Thanks, Mester Benson. Just as far as the gate. I'd best be off home mesen.'

'Ow's it feel to be a working man, then, eh, Danny?' Will Benson laughed wheezily. There wasn't much that escaped the carrier. News travelled on his cart alongside the pots, pans and provisions.

'He dun't start till Monday, Grandad,' Kate said.

'Holiday, is it, lad, 'afore you even start? Eh, but Ah dun't know what things is coming to. Why, in my day . . .'

'Oh, Grandad!' Kate giggled and wriggled her fingers against the old man's ribs to tickle him, but she could not feel his body beneath the thick coat he wore. Although spring had arrived, it was still cold riding on the front of his cart in all weathers when the wind whipped across the flat Lincolnshire fenland. Kate loved her grandfather. As long as she could remember, he had spoilt her and could be relied upon to take her side, even against her mother. He always looked so smart, Kate thought looking up at him now, with his black trousers and pin-striped jacket and matching waist-coat, a gold watch-chain looped across his narrow chest. She only had to ask for him to pull the watch out of his pocket and hold it to her ear to listen to its tiny tick-tick-tick. And his boots, resting on the foot-board, shone so that she could almost see her face in their hard, rounded toe-caps. She liked it in summer when he wore a rakish boater-shaped hat, but today he still wore his winter cap against the cold. His smooth hair was almost completely white with only a few strands of the ginger colour it had once been still showing. Will Benson's old eyes twinkled down at her and he wiggled his white moustache. 'You'll be losing yar playmate then, eh, Katie?'

Remembering suddenly, the smile fled from her face.

'Grandad – ya've got to speak to me mam. She's going to send me away. To boarding school. Ya won't let her, will ya, Grandad?'

Will Benson slapped the two horses with the reins and above the rattle of the cart's wheels he asked, 'What? What's that you say?'

Raising her voice, Kate repeated, 'Me mam's sending me to boarding school in Lincoln, come September. I dun't want to go, Grandad. I'll hate it!'

'Huh!' Will made a disapproving noise and muttered something that sounded like 'We'll see about this'. Above the noise of the cart-wheels, however, Kate could not be sure exactly what he had said.

But she was sure the moment he opened the back door of the farmhouse and stepped into the back scullery.

'Esther,' he bellowed. 'You here, Esther?'

'In here, Dad,' came her mother's voice. Kate followed her grandfather into the kitchen.

Esther Godfrey was standing at the large kitchen table. A thick blanket was spread upon it and an old sheet, worn to transparent thinness, on top of that. Two flat irons were heating on the range while she worked with a third ironing the previous morning's wash. From the wicker cradle in the far corner came the baby's mewling.

'Oh, there you are, Missy! And just where did you disappear to?' her mother began and Kate was sure she added under her breath, 'As if I need to ask!'

Peeping round the comforting figure of her grandfather and using his presence as a buffer against her mother's wrath, Kate said, 'I've been on the beach with Danny.'

She saw her mother's mouth tighten. 'I thought as much. Into the scullery and wash yar hands. Dinner's in ten minutes, now yar grandad's here.'

Kate obeyed, but left the door ajar so that she could peep through the crack and listen to their conversation.

In a tone that Kate could not remember having heard him use before, Will said, 'What's this Katie tells me about you sending her away to school?'

She saw her mother glance up in surprise, the iron suspended in mid-air before it thudded down on to one of the baby's white frocks.

'Well?' Will Benson's tone was sharp.

The iron came up again, the tiny dress was flicked over and the iron thudded down once more. In the grate of the huge black range a log fell, sending a shower of sparks up the flue.

'I'm thinking about it – that's all.' Her mother's tone was terse. 'Nothing's settled – yet.'

'Ya shouldn't be even *thinking* about sending the bairn away. A country bairn in a *city*! Lass'll pine away. Besides, how can you afford the fees them fancy schools charge?'

'I've scrimped and saved – that's how. I've still got me box under the bed and there's not a week goes by but I don't add a shillin' or two. I can afford it, Dad, I've minded that.'

Will grunted, casting about for another objection now that one had been foiled. 'Ya trying to turn her into something she's not . . .'

'Dad – I've got to get her away from here. Now she's growing older. You know why. It's for her own good.'

And although Kate strained her ears, it seemed as if her grandad made no reply to her mother's puzzling statement.

Two

'Kate. Kate, where are you?'

'Here, Dad, in the wash-house.'

Jonathan Godfrey appeared in the doorway. 'Samphire's about to calve. Do you want to watch?'

'Me mam's set me to mash these 'tates for the little pigs. Then she said I'd to go to bed.'

'Bed? This early?' His blue eyes sparked with mischief, the tanned skin around them wrinkling with laughter-lines. He brushed back the lock of fair hair that fell in a gentle flick over his forehead. 'What have you been doing to deserve such dire punishment?'

Kate breathed in the smell of steaming potatoes, just out of the copper in the corner of the wash-house. As she thumped the wooden masher down, splitting open the brown skins and releasing the creamy potato, her hair fell forward like a curtain, hiding her face. 'I was late back from the beach,' she muttered.

'And?' he prompted. 'There's got to be more than that.'

'I forgot to feed the hens 'afore I went to play with Danny.'

'Ah – with Danny.' She thought she heard him sigh softly, but his eyes were twinkling at her as he added, teasing gently, 'And forgetting the hens. Dear me, that explains it.'

She smiled ruefully and continued mashing the potatoes with a steady, easy motion.

'Well,' he was saying, 'I could do with a little help . . .'

She tossed back her hair, her eyes shining. 'Aw, thanks, Dad.'

He put his forefinger to his lips. 'Not a word to your mother.' He turned to go. 'Samphire's in the little barn, Kate. There's more room there than in the cowshed.'

The girl nodded, understanding immediately. This particular cow out of their small herd of four was temperamental at the best of times. She had to be hoppled sometimes just to be milked; calving, she'd be even more difficult. They'd need plenty of space to avoid her kicking hooves.

A little later Kate crossed the yard to the small barn lying between the cowshed and the stables. As she stepped into the dim interior and pulled the door closed behind her, a rat scuttled along a rafter above her head. She glanced up and smiled briefly.

'I ain't time to be chasing you, Mester Rat. You're safe from me big stick just now!' she murmured, thinking of all the times she and Danny had made a game of chasing rats. As her eyes became accustomed to the gloom, Kate moved softly across the thick carpet of straw towards where her stepfather stood beside the cow. Samphire was making a dreadful noise, bellowing and stamping. Suddenly she pushed sideways towards Jonathan Godfrey, pinning him against the brick wall.

'Dad!'

'Keep back, Kate,' he gasped. 'Don't get near her back legs – whatever you do.'

With all his strength he shoved at the cow and, gaining a little space, moved swiftly out of the way.

'You all right, Dad?'

'She's winded me a bit, that's all,' he said, wiping the sweat from his forehead with the back of his hand. 'I can't seem to pacify her, Kate. Your mother's the only one who can quieten Samphire.'

14

After a moment's hesitation, for it would mean she would be banished from the barn, the girl asked, 'Shall I fetch me mam?'

'You can't. She's gone to the Grange to see Squire Marshall. It's rent day.' He glanced down at her and for a moment the worried expression on his face lightened as they exchanged an amused glance.

Esther Godfrey was meticulous in money matters. Her quarterly rent for the tenancy of Brumbys' Farm, which was solely in her name, must be paid exactly on the day it was due.

Turning back to watch the restless cow pulling at the rope which tethered her to the wall, Jonathan's face sobered again as he said, 'I'm rather afraid the calf is breech.'

'Ya'll have to turn it, Dad.'

She saw the beads of sweat standing out on his forehead. Again he swept his hand across his brow. He took a tentative step towards the cow and stopped. Kate watched him. It was obvious that her stepfather was unsure what he needed to do. After all, she thought, with sudden sympathy for him, he had only been involved in farmwork since marrying her mother four years earlier. His trade had been building traction engines in Lincoln.

Kate touched his arm. 'Ya need to put yar arm inside her and . . .'

The sweat was running down the side of his face now at the mere thought.

'I've watched your mother – but . . .' His anxious glance flitted towards the cow and back again to Kate. His anxiety was becoming almost fear.

'Wait, Dad, just wait here and watch her. Dun't do anything . . .' Kate turned and ran towards the door.

'Kate – wait! Where . . .?'

15

But she was out of the door and running round the corner of the building and out of the yard gate.

Danny – she must fetch Danny. He would know what to do. In the lane she turned to the right and sped towards the Point. Arriving at the top of the steep incline, known as the Hump, over a natural bank in the road, she paused to catch her breath and survey the scene below her. To her right the setting sun slanted golden streaks across the fields harrowed smooth and flat after the recent spring sowing. The River Lynn meandered through the fields to the Point where it joined the sea. To her left was the pub and beyond it, the marsh and then the sea. Directly in front of her was a stretch of grass between the river bank and the line of four cottages where Danny lived.

The three Harris brothers, Peter, Luke and Georgie, were playing cricket on the grass, but Kate could not see Danny among them.

She plunged down the bank and, lifting her skirt to her knees, sprinted across the grass. 'Georgie – Georgie! Where's Danny?'

'Hello, young Kate. Come to play cricket, 'ave ya?'

'Dun't let her play again, Georgie,' shouted Peter, though he was grinning as he said it. 'She batted our ball into the river last time,' They were all older than Kate and Danny; fine, strapping young men with broad, muscular shoulders and faces tanned a healthy bronze from working out in all weathers. None of them had married as yet and still lived at home with their parents in the end cottage. 'Can't find a lass to match me mam's cooking' was their unanimous verdict, but if the snatches of conversation Kate overheard sometimes were true, they all three had 'an eye for the lasses' but preferred to stay fancy-free, at least for the present.

'Where's Danny?' she demanded.

The young man clasped his hands over the place where

he believed his heart to be and dropped to his knees on the grass. 'Danny – always Danny! And here am I pining for one little kiss . . .'

'George – me dad can't manage Samphire. She's calving.'

At once the young man stopped his teasing. 'He's up near the Point helping his dad mend the nets, I reckon . . .'

But she was gone like the wind, calling back over her shoulder, 'Thanks, Georgie.'

She ran along the curving river bank until she came to the place where the river widened out into intertidal mudflats, channelling a wandering route to the sea. Moored on the river bank was Robert Eland's fishing boat, and on the headland, the very Point itself, father and son bent their heads over the nets, examining them for holes.

'Danny, Danny!'

The two men looked up and Danny waved. 'Summat up, Katie?' he asked as she reached them.

'Hello, Mester Eland . . .'

The older man nodded briefly.

'Can you come and help us, Danny? Me dad can't manage Samphire. Her calf's coming breech.'

'Oh heck!' Danny muttered and then glanced at his father. 'Dad . . .?'

The older man was silent, threading the nets expertly through his fingers. His eyes were downcast and his mouth was completely hidden by a thick, grey-speckled beard and moustache, so that Kate had no way of reading any expression on his face. It was impossible to see if he ever smiled, and the visible part of his face was weather-beaten and lined, his forehead seeming to have a permanent frown. He was a quiet man who gave the impression of being dour, even moody. Though Robert Eland rarely came to Brumbys' Farm – hardly ever did he help with the harvest for he preferred the sea to the land – Kate's stepfather would often meet him in the Seagull to play dominoes over a pint or two. 'He's a good man when you get to know him,' Jonathan would say, to which Esther would reply, 'You never see bad in anyone', and Kate's gentle stepfather would smile fondly at his wife.

Danny thought the world of his father; he was forever saying, 'Me dad ses' or 'It was summat me dad said'. And that – for Kate – was good enough.

'Where's yar mam?' Mr Eland was asking Kate now.

'Gone to the Grange. We don't know how long she'll be and the cow's in a bad way . . .'

There was a moment's pause before he said, 'All right, then. Off ya go, lad.'

'Thanks, mester,' Kate called over her shoulder for already her feet were flying across the grass back the way she had come.

'Wait for me,' Danny called after her, but, as always, he arrived at Brumbys' Farm hot and breathless and a minute or two after Kate.

'Get me – some hot – soapy water, Katie,' he commanded, still trying to regain his breath, but having summed up the situation in the barn at a glance. In a few moments Kate was back with hot water from the side boiler in the kitchen range and a scattering of soap flakes from the wash-house dissolving in it.

Danny had taken off his shirt. His braces hung loosely down the sides of his trousers. He looked very thin, his shoulder-blades and ribs sticking out, but Kate knew his slight physique belied a wiry strength. He might not be able to run as fast as she could but he could beat her at arm-wrestling any day of the week.

'We'll have to hopple her, Mester Godfrey,' Danny was saying, 'else she'll kick me shins to bits!'

Kate reached for the leather thong from the wall and handed it to Danny.

'Kate – we'll need some thin rope. Plough line'd be best, if you can find any.'

Kate screwed up her mouth and wrinkled her smooth brow. Then her thoughtful expression cleared. 'Wait a bit . . .'

In the stable next to the barn the two cart-horses tried to nuzzle Kate as she squeezed past them. 'Move over, Boxer. No, I ain't no sugar – not this time. I'm busy. Oh, move over, do – I need that plough line on the wall.'

She pushed at the huge horse's flanks and obligingly the animal side-stepped and allowed the girl into his stall to reach the line. Giving him a swift pat on his nose, Kate said, 'I'm sorry, old feller, I can't stay. Poor old Samphire needs help.'

Closing the stable door, she ran back to the barn and, stepping inside, saw Danny standing on a box pushing his thin arm, made slippery with the soapy water, into the cow. Samphire lowed and tried to move but because of the thong looped around her back legs she could not kick. Sweat ran down Danny's forehead and his face was contorted with pain.

'There – ain't much – room in here,' he gasped. 'If I can – just . . . aaah.' As he spoke one small back leg of the unborn calf popped out.

'Well done, Danny.' Jonathan Godfrey moved forward as if to help, but as he did so the cow jerked her rump and knocked against Danny, causing him to lose his precarious footing on the box. He let out a gasp of pain as his arm, trapped deep within the cow, was twisted into an awkward position.

'Get back, Dad,' Kate hissed and darted forward to set the box straight and help Danny back on to it. 'You okay?'

she said softly. Anxiously, she looked up into Danny's brown eyes, full of pain. He bit his lip but nodded resolutely.

Again he was moving his hand deep inside the cow, trying to release the unborn calf's other back leg. Danny took a deep breath and grunted with the effort. Slowly Kate moved closer to the cow. She began to murmur soothingly to the animal as she had heard her mother do so often. At the same time she ran her hands gently up and down the cow's back. 'There, there, old girl. We're trying to help you. Soon be over.'

'Aaah,' Danny gave a gasp of pleasure and relief as the second tiny back leg appeared. Thankfully, the boy eased his arm out of the cow. As he did so, he grabbed the tiny, protruding legs.

'Quick, Kate. Give us the line.'

Kate handed it to him and swiftly he tied one end round the calf's legs and passed the other end to Kate.

'Hold it taut, Kate, we don't want him tucking 'em back in.'

Danny stepped down from the box. There were red pressure bruises all the way down his arm and he winced as he bent over the bucket of soapy water to wash away the blood and slime.

'Have you hurt your arm, Danny?' Jonathan Godfrey asked in concern.

'It'll be right, mester. Just twisted it a bit when I fell off the box.'

'That was my fault,' the man said with contrition.

Danny stood up and Kate could tell that the grin he gave was a little forced. 'Right then, let's have a go.'

All three of them grasped the line and, with one accord, pulled on it. As if sensing that they were trying to help her, Samphire appeared to pull in the opposite direction, though her lowing sounds became more frantic and high-pitched.

'It's no good,' Jonathan Godfrey gasped as they paused for breath. 'You'll have to fetch the vet.'

The two youngsters looked up at him askance. 'The vet?' They both spoke at once, and Kate added, 'Me mam'd have a double-duck fit if we was to waste money on a vet.'

The man gestured helplessly towards the cow, now looking round at them reproachfully. 'But we can't manage. We'll lose calf *and* cow if we don't get some expert help soon.'

'Let's give it just one more try, Mester,' Danny urged. 'Then I'll go for the vet.'

'Me mam'll go mad!' Kate muttered, grasping the rope and pulling with every ounce of her strength.

'Come – on!' she heard Danny gasp and echoed his entreaty in her mind.

Suddenly there was a loud sucking sound and the calf slithered out on to the mound of straw beneath the cow's hind legs. The man and the two youngsters, still pulling hard, fell back together in a heap. They disentangled themselves and sat up. In front of them was the newborn calf lying in the straw. Samphire, her cries of pain stilled, looked round in surprise as if to say, 'Where did that come from?'

Kate laughed aloud and scrambled on all-fours to where the wriggling creature lay. She picked up handfuls of straw and wiped the calf.

'Oh, he's lovely. Look, Dad, he's . . .'

At that moment the door of the barn was flung open and her mother stood there. 'What on earth . . .?' began Esther Godfrey. Her glance rested briefly on Danny and her mouth tightened noticeably, but she directed her anger at her daughter.

'Kate! I thought I told you to go to bed. How many times do I have to tell you . . .?'

'Esther,' Jonathan's deep voice interrupted in gentle

reproach. 'The youngsters have been helping me. I couldn't have managed without them.'

Kate saw her mother open her mouth but at that moment she saw the calf struggling to its feet, and whatever sharp retort she had been about to make was stilled. Then once more her gaze came to rest upon Danny's head, bowed over the plough line he was looping into a neat coil.

'Thank you for your help, Danny.' Her mother's tone was stiff and unfriendly and as Danny's head jerked up, Kate saw that there was puzzlement in his dark brown eyes and a red flush of embarrassment creeping up his neck.

Handing the coiled line to Jonathan Godfrey, he nodded briefly to Kate and went towards the door.

Once more Jonathan's deep voice prompted gently, 'Esther, the lad saved the calf and probably your cow as well.'

Esther seemed to be struggling with some inner conflict, but as Danny passed by her, she reached out her hand, touched his shoulder briefly and said, 'I *am* grateful, Danny, really.'

The boy hesitated and, for a moment, stared up at her. Then with a muttered 'Missus', he moved on out of the doorway.

As they heard his boots crunching across the cinders in the yard, Esther's attention came back to Kate. 'I don't want you to see so much of Danny from now on, Kate. He's growing up and come Monday he'll think of himself as a working man. He's no longer a boy.'

Kate stared wide-eyed at her mother, her mouth slightly open in shock. Why was her mother behaving so strangely? Danny had always been her friend. He was only a few months older than she was and they had both lived all their young lives at Fleethaven Point.

'Why have you gone all funny with Danny, Mam? You've never stopped us bein' friends before. I can't just . . .'

'Mebbe that's where I made me mistake – I should have put a stop to it a long time ago!' her mother muttered, then she raised her voice and added, 'Dun't argue with me, Missy, ya'll do as I say. Now off to bed with ya.'

'Mam . . .?' Kate began but her protestations were cut short by Esther flinging her arm out and pointing towards the house.

'Bed!'

Three

The next morning at breakfast, Kate was subdued and silent. Had her mother really meant what she had said about Danny the previous night?

'Look after Lilian while I get the dairy work done, will ya, Katie?' her mother asked, bustling between kitchen and pantry where the milk stood waiting in churns. 'Just wheel her up and down the lane, mind. No sneaking off to the Point.'

So – she had meant it. Kate bit her lip, but decided not to argue – at least, not at present.

'Can't I c'lect the eggs, Mam?' Kate hated wheeling the baby in the black baby car; its handle was too high for her and it was heavy to push on the uneven surface of the lane.

'Later – when you've got the baby to sleep for the morning.'

There was no escape. For the remainder of the Easter holidays, it seemed as if her mother deliberately kept her busy. Collecting eggs, feeding the hens, fetching the cows from the meadow for milking twice a day and running errands – anywhere except to the cottages at the Point. And, of course, wheeling Lilian. The baby's blue eyes stared resentfully up at her from inside the huge hood of the baby car, the tiny mouth puckered, ready to whimper.

'Talk to her, Kate,' her mother would say. 'It'll soothe her.'

But Kate could not bring herself to talk to the baby like her mother did. To the young girl it sounded daft!

She had no opportunity to see Danny. Now he had started work and she would soon be back at school, Kate realized there would be even less chance of meeting him.

'Look sharp,' her mother shouted from the bottom of the stairs as Kate dressed on the first morning of the new school term. 'Yar dad's getting the trap ready to take you.'

Tears threatened as Kate realized afresh that only she needed taking to school now. This morning there would be no Danny appearing on top of the Hump and running down towards Brumbys' Farm for a ride to school in their trap. There would be no playing their usual game.

'Go on, Dad, get going. Mek him run. 'E shouldn't be late.'

Smiling, Jonathan would flick the reins to make the docile pony inch forward, the animal seeming to know it was all in the game and that he shouldn't set off too quickly but give the boy a fair chance of catching them.

'Come on, Danny, faster, faster . . .' Kate would stand up in the trap shouting back to him, her merry laughter bouncing on the breeze. 'We'll leave ya and ya'll be late an' get the cane.' Then she would say to Jonathan, 'Let him catch us now, Dad, he's out o' puff.'

Jonathan would ease back on the reins to halt the pony and the boy would clamber up into the back of the trap, breathless and red in the face, but laughing. Always Danny Eland seemed to have a broad grin on his tanned face.

But this morning there would be no game and no laughter because there would be no Danny.

Kate sat stiff and silent in the trap, looking back down the empty lane. Her gaze took in the flat fields stretching westwards as far as she could see, trees dotted black against the low horizon. The lane wound gently following the natural line of the sand-dunes all the way to the outskirts of Lynthorpe.

Just before they reached the first houses, Jonathan turned the trap to the left and took a lane leading inland. 'We mustn't forget to pick Rosie up.' He smiled down at Kate, but her normally happy face was solemn.

She felt lost without Danny.

When the trap pulled up outside the smithy, however, and little Rosie Maine came running up, Kate's spirits lifted a little. It was impossible not to be cheered by Rosie – she was such a bright chatter-box, with white-gold bouncing curls, merry blue eyes and a round chubby face that always seemed to be smiling. Jonathan held out his hand and the child climbed up the step into the trap. She flung her arms about Kate's neck and hugged her hard. Then she sat down and pulled her skimpy dress over her knees. Already, the shapeless shift dress seemed too short for her. Over it, she wore a grey hand-knitted jumper that had been washed so many times, the wool stitches had matted together.

Rosie swung her bare legs and giggled as she pointed at her canvas shoe. 'Look, me big toe's poking through. I got a new pair at Easter, but me mam ses I'll only spoil 'em if I wear 'em for school.'

She wriggled closer to Kate and slipped her hand through the older girl's arm. 'Ooh, I 'ave missed you, Kate, these holidays. I didn't even get down to see me Grannie Harris and to come an' play with you. Me mam's been a bit poorly. She's having another babby, y'know.'

Rosie's mother was always having another baby, Kate thought. Rosie, at five, already had two younger brothers and now there was another child on the way.

'She's been sick ev'ry morning this week, but that'll go after the first three months,' the child added, frighteningly knowledgeable for one so young. Rosie paused and looked about her as the trap rattled on. 'Funny without Danny, in't it?'

'Yes,' Kate mumbled, but could not trust herself to say any more. Rosie was the last person she wanted to see her tears. The child idolized her and Kate loved Rosie as she might a younger sister – more, if she were honest, than she loved her real sister, well, half-sister.

Rosie chattered on. 'We might be coming to live at the Point, in that cottage that's empty near me Grannie Harris's. I'll like that.'

Jonathan Godfrey looked down at the excited little girl. 'Your father will still work at the smithy, though, won't he?'

Rosie's father, Walter Maine, had been wounded in the war and had lost a leg. When he and Enid Harris from Fleethaven Point had married some six years earlier, Kate had been their bridesmaid, and the newly married couple had made their home in the two small rooms above the smithy where Walter worked.

'Oh yes.' The bright curls bobbed as Rosie nodded vigorously in answer to Jonathan's question. 'But there bain't room there for all us lot now, Mester.'

Kate saw the slow smile on her stepfather's face, and despite her unhappiness at missing Danny, she wanted to smile too. She well knew the cramped conditions the Maine family lived in, even though they had brought it upon themselves by having so many children. But it would be nice to have little Rosie living nearer.

'You tell your dad and mam that if they want to borrow the horses and a wagon to move, they'd be most welcome.'

The child's pink cheeks shone and her pretty mouth stretched wide in a grin. 'Thanks, Mester, I will,' and as the trap pulled up outside the school gate, Rosie jumped down and was gone, running into the playground.

'She's like a little whirlwind,' Jonathan murmured, and Kate smiled thinly in return.

'Bye, Dad. See you tonight.'

'Kate?' The soft tone made her look back at him. 'Be careful coming home tonight.' He paused, as if knowing that what he felt obliged to say would cause her more pain, 'You – you'll be on your own when you leave Rosie at the smithy.'

Kate closed her eyes against the tears and swallowed the lump in her throat. Not trusting herself to speak, she nodded, turned and ran into the playground without looking back.

All through the long morning, Kate's glance kept wandering to the place where Danny used to sit, now occupied by a fat, spotty-faced boy. It gave her a shock every time she glanced across, half-expecting, half-hoping to see Danny, to see instead the ugly boy sitting at Danny's desk. She didn't want anyone else sitting in the place that had been Danny's. She would have preferred it to remain empty rather than that anyone else should sit there. At playtime she sat morosely in the corner of the playground, refusing to join in any of the games, dreading the end of afternoon school when she must face the long walk home alone.

When the bell clanged for the end of the school day, Rosie skipped and hopped at her side, keeping Kate company as far as the smithy, chattering incessantly. Kate made no reply and finally the younger child looked up and said, 'Kate, a'ya cross with me?'

''Course not.'

'Then what's the matter?'

'Nothing.'

'Yes, there is.' Rosie danced lightly around Kate. 'You bin in trouble at school?'

'No.'

Silence.

They had reached the blacksmith's, Rosie's home, but

the child grasped Kate's hand and tugged at it insistently. 'What, then?'

The pent-up emotion of the last few days and the loneliness of this day burst out. 'I dun't want to go away to school. I dun't even want to go on going to school. I want to work – like Danny. I want to *be* with Danny.'

She saw Rosie's eyes widen and her mouth open, but Kate snatched her hand away and ran, leaving the child standing in the lane staring after her.

Kate ran and ran until she came to the lane alongside the dunes, but instead of following it, she scrambled up the slope, catching hold of the tough, spiky marram grass, and down the other side. Across the flat marsh, jumping the creeks, frightening a skylark into the air to defend its territory against her pounding feet, until she crested the rise of the easterly dunes and came to the beach. Her heart was pounding as she gulped air, her lungs bursting, but still she forced herself onwards, across the soft, dry sand until she came to the water's edge where she sank down, sobbing and breathless. She pulled her knees up to her chest, wrapped her arms around her legs and buried her face against her skirt.

The incoming tide came closer, receded and then crept closer still, its waves probing with gentle frothy edges until she became aware of its coldness soaking through her skirts. Sudden anger spurted and she smacked the flat of her palm on the encroaching water, sending a shower of salt water over herself. 'I won't be sent away. I won't go – I won't!' Now the tears that she had kept locked inside all day long spilled over.

The sea retreated but came again; a stronger, bigger wave catching her unawares so that she lost her balance and fell backwards into the shallows. Soaked to her skin, Kate scrambled to her feet. Sobbing, the sea-water squelching in her shoes, she began to run.

'Why, lovey, you're wet through!' Beth Eland reached out with gentle hands and pulled Kate into her warm kitchen. 'Whatever happened? Did ya fall in a creek?'

Kate sniffled and shook her head as she allowed herself to be led towards the rickety wooden chair set before the glowing range. A log settled in the grate sending up a welcoming shower of sparks.

Kate hesitated before she sat down, glancing up at Danny's mother. As if reading the girl's thoughts, the woman smiled gently and said, 'Go on, Mester Eland won't mind you sitting in his chair this once. Now, off with these wet things.'

Mrs Eland slipped the shawl off her own shoulders and wrapped it round Kate. 'I'll rinse ya pinny out and hang it on the line, else that mud'll stain it. Eh, dearie me, even ya shimmy's wet through.'

She took Kate's salt-stained clothes to the deep white sink under the window and worked the handle of the pump. Water splashed into the sink.

'I dun't know how I'm to get these dry in time for you to go home, Katie,' Mrs Eland murmured worriedly, taking an enamel jug from a shelf of pots and pans running along one wall and coming back to the range to ladle hot water from the side boiler.

Kate, her teeth chattering, held out her hands to the log fire, and wriggled her toes into the worn peg rug that covered the hearth. She felt the woman's anxious glance on her.

'Eh, ya shivering. I'll just get these clothes in to steep and I'll make you some hot milk with a spoon of honey in it.'

Kate nodded and sniffled. She was still unable to speak.

After her drenching in the sea, she had run along the beach. Sobbing and breathless, she had climbed the easterly dunes, crossed the marsh and come to the Point, deliberately avoiding going anywhere near her own home.

Danny, she must find Danny.

Now she lifted her tear-streaked face, her long hair straggling down her cheeks, to look up at his mother. 'Where's Danny?' she asked.

Mrs Eland bent over her as she gave Kate a steaming mug of milk and honey. 'There now, drink this. It'll warm ya. Danny? Why, he's not home from work yet.'

Kate wrapped her cold hands round the mug and sipped the hot liquid. 'How long will he be?'

The woman stood looking down at her, her brown eyes full of concern and something else Kate could not quite understand. There was more than just sympathy for her bedraggled state; there was a sadness in Beth Eland's eyes. 'Katie, ya'll have to forget our Danny now and make new friends at school. Ya going to a new school soon, aren't ya?'

The child's green eyes flashed with renewed vigour. Her mouth was set in a line of rebellion. 'I dun't want to go. I won't go!'

Mrs Eland sighed heavily. 'If it's what yar mam wants . . .'

Kate gazed up appealingly at the older woman. 'Couldn't you speak to me mam? Mebbe she'd listen to you . . .'

'No!' Beth Eland's sudden sharpness startled Kate and the mug she held wobbled, splashing hot milk on to her bare leg. The woman's eyes softened, but there was still a deep-rooted pain in their depths. 'Yar mam and me dun't talk to each other, child. Ya know we don't. Not since – not for a long time.'

She turned her back on Kate and went back to the sink, plunging her hands deep into the water and wringing out Kate's dress and pinafore, twisting the fabric in her grasp with a pent-up anger.

'But . . .' Kate began and then fell silent. Mrs Eland's back was rigid; it was obvious that further pleas would be fruitless.

*

31

'Where on earth have you been?'

Kate faced her mother's anger squarely. Inwardly she was trembling but she clenched her jaw stubbornly, her bottom lip pouting.

The tirade continued. 'We've been worried sick. Your father's been up and down that lane three times searching for you, right as far as the school. He even knocked on the school-house door to ask the headmistress . . .'

Kate's insides quivered afresh. That would mean more trouble at school in the morning. She lifted her chin defiantly. 'I got me clothes soaked and I – I . . .' She hesitated but there was no point in lying. Her mother was sure to find out the truth. Mrs Eland wouldn't tell her, but Grannie Harris very well might.

When Danny's mother had rinsed her clothes and hung them outside in the wind to dry she had come back into the cottage and stood before Kate once more. Her eyes were gentle and concerned again; the sudden, unusual hostility of a few moments before gone as swiftly as it had come.

'You ought to be going home, Katie. Yar mam will be worried.'

Kate had looked away, staring into the flames. 'I dun't reckon she'll miss me, not now she's got the babby.'

She felt the soft sigh on her cheek and was surprised to feel the touch of the woman's lips brushing briefly against her forehead. 'Oh, Katie love,' Beth Eland murmured and then, more briskly, 'I'll just nip next door. Mebbe Grannie Harris has some old clothes her girls have grown out of . . .'

A few moments later Mrs Eland returned with her arms full of an odd assortment of clothing. Panting slightly, she dumped the bundle on her kitchen table and for a moment the anxious look in her brown eyes was lifted as she laughed. 'Eh, Katie, Grannie Harris is such a hoarder. I reckon some of these clothes are Enid's!' Enid was Grannie Harris's daughter and Rosie's mother. Kate knew the garments must be years old!

Mrs Eland held up a shapeless dress. 'It's a bit big, but it might fit you. Fancy her keeping it all this time . . .'

They giggled together when Kate, a few moments later, stood before Mrs Eland, the long dress flapping around her ankles, the waistline somewhere around her slim, girlish hips. The older woman put her hand to her mouth as if to stifle her laughter. 'It looks dreadful, Kate, but it'll have to do. Ya can borrow my shawl and a pair of woollen stockings. You'll look like a scarecrow, but at least it'll get you home . . .'

The laughter faded for they both knew what awaited Kate then.

And now she was standing before her mother's wrath.

'I am waiting for an answer, Missy.'

'I – came home on the beach and fell in the sea. I went to the Point.'

Her mother's frown deepened and some instinct made the girl bend the truth a little and omit mentioning Danny's mother. 'Grannie Harris lent me these clothes,' she finished, praying fervently that neither Mrs Eland nor even Danny would bring her own clothes back to Brumbys' Farm when they were dry.

'Ya'll get ya'sen to bed this minute and no tea or supper.'

'But Mam . . .'

'I dun't know what I'm going to do with you, Kate Hilton. You've grown so wilful and disobedient, ya'll be the death of me. Mebbe your new school will mek you toe the line.'

Four

'Kate? Kate, are you asleep?'

It was her stepfather whispering from the doorway. Kate lifted her head from under the bedclothes. 'No, I'm not asleep, Dad.'

The door creaked as he pushed it wider open and stepped down the one step into her bedroom. He was carrying a glass of milk and a plate with a wedge of crusty bread spread thickly with fresh butter.

In the dimness of her bedroom – it was dusk outside her window now – he smiled down at her. 'Your mother's busy outside with the milking. Don't you tell her I've brought you this, will you?'

Kate sat up and reached for the milk eagerly. Crying had dried her mouth and left a salty taste on her lips.

'I'm sorry,' she said between gulps, 'you – went looking – for me.'

He sat down on the bed, holding the plate ready for her. 'You should have come straight home, Kate. I told you this morning. It was the first time you've had to walk all that way on your own . . .'

As his words reminded her, fresh tears started.

'We were worried, that's all.' His tone was firm, making her understand that she had been thoughtless, but he stroked the hair back from her forehead with a gentle gesture that took the sting from his reproach.

'Me mam's not really going to send me away to school,

is she?' Kate asked, her green eyes wide and appealing. She struggled inwardly, wanting to ask if it was because of the new baby. But Lilian was his child – and she wasn't. Even though this gentle, kind man was as good to her as any real father could have been, Kate thought, still she was not his child.

She bit deeply into the thick bread and butter and filled her mouth to stop it speaking.

He sighed and stroked her hair again. 'You're growing up, Kate. You're almost a woman and – and your mother's worried about you spending so much time with – with – well – boys.'

She saw him hesitate and thought that perhaps he was embarrassed to touch upon delicate, feminine matters.

A mischievous grin quirked at her mouth even through her recent tears. 'Me mam has told me about the birds and the bees. I mean, I know I mustn't let boys do to me what the old boar does to the sow when he visits.'

Her grin widened at his shocked gasp. 'Kate!'

'Oh, I've often watched,' she said airily, wiping the crumbs from her mouth with the back of her hand.

'You shouldn't talk like that. It's not the sort of talk for young girls . . .'

He paused and she saw he was staring at her through the gloom. 'What?' she prompted.

He sighed and she felt the waft of his breath on her face. 'Maybe,' he said slowly, thoughtfully, 'that's what your mother means. You need to learn to be more – more ladylike.'

Kate gave a snort of laughter and then clapped her hand over her mouth to stifle the noise. 'Me? Ladylike?' The thought was so comical that for a moment it drove away her tears.

'Your mother's only trying to do what's best for you.' Her stepfather patted her hand, picked up the empty plate and glass and stood up. 'I'll see what I can do, Kate. But I can't promise to make her change her mind, you know that, don't you?'

'Yes, Dad. But if you'd try.'

'I'll try,' he agreed, but she knew that was as much as he was able to promise.

There was one thing about her mother, Kate was obliged to acknowledge, she didn't bear malice and stay angry for days on end. The next morning when Kate appeared at the breakfast table, washed, dressed and ready for school, Esther Godfrey greeted her daughter with a smile and planted a kiss on her forehead. 'Ya lunch box is ready on the side there. Dun't forget it. D'ya want more milk on ya porridge?'

'No thanks, Mam.'

Kate sat at the kitchen table and ate while her mother picked up the baby from the cradle in the corner, sat in the Windsor chair by the fire in the range and opened her blouse front. The baby nuzzled greedily and began to suck loudly. Deliberately, Kate concentrated on her porridge.

'Shall ya come to church with me on Sunday, Katie? It's time I was churched after having Lilian. Ya Dad'll mind her for once.'

Eagerly, Kate said, 'Ooh yes, Mam. I'd like that.'

She was rewarded with one of Esther's radiant smiles. 'That's settled, then.'

Happily, Kate finished her breakfast. On Sunday, for a few precious hours, she would have her mother all to herself.

She didn't see Danny again until Morning Service on the Sunday. He was sitting in his usual place beside his mother on the opposite side of the church. Kate, being first in the pew and landing up against the white-washed wall, knelt on the hassock and covered her face with her hands. Slowly she spread her fingers a fraction and peeped between them to study Danny's bent head. Although he was dressed in his Sunday best suit, the collar of his white shirt stiffly starched, his face looked thinner than just a week ago and there were dark shadows under his eyes.

All local children worked from an early age – it was the way of all their lives – but Kate guessed that Danny's first full week as a working man had been tough and exhausting. It was written on his young face.

As the congregation stood to leave at the end of the service, Kate shifted from one foot to the other impatiently.

'Stand still, Kate, and stop jiffling. I've to see the vicar about our Lilian's christening,' her mother whispered. 'Just be patient, will ya?' Behind her mother's back, Kate pouted. Now she would not be able to catch Danny before he left with his mother to walk the two miles home.

The vicar greeted Esther Godfrey warmly and patted Kate on the head with annoying condescension. 'So, Mrs Godfrey, you want to bring your little one to be baptized.'

'We thought between harvests, Vicar. About the end of July.'

'Mmm, yes, yes, I think we could fit you in after Morning Service. Shall we say the last Sunday in July?'

Kate watched her mother nod agreement, shake the vicar's hand and walk swiftly down the path to their pony and trap.

Kate skipped beside her. 'Walk properly, Kate. You're no longer a child.'

Kate sighed, but obeyed.

It was a fine, warm morning and once on the coast road the pony trotted smartly, the breeze lifting his silky mane.

'There's Danny – and Mrs Eland. Can't we give them a ride home, Mam?' Kate shouted above the noise of the wheels. The only reply her mother made was to slap the reins to make the pony go even faster. Esther Godfrey stared straight ahead, not even glancing down as they passed the pair.

Kate saw Mrs Eland and Danny step on to the grass verge to allow the trap to pass. Danny looked up at Kate, grinned and waved, but Mrs Eland – just like Kate's mother – stared stonily ahead and made no acknowledgement that the trap had even passed near them.

The day Kate had so looked forward to had ended in disappointment.

'We're moving to the Point on Saturday.' Rosie's cherubic face was one broad grin as she clambered up into the trap for her daily ride to school with Kate the following morning. 'We're coming to live in the end cottage.' She flung herself against Kate. 'Won't we have fun? I'll be able to come and play every day and help you on the farm, c'lecting eggs and feedin' the hens, won't I? Do say ya'll let me, Katie?'

Kate could not prevent tears filling her eyes.

'What's the matter? Dun't you want me to come and live near you?' The merry smile died and Rosie's lower lip quivered.

Swiftly, Kate hugged the younger child tightly. ''Course I do. But – but I might not be there mesen.' She glanced at her stepfather. The indulgent smile that had curved his gentle mouth when the excited Rosie had climbed into the trap faded. He looked away and flicked the reins to make the pony walk on.

'What d'ya mean?' The little girl was mystified.

'Me mam might be sending me away to school. I'll only be here in the holidays.'

Rosie blinked rapidly. 'You – you mean you won't come home at night?'

Kate, unable to speak, shook her head.

Rosie, sitting beside her, snuggled closer and took Kate's hand in her small one. She patted it and then held it tightly for the rest of journey to the school. Neither of them spoke again. Not even Rosie could think of anything to say.

Moving day for the Maine family caused great excitement for everyone who lived at the Point.

The Godfreys lent their farm wagon and the two horses – Boxer and Bonnie – to pull it. Jonathan Godfrey drove it to the smithy, helped Walter Maine to load all their belongings and then, with the high load wobbling precariously, drove back along the coast road towards the Point. Later in the afternoon Kate went with her mother in the pony and trap to fetch the rest of the Maine family.

'Enid, you look done in,' Kate heard her mother say in a voice that forbade any argument. 'Ya'll come back to the farm and rest awhile and let the others unload and settle things in. Kate can look after the bairns.'

'But, Mam, I want to . . .' Kate began, but a look from her mother quelled her protest.

It was Saturday afternoon and Danny might be home early from work. She had thought that helping the Maines to move would give her an excuse to go to the Point. Now she had to stay at home and play with Rosie and her two younger brothers.

'I'm three months gone, Esther,' Enid was saying quietly to Kate's mother.

Esther clicked her tongue against her teeth in an expression of exasperation. 'Well, your Walter might have lost his leg in the war, Enid, but he certainly didn't lose owt else, did he?'

Enid snorted with laughter and clapped her hand over her mouth. For a moment the tiredness left her eyes as the two women exchanged a joke that the children could not share.

'You're having 'em a mite too fast for your health, Enid. You're thinner than ya used to be.'

'I reckon it's livin' in the town,' Enid murmured. 'I've never really liked it above the smithy. The smell of the forge never leaves the place.'

At Enid's words Kate could almost hear the sizzling of the iron and smell the burning hoof as Walter shod a horse.

'Well, you're moving back to the Point not a moment too soon to my idea, and ya'll have ya mam nearby to keep an eye on ya.'

'She can't wait to have a brood of little ones running around again.'

Kate watched moodily as the two women smiled at each other.

'Take them into the front garden, Kate,' her mother ordered as she drew the trap to a halt in the yard of Brumbys' Farm. 'But keep them away from the pond at the side of the house, mind.'

It was early evening before Kate took the three children down the lane and over the Hump to the Point. The youngest boy had to be carried and was asleep against Kate's shoulder by the time they arrived at the cottages. His brother dragged his feet with tiredness, but Rosie seemed to have boundless energy, running ahead of them to stand on top of the Hump shouting back, 'Come on, oh, do come on,' then running down the other side of the bank and across the grass towards her new home.

Georgie and Peter Harris were lifting the last heavy box from the cart.

'Now then, our Rosie. Ya've a little bedroom all to ya'sen. Come and see.'

Rosie squealed with delight, clapped her hands and ran into the cottage.

Georgie grinned at Kate. ''Tis only like a big cupboard, but she'll love it.'

Kate smiled.

''Spect ya've had ya hands full with these three all day,' George continued as Enid came out to collect the boys from Kate.

'Thanks ever so for having 'em, Kate,' she said. 'I dun't know what we'd have done with them under us feet all day.'

Kate opened her mouth to reply but Rosie appeared in the doorway. 'Come and see my bedroom, Katie, it's . . .' she paused as her darting eyes caught sight of something beyond Kate and her rosebud mouth shaped itself into an 'oh' of surprise. 'Look, look,' she pointed. 'There's Danny.'

Kate turned to follow the line of Rosie's pointing finger to see Danny free-wheeling down the steep incline of the Hump on a bicycle, his legs sticking straight out on either side. He came rocketing on to the grass, hit a bump and promptly fell off, legs, arms and bicycle all in a heap.

The two girls gave cries of alarm and ran towards him, while Georgie and Peter just stood and laughed.

Kate pulled the huge bicycle away while Rosie squatted down beside Danny. He lay on the grass, his eyes closed, not moving.

'He's not dead, is he?' Rosie whispered.

'Don't be daft, Rosie, he's pretending.' But a cold sliver of fear made her say sharply, 'Danny!'

Still he did not move. Kate flung the bicycle down again, dropped to her knees and bent over him. She took hold of his hand and chafed it. As she bent closer, Danny jerked his head up and planted a kiss on her cheek. Startled, Kate fell backwards, but Rosie shrieked with laughter. 'He kissed you! He kissed you!'

Rosie jumped up and began to pull at his arm. 'Get up, Danny. I want a piggy-back.'

Danny gave an exaggerated groan, but winked at Kate. 'Children!'

He made a big performance of rising, holding his back as if it pained him and bending double. Rosie giggled. 'You're p'tending, like Katie ses. You're p'tending.'

Danny's brown eyes were full of mischief. 'Come on then, up you get.' Obligingly, he bent down so that the little girl could climb on to his back, her chubby arms tight around his neck.

Danny galloped towards the cottages with Rosie bouncing up and down on his back and shrieking with laughter, leaving Kate to pick up his bicycle and wheel it after them.

The Sunday morning of Lilian's christening was fine and bright, but breezy. Scudding clouds made the sunlight fitful, sending shadows running across the fields of waving corn.

'We'll have tea out on the front lawn,' her mother decided. 'Kate, help yar dad fetch the trestle tables from the Grange. Squire said I could borrow them. Then when you come back, you must get changed and ready for church. Jonathan, are your folks going straight to the church?'

Orders and questions came in quick succession from Esther Godfrey's lips, scarcely allowing time for any reply. 'When we get back from church, Kate, I want you to help me carry all the food out into the garden.' Her mother seemed to have been baking during the whole of the previous week and now mountains of pasties and tarts, cakes and plum bread stood ready in the pantry. 'Oh, I do hope it dun't rain,' Esther added, glancing anxiously at the sky.

'Danny says it's going to be fine all day.'

Her mother's green eyes flashed. 'When did you see *him*? I told you not to go to the Point . . .'

'I don't, Mam, honest,' Kate said reasonably, trying to pacify her mother's quick temper. It wasn't much use going there anyway, now he was working, but she kept these thoughts to herself. 'Have you asked the folks from the Point to the christening?'

'The Harrises and the Maines.'

Kate looked up at her mother. 'Not Danny and his mother and father?' As soon as she had let the words slip from her lips, Kate could have bitten off the end of her tongue.

'We dun't have owt to do wi' them.'

'You mean you and Mrs Eland dun't speak. Everyone else does. Dad sees mester in the pub and me an' Danny . . .'

'Aye, you and Danny, you and Danny! That's all I seem to have heard for years.'

'Why dun't you like him now? You used to – to . . .' Kate hesitated. Vague memories, elusive and fleeting, were nudging at her mind. 'You used to make him welcome. When me real dad . . .'

'Stop it! You hear me? I dun't want to speak of him. 'Specially not today.'

'Why, Mam? Just tell me why?'

Suddenly, Esther Godfrey seemed weary. She sighed and turned away, more in sadness than in anger now. 'Dun't ask me, Katie love, please dun't ask me. Ya wouldn't like the answer.'

Five

'I'm going with me grandad,' Kate announced firmly and slipped her hand through Will Benson's arm.

'Ya grandad's riding in the trap with me and the baby, Grannie Harris, Enid and Walter,' Esther said. 'It's all arranged. The rest of you will have to walk to the church.'

'What about Rosie? She can't walk all that way.'

'Enid's bairns aren't coming to the church, but they'll come here after.'

'Who's looking after them?' But Kate knew the answer almost before she asked the question.

'The Elands,' was her mother's terse reply.

That meant Rosie would be with Danny. Her two best friends and she could not be with them. I'd rather be playing with them, Kate thought morosely, than going to the christening of a squealing infant!

When the whole party arrived at the church porch, two women were waiting there.

'Jonathan! My dear boy.' The older one of the two women stretched out her arms and enveloped him.

'Hello, Mother.'

Kate watched as her stepfather succumbed to the woman's rapturous hug and then he turned to the younger woman and kissed her on the cheek. 'Hello, Peggy. How are you, love?'

Jonathan Godfrey's tone, always gentle and kindly, had

an even deeper note of tenderness when he spoke to his sister, so that Kate stared at the tall, slim woman with interest.

Introductions were made all round.

'I'm so sorry your father couldn't come, Jonathan,' Mrs Godfrey was saying. 'He has a wretched cold and it's settled on his chest. He's cough, cough, cough . . .' She cast her eyes skywards in a gesture of resignation. 'He keeps me awake half the night, too,' she added, but she was smiling as she said it and there was no rancour in her tone.

The party moved into the church and sat at the back near the font while Morning Service continued. Lilian whimpered and grizzled all the way through and when it came to the point of the christening where the vicar splashed water on to her forehead, the baby set up a loud wail that embarrassed Kate. She wished she could rush out of the church. Instead she shrank towards her grandfather, leaning against his arm, to be rewarded by him smiling down at her. Although baby Lilian was as much his grandchild as she was, Kate did not feel her place in Will Benson's affections had been usurped by the new arrival.

'Come on, me little lass,' Will whispered as the party emerged from the church and everyone gathered around Esther and the baby, 'let us slip away. We'll walk back home on the beach, shall we?'

'Oh yes, Grandad,' Kate agreed eagerly, then her expression sobered as she looked down at his polished boots. 'But won't the sand spoil ya boots?'

Will Benson chuckled, 'Mebbe, mebbe so. But they'll shine up again with a bit of elbow grease. Come on, lass, afore an argy-bargy about who's ridin' in the trap starts.'

For Kate it was the best time of the whole day, her walk on the beach with her grandfather.

As they walked at the water's edge towards home, she could see two figures in the distance. As they drew closer,

Kate could see Danny digging in the sand, while Rosie, barefoot, skipped and danced around him. She saw the child run towards the sea and then heard Rosie shriek with delight, as the waves rushed up the beach towards her. 'Ooh, it's cold. It's freezin'!' The little girl hopped about on the sand, but seconds later she was dancing towards the water once more, daring it to catch her again.

Danny lifted his face to watch Rosie's antics, an affectionate smile curving his mouth. He caught sight of Kate and his smile broadened. He straightened up and waved to her.

Poised on her toes, Kate said, 'Grandad, I'm just off to see Danny and Rosie.'

To her surprise, her grandfather frowned. 'I dun't think you ought to, lass. Ya mam . . .'

'I'll not be a minute, Grandad, honest. You go on and I'll catch you up afore you get home. You know how fast I can run.'

The old man laughed. 'Aye well – all right, but dun't be long, mind?'

But already Kate was running towards her friends.

'Kate! Kate!' Rosie squealed with delight. 'Danny's building me a sand-castle. Look – with a moat an' all. When the sea comes in, it'll go all round it. In't he clever?'

'Why don't you collect some shells to decorate the sides of the castle, Rosie?' Kate suggested, exchanging a glance with Danny. She had lost count of the number of sand-castles they had built together, digging deep moats and adding shells as windows and doors and turrets. Then standing and watching as the sea slowly demolished their efforts.

As Rosie began to collect stones and shells, Kate said, 'I can't stay. I've got to help with the guests.'

The smile on Danny's face faded and he lowered his gaze. He resumed his digging, piling the sand higher and higher.

Kate stood awkwardly for a moment, suddenly embarrassed because the Elands had not been invited to the christening.

'I'll try and get out later.'

He shrugged his thin shoulders.

Kate bit her lip. She badly wanted to stay and talk to him. She didn't like Danny going quiet on her. It wasn't like him. She glanced towards the sand-dunes. Her grandfather had disappeared. He'd be picking his way across the marsh now. Soon he'd be at Brumbys' Farm and her mother would want to know where she was.

'I wish I could stay now, but I daren't.'

Danny banged the back of the spade against the sides of the castle, flattening the sand. Still he would not look at her again.

Rosie came back clutching several shells to her chest. 'Where shall I put 'em, Danny?'

'On the sides. Look – like this.' He squatted down, and, taking a couple of the shells, he pressed them into the sand-castle.

For a moment Kate stood watching them, feeling excluded from their game.

'I'll – see you later.'

Danny nodded absently. 'Yeah, see ya.'

Kate turned and began to run, her flying feet sending up little showers of sand as she went.

Back at Brumbys' Farm she was set to work to help her mother cater for the party, running from house to front garden and back again so many times until sweat plastered strands of her long hair to her forehead.

'So you're Kate.'

She was standing before Mrs Godfrey, holding out a plate piled high with plum bread. Her stepfather's mother was

47

very smart to Kate's idea. She wore a loose-fitting flowery dress with a full-length coat over it, the sleeves gathered with smocking just above the wrist. From beneath her close-fitting hat, two neat brown curls peeped out. Her shoes were dainty, with pointed toes and a T-bar strap across the top of her foot. Her complexion was pale, made more so by face-powder, and red lipstick accentuated her wide mouth.

The woman took a piece of the plum bread. 'Is this all your mother's baking?' When Kate nodded, she added, 'She'd make her fortune if she opened a shop in the High Street. What do you think, Peg?'

Jonathan's sister nodded. 'It's lovely.'

Kate smiled at her. 'I do like ya frock.' She had been admiring the younger woman's outfit ever since she had first seen Peggy and Mrs Godfrey in the church porch. The dress was low-waisted, the skirt knee-length and made in a blue silky material and was decorated with intricate embroidery. Kate longed to feel it. The cloche hat which Peggy wore, its brim almost hiding her eyes, was trimmed with flowers made out of the same material. She wore a long pearl necklace, one strand tight around her neck, the other dangling down almost to her waist.

'Why, thank you, Kate,' Peggy said in her soft voice.

Kate couldn't take her eyes off the two women in their finery. In comparison, her mother's long black skirt, reaching almost to her ankles, and her crisp, white blouse seemed plain.

'Peggy works in one of the big stores in the High Street,' Mrs Godfrey was saying with an obvious note of pride in her voice. 'She spotted this fabric when it first came in and bought a length.'

Kate's puzzled glance went from one to the other. Peggy smiled. 'Mother's a dressmaker, she made this dress and trimmed the hat.'

Kate gasped. 'Did you mek them flowers?' She pointed at the hat.

'Yes, dear,' Mrs Godfrey said modestly.

'They're lovely,' Kate said, hardly able to take her eyes from them. Her gaze dropped to the face beneath the hat. Peggy was pretty, Kate thought, with a smooth skin and a well-shaped mouth. And she was kind, like her brother, Jonathan, but sometimes when her face fell into repose and she thought no one was watching her, she seemed, to the observant Kate, to have an air of sadness about her.

Mrs Godfrey was leaning towards Kate, smiling and nodding, 'When you come to school in Lincoln you'll have to come and see us and Peggy will take you shopping. There, you'd like that, wouldn't you? You'll love the bustle of the city. There's always something going on. Not like here . . .' The woman glanced over her shoulder across the flat farm fields and shivered slightly. 'Whatever do you find to do here?' she murmured, then added more briskly, 'You'll have such a good time. There's the shops and the markets and the theatre and the pictures. Peggy will show you around, won't you, Peg? You'll love it, Kate, really you will.'

'Of course you must come and see us, Kate.' Peggy's smile was genuine and warm. Dutifully, Kate nodded. Though she knew they meant it kindly, the talk of city life sounded a little frightening. It didn't make her feel any happier about leaving all the things that were familiar, to go to boarding school.

Not one jot.

When all their guests had departed, Jonathan drove his mother and sister back into town to catch the evening train. As they made their farewells, Mrs Godfrey hugged Kate to her, enfolding her in a waft of flowery perfume.

'Now, don't forget. When you come to school in September, your Aunty Peg will come to the school and fetch you to our house for tea one Sunday.'

'Thank you,' Kate said politely, and was rewarded by one of her mother's brilliant smiles. 'Thank you very much.'

'Isn't Aunty Peggy married, Mam?' Kate asked as they stood at the gate waving at the trap disappearing along the lane.

'No.'

'She's ever so nice, isn't she?'

'Well, of course, she would be.' Esther smiled, putting her arm about Kate's shoulders as they went back towards the farmhouse. 'She's ya dad's sister.'

Kate giggled inwardly. In her mother's eyes, any relative of Jonathan's couldn't help being nice.

As they went into the scullery, they both heard Lilian's wailing.

'Oh, there she goes!' Esther sighed. 'And there's all the pots to wash . . .'

'I'll do them, Mam. You go and see to her.'

'You're a good girl, Katie, I dun't know what I'd 'ave done without you today. I'll just feed her and then I'll give you a hand.'

Kate stifled a yawn. She was tired, but guessed her mother was even more weary. 'It's all right, Mam, I'll manage.' She picked up a pile of dirty plates and went through to the deep white sink in the back scullery, while her mother sat in the Windsor chair to feed Lilian. Kate would do anything to escape the sight of the baby guzzling at her mother's overflowing breast. She would even face the mountain of washing-up single-handed to avoid seeing the tender expression on her mother's face as she gazed down at the greedy Lilian.

Half an hour later, her stepfather came in through the back door.

'All on your own, Katie? Where's your mother?'

'Upstairs. Lilian won't settle.' She set another of her mother's best cups carefully on the draining-board.

Jonathan picked up a tea-towel and began to dry the pots. He grinned at Kate, the familiar, lopsided smile crinkling his eyes. 'All the excitement of getting herself christened, I expect.'

There was silence between them, the only sounds being the clatter of china as together they washed and dried it, setting it carefully on the kitchen table for Esther to put away herself in the cabinet in her front parlour.

He was an unusual man, Kate mused. Not many men would help with the household chores the way he did.

'Babies – little babies – ' he began hesitantly, 'are not much fun. She'll be different when she's grown a little.'

'I shan't be here that much, shall I?' Kate muttered.

The silence lengthened and she felt he was searching for the right words. 'Kate, you mustn't think . . .'

'At last!' Esther stepped out of the kitchen into the scullery. 'I thought she'd never settle!'

Kate saw the glance that passed between her mother and stepfather.

'You all right, love?' His blue eyes were full of tender concern.

Her mother moved and stood close to him, reached up and, placing her palms against his chest, kissed him gently on the mouth. Still holding the tea-towel in one hand and a plate in the other, his arms went around her and they stood together, oblivious now of Kate's presence. Whatever he had been going to say to her had flown from his mind the moment her mother had stepped into the scullery.

Kate bent her head over the soapy washing-up water, her hair falling forward to hide her tears.

*

51

'It's all settled – you start in two weeks' time.'

Her mother was standing before her dressed in her best costume and pulling off her gloves. 'I've been to Lincoln on the train today and seen the headmistress – Miss Denham. I'm to take you on the Wednesday – the day after the term actually starts. She says that will give everyone else time to have settled back into school.'

Kate felt the colour drain from her face, but no words would come. All she could do was stare at her mother in shock.

But Esther Godfrey, full of her day in the city, of her success with the headmistress of the St Mary's School for Young Ladies, was not even looking at her daughter. Now she was turning away to talk directly to her husband. 'Has the baby been all right? It's a long time to leave her, but I had no choice. It's a good job I've started weaning her.'

'Did you see Mother and Father?'

'Yes – I had a nice dinner with them and a long chat with them about the school. They reckon she'll be fine there, and they'll take her out on a Sunday afternoon. The headmistress said that was when the girls are allowed out with family or friends. Well chaperoned, of course.'

'Peg would fetch her. Did you see Peg? Is she all right?'

'No, she was at work, but I asked after her and she's fine.' She paused and Kate saw the mischievous smile curve her mother's lips. 'I must say, I like your dad. I reckon he took quite a fancy to me.' Almost coquettishly, Esther smoothed tendrils of her hair that were escaping from the combs.

Jonathan caught her by the waist and planted a kiss on her mouth. 'Well, of course he would.'

'He's like you, ain't he? I mean, you're like him.'

'I would like to think so. I admire my father – he's kind and gentle and all his pupils adore him . . .'

'Is he a teacher?' Kate butted in, desperately seeking some kind of hope. 'Will he be there – at the school I'm going to?'

Her mother and stepfather looked round at her, surprise on their faces. They had been so busy planning, deciding her future, that they had forgotten she was even in the room.

Jonathan shook his head, 'No love. He teaches at a boys' school. He won't . . .'

'Then I won't go,' Kate stormed. 'I won't!'

She whirled around, rushed out of the kitchen and through the scullery and dragged open the back door. Then she was running – across the yard, out of the gate, across the lane and up the dunes through the trees – ignoring the shouts of her stepfather behind her.

'Kate! Kate, don't, love. Please don't!'

She stayed in the sandy hollow until the sun had sunk behind the dunes, waiting. Waiting for the time when she knew Danny would be home from work. Then she climbed out of the hollow and, taking a diagonal line across the marsh, came out at the back of the line of four cottages at the Point. She could hear shrieks of laughter coming from the stretch of grass in front of the cottages and recognized Rosie's high-pitched excited chatter organizing her younger brothers in their game. She listened intently. Was Danny there, too?

She moved towards the back door of one of the centre cottages where Danny lived. His mother came out of the little wash-house set at right-angles to the back door and almost dropped the basket of washing she was carrying.

'Why, Kate! You made me jump.' Mrs Eland peered closely through the shadows at her. 'You in bother again, lass?'

Kate shook her head and qualified the negative response

53

by saying, 'Well, not exactly.' There was no doubt she would be in trouble for having stayed out so late. 'Where's Danny?'

She heard Beth Eland's soft sigh. 'He's with his dad up at the headland. They're at the boat.'

As Kate turned away, the older woman said, 'Kate – you – you ought to be finding ya'sen other friends now Danny's working, y'know.'

Kate stood still. Her heart was pounding in her chest as if she had been running a mile. Oh, no! Not Danny's mother too! And it wasn't the first time she'd said as much, either. She turned slowly to stare at Beth. The older woman's brown eyes were troubled. 'It'd be – for the best, lovey,' she added softly.

Was everyone trying to keep her away from Danny? Kate couldn't believe it. She gave a sob and, turning away, began to run. She did not stop until she reached the point of land where the river widened out into the sea.

'Danny. Danny!' she shouted, standing on the grassy headland directly above the muddy river bank. The tide was receding and the Elands' fishing boat was almost stranded on the mud where Robert Eland had moored it earlier in the afternoon at high tide.

She shaded her eyes against the bright gold of the setting sun, low in the western sky. A shadow moved on the boat. 'Katie? What you doing here? Summat wrong?' He clambered over the side and swung his way up the wooden planking of the small jetty that straddled the mud to the boat.

'What's up, Katie?' He peered at her through the gloom and although she could not see the expression in his eyes, she could hear the concern in his voice. It caused a lump in her throat and tears to prickle her eyelids. At least Danny cares, she thought. The words came tumbling from her lips in a jumble, falling over themselves in her eagerness to tell him of her distress.

'Me mam's been to Lincoln – to that school – it's all arranged. I'm to go in two weeks. She's sending me away!' The last was on a wail of despair.

He came and stood in front of her. He put his arms about her and she clung to him, burying her face against his shoulder. They stood on the headland, silhouetted against the red gold of the setting sun. She felt his hands, rough and calloused with the heavy work he now did daily, but surprisingly gentle, stroke her hair. 'Don't cry, Katie. It'll be all right. Perhaps you'll enjoy it when you get there . . .'

'I won't!' Her words were muffled against him but none the less vehement. 'I'll hate it! I'll miss you so much!'

Involuntarily his arms tightened about her. She lifted her face up and tilted her head back and then wound her arms around his neck. They gazed at each other.

'Katie . . .' he began, but whatever he had been going to say, the words remained unspoken for at that moment a shout made them both turn to see Kate's mother, her skirts held high, running towards them. 'Keep away from her, Danny Eland. Dun't you lay a finger on her else I'll . . .'

Kate gasped, shocked to see the rage on her mother's face. Two spots of vivid colour burned in Esther's cheeks and her hair was coming loose from its combs and falling down her back.

She reached them and grasped Kate's arm roughly, jerking her away from Danny.

'Mam, you're hurting. Don't . . .'

'I'll hurt you, me girl, if I ever so much as catch you with him again.'

Kate began to struggle against Esther's grip. This was Danny her mother was talking about; Danny Eland, her life-long friend.

'Mam . . .' she began, but Esther was dragging Kate away from the headland, away from Danny. Kate half-turned back to him, tried to twist out of her mother's grasp. 'Danny . . .' She gave a cry of anguish, but her mother's hold on her arm only tightened.

He made no move. He was standing on the headland, silhouetted against the burnished evening sky, a lonely, bemused figure, as much at a loss to understand what was happening as Kate herself.

Doors were opening in the cottages and faces peering out as Esther Godfrey hustled her daughter homewards. Grannie Harris and next door to her, Mrs Eland, stepped out on to the grass.

As they drew level, Esther shook her fist. 'Keep him away from my girl, Beth Eland. Keep ya bastard away. If ya don't . . .' She paused to drag in a painful, heaving breath. There was menace in her tone as she added more quietly, 'If ya don't – I'll see he knows the reason why!'

Six

The day she had been dreading had arrived.

The summer had passed all too quickly and already it was September. 'I'll miss the Harvest Festival and the Harvest Supper at the Grange.' All her protests were in vain. Her mother was adamant and there was nothing Kate, nor her stepfather, could do about it. Esther Godfrey remained inflexible even in the face of her own father's wrath. From the kitchen Kate had listened as Will Benson had stood in the doorway of the pantry, whilst Esther churned the butter.

'The city's no place for that lass,' he had railed. 'She'll be miserable . . .'

'She will be if you keep putting the idea into her head,' her mother had snapped back.

'But, Esther . . .'

'No "buts", Dad. Kate's going to boarding school for a couple of years and that's that.' The handle of the barrel churn flew round under Esther's angry hand, until they could hear the flip-flop of the thickening butter.

'Huh.' Will Benson turned away from the pantry door. 'Well, I reckon ya'll regret it, lass. Dun't say Ah didn't warn ya.'

'I won't,' Esther said, grimly determined.

Coming back through the kitchen Will took hold of Kate's arm and led her out into the yard. 'Come and see me off,' he whispered. When they were outside he stood before her and put his hands on her shoulders, looking down at her with what looked suspiciously like tears glistening in his eyes.

'Katie love, there's nowt more Ah can do.'

Kate shook her head sadly. 'Dun't worry, Grandad. You tried.'

'Now listen to me, lass. The village where I live – Suddaby – you know it, dun't ya?'

Kate nodded.

'Well, it's between here and Lincoln. If ever you need help, you send me word and I'll come to ya.' He gave her a gentle shake as if to emphasize his words. 'Remember now, won't ya?'

Kate looked up at his worried face, feeling suddenly the older of the two, as if it were her grandfather who needed the reassurance that she would be all right. She forced a smile to her mouth and said as brightly as she could manage. 'I'll remember, Grandad. Dun't you worry. Mebbe me mam's right and I'll love it when I get there.'

They were brave words but there had been a hollow ring to her feigned confidence.

Now it was the morning she must go.

She took a last look around the big bedroom that had been hers alone until now, for only last night her mother had talked of moving the baby into the big room, 'Now that Kate will only be home in the holidays'.

So, already it was no longer 'her' room. Kate's glance roamed over her well-loved toys; the rocking horse standing in the corner, forlorn and neglected for Kate had long since outgrown him. No doubt Lilian would soon be big enough to ride him again and she'd soon have her fingers into all Kate's other toys too; the doll with the china face, the wooden doll's house her stepfather had made for her. The whole of the front opened in two big doors revealing four rooms, hallway and landing. Two miniature pot dolls inhabited the house and the tiny furniture was all made to scale.

The girl turned away and went downstairs feeling strange and awkward in her new school uniform; a long-sleeved winceyette blouse with a tie in the school colours of brown and gold and a brown pleated gym-slip falling straight from her shoulders to just below her knee. The matching braid girdle tied around the waist made her feel bulky and shapeless.

'I feel like a sack of 'tates tied round the middle,' she muttered gloomily. Thick brown woollen stockings held up by suspenders buttoned on to a Liberty bodice made her legs hot and in her sturdy winter boots her feet were sweating.

At the bottom of the stairs she turned to the right and went into the best parlour with its plush chairs and polished brass fender. An organ stood in the corner, but no one ever played it. In the middle of the floor her trunk stood open all neatly packed and ready to be closed when the last-minute things had been added.

Her mother had been sewing for weeks making blouses, pyjamas and even the serge gym-slip. 'Three of everything!' Esther had exclaimed when the list had arrived. 'I can't afford them fancy prices to be buying all ya need ready made. My sewing's as good as anyone's – I'll have to make as many things as I can.'

Now everything was packed in a huge trunk ready to be loaded into the trap. Her stepfather was to drive Kate and her mother to the station in Lynthorpe where they would catch the train to Lincoln. 'Be sure to get a porter to organize taking her trunk up to the school when you get to Lincoln,' he told them.

'I don't need to be tipping no porter to carry something we can carry oursens . . .' her mother began indignantly.

'Esther,' Jonathan said quietly, 'it won't look good at the

school. Believe me. If you want your daughter to become a "young lady", she's got to start acting like one.'

'Dun't mean she's got to be idle,' her mother muttered but as Jonathan opened his mouth to speak again, she put up her hand palm outwards. 'All right, all right, we'll do as you say.'

And now there was only an hour left before they must leave.

Kate turned and left the parlour and walked back through the narrow hallway, the stairs leading up on her left, and to her right was the front door which opened out on to the garden. Then she passed through the living room, pausing only to glance round, just looking at all the familiar things as if for the last time. The furniture was old-fashioned but everything was polished and sparkling. A red chenille cloth covered the table and red velvet curtains hung at the window. On the mantelpiece brass ornaments shone and twinkled. Slowly she came to the kitchen.

Huge hams from the last time they had killed a pig hung from hooks in the ceiling and to her left was the door leading down two steps into the pantry where all the dairy work and the butter-making was carried out. In the centre stood a plain, scrubbed table and on the far wall was the huge range, the centre of the home almost, Kate thought. It heated the water, boiled and cooked all their food, and its fire warmed them on cold winter days and nights. They even bathed in turn in front of it every Friday night in the tin bath that hung on a peg in the wash-house.

Her mother had let down the clothes airer on the rope from the ceiling and Kate paused a moment to watch her hanging freshly ironed clothes over the wooden slats.

Kate moved on out of the kitchen and through the back scullery. She opened the back door and stepped into the yard.

Her mother's voice followed her. 'Dun't you go getting ya new uniform messed up.'

'No, Mam,' came the automatic reply.

It was a soft, September morning when the heat of the summer was gone and there was a freshness in the air. Kate lifted her head and breathed in all the smells of the farmyard, the scents of home. The cows, the horses, even the pigs and always the breeze carried a hint of the sea as a background perfume.

'Goodbye, Boxer, goodbye, Bonnie.' She patted each of the heavy horses in turn and they nudged at her shoulder over the half-door of their stable. 'I ain't no sugar,' she apologized and added ruefully, 'Not in this stupid dress, I ain't.'

She looked in at the pigs and then wandered round the side of the house past the pond with the huge weeping willow tree bending over and trailing its fronds in the water and round to the front of the house which faced westwards. She stood a moment among the fruit trees laden now with the fruit which usually she helped to pick.

This year she would not be here.

She gazed out across the flat fields beneath the huge expanse of sky. Stooks of corn stood sentinel in the fields waiting to be collected and brought to the farmyard to be stacked. She would not be here to hear the familiar cry, 'Harvest home, harvest home', when her mother placed the last sheaf on the last load. She would not be able to join the gleaners who scoured the fields for every last wisp of corn.

She turned away and went back through the yard and out into the lane. She stood for a moment poised on her toes, holding her breath. She glanced back over her shoulder but there was no one in the yard. Then she began to run.

'I'm sorry, lovey. Danny's not here. He's at work.'

'I was afraid he might be. I – I came to say goodbye.'

'Oh,' Mrs Eland said. 'Oh, I see.' She was looking at Kate with her brown, sad, eyes. Her black hair was drawn severely back from her face into a bun at the nape of her neck. Already there were wisps of grey at her temples even though, Kate guessed, Beth Eland must be a similar age to her mother, – only in her early thirties.

Returning the woman's steady gaze, Kate thought – and not for the first time – that Danny's mother could be really beautiful, as striking as her own mother, if she were to take a little trouble over her appearance. She had a lovely face, with high cheek-bones and dark eyes fringed with long black lashes. Her figure was a little too buxom to be fashionable, but to Kate it made Mrs Eland seem all the more warm and motherly. She was reaching out now and touching Kate's face in a gentle gesture. 'Tek care of ya'sen, lovey.'

Kate nodded and said flatly, 'I'll see you at – Christmas.' It seemed an age away and though Danny's mother said, 'It'll soon be here,' even her tone lacked conviction.

At the cottage next door, Kate found herself swept against Grannie Harris's ample bosom. 'Eh me lass, we'll miss you, all on us. 'Specially Rosie. There's nobody like Kate Hilton in young Rosie's eyes.'

Kate's summer had been spent with Rosie. The child had been her constant companion.

'Let's go and find her. She'd never forgive me if I let you go without seeing her.'

Rosie's tears almost shattered Kate's resolve not to cry. 'Don't go, Katie, don't go 'way. Who'm I going to play with? Who's goin' to take me to school?' She wound her chubby arms around Kate's neck, almost strangling her, and sniffled pitifully.

'I must go, Rosie. Really I must. Me mam'll be waiting

for me,' Kate pulled herself out of the child's grasp, turned and ran.

She could still hear Rosie's sobs as she crested the Hump and plunged down the other side towards home.

'There you are. It's time to go. Mek haste, Kate.' Her mother was dressed in her best costume, with a smart new hat perched on top of her hair which, as always, was piled high on her head, luxuriant and thick – a rich auburn colour like Kate's own. There was not a trace of grey showing in her mother's hair, Kate thought.

Her stepfather was still in his working clothes for he was only coming as far as the station.

'Aren't you going to say goodbye to your sister?'

Dutifully, Kate bent over the cradle and kissed the baby's forehead. Lilian's tiny fingers clutched at Kate's flowing hair and tugged at it.

'Ouch!'

The baby crowed with delight, but when Kate prised open the small hand and stood up, Lilian began to whimper at the removal of her plaything. Kate stood looking down at the child with distaste. She'd rather have little Rosie for a sister any day!

'We're all loaded up,' Jonathan Godfrey came into the kitchen, 'and Enid's just arrived to take Lilian till I get back.' His voice had a forced joviality that did not deceive Kate. But far from upsetting her, it actually comforted her to think that he cared.

As the trap rattled down the lane towards the town, Kate watched Brumbys' Farm become smaller and smaller. She bit down hard upon her lower lip. She refused to let her mother see her cry.

What hurt most of all was that she had not seen Danny.

The one person she loved best in all the world and she had not even been able to say goodbye to him.

She pushed her hand into the pocket of her coat and felt the reassuring wrinkled surface of the whelk shell he had given her.

Seven

The school was a tall grey building set in a row of imposing town houses. From the street, stone steps led up to the heavy front door and the long windows seemed to be watching their approach.

It had been raining when they stepped off the train, and although Esther had tried to hold the umbrella over both of them as they walked from the station, by the time they reached the school Kate's long hair was straggling down her back in untidy wet strands. There was a peculiar fluttering feeling inside her stomach, just below her ribs, like a captive bird struggling to get out.

A maid opened the door; a young girl in a long black dress with a white apron and mob cap covering her short hair. Her face was pale and pinched. She was young enough to be a pupil, but obviously she was not one of them.

'Wait here. I'll tell Miss Denham.'

They were left standing in a hallway that stretched up and up three storeys high. From the centre of the hall the stairs rose to the first floor and divided into two and then again up to the second floor, dividing again. On each level the landings ran around the open square so that even from the topmost floor it was possible to peer down and see who was standing in the hall below.

Kate heard the echo of whispering and looked up to see herself being observed by three pairs of curious eyes, their owners leaning over the balustrade on the second floor.

Somewhere a bell sounded and the three girls scuttled down the stairs to the first floor and disappeared.

The maid returned. 'This way,' and they followed her through a huge oak door at the left-hand side of the hall and into a book-lined study.

From behind a wide, leather-topped desk rose the tallest woman Kate had ever seen. She towered above both Kate and her mother and her height was accentuated even further by her grey hair scraped up from her face into a bun on the top of her head. Miss Denham stood tall and straight-backed, and her shape looked as if her body were trussed up in a corset, moulded by bones and padding, all tightly laced. Her bosom was high and rigid and her waistline, though by no means slim, curved in and then out again to generous hips. Her hairstyle and dress, a grey striped close-fitting gown with a white collar and a small velvet bow at the neck, were out of date for the shapeless fashion of the twenties. But if intimidation of the girls in her charge was her endeavour, then, in Kate's wide eyes, Miss Denham succeeded.

'Good morning, Katharine. I am Miss Denham, and I am the Principal of this school.' The voice was deep, almost masculine, but it fitted the frame from which it issued. Kate felt the woman's cold grey eyes taking in every inch of her appearance from the top of her very wet head right down to the muddy toes of her lace-up boots. The woman was pointing now at Kate's feet.

'I trust, Mrs Godfrey, that you have equipped your daughter with something more appropriate in the way of footwear than – those?'

At her side Kate felt her mother almost bristle with indignation. 'Naturally, Miss Denham, I have – equipped – her with every item on the list of requirements ya gave me.' Esther Godfrey was standing stiffly before the woman and staring fearlessly up at her. In that moment Kate was fiercely proud of her mother until she remembered that it was her mother's fault that they were here in the first place!

Miss Denham pulled a bell-rope and before the tassel on the cord had stopped swinging the little maid appeared in the doorway.

'Say goodbye to your mother, Katharine, and go with Mary.'

Kate gave a little gasp, turned and flung her arms around her mother, pressing her face into Esther Godfrey's bosom. 'Mam, dun't go. Not yet.'

Her mother's arms came tightly around her. She rested her cheek against Kate's hair. 'Oh, Kate,' she whispered. 'You'll be all right, really you will. Write to us . . .' For an instant there was a slight tremor in Esther's voice, as if suddenly she had doubts herself.

'Mrs Godfrey,' Miss Denham's manly voice cut in, 'you are not helping the child.'

Kate lifted her head and looked up into her mother's eyes; eyes that were troubled now. 'Mam, please don't leave me here . . .'

'Katharine!' Miss Denham barked, so that Kate jumped physically. 'Control yourself. We do not condone such emotional behaviour here. Now,' the voice quietened a little, 'I repeat, say goodbye to your mother, and pray conduct yourself with a little more decorum.'

Kate was so shocked that before she really realized what was happening she was being kissed on the cheek by her mother and then ushered out of the door by Mary, who shut the study door with a heavy thud of finality.

'This way, Miss.'

There was nothing Kate could do but follow obediently.

*

The three pairs of inquisitive eyes were staring at her again, this time much closer.

Kate was sitting on a high bed and the three girls were ringed around the end just staring at her.

The long room, with a high ceiling, had five beds down each side. Beside each bed were a small chest of drawers and a narrow wardrobe. There were windows at the end of the room but set so high up in the wall it was impossible to see out of them. They were barred and the little of the glass that could be seen was opaque with grime on the outside so that not even the sky was visible. The floor was bare of any carpet or rugs and was so highly polished that it squeaked under Kate's boots when she walked on it.

'What's your name?' one of the watchers asked at last.

Kate looked at each of the three girls in turn. They were all dressed in similar uniform to her own, yet there was a subtle difference about theirs somehow. They all had short hair, cropped to a length just below their ears.

'Kate. Kate Hilton. What's yours?'

Another spoke but ignored Kate's question. 'Is that your *proper* name? The one you were christened?'

'N-no. I – was christened Katharine, but I'm called Kate.' And Danny calls me Katie, she almost added, but bit her lip to hold back the confidence.

'Huh,' the second girl said scathingly. 'You'll be called Katharine here.'

'And you'll have to have that hair cut.' The third girl spoke for the first time, touching her own neatly cropped hair. 'We all have to have it cut the same way.'

'Or plait it, Isobel. She could have it plaited,' the first one volunteered.

'Not unless she can do it neatly.'

Kate gasped in horror. 'They aren't cuttin' mine!' she said vehemently, but the girls only laughed.

The door opened and a woman entered. She was dressed in what appeared to Kate to be a nurse's uniform. She wore a long navy blue serge dress and a pristine white apron with a bib. Her hair was completely hidden by a starched square of white cloth folded around her head and falling into a triangle at the back.

'Matron – this is the new girl, Katharine Hilton.'

'But she likes to be called Kate.'

The woman's eyebrows almost reached the edge of her cap. 'Really?'

Now four pairs of eyes regarded her.

'Come with me—' the Matron paused and then added with emphasis, 'Katharine.'

The three girls stifled their giggles swiftly as Kate slid slowly off her bed and walked between them towards the Matron.

'Look at her blouse – it's home-made,' came a whisper.

'So's her gym-slip – just look at her boots!'

'Have you unpacked and put your clothes away?' the matron was asking.

'No, me trunk ain't got here yet.'

Another whisper. 'Listen to how she speaks! How common!'

Kate spent the next half-hour in the Matron's room listening to a list of school rules which she knew she would never remember. Then the Matron took her downstairs to the first floor and into a classroom to meet her teacher. When they entered, there were seven other girls in the room, all sitting in a semi-circle around the teacher, sewing. But at once they all stood up and chanted, 'Good afternoon, Matron,' and only sat down again when the Matron had acknowledged their greeting and added, 'You may sit down, girls.'

'Miss Ogden – this is Katharine Hilton. She will be in your class from tomorrow morning.'

The teacher rose and came to greet Kate, stretching out her hands to take Kate's. For the first time since she had arrived at this place, Kate found herself looking into a face that was smiling and welcoming. Miss Ogden was a pretty, dark-haired young woman with a kind smile and merry, dancing eyes. 'Welcome to Class Two, Katharine. We'll introduce you to everyone tomorrow.'

Kate glanced briefly at the other pupils and her heart sank when she saw that the three girls whom she had met half an hour earlier were sitting there, their heads bent demurely over their sewing.

'We'll see you at dinner this evening,' Miss Ogden said as the matron ushered Kate out of the classroom door and continued to show her around the school.

The ground floor consisted of the Principal's study and private sitting room, the dining room and, at the rear of the house, the kitchens where the cook reigned over her kitchen maid and the parlourmaid who had answered the door. On the first floor were three classrooms, an art room and a domestic science room. Upstairs were three large dormitories with ten beds in each, Miss Denham's bedroom and those of her two assistant teachers and the Matron. There was also a small room set aside as the sickroom, whilst up in the attic were the domestic servants' bedrooms.

'There, now you have seen everything, Katharine, I expect you not to get lost. Miss Denham cannot abide unpunctuality either for lessons or meals, or indeed for anything. Dinner is at half-past six. You may go and unpack your trunk which I believe has now arrived from the station.'

With the briefest of nods, she dismissed Kate.

'We speak French at meal-times.' In the dining room, Miss

70

Denham was towering above her. 'I presume you know a little French?'

'No, Miss, I dun't.'

'She can't speak English properly,' came a voice from somewhere behind her, but Miss Denham chose to ignore the remark.

'You'd better sit next to me this evening, but from tomorrow you will sit at Miss Ogden's table.'

With an outward meekness she did not feel inside, Kate followed the Principal, thinking that she would rather sit near Miss Ogden, French or no French.

Miss Denham's deep voice boomed out above their bowed heads, saying the Grace in French. Then there was a scraping of chairs on the bare wooden floor and everyone sat down.

Two girls from each table went to the serving hatch at the end of the dining room and returned carrying plates with a portion of meat on each. The procedure was repeated until everyone was served. Then, starting with the teacher at the head of each table, the vegetables were passed round and everyone helped themselves. Only when everyone was served was the signal given that they might start eating.

Conversation was not allowed, the rattle of knives and forks being the only sound in the room.

Kate felt the knot in her stomach, just below her ribs, tightening. She took a mouthful of meat and began to chew. The meat was tough and tasteless. Her mouth was dry; she could not swallow it.

'Please may I have a glass of water?'

The Principal spoke but the words were completely unintelligible to Kate. '*En français, s'il te plaît.*'

Kate stared blankly at her. Even sitting down the woman looked tall and imposing, with lips so pursed there was hardly any mouth at all. Further down the table came a stifled giggle which prompted a stony glare from Miss Denham.

There was no way Kate could understand what was being said to her and even less chance of her replying. She bent her head and ate some of the vegetables instead. They had been over-cooked to a mushy pulp. She felt the bile rise into her throat with revulsion. Setting her knife and fork neatly together at the edge of the plate, Kate folded her hands in her lap.

She would eat no more.

'*Mange*!' In the silence of the room, Miss Denham's voice boomed, audible to all.

Kate fixed her gaze upon a picture on the wall opposite to where she was sitting, yet she could feel every eye in the room was turned in her direction. She was aware that only one face was perhaps turned upon her with any expression of sympathy and that was Miss Ogden's, who was seated just below the picture.

'Katharine Hilton, *mange – maintenant*!'

The nervous knot in Kate's stomach hardened into anger. Her green eyes swivelled from the picture and sparked fire.

'I dun't know what you are saying to me. I dun't understand French.'

A shocked gasp reverberated around the room.

Kate stood up, her chair scraping on the wooden floor.

'*Assieds-toi, immédiatement*!'

Kate realized she was probably being ordered to sit down, but she had said she could not understand and now she had to carry it through. She left her place and marched down the length of the room, pulled open the heavy door and went through it. It swung to behind her with an echoing thud. The hall was dark and dismal, with only low wall lights burning. Kate shuddered, lifted her skirt above her knees and scampered up the two flights of stairs to the dormitory.

It was worse there. The long room was in complete darkness with only a glimmer of light coming from the high, barred windows at the far end. Kate rushed towards them. If only she could see out, she might feel better. If she could see the garden, trees, hear the birds . . .

She stood below the windows craning her neck backwards, but all she could see was pale grey light through the grime.

'I can't even see the sky!' she wailed aloud. She leaned her cheek against the wall and sobbed.

It seemed as though she was in the darkness on her own for an age, huddled on her bed, before she heard voices coming up the stairs and along the landing, nearer and nearer.

Then they were in the room. Someone lit the gas light near the door and they were crowding round the end of her bed, gaping at her. Some had expressions of something akin to admiration. 'Fancy walking out like that. I'd never have dared!'

Others with derisory glee. 'You're in for it. Miss Denham wants you in her study. Now!'

And one or two with hostility: 'You'll get us all into trouble if you carry on like that.'

'What can you expect from a country bumpkin? No manners and can't even understand a word of French!'

'Ya'd better go down, likely ya're in fer ca-ane.' It was a cruel impersonation of the Lincolnshire dialect so strong in Kate's speech.

Rage flooded through her again. She dashed away her tears with the back of her hand and swung her legs off the bed. 'I aren't afraid of *her*!'

'Just listen to her! "I aren't!" Wherever did she go to school?'

'A better school than this 'un,' Kate uttered as a parting

shot as she marched out of the room, the sound of their heartless laughter following her down the stairs.

Outside the door of Miss Denham's study, her boldness deserted her. Again the knot of nerves was fluttering just beneath her ribs and rising into her throat. She swallowed and her empty stomach gurgled.

She knocked on the door and on hearing 'Enter' – thankfully spoken in English now – she went in.

Miss Denham sat behind her desk with Miss Ogden standing on one side of her and the Matron on the other. Miss Ogden looked at her sadly, whilst outrage was apparent on the other two faces.

'Katharine Hilton, your behaviour at the dinner table this evening was disgraceful,' Miss Denham began. Kate returned the woman's stare steadfastly, though her insides were churning and her knees were trembling. 'Have you anything to say for yourself?'

'I felt sick, Miss.'

Out of the corner of her eye she saw Miss Ogden's hand flutter briefly towards her, almost as if she wanted to reach out and touch her. 'Oh, you poor child . . .' she heard the teacher mutter, but the gesture of understanding was quelled by a look from the Principal.

Miss Denham turned her cold gaze back upon Kate. 'Normally I would cane you for such behaviour, but because it is your first day here, this time,' there was heavy emphasis on the two words 'this time', 'we will say no more about it. However, you will go straight to your dormitory and to bed instead of participating in games hour before bedtime. You may go.'

Kate went – thankfully. She was relieved to find the dormitory empty, and having paid a visit to the bathroom she undressed and lay down in the narrow, hard bed.

The sounds of the large building were all around her:

voices, footsteps, doors banging, and the chimes of the cathedral clock only a short distance away. When the other girls came to bed, Kate lay with her head buried beneath the covers and pretended to be asleep. No one spoke to her or about her. It was as if she were not even there. When the room was in darkness she lay listening to the breathing of the nine other girls in the room and knew sleep would be impossible. She felt closed in and longed for the cool marsh breezes and the sound of the sea – and Danny.

At the thought of Danny she stuffed the sheet into her mouth to stifle a sob.

Then she remembered the whelk shell; a little piece of home. Quietly, she turned back the covers and swung her feet to the floor. She was half-way between her bed and the wardrobe when light flooded into the room and Kate turned, blinking in the sudden brightness, to see the Matron standing in the doorway.

'What are you doing out of bed, girl?'

The polished floorboards were icy beneath her bare feet. Kate shivered, not so much from cold as from knowing that every girl in the room was wide awake and listening.

'Well?' snapped the Matron.

'I was just getting summat from me coat in the wardrobe.'

Blanket-muffled laughter sounded.

'What is it you want?'

Kate hesitated, searching desperately. 'Me – me hanky.'

'Have you not got a clean one in your bedside drawer?'

'I – dun't know.'

'Oh, very well, but hurry up.'

Trembling now, Kate opened the door of the wardrobe which squeaked loudly in the silence. Praying fervently, she reached into her coat pocket and felt the hard roundness of the whelk shell and beneath it – 'Oh thank you, thank you' – the softness of her white handkerchief.

Fumbling a little, she wrapped the shell in the handkerchief and held it tightly in the palm of her hand before she withdrew it from her pocket. When she turned back to face the Matron, only one corner of the hanky showed in her hand.

The woman nodded briefly and closed the door, plunging the room into darkness once more.

Kate climbed into bed and buried her head beneath the covers to unwrap the shell.

Only then, with the sound of the sea in her ear, did she fall asleep.

Eight

'Katharine Hilton!' Matron's voice rose above the hubbub as the girls scurried to and from the bathroom the next morning. 'Your bath nights are Tuesdays and Fridays, and you will wash your hair each Friday.'

Kate felt the woman's eyes take in the long flowing auburn hair that tumbled untidily down her back, so long that she could almost sit on it.

Her mouth pursed, Matron said, 'You will plait your hair before you come down to breakfast.'

It was an almost impossible task for Kate to plait the long hair herself. She made a valiant effort, although strands escaped and the skeins of hair were woven in and out unevenly. If only her mother's nimble fingers were there; she could plait the length of Kate's hair in seconds.

The day seemed interminable. Kate struggled with the sums and every time she opened her mouth to speak, there came a wave of suppressed giggles around the room. Miss Ogden, helpless to reprimand the covert cruelty, tried to bring comfort to the lonely new girl by praising her sewing, but that only seemed to alienate her further from the other girls.

' "Look at the back of Katharine's work" ', mimicked Isobel, when Miss Ogden left the room for a moment. ' "See how neat it is?" Pity her hair isn't as neat.'

Isobel's two followers giggled dutifully. It was soon obvious to Kate that Isobel Cartwright was a natural ring-leader.

The two girls who were her closest friends – Brenda and Hazel – followed her around and she ordered them about like a mistress giving orders to servants. Isobel had short hair, cut to the regulation length, and yet there seemed a subtle difference in the style. Kate couldn't understand what it was that made it different from all the rest. Then, when school had finished on the Friday afternoon, Isobel was missing. Kate overheard Brenda saying that she had gone out in a car.

'Her mother's taken her out to tea in town – and to have her hair done. They've got a chauffeur. You should have seen him, Hazel. He looked so smart in his grey uniform and peaked cap.'

'However does Isobel get permission to go out in the week?'

Brenda leaned closer, but Kate still heard her whispered words. 'It's probably because her father's a governor of the school. Even Miss Denham doesn't want to upset the Cartwright family!'

'Yes, but to be allowed to go out of school to have her hair done in a salon . .!' Hazel sighed enviously.

The subject of hair made them turn and look at Kate. 'It's your bath night tonight,' Hazel reminded her gleefully. '*And* you've to wash your hair.'

'How do you get it dry?'

'In front of the range,' Kate told them.

The two girls exchanged a glance and then clutched each other as they shook with laughter. 'There's no range here. You'll have to go into the kitchen and put your head in the oven!'

Isobel returned from town with her hair beautifully styled and shining golden. She really was quite a pretty girl, Kate thought charitably, except for a sulky pout to her mouth and a way of holding her head as if she were looking down her nose at everything and everyone. And her cold blue eyes missed nothing.

That evening Kate tiptoed into the bathroom carrying her towel, a huge bar of carbolic soap and a flannel. There was a line of six wash-basins along one wall and two baths in separate cubicles. Sighing with relief, she realized she had the bathroom to herself. She moved into one of the cubicles and looked at the huge cast-iron bath standing on clawed feet and fitted with brass-coloured taps. She'd never seen anything like this before; it was very different from bath-night on a Friday night at home when her mother banished her stepfather from the kitchen and tugged the zinc bath in front of the range, drawing water from the side boiler. Kate and her mother would wash each other's hair before the girl stepped into the bath. Esther, her own hair wrapped in a towel, would pour more hot water into the tub so that it swirled around Kate, warming her. Then she would kneel and soap her daughter's back, talking to her about school or the farm.

Sitting in front of the kitchen range, in the rosy glow of the firelight, had been warm and intimate. It was a time Kate had cherished; a time when she had her mother to herself – even after Lilian had been born.

But this bathroom was so cold that Kate shivered. The floor was bare stone, the walls painted a dull green with only a line of patterned tiles running round the wall just above the bath. Somewhere above her, pipes gurgled noisily as the hot water was pumped up from the boiler in the cellar. She washed her hair in one of the basins first and wound it up in her towel, turban-fashion, on top of her head. Then she moved into one of the cubicles. The bath was so huge that Kate thought if she filled it too full and slipped when climbing in over the high side, she might well drown in it and no one would know.

The bathroom door opened and Isobel looked in. 'Oh, sorry . . .' she began, then, recognizing Kate, added, 'Oh, it's you. What's the matter? Never seen a bath before? You fill it with water, get in and wash your dirty self all over!'

Kate turned her back on the girl and learned over the side of the bath. With nervous fingers she twisted the top of the huge tap and jumped when water gushed out suddenly. She heard Isobel laughing as she went into the next cubicle and ran her own bath.

When the water had reached a depth of about twelve inches, Kate turned off the taps. From the next-door cubicle, the water still gushed into the bath and continued for such a long time that Kate thought it would never stop. As she sat in the water and began to soap herself, she heard the taps being turned off and Isobel splashing. Only a minute or so later, she heard a swish of water as the girl next door stood up and climbed out of the bath. The plug on its chain was pulled out and the water began to empty from the bath. What a waste, Kate thought, me mam would have a ducky fit! Fancy filling a bath up that much and spending about a minute in it and then getting out and emptying it. Isobel wouldn't do that if she had to fill the bath by the bucketful as they did at home. Kate splashed water on to her body to wash off the soap, then put her hands on the top edges of the bath and levered herself up. At that moment, Isobel popped her head round the corner again, dressed in her pyjamas and dressing-gown, ready to leave. Her cool gaze lingered on Kate's slim body, the small breasts scarcely formed and her long legs, thin and coltish. Embarrassed, Kate stood in the bath wishing she had a towel to put around her to cover her nakedness, but the only one she had brought was wrapped around her head.

'You'd better hurry up. We're only allowed ten minutes

each. There's others to bath after you, you know,' the girl said brusquely.

She turned away and Kate heard the bathroom door open. From her position in the cubicle, Kate could not see what Isobel was doing, but the next moment the whole room was plunged into blackness.

Upon leaving Isobel had turned off the gas-light near the door, deliberately leaving Kate standing in the bath, shivering in the darkness.

'Isobel, don't,' she shouted, but the door slammed.

Kate bent and put out her hands trying to find the edge of the bath. Her feet slipped and she felt herself falling. She let out a yell as she hit her head with a thud against the bath and slipped back down into the water, which sloshed up and down the bath and splashed over the edge on to the floor. She felt the towel unwind and fall from her head.

'Isobel,' she roared, more angry now than frightened or hurt. She grabbed the sides of the bath and heaved herself upright and as she did so, someone pushed open the door and light from the corridor filtered into the bathroom.

'What on earth are you doing, girl? Did you put this light off?' Matron snapped as she relit the light to inspect the bathroom. 'Just look at the mess you are making! Mind you clear all this up. And where's your towel?'

Kate, her hair plastered to her back and running rivulets down her body, bent and picked the dripping towel out of the water.

'Well, you're not going to get very dry on that, are you, you foolish child?' The matron shook her head impatiently. 'Wait there . . .' She disappeared, and Kate stepped carefully out of the bath and wrung her wet towel out, twisting it viciously between her hands, wishing it was Isobel Cartwright's neck.

Matron returned with a towel. 'Here, dry yourself quickly

and let's have no more of this nonsense. And don't go turning lights off until you know how to relight them. Fancy trying to take a bath in the dark!' She shook her head in exasperation and disbelief that anyone could be so stupid.

Kate opened her mouth to retort that the light had been turned out while she was in the bath, but then she closed it again without speaking. She was no tell-tale. She never had been and she wasn't going to start now, however much she hated Isobel Cartwright.

The Matron turned away and left the room, leaving Kate to dry herself and wipe the floor. There was nothing else to use but her own towel which was now not only soaking wet but grubby too.

When she returned to the dormitory, she found all the girls knew of her embarrassment. She glared at Isobel, who smirked as she said, 'Tell Matron, did you?'

'No,' Kate answered shortly. 'I aren't a tell-tale . . .' There were further giggles. 'But I'll get you back, Isobel Cartwright,' she added, wagging her forefinger at the other girl. 'I dun't care how long I have to wait – but one day I'll get you back. You see if I don't!'

'Oooh, I'm sha-aking in me shoes,' Isobel mocked.

Kate turned her back on them all and began to dry her hair, rubbing it vigorously with a towel.

On the first Sunday after her arrival, Kate discovered that all the pupils walked in crocodile fashion up the steep hill to the cathedral for Morning Service, accompanied by the Principal and the two assistant teachers.

The moment she stepped through the huge doors, Kate felt her heart begin to thud. The interior of the holy place was immense! Her hobnailed boots echoed hollowly on the flagstones and she could feel Miss Denham's disapproval boring into her back.

Awe-struck, Kate gazed around her as she took her place in a pew. Stone pillars supported the high arched roof and in front of her the rich wooden carving of the angel choir gave warmth to the austere stonework. Light shone through the stained glass windows, mottling the flagstones.

Unbidden, and for no reason that she could understand, a feeling of peace crept through her. Although she was still sitting among them, for an hour or so she was safe from the taunts of her fellow-pupils and Miss Denham's scolding.

For the first time since she had arrived in Lincoln, Kate felt a sense of security as she gazed around her in wonderment. She forgot her own misfortune as she marvelled at the beauty of the building and listened to the pure voices of the choir, the music reverberating sweetly through the vastness.

Miss Denham walked up and down the aisle twice during the service, her sharp eyes lingering on whisperers, who, reddening, subsided at once.

Kate knelt for the final prayer. 'Please let me go home,' she prayed silently and fervently, squeezing her eyes tightly shut and pressing her hands together so hard her wrists hurt. 'Please make something happen so I can go home . . .'

There was shuffling all around her and she opened her eyes to see that everyone was rising to leave. She sighed and scrambled to her feet. As they filed out of the cathedral, Kate felt bereft as if she were being dragged from a place of sanctuary.

'There's a uniform inspection!' Hazel came running into the dormitory, slamming the door behind her. 'Miss Denham *and*

Matron! They're in "B" Dormitory now. They'll be here next. Quick!'

'Oh help!' wailed one girl down the far end of the dormitory. 'I've lost my house shoes. I'll be for it.'

'I saw a pair in the bathroom last night. Did you leave them there?'

The girl's face brightened. 'Ooh thanks, Hazel. I think I did.' And she scuttled out of the room to retrieve her lost property.

Kate watched all the girls in the room opening drawer after drawer of their bedside cabinets, refolding and tidying the contents. Wardrobe doors were flung open and the clothes hanging there straightened, shoes set neatly beneath.

Brenda was untying the braid girdle around her waist. 'I think my gym-slip's too short. If I loosen my sash will it make it a bit longer?' she asked Isobel.

'It might do,' Isobel said doubtfully.

'Do you think she'll do a gym-slip inspection?'

'Bound to. She always does at the beginning of term.'

'Oooh!' Brenda wailed. 'Does that look better, Isobel?'

Isobel inspected her friend's tunic. 'A bit,' she said, sounding none too hopeful.

The door opened and the girl who had gone to find her shoes came in. 'They're coming,' she hissed.

As the Principal and Matron entered, every girl was standing by her bed, almost to attention. Miss Denham carried a ruler and a pair of scissors.

'Kneel,' Miss Denham commanded.

Mystified, Kate glanced round to see every girl kneeling down, not against the bed as if to pray, but in a line down the centre of the room.

'Katharine . . .' came the warning voice, and swiftly Kate knelt down at the end of the line.

Miss Denham passed down the line, placing the end of

the ruler on the floor and measuring the height of each gym-slip hem from the floor. It was about two inches. Kate glanced down, knowing, with a sinking heart, what she would see. Her own tunic was longer than everyone else's, its hem wrinkling against the bare boards.

She watched as Miss Denham paused in front of Brenda, measuring carefully. Kate could see that the girl was bending her body forward slightly so that the hemline came a little nearer the floor. Miss Denham passed on without comment and Kate could almost hear Brenda's relief.

They were standing before Kate and there was no need for the ruler. 'Stand up, Katharine,' the voice boomed. As she did so, Miss Denham grasped the hem of Kate's gym-slip and, turning it up, inserted the scissors into Esther Godfrey's neat stitching and cut the thread. There was a tearing sound as she ripped the hem undone.

'Go down to Miss Ogden's room and ask her to supply you with needle and thread. You will sew up this hem to the correct length tonight. And another thing, Katharine, I am not satisfied with the neatness of your plait. You know the rule, unless you can plait your hair neatly in a single plait down your back, you must have it cut short.'

Kate's face flamed and when the two women had left the room, noise broke out on all sides.

'Phew! That was a close one. I thought I'd had it!' said Brenda.

'She didn't even look at my shoes,' the other girl said petulantly, then cheered up. 'Still, at least I've found them.'

'Ya'd better get goin', Ka-ate,' Isobel mimicked. 'Else ya'll be up 'alf the night a-plaiting yar hair.'

Kate turned and left the room, the sound of their laughter following her along the corridor.

*

The days crawled by and she had been at the school two weeks. Two weeks in which she had hardly been able to eat. Fourteen days of sitting beneath Miss Denham's gaze, for the Principal had ordered her to sit beside her for every meal instead of moving to Miss Ogden's table.

Miss Ogden had been the only person to show even a glimmer of kindness, but that was made tentatively, as if she herself feared reprisals should she show too much sympathy towards the new girl. In the classroom Miss Ogden was patient, and Kate felt as if the young teacher would have liked to display more understanding but dared not show favouritism in front of the rest of the class. As for the other girls – led on by the three who had assumed the role of her tormentors, Isobel, Brenda and Hazel – there was not one friendly word from any of them.

Meals were purgatory. Under Miss Denham's glare Kate struggled to eat the unappetizing food, while her stomach churned rebelliously and constantly threatened revolt.

Then came the day of the gooseberries.

Nine

The meal had been going quite well. She had managed to eat all the first course – steak and kidney pie. For once the meat was tender and the pastry not too soggy. But when a bowl of gooseberries was placed before her, Kate looked around for the custard. There was none. She bit her lip and said tentatively to the girl next to her. *'Passez le sugar, sivoo play.'*

'Sucre, sucre,' boomed Miss Denham's voice to her left. *'Tu n'as pas besoin de sucre.'*

Kate looked down at the small green bullets in the dish. Reluctantly, she picked up her spoon and selected two of the gooseberries that looked a little softer than the rest. The moment she put them in her mouth the sourness attacked her taste-buds so that her mouth salivated and her stomach erupted. Before she knew what was happening, she had vomited into the dish in front of her, bringing up all the first course.

Next to her, a girl screamed and pushed back her chair, 'Oh how disgusting!' while Miss Denham rose and grabbed Kate's arm in a vice-like grip and hustled her, still retching, down the room past all the staring faces. Kate found herself dragged through the hallway and pushed into a small lavatory. The door slammed behind her and miserably she leaned over the bowl and retched until there was nothing left to bring up but evil-tasting, yellow bile. Yet still her mouth salivated and her stomach heaved.

At last she leaned against the wall, weak and trembling, a cold sweat breaking out all over her.

A knock came on the door and Miss Ogden's gentle voice said, 'Katharine, are you all right?'

When Kate did not answer, the door opened and pushed against her as she stood behind it. 'Katharine...? Oh, my dear girl...'

The teacher drew Kate out of the small, dark room. 'Are you feeling better now? Come along, let me take you up to Matron.'

But the Matron was as unsympathetic as Miss Denham. 'Clean yourself up, girl. How dare you create such a disgraceful scene? You're doing it on purpose, just to cause disruption. Change your dress and then you are to report to Miss Denham's study.'

Half an hour later Kate was standing in front of Miss Denham's desk. The Principal rose majestically. 'Come with me.'

Meekly, Kate followed and found herself in the huge dining room being seated at the table once more. All evidence of her humiliation had been removed, but the floor showed damp patches where it had been wiped clean.

A maid entered from the kitchen and placed a plate of food in front of her. It was the first course.

'You will stay here and eat the whole meal again and you will not leave until you have done so.'

Kate watched the woman turn and leave the room. The door closed behind her.

Left alone, without Miss Denham's critical gaze upon her every mouthful, strangely Kate found she could eat – at least the first course – but when another dish of gooseberries came, she hesitated. She picked up her spoon and ate one. The gooseberry itself was just as sour as before but now the juice in which the fruit lay was sweet – much sweeter than before. Someone had realized what was happening and had taken pity on her. Kate felt a warm gratitude towards the unknown person beyond the kitchen door.

When Miss Denham returned, Kate was sitting with two empty plates in front of her.

The woman stood over her. 'There, you see, you can eat it when you try.'

Kate stared back at the woman, deliberately keeping her face expressionless. When dismissed, the young girl stood up and, holding her head high, walked out of the room. There was no way she could win against the authority of this horrible woman, but Kate Hilton was certainly not going to be cowed by her.

But oh, how she longed to be back home running along the beach with Danny panting after her shouting, 'Wait for me, Katie, wait for me!' or to feel the chubby arms of little Rosie Maine winding themselves around her neck and hear her merry voice pleading, 'Come and play with me, Kate.'

Before returning to her classroom Kate went up to the dormitory and felt in the pocket of her coat for the whelk shell, standing several minutes with it pressed against her ear so that even in this dismal, lonely room she might still hear the sound of home.

On the third Sunday, Peggy Godfrey arrived at the school to take Kate out for the afternoon.

Two whole hours of freedom, thought Kate ecstatically. It was her first escape from what she thought of as her prison.

They walked down the hill and along a straight road past a park on the left-hand side until they came to a side street where Mr and Mrs Godfrey lived at number eight. The houses were terraced, with a small frontage outside the bay window and front door. A passage ran between every second house leading to both back yards.

'Kate, how lovely to see you.' Jonathan's mother was smiling a welcome as she opened the front door and Kate found herself stepping straight into the best parlour.

'Come through to the living room, dear. Take no notice of all this.' She laughed and waved her hand to encompass the front room. Kate glanced around as she followed Jonathan's mother. The room was littered with paper patterns and pieces of material. In the centre of the room on a small table stood a sewing machine.

'I use it as my workroom,' Mrs Godfrey was explaining, and Kate remembered that at Lilian's christening Peggy had said her mother was a dressmaker. 'My ladies come here for fittings so I have to have somewhere nice and we never use the front room for anything else except at Christmas.'

Mrs Godfrey led the way through to the back living room, 'Here we are, dear. Look who's come to see us, Henry.'

Kate stepped into the room, where the smell of their recent Sunday dinner still lingered.

'This is Mr Godfrey.' Mrs Godfrey was gesturing towards a man sitting in an easy chair near the fire. He lowered the newspaper he was reading and stood up, and Kate found herself looking into the kindly face of her stepfather. An older face, of course, but the likeness was so astonishing that she could not prevent the words escaping her lips.

'Oh, you're just like me dad.'

The others laughed and Mr Godfrey's deep voice said, 'That's not the first time I've been told that.' He smiled gently down at her, his eyes crinkling just like his son's.

'Sit down, sit down. I hope you can stay to tea, dear,' Mrs Godfrey was saying. 'Peggy has made a trifle, haven't you, Peg?'

Taking off her coat and hat, Peggy nodded.

'And how do you like the school, young Kate?' Mr Godfrey asked.

As she felt the eyes of the three adults upon her, Kate bit on her lower lip to still its sudden trembling. She glanced from one to another and saw the genuine concern written on all their faces; such an expression of friendliness which she had not seen since her arrival in this city.

'It's awful,' she burst out, and the tears held in check for so long now spilled over and flooded down her face. At once Mrs Godfrey pulled her down on to the settee and sat beside her, putting an arm around her shoulders. Shocked, Peggy stood in front of them wringing her hands. Mr Godfrey sat down in his chair again, but laid his newspaper aside and sat forward, his forehead creasing worriedly.

'Tell us all about it, love,' Mrs Godfrey insisted. And out it all came tumbling.

'Well!' and 'Oh, how could they!' and 'I can scarcely believe it!' were the only interruptions they made and when she had finished and leaned her head against Mrs Godfrey's shoulder, it was Peggy who said, 'We can't let her go back there, Mother.'

Mrs Godfrey glanced worriedly at Kate and then at her husband. 'What do you think, Henry?'

Mr Godfrey shook his head, 'It used to have a very good name when Miss Peterson ran it . . .' He paused and Kate saw the glance that passed between husband and wife.

Mrs Godfrey put her arm around Kate, 'Come along and have your tea, dear, and then we'll think what to do.'

As she sat at their tea table, hunger overwhelmed her. There were delicately cut cucumber sandwiches, a trifle with cream, and cakes – a chocolate one with chocolate icing and a sponge cake with jam in the middle.

'Help yourself, dear.'

Six sandwiches, two helpings of trifle and three pieces of cake later, Mrs Godfrey said, 'Better now?'

Kate nodded, feeling comfortably full for the first time in weeks.

'Now,' Mrs Godfrey turned to her husband. 'What ought we to do, Henry?'

'I've been thinking, whilst we've been having tea,' he said slowly. 'I'm afraid we didn't ought to let you stay with us. It wouldn't be right. The school would be angry and your mother wouldn't thank us for interfering. But,' he added hurriedly, 'we'll write to Jonathan – yes, that's what we'll do. We'll tell him everything you've told us and he'll talk to your mother.'

'Couldn't you go and see this – this Miss Denham, Father?' Peggy put in quietly. 'Perhaps she'd listen to you.' She turned to Kate to explain. 'Father's a deputy headmaster at the boys' school in the city.'

Kate nodded. 'I thought it was *his* school I was coming to,' she said simply, but the note of wistfulness was not lost upon the three adults. Mrs Godfrey patted her hand.

'I'd go and see this Miss Denham if I thought it would help,' Mr Godfrey was saying. 'But from what you tell us, Kate, the woman would undoubtedly see it as interference and it could make things even worse for you.'

Kate bowed her head and her long hair fell forward hiding her face. She knew what Mr Godfrey was saying was reasonable; that was exactly how Miss Denham would react. And she doubted whether a letter to her stepfather would help either. He might be sympathetic, but would her mother be?

Slowly Kate rose from the table. 'Thank you for the tea, Mrs Godfrey, it was lovely,' she said in a small voice.

'Now, you can come here any time you like. Every Sunday for your tea. And in the week too, if they'll let you.'

Kate shook back her long hair. 'I dun't think they'll let me come for another two weeks.'

'Well, come whenever you can. We'll be here. Now, Peggy will walk back with you.'

As they walked up the hill, Peggy said, 'I'm sorry you're having to go back. I'd have let you stay with us if it had been up to me. But Father's in a difficult position, being in the teaching profession too. And Mother's afraid of upsetting your mother. She thinks the world of our Jonathan, you know, and doesn't want to do anything that might cause trouble between him and his wife. You do see, don't you, Kate?'

Inwardly Kate sighed. Yes, she did see – only too well!

'Matron wants you, Sicky.'

'You'd better get along to her room instead of standing there gaping.' Her three tormentors – with Isobel Cartwright as the ring-leader – had brought her the command and now they stood close together, their heads bent towards each other, giggling and whispering.

Kate's stomach contracted. She had no choice but to obey the summons. She tucked the shell she was holding under her pillow and slipped off the edge of the high bed. With an exaggerated movement the girls stood back out of her way.

'Dun't get near 'er,' Isobel mimicked. 'She'll be sick all ovver ya.'

'She will be sick when she knows what Matron wants her for.' They all laughed again.

As Kate moved away from her bed, Isobel pounced forward and thrust her hand under the pillow. 'Let's see what you're hiding under here . . .'

Kate whirled around and lunged at the girl, but too late.

93

Isobel held up the whelk shell. 'Look, Sicky's got a pwetty shell. Ah! Here, Brenda, catch.'

Isobel tossed the shell high over Kate's head and Brenda caught it deftly. Kate turned and caught hold of Brenda's arms. 'Give it me!' she cried. 'Give it back. It's mine.'

Brenda threw it to Hazel and the three of them encircled her, throwing it from one to the other.

Kate was almost weeping with frustration. 'You've no right to tek me shell.' The anger welled up in her and she screamed. 'Give it me back!'

The door was flung open and the Matron marched into the room. 'What is all this noise about?'

Immediately Isobel put her hand holding the shell behind her back and turned innocent eyes upon the Matron.

Matron's gaze came to rest upon Kate's hot face and dishevelled hair. 'Katharine Hilton – come with me this instant.'

Without waiting to see if the girl obeyed her, the woman turned and left the room. Kate swung back to Isobel. 'Give me my shell.'

The hand remained behind the girl's back. 'Shell?' the girl drawled, her cold eyes narrowing, 'What shell might that be?'

'You'd better get along to Matron's room else you'll be in more trouble,' Hazel warned.

Kate hesitated, then, casting a vicious glance at Isobel, she muttered through her teeth, 'You wait, Isobel Cartwright, just you wait!'

Pushing Hazel aside, Kate stormed out of the dormitory.

The Matron was standing in the centre of the medical room with a large pair of scissors in her hands. 'Now, my girl. Since you cannot, apparently, keep your hair neatly plaited, it's time we cut it to regulation length.'

Horrified, Kate wheeled around to run from the room but found her way barred by the daunting figure of Miss Denham advancing into the room behind her.

Still in a temper from the girls' teasing, Kate fought back. 'No, no. You aren't going to cut me hair. You've no right. I won't . . .'

The door closed and the immovable figure of Miss Denham leaned against it. 'You, Katharine Hilton, will do exactly as you are told and we will have no more of this wilful behaviour.'

Hardly before Kate knew what was happening, Miss Denham had caught hold of her shoulders and pulled her towards her, enfolding her in a vice-like grip. Kate's face was pressed suffocatingly against the woman's massive bosom. She felt the painful tug on her scalp as the Matron grasped a handful of hair and she heard the scissors cut into her silken curls. Snip, snip, snip and her beautiful auburn tresses slipped to the floor.

When Miss Denham released her, Kate could feel the sudden chill on her neck and she put up her hand to feel the jagged ends brutally cropped just below her ears. Suddenly all the fight went out of her. Her knees gave way and she sank down, reaching out with trembling fingers to touch the shorn locks lying on the floor.

'Get up, Katharine, and sit in a chair whilst I neaten . . .'

Her spirit returned. She scrambled up and struck out at the woman, knocking the scissors out of her hand and sending them slithering across the floor. 'Ya'll not touch me hair – not again.' Her fury gave her strength. She pushed past Miss Denham, dragged open the door and ran. Down the two flights of stairs, through the hall, out of the huge heavy front door and down the steps into the street before anyone could stop her.

On the pavement, poised on the balls of her feet, she

hesitated and glanced back at the grey building towering menacingly above her. Then, her decision made, she picked up her skirts and began to run up the hill towards the cathedral.

Ten

She was wet, cold, hungry – and lost!

Kate had waited in the cathedral until dark, joining the Evensong worshippers and leaving amidst them, hoping that no one would recognize the school uniform and question why she was there on her own – and without coat or hat.

No one did.

She wandered around the precincts of the towering building until she came to a statue of Lord Tennyson. Tired, she sat down and leaned her back against the base.

'What are you doing here, little girl?' The voice spoke directly above her. Kate blinked. For one foolish moment she thought it was the statue speaking to her. Looking round, she saw an elderly man dressed in a long black cassock peering round the corner of the statue.

Kate scrambled up and began to back away from him. Her heart was pounding and at once she was poised on her toes ready for flight. But the man's tone was friendly. 'Don't be afraid. I won't harm you – or be angry. I just wondered – I mean – are you all right? Shouldn't you be going home?'

'Yes,' Kate replied firmly, although he could not fully understand the meaning behind her words. 'That's exactly where I should be – home!'

'Then why . . .?'

'I dun't know which way it is. At least – I know I need to go east, towards the . . .' she stopped. She had been going to say 'towards the sea', but perhaps the old man would question that. It was a long way to the sea. Kate took a deep breath and said, 'I came to Evensong,' which was the truth but not the whole truth,' and when I came out, I didn't know which way to go. So, I was waiting for the stars to come out so I could see the North Star and then I'd know.'

The old man chuckled. 'You seem a very knowledgeable young lady. Finding your way by the stars, eh? Well, well, I never did.'

'Danny,' the very mention of his name brought a lump to her throat, 'he's my friend – he taught me.'

'Did he indeed?' The elderly man glanced upwards into the darkening sky. 'Well, my dear, it's very cloudy tonight. It looks like rain. I don't think you're going to see the stars at all tonight.'

Kate tipped her head backwards, feeling the jagged edges of her newly cropped hair against her neck. She sighed. He was right – there would be neither moon nor stars this night.

She looked back again at the old man. 'Do you know which way is east?' she ventured.

The man nodded. 'Yes, my dear. In fact I'll take you and set you on your way. Once on the road, you just keep straight on.'

They fell into step together and he continued, 'All the main roads which lead into Lincoln were originally built by the Romans and they all lead straight and true towards the cathedral. Now here we are, this will lead you to Wragby Road.' He glanced down at her. 'Is that the one you want?'

Kate hesitated, not wanting to tell the old gentleman a deliberate lie. 'I'm trying to get to Suddaby . . .'

'Suddaby? Why that's miles away . . .'

Kate knew a moment's fear. She'd made a mistake, but she'd had to take the risk to find out the right road.

'Me grandad lives there, he'll be meeting me,' she told him, silently begging forgiveness for the small lie.

'But you have no coat. I really don't like to think of a young girl like you walking all that way alone and in the dark. Won't you . . .?'

'I'll be fine – honest,' she assured him and began to move away.

'Take care, then, my dear. Take care.'

'I will. Thanks, Mester.'

She knew it was a long way to the coast and Fleethaven Point – forty miles or more – but she was not afraid of the distance. All she wanted was to be away from that dreadful school and back home with her family – and with Danny. But she had not, in her moment of precipitate flight, thought of the trouble she would face when she did reach home. For the first time her footsteps slowed. She could almost hear her mother's voice raised in anger and see her stepfather's anxious face.

Then the idea, which had come into her mind as an excuse to the priest, now took root. Her grandad. She would go to her grandad. Hadn't he told her to do just that if she needed help?

And she needed help now.

It was then that she felt the first spots of rain. They were huge droplets, heralding a downpour. Kate looked around anxiously. The city was three miles behind her now and open fields bordered the road on both sides. Only here and there did lights shine into the dusk from the windows of cottages and farmhouses.

She trudged on, bending her face against the rain falling heavily now, quickly soaking through her gym-slip and blouse. The thin-soled house shoes she was wearing offered no protection. She wished she still had her sturdy boots but the matron had thrown them away with a look of disgust upon her face. Kate's hair – what was left of it – was wet through and rivulets of water were running down her neck.

On her left a clutch of farm buildings loomed in the darkness. Holding her breath, Kate tiptoed to the farm gate. Hoping that it was too wet for even the farm dogs to be prowling around, she felt her way stealthily around the wall of the nearest building until she came to an open door. Inside the darkness was even blacker, but as she walked forwards carefully, her hands outstretched in front of her, she felt her feet rustle in straw – deep, dry straw. She took off her wet tunic and spread it out. Then she burrowed beneath the straw and curled up. Although she was still wet and hungry, now at least there was a little warmth. Exhausted, she was asleep in seconds.

She awoke to the sound of rain pounding on the roof and to see daylight filtering through the wooden boards of the barn walls. Scrambling up, she struggled into her damp gymslip. She must go; the farmer might set his dogs on her for trespassing. Opening the barn door a crack, Kate peeped out. There was no one about and she was out of the barn, into the road and running before anyone had seen her.

It was still raining – 'siling' as her grandad would say. At the thought of her grandad, her spirits lifted.

She could almost hear his voice. 'If ya needs me, lass,' he'd told her, 'just send word and Ah'll come.'

Well, she'd do better than that; she was going to him.

It wasn't long before she was soaked. The wet seeped through her clothes and was cold against her skin. She walked briskly in an effort to keep warm, but the wind whipped bitingly across the rolling countryside of the Wolds and she was soon shivering. She was sure she had kept to the main road the old man had shown her but she could not find a signpost that bore the name of Suddaby.

It was at that point that she began to be afraid she was lost.

She was taking little running steps every so often and sobs punctuated her rapid breathing. Her head began to ache and her throat was parched; she was hot and then shivering with cold and the next moment sweating again. She looked around for a farmhouse or cottage, but the road stretched ahead through open country. There were no buildings of any kind now, only fields ploughed in neat furrows on either side as far as she could see.

Kate began to pray. 'Oh please, please help me . . .'

She was so tired, her legs ached and . . . Faintly, behind her, came the sound she most wished to hear at this moment; the sound of cart-wheels – a carrier's cart.

'Oh, Grandad, Grandad,' she sobbed thankfully. Turning, she stood watching the carrier approach, knowing what a pathetic, bedraggled creature she must appear to him. The cart slowed and she lifted her eyes to the man on the seat at the front.

'Well, little maid, and what be you a'doin' out on ya own a day like this'n?'

It was not her grandad. If she had not been exhausted and cold and almost on the point of collapse, her common sense would have told her that it would be too much of a coincidence to even hope that it could be her grandfather. This was not his route anyway. But in her confused state, it had seemed like an answer to her prayer.

She stood, bemused, staring up at the carrier's wrinkled face. 'Want a ride, young'un?' he asked kindly. 'Ya fair soaked and no mistake. Ain't ya even got a coat?'

He reached down his gnarled hand and, putting her small, cold hand into his, Kate found herself hoisted on to the seat beside him.

The carrier reached back into his cart. 'Here, wrap ya'sen in this.'

Gratefully, Kate wrapped the waterproof cape around her. The carrier flicked the reins and his two horses moved forward. 'Where be you a'goin'?'

'Suddaby,' Kate answered, speaking for the first time. Her voice was a rasping croak and it hurt her throat to speak. 'Me grandad's the carrier there. He . . .'

'Who? Not old Will Benson?'

Kate nodded and pulled the wrap closer around her. Now she was not walking, she was shivering uncontrollably, and yet her head felt burning hot.

'Well, dun't that beat all! Ah knows old Will real well. Ah'll tek you straight there, young'un, though we've a bit of a ride ahead of us.'

She felt his glance upon her. 'Should you like to ride in the back – under cover? It'd be warmer for ya.'

'Yes, please.'

She lay on a piece of old matting on the floor of his carrier's cart, dozing fitfully. Real sleep was impossible for the jolting of the cart, the rattle of its wheels and the hardness of the floor. She was alternately sweating and shivering, her head ached and there was a growing tightness in her chest. Above her, pans clanged together and pots clinked with every movement.

It seemed as if the journey would never end and then suddenly she felt the cart halt and the carrier was lifting the flap and saying, 'We're here, young 'un, at ya grandad's, but he bain't here. He's out on his rounds, so Mrs Raby, his neighbour, ses.'

Kate roused and pulled herself to the back of the cart. She saw the carrier standing there and with him a tall woman with a grey bun on the top of her head. Sweat prickled her skin and she could not breathe.

102

Miss Denham! Miss Denham had followed her.

It was then that Kate began to scream.

Their voices were rising and falling, coming and going around her. She felt herself lifted and carried and then laid on a sofa.

'Poor mite – she's ill. Ya can see that,' came the woman's voice.

It was nothing like the voice of Miss Denham. There came the touch of a work-worn yet caring hand upon her forehead. That was certainly not Miss Denham. Kate sighed with thankfulness and closed her eyes. Their conversation floated around her.

'Who is she?'

'Dunno, really. She ses she's Will Benson's granddaughter.'

'Naw. Lass is ramblin'. Him an' his wife never had no bairns, so how can he have a grandbairn?'

'Dun't ask me – ask him.'

'She must be something to him, though. I'd better look after her, else Will'll have me guts fer garters.'

Kate shivered and drew her knees up, curling herself into a ball for warmth. The woman must have noticed for at once she began issuing orders.

'Get me some kindling fer the fire an' fill the kettle . . .'

'Hang on a mo,' came the carrier's reproachful voice. 'I've to be on me way. There's me round to see to. I've come out o' me way to bring her 'ere as it is.'

'Nathaniel Wallis, if this is some relation of Will Benson's . . .' The words hung in the air like a threat.

'Aye, aye, all right, Millie, you win. I'd not like to get wrong side o' Will Benson and no mistake.' The man chuckled and Kate heard his footsteps leave the room.

'Now, me little lass.' The woman was bending over her, a rough kindness in her voice. 'Let's get you out o' them wet things . . .'

In her delirium, Kate imagined it was Mrs Eland helping her out of her wet clothes after her soaking in the sea; Danny's mother who was sponging her face, tucking a warm blanket around her and holding a mug of warm milk to her lips.

Then Danny would soon be home too . . .

'Danny?' she tried to ask and did not recognize her own feeble squeak of a voice.

'There's no Danny here, little lass,' the woman said.

Kate opened her eyes and struggled to focus them. It was not Mrs Eland. Then where . . .?

'Dun't fret. Yar – Will Benson'll soon be home.'

That was it, Kate thought dreamily. Her grandad. She had come to find her grandad.

It seemed only moments later that she heard his voice and then he was there kneeling beside the sofa and stroking her head and saying, 'Oh, me little Katie, me little girl. What have they done to ya?' And Kate knew she was safe at last.

She put her arms round his neck and felt his cool cheek against her hot forehead. 'Ee lass, ya burning up.'

'I've sponged her, Will, and made her drink, but she's poorly. Reckon ya should get her home and tell her folks to get the doctor – ne'er mind the cost.'

'Mebbe she'd better stay here . . .'

Kate gave a whimper at his words. 'No, Grandad. Tek me home. Please – tek me home!'

'All right, lass, all right.' He turned to the woman. 'She'll be all right if we wrap her warm in blankets, won't she?'

'Well . . .' The woman hesitated, reluctant to take responsibility, but as Kate's eyes filled with tears she said, 'I reckon she'll mek 'ersen worse fretting if you dun't tek her home, Will.'

Kate closed her eyes with thankfulness. Soon, soon she would be home. Above her, she heard the woman ask, 'Just who is she, Will? She ses she's yar grand-daughter. I thought she must be rambling, but now I ain't so sure.'

'You mind ya business, Millie Raby, and let me mind mine,' came her grandfather's sharp reply.

'Oh, sorry I spoke, I'm sure. After I've looked after the little lass most o' the afternoon an' all.'

Will sniffed and muttered gruffly, 'I'm sorry, Millie, I meant nowt. But I'm fair worried about her. She's ill. And I'd like to lay me 'ands on who's cut all her lovely hair off. That Ah would!'

Millie Raby's curiosity overcame her pique. 'So you do know her then?'

'Aye, I do,' Will said shortly and then added, 'She is me grand-daughter. She's Esther Everatt's daughter.'

Mrs Raby gave a gasp of surprise. 'Esther ... Well, I nivver! Esther Everatt! Esther's bastard, is she?'

'No, she's not,' Will's voice thundered, almost shaking the sofa where Kate lay. 'Esther was married a good year afore this little lass was born.'

'Well, I was just remembering about Esther an' how she left this village all sudden-like ...'

'Well, ya can stop remembering and putting two and two together and mekin' five. Help me get the lass into me cart. I'm tekin' her home where she belongs. An' this time she'll stay there, else Ah'll know the reason why!'

The woman gave a low chuckle. 'Well, Will Benson, they ses as how ya reap what ya sow. It looks to me as if ya wild oats from years back have brought you a bitter harvest.'

'That's where ya wrong, Millie Raby. Wild oats I might

'a sown, but if this little lass is me harvest I couldn't have asked for a greater blessing.'

Kate heard the words of their strange conversation but in her weakened state had no way of knowing if it was all part of her delirium. She was only blissfully aware that her grandfather was here and she was safe, and that he was picking her up tenderly and laying her in blankets in the back of his cart.

'Thank 'ee, Millie. Ah'll not forget ya help this day.'

'Eh, Will . . .' Kate saw the woman put her hand on his arm for a moment. 'We've been neighbours for more years than I care to remember, and I know I'm a nosey old beezum,' she cackled with laughter at the insult to herself, 'but ya secret's safe with me, I promise.'

Through the haze of her drowsiness, Kate heard her grandfather's chuckle. 'Aye, ya not such a bad old stick at that, Millie Raby.'

'Get away wi' ya and get yon lass home.'

This time, despite the rattling of the cart and warm and cosy in a mound of blankets, Kate did sleep, only rousing now and then to call to her grandfather. 'Are we there yet, Grandad?'

'Not far, lass, not far now.'

'Is Danny there, Grandad?'

A pause and then he answered, 'Aye, Danny'll be there.'

'I can't eat the gooseberries, Grandad. Dun't mek me eat the gooseberries.'

'What's that you say, lass, I dun't understand you . . .?'

Kate was asleep again and the next time she awoke she could hear the sea. It was her whelk shell. She was hearing the sea in her shell – the shell Danny had given her. She felt for the pocket of her coat. But she was not wearing her coat.

'Me shell, Grandad. I've lost me shell. Isobel's got me shell . . .'

But now she could smell the salt air and hear the waves across the marsh. It wasn't her shell. It was real.

Then Kate knew she was home.

Will himself carried her from his carrier's cart and into the farmhouse, straight up the stairs and into her own bedroom. Tenderly he laid her on her bed. Her mother and stepfather followed, bewildered and anxious.

'Oh Katie, my darling girl.' Her mother was bending over her, caressing her with gentle, loving hands.

'Mam, dun't be angry, dun't send me back. I dun't mind if you love Lilian more, but please dun't make me go back.' Then Kate began to cough, a tearing sound from deep in her chest.

Her mother's voice was a frantic whisper. 'Dear Lord! What has happened to her? She's so thin and who's cut her hair?'

'Now listen to me, Esther,' Kate heard her grandfather say, 'this lass stays put and if you try to send her away again, ya'll have me to answer to.'

Kate looked up into her mother's face and felt her hand upon her forehead. 'Ya needn't worry, Dad,' Esther was saying. 'But someone'll answer for this. Oh yes, someone will definitely have to answer me a few questions.'

'Mam – I haven't got to go back, have I?'

'No, my love, dun't fret. Ya never going back there.'

Kate closed her eyes. The sound of their voices came and went and she felt herself undressed and put between the sheets with hot bricks wrapped in cloth placed at her feet and on either side of her. As she began to sweat the fever out, she fretted no more. She was home for good. Her mother had promised.

And for all Esther Godfrey's strictness, she never broke her promises.

Eleven

She was having strange dreams; she was trying to run but her feet were like lead, her heart was thudding in her chest and she couldn't move. Then it felt as if someone at the end of her bed was lifting her legs.

'Mam, dun't lift me legs. It feels funny. Dun't lift me legs.'

'Katie love, I'm not touching your legs,' came her mother's voice as if from a great distance, and she heard her step-father's gentle voice too. 'It's the fever, Esther. She delirious. Bathe her forehead again.'

Then Kate felt the cool dampness on her forehead and the throbbing eased a little. 'Me shell – she's got me shell. She wouldn't give it back . . .' she murmured.

She awoke once to see Dr Blair's kindly face bending over her as he gently spooned liquid between her lips. 'There, there, my dear. We'll soon have you up and running about again . . .'

She heard him speaking to her mother in his deep voice. 'She'll be fine, Esther, really. It's clear the child hasn't been eating properly and she's exhausted. She obviously got very chilled trying to get home, but there's no real harm done. All she needs is a few days in bed. She'll feel a little weak when she first gets up, but with Fleethaven's good fresh air and your good food . . .'

Then her mother's voice. 'Thank goodness. I – I thought she'd got pneumonia.'

'No – nothing like that, I assure you, but Kate's been very distressed about something, Esther.'

'Yes – and as soon as she's better, I mean to find out exactly what's been going on.'

Another time Kate opened her eyes to see Rosie standing beside her bed clutching a posy of wild flowers. The child's face was unusually solemn, and her voice was only a whisper. 'Katie, I've brought you some flowers – to make you better. Do get better, Katie.'

'Danny? Where's Danny?' Kate croaked. 'Why hasn't he been to see me?'

The child hopped from one foot to the other. 'He – he wanted to come – but he wasn't sure . . .'

'Tell him I want to see him.'

Kate closed her eyes again. When next she opened them, Rosie had gone and her mother was once again sitting beside her bed holding her hand. Every time Kate awoke, her mother was there.

After a couple of days sleeping most of the time, Kate, although still weak, began to feel better. It was her mother who had dark shadows beneath her eyes now.

'Oh Katie,' she said, putting her arms about her daughter and holding her close. 'You had us all frightened. Kate, listen to me a minute. When you were rambling, you said something about me loving Lilian more than you.'

Kate buried her face against her mother's shoulder. 'I dun't remember.'

Her mother stroked the short cropped hair and murmured, 'They say ya speak the truth when you're in that sort of state. But that was not the reason I wanted you to go away to school. I love you dearly. I would never love one of me children more than the other. But a baby takes up a lot of time and attention and I can see it must 'ave felt like that for you, specially because ya'd been the only one for so long.'

When the girl did not answer, Esther said, 'Do you understand, Katie?'

Against her mother's shoulder she nodded, then drew back and looked into her face. 'Then why did you send me away?'

Esther Godfrey sighed heavily. 'Oh, Katie, there are things you dun't understand . . .'

'Then tell me.'

Her mother avoided Kate's direct gaze and unusually for her she stumbled over her words. 'I was worried – you see you're getting older now – and there are so many dangers for a young girl – a young woman almost . . .'

'Mam, just tell me.'

'I – I was afraid you were getting too close – too involved with – with the boys at the Point.'

'You mean Danny, don't you?'

'Well – yes. He's a young man now and – and young men start to – well – want things from girls.'

Softly Kate said, 'Danny wouldn't hurt me, Mam,' and then added with a little of her old spark, ''Sides, if he tried anything, he'd soon get a kick right where it hurts!'

Kate saw Esther's mouth twitch with laughter, despite the anxiety clouding her eyes. Then her face sobered again. 'Kate, I want you to give me your solemn promise that you will never, ever, let Danny . . . touch you.' Knowing just what a promise meant to her mother, that they were never given lightly, Kate hesitated. 'Why, Mam?' she pressed.

'He – he's not for you, Kate, not in that way. Friends, yes, but there – there can't be anything else.'

'Oh Mam, surely you don't think I'm stupid enough to let anybody – including Danny – touch me before I'm wed. You've drilled that into me ever since – well, as long as I can remember.'

Kate watched her mother's face, saw conflicting emotions

crossing it, as if there was a fight going on inside her head. 'What *is* it, Mam?'

'Nothing – nothing. It'll be all right, if ya'll promise me that.'

Kate sensed it wasn't 'nothing'. There was something her mother wasn't telling her. But there was nothing the young girl could do to prise whatever it was out of her mother. Instead she said airily, 'Oh yes, I can promise you that much, Mam.'

For the moment her pledge seemed to satisfy her mother.

What Kate did not voice, and what she had only just realized herself as a result of this conversation with her mother, was a silent vow she made to herself.

One day I'll marry Danny Eland.

It seemed that having gained Kate's promise, her mother's fears regarding Danny were allayed. The very next day Kate heard her voice calling from the bottom of the stairs, 'Kate, Kate you've got a visitor. Up you go.'

She heard footsteps on the stairs and even before the door of her bedroom was pushed wider, she knew it was Danny.

He stood in the doorway, grinning at her, his dark hair tousled, his skin weathered brown and glowing with health. Then she saw the smile fade. 'Oh, Kate – ya pretty hair,' he sympathized, moving into the room and coming to perch on the end of her bed. 'Did ya mam have to cut it off because of the fever?'

Kate shook her head. The nightmare was back; the scissors, the strong arms and her face pressed against Miss Denham's corseted bosom.

'I – I dun't want to talk about it . . .'

His grin was back. Comfortingly he said, 'Well, it'll grow again. 'Sides, it's lovely and curly when it's short, in't it?'

'You're just saying that to cheer me up.' But she too was grinning now. Then the smile wobbled a little. 'Danny – when I ran away from the school, I left the whelk shell you gave me.'

'Dun't worry about that – plenty more on the beach. I'll bring you another.'

'But that was special,' she murmured, leaning back against the pillows, 'it was the biggest you'd ever found – and I've lost it.' Because she was still weak, easy tears filled her eyes.

'Dun't bother ya'sen,' Danny said. 'I'll keep looking till I find another just as big. Hurry up and get better, then we can look together, eh?'

Suddenly, the boarding school was all a horrible nightmare. She was back home and all the days of the rest of her life stretched ahead – with Danny.

Soon Kate was allowed downstairs and with each day she grew stronger. Then came the morning her mother appeared dressed in her best costume with a smart hat perched on the top of her hair.

'I'm off to Lincoln today, Kate, to give that Miss Denham a piece of my mind.'

'Oh, Mam, do – do you think you ought?' Kate quailed at the very thought of her mother standing toe to toe with the enormous, overpowering figure of Miss Denham.

Her mother was smiling down at her, but her green eyes were flashing defiance. She touched Kate's cheek gently with her fingertips. 'Dun't you worry, my love. I've never been frightened of anyone in me life – I ain't likely to start now.'

But Kate was in a state of agitation all day. Her poor stepfather spent the whole time trying to pacify the baby and calm Kate. 'You needn't worry about your mother,' he told her, his lop-sided grin crinkling his eyes. 'She's a match for anyone.'

'You don't know Miss Denham,' Kate muttered, and her insides quivered at the mere thought of the woman.

'I know what might help,' her stepfather said suddenly. He was obviously trying to think of something he could do to take Kate's mind off her mother's trip. He left the kitchen and went through into the living room. Mystified, Kate followed and stood watching as he opened the front of his bureau. He searched beneath a pile of papers.

'I really must get down to filling in these forms about this year's crops for your mother. She hates anything to do with officialdom.' He glanced back over his shoulder, winked at Kate and then continued his search. 'Ah,' he said triumphantly, pulling two sheets of writing paper from the heap. 'Here it is! Right, let's go back into the kitchen where it's warmer. I want you to read this letter.'

Back in the kitchen, he told Kate to sit in his chair by the fire and handed her the letter. 'It's from my mother,' Jonathan told her. 'We received it whilst you were so poorly, but I always intended you should read it when you were stronger.'

Kate unfolded the pages and began to read. The letter was written in a bold flourishing hand and was dated the day of her visit to their home.

My dear Jonathan, Kate came to see us today and the poor child is in a dreadful state! She looks thin and pale – nothing like the healthy child we first met at little Lilian's christening. She is obviously very unhappy at that school and if what she told us is true – and I can hardly believe a young girl of her age could make up such tales – then you and Esther should remove her from there at once.

We felt we should not interfere directly, but your

father did hear some very disquieting news only last week, funnily enough. We didn't say anything in front of young Kate, but we certainly think you and Esther should think things over very carefully. It seems this Miss Denham has only been there for a term. Miss Peterson, the previous Principal – a lovely woman – was taken ill very suddenly and sadly died. The appointment of Miss Denham seems to have been made with unseemly haste and – to my mind – with disastrous results! Already three parents have removed their girls from the school.

Kate raised her head and met her stepfather's eyes. He nodded as if in answer to her unspoken question. 'Of course, you were already home by the time we got this letter. In fact, you were home before the telegram arrived.'

'Telegram?' This was the first Kate had heard about a telegram.

Jonathan sat down in front of her and took her hands in his. Leaning forward he said, gently, 'You were very wrong to run away, you know, Katie. You worried my mother and father – and Peg – very much.'

'How – how did they know?'

'Miss Ogden went to see them that Sunday evening, just after my mother must have written and posted this letter to us. Miss Ogden thought you might have gone there. The school knew their name and address because you'd been allowed to visit their home. They had the police looking for you all over Lincoln throughout the night.'

'The – the police?' Kate felt herself growing red with shame. 'Oh, Dad, I'm sorry. I – I didn't think they'd bother to look for me.'

'Why didn't you write to us, Katie, and tell us what was going on?'

She hung her head, but now there was no long hair to hide behind. 'I didn't think me mam would believe me.'

'We'd have come to see you,' he said softly. 'We both know you would never tell lies. We'd have seen for ourselves,' his glance flickered towards her shorn hair, 'how you were being treated. As for whatever else happened, well, if you ever want to tell us . . .'

Kate shook her head. 'I dun't want to talk about it. Mebbe some time, but not now.'

'I understand,' he said gently.

'I am sorry, Dad.' She looked up at him again, tears brimming her eyes.

He smiled at her and ruffled her short hair. 'We'll say no more about it. You're safely home now and that's all that matters.'

At that moment the baby began to whimper and the whimpers became louder until she was squealing. Jonathan cast a comical look at Kate and went to the cradle to pick Lilian up. Putting her against his shoulder, he patted her back. The baby gave a loud burp and the squealing subsided, but only to a continuous grizzle.

Jonathan nuzzled Lilian's downy head, 'Who's Daddy's pretty little girl, then?' he murmured, but Kate's sharp hearing caught his words and she felt the familiar shaft of jealousy. Jonathan glanced at her and Kate dropped her gaze, afraid that he might read in her eyes the feelings she tried hard, yet failed, to quell.

Jonathan's deep voice came softly. 'I hope she grows up to be like you, Kate. You were a lovely little girl when I first met you. Not that you're not now, of course!'

Kate felt a warm glow spread through her and she raised her face again, the fleeting resentment banished by his affectionate words. 'How old was I?'

'Let me see, you'd be about four. A bright little thing you

were, always laughing and chattering. Much the same as you are now – at least, as you were before you went to that wretched school,' he admitted regretfully.

Kate frowned, puzzled. 'But me dad, me—' She stopped, changing the words carefully, conscious of the hurt she might inflict upon her beloved stepfather. 'Me other dad – was here then, wasn't he?'

'He was away at the war. I came to Fleethaven Point to see Grannie Harris when I was on sick leave. Let's think, nineteen-sixteen, it would be. I'd been with her eldest son, Ernie, when he was killed in France and he'd told me all about his home and his family. And about "the Missus at Brumbys' Farm". That's what he called your mother.'

'So you came to see them?' Kate watched the expression on her stepfather's face sober. His eyes took on a faraway look and there was pain in their depths.

'I came to try to bring the Harrises what comfort I could. And then – I stayed for a while. But of course I had to go back eventually. After the war, your father came back. He was very . . . ill, at first.'

'I can just remember him,' Kate said softly. So that was what Danny had meant when he had said Jonathan Godfrey had 'come back' after her father had drowned. But it was all still a little hazy. She didn't quite understand what had happened.

'Did you and me mam . . .?'

At that moment the back door was flung open and her mother called, 'I'm back.' Then she was in the kitchen and the moment for Kate to share further confidences with her stepfather was lost.

He had been quite right; Kate need not have worried. Her mother returned triumphant.

'Ya didn't say that to her, Mam, did ya?' Kate hugged her knees to her chest in delight, imagining the scene as her mother recounted the interview between herself and Miss Denham. Esther Godfrey's eyes still sparkled with the light of battle as she stood, hands on hips, smiling at her daughter. 'Indeed I did, Katie. I told her she was an old beezum!'

'What did she *say*?' Kate's question was high-pitched with excitement, while Jonathan smiled indulgently at his wife, ferocious in the defence of her young.

Esther's grin widened and her eyes twinkled merrily. 'She said she could see where you got your rebellious streak from, and I said, "Well if there's many folk like you in the world, she's going to need it!" ' Her expression softened and she ruffled Kate's short hair. 'I'm glad you've got a bit of my spirit, lass, even if it does mean we clash now and then.'

'Did ya get all me things back? All me clothes I left?'

Esther nodded. 'I left the trunk at the station, though.'

'I'll pick it up tomorrow,' Jonathan promised.

'Oh.' Kate knew there was disappointment showing on her face.

'What is it, love?' her mother prompted.

Kate glanced from one to the other. 'Well, just before I left, three of the girls, they'd got summat of mine and – and they wouldn't give it back . . .'

'Do you mean this?' From her coat pocket, Esther drew out the huge whelk shell.

Kate drew in her breath sharply and, tears glistening in her eyes, she reached out with trembling fingers to take the shell once more into her hands. 'Oh, Mam, thank you. Thank you. Yes, yes, that's it. The whelk shell Danny gave me. Oh, thank goodness you found it. Was it amongst me things?'

'You were rambling about a shell when you were ill and when Danny—' Kate saw her mother glance swiftly at Jonathan and then away again. 'When Danny came to visit you,

117

he told me all about it. I realized it was ... important to you.' Her mother's voice dropped and she gave the faintest of sighs.

There was a pause and Kate prompted, 'And?'

Esther was smiling again, 'When I was taken up to the dormitory to pack your things up, I searched especially for the shell. It wasn't there. So,' Esther continued, enjoying the retelling of her tale, 'I demanded that it be found.'

'Oh Mam, you didn't!' Kate squeaked, but she was laughing with joy at the scene her mother was painting.

'I did,' Esther said firmly, and once more her eyes were sparkling. 'I waited until every girl in your dormitory was fetched from class and made to go through her belongings. And,' she finished triumphantly, 'it was found in the chest of drawers belonging to Isobel Cartwright.'

Kate was not surprised and said so. 'She was one of the three girls who were so horrid.'

'You can forget all about that dreadful place, Katie love, and all the people in it. You won't ever have to see any of them again,' her mother said. 'You're safe home with us now. And I – I won't send you away again.'

Kate bounced up from the chair and hugged her mother. Esther's arms came tightly around her. Everything was all right – her mother really did love her.

And yes, she was safely home; with her mother, her stepfather – and Danny.

Twelve

'Mam – I must go and look at the sea, I just must!'
'Well – all right then. But no paddling, mind. I
know you, Kate Hilton. Get a bit of winter sunshine and ya
reckon ya can act like it's midsummer!'

Kate grinned at her mother and was rewarded by Esther
Godfrey's wonderful smile. 'Eh, but it's good to see you
better, love. You're still a bit thin and pale, though. I dun't
want you taking risks and getting another chill.'

'I won't, Mam. Just look how I'm muffled up in this coat
and scarf – and a hat!' she finished scathingly. Kate had
never before worn a hat even when it snowed.

'And don't sit on the wet sand,' her mother shouted after
her as Kate went through the farm gate and across the lane.
She turned back briefly, smiled and waved. She'd never
known her mother fuss so much. But then, she realized, she
had never been so ill before; always a robust youngster,
she had shaken childhood illnesses off quickly.

Kate climbed the dunes through the trees and at the top
stood to look across the marsh towards the far dunes and
the sea beyond. With a whoop of delight she ran down the
slope and began to run across the marsh, delighting in the feel
of the spongy turf beneath her feet, the sharp breeze on her
cheeks bringing the colour back to them. To her surprise and
disgust, her breathing soon became laboured and she was
forced to slow down, even to stop for a few moments to
regain her breath.

119

She could no longer run.

She pulled in deep breaths, but it was like trying to breathe in through a feather pillow and there was an ache in her chest. Slowly she threaded her way across the marsh, jumping the meandering streams but having to rest after each exertion. She came to the far dunes and found that she could only climb to the top in three stages, resting twice on the way. But when she gained the beach and saw the sea, it was worth all the effort.

Would she ever run like she used to do? 'Like the wind', as Danny used to say with grudging admiration?

Kate walked slowly along the beach. She even felt the cold more now. Hunched into her thick coat, the woollen scarf around her throat and mouth, she trudged miserably back across the marsh towards the cottages at the Point. She knocked on the Elands' back door and when it opened she found herself enveloped in Beth Eland's embrace, her face pressed against soft, plump breasts.

'Oh lovey, it's so good to see you. How I longed to come and visit you when I heard how ill you was! Ne'er mind, you're here now. Come in near the fire and let me look at you.'

She drew Kate into her warm kitchen and held her at arm's length, her soft brown eyes searching Kate's face. 'Ya still look pale, Katie. Here, tek ya coat off else ya'll not feel the benefit when you go out again. Sit down and have some of my scones, fresh out the oven.'

In a moment, Kate was biting into a thickly buttered scone, the crumbs scattering down her pinafore while Beth stood smiling down at her.

Kate looked up at her. 'Where's Danny? He's not been to see me again. He came that once while I was in bed, but he didn't come no more.'

The smile on the woman's face faltered a little. 'Oh – er – well, yes. He's at work. He – he dun't get much time,

Kate . . .' her eyes flickered away and she fingered the hem of her apron nervously. Then Mrs Eland's face brightened as, seeming to change the subject, she said, 'You sit there, I'll just nip next door and fetch Grannie Harris. She'll want to see you . . .'

'Oh, I see Grannie every day nearly when she comes for the milk and eggs for everyone at the Point.' Kate took another bite, munched a few seconds, swallowed and then said, 'You have ya milk and eggs from us, dun't ya, Mrs Eland?'

Beth's gaze flickered away. 'Um, well, yes.'

Kate stared at her with candid eyes. 'But you never come ya'sen to fetch them, d'ya?'

Beth Eland shook her head, a kind of sadness in the movement.

'Why?' the girl persisted.

'Dun't ask me, Katie,' she whispered. 'Please – dun't ask me.'

It was the same strange reply her mother had once given to a similar question.

There was something odd, Kate thought, realizing something she had always known but had never really thought about before; the fact that in such a small community her mother and Beth Eland never spoke to each other, although each of them was friendly with everyone else. Perhaps they had quarrelled years ago and they were both too proud to make the first step to reconciliation.

Mrs Eland had turned away and was busying herself at the range, stirring something in a cooking pot. Kate jumped up from the stool and went to her, putting her arms around the woman's plump waist and hugging her. She didn't want to upset Danny's mother. Kate liked her – loved her – and not just because she was Danny's mother. Mrs Eland was always so kind and gentle towards her. The woman turned

121

round, holding the girl close once more, her smile as warm as always.

'I'd best get back,' Kate said now. 'It's one of me grandad's days for visiting. Will you tell Danny to call for me on Sunday after dinner?'

The haunted look was back for a moment in the woman's soft brown eyes. 'Aye, all right. I'll tell him,' she promised, but now there was no smile.

'Oh Katie, it's so good to see you looking better.' Bustling between pantry and the living-room table where they were to have dinner the moment Will Benson arrived on his carrier's cart, Esther paused to give Kate a swift hug. As her mother disappeared into the pantry, Kate resumed laying the knives and forks on the table. Emerging once more, carrying a large oval dish for the beef which was still sizzling in the range oven, Esther said, 'You'll soon have to be thinking what you're going to do, though. Do you want to go back to school here?'

Kate shook her head and then glanced at her mother, trying to gauge how what she wanted to tell her might be received. The young girl paused and took a deep breath. 'I'd – like to take a job in town – in the biggest shop there, if I could have a bicycle to get to and from work. And then when classes start at the Evening Institute next autumn, I thought I might learn dressmaking and tailoring. And after that . . .' Her words came faster, tumbling over each other in her enthusiasm.

'You seem to have got it all planned.' Her mother's face – usually so transparent in its expressions – gave no indication of her thoughts. 'Seems eminently sensible to me.' Her stepfather looked round from behind his newspaper and smiled benignly on them both. Esther glanced at him briefly but then her gaze came back to rest on her daughter. Kate felt Esther's scrutiny, but met her mother's gaze squarely. Kate had plans – ambitions. Modest as they might be, the planning of them gave her a thrill of excitement in the pit of her stomach. But she desperately wanted her mother to approve of them.

Kate imagined herself sitting in a room very like Jonathan's mother, Mrs Godfrey – in front of a sewing machine and creating beautiful garments for wealthy ladies. By working in a shop in town she would have the chance to handle and sell fine fabrics. At evening classes she could learn how to turn the fabric into lovely dresses and costumes.

She could hardly wait to begin.

She had now fully recovered from her illness and the terrible experience she had suffered. Her hair had grown a little but at least it was now expertly cut into a neat style and curled prettily around her face. Her complexion was still a little pale for the winter months had not allowed her to be out of doors as much after her illness as she would normally have been, but now her green eyes were shining with excitement at her plans.

Then suddenly her mother was smiling. 'I agree with yar dad. They are sensible plans. I'll have a word with Miss Davenport who works at that big drapery shop, if ya like. She's always been so helpful when I've gone in there.'

'Oh Mam, would you really?' Kate flung her arms about her mother's waist and dragged her into a dance around the kitchen table. 'Oh, thank you, *thank* you!'

Kate's happiness was complete. She was back home at Fleethaven Point. She knew her mam loved her even though baby Lilian took up so much of her attention, and, best of all, she was back with Danny.

*

'Danny, do you know why your mam and mine dun't speak to each other?'

'Haven't a clue,' he replied airily and grinned at her.

'Danny – be serious a minute.'

They were walking along the beach as they did now every Sunday afternoon.

'Me – serious?' He flung his arm around her shoulder. 'How can I be serious when I'm that happy to see you looking better, I could burst.'

'Stupid!' She shoved him away, pleased yet shyly embarrassed by his display of affection.

'Ya blushing, Katie Hilton. Ya blushing,' he teased and then dodged out of her way as she aimed a playful cuff at him.

She voiced her thoughts about the strangeness of two people in such a small community deliberately ignoring each other.

Danny wrinkled his brow. 'D'you know, I never thought about it afore. But now you come to mention it, it's always been like that.' His grin broadened. 'Mebbe when they was young they fell out over some bloke.'

Kate regarded him solemnly. Danny had said it as a joke, but Kate was not joking. 'Well, there's summat, an' I'll tell you summat else.'

'What?'

'Whatever the reason is, no one's telling. When I ask questions, they all clam up and say, "Dun't ask, Katie, dun't ask." '

'Well, ya're such a nosey little blighter. If they dun't want to tell ya, that's their business. It's got nowt to do with us and it's not going to come between us.'

He flung his arm around her shoulder again and they walked along in companionable silence.

Somewhere in the universe, sadistic Fate laughed.

Thirteen

1930

'Are ya coming out on me boat?'

Kate skidded to a halt on her bicycle, sending a shower of small stones on to the grass verge. She looked up to see Danny standing on the bank at the side of the lane.

'What? Now? Bit late at this time of day, isn't it?'

'It won't be dark for a couple of hours yet. Oh, do come, Katie.'

He leaped down from the bank into the road and came towards her. In the four years since she had started work in Lynthorpe, they had both altered. At eighteen, Danny was no longer a boy but a man with strong, sunburnt arms and a brown-skinned face that still seemed to be always grinning. He was not very tall, not much taller than Kate, yet his shoulders had broadened. He tried to slick back his hair, but the wind ruffled it into unruly black curls.

Kate's own hair had grown again, falling in waves and curls to her shoulders; and cycling into Lynthorpe every day, whatever the weather, kept her blossoming figure lithe and her skin glowing with health.

Kate looked at Danny closely. There seemed to be an air of excitement about him. Then she remembered. Trying to hide a smile, she said, 'I'm a bit tired for all that rowing...'

Triumphantly, Danny interrupted, 'Ya dun't have to row any more.'

Now the laughter was bubbling up inside her, but she

125

quelled it, allowing Danny his moment of glory. 'I've finished fitting the engine in it.'

'Engine? Really?' She could no longer prevent the smile twitching the corner of her mouth.

He leaned closer. 'You knew!' he accused, but he too was laughing.

'I'm sorry – I didn't want to spoil your surprise, but Dad mentioned it.'

Danny nodded. 'Ya dad's been very good helping us. He's clever with motors – wish I was. Me dad ses we'll keep the oars on board – just in case. Reckon he doesn't trust my mechanical efforts yet.' He paused then added, 'Well, a' ya comin' or not? I've been waiting for you this past half an hour. You're late, aren't ya?'

'Mr Reynolds called me into his office just as I was leaving.'

'Oho – been a naughty girl, have ya?'

''Course not . . .' she began indignantly, then saw his teasing grin. She punched him lightly on his shoulder, feeling the hard muscle beneath her hand.

'So what had you done to have old man Reynolds after ya?' Danny asked her. 'Left a bit of ribbon dangling out of a drawer again?'

Kate giggled as Danny reminded her of the times she had been on the receiving end of one of Mr Reynolds's lectures.

Mr Reynolds was the owner of the drapery store where Kate now worked. He was a short man, always dressed in a black morning jacket with pin-striped trousers. His thin neck poked up out of a stiffly starched collar. His cold blue eyes peered at all his staff through steel-rimmed spectacles which enlarged his eyes and made his scrutiny appear even more critical than it was. He was a martinet; every morning he toured the store and not a thing missed his sharp glance.

'No,' Kate said, her eyes gleaming. 'He's going to promote me.'

'Again? But it's only a couple of months since he put you in charge of a department. Ya'll be manageress of the whole shop soon,' he teased, but he was smiling as he said it.

'He wants me to go into the sewing room – as supervisor. Miss Poole's retiring.'

'But what about the other girls already there? Their noses'll be out o' joint if you're put in over 'em?'

Kate sniffed. 'Quite likely,' she said shortly.

She felt Danny's glance on her. 'Ya're a hard one, Kate Hilton, when it's summat ya want.'

She grinned at him, her eyes sparkling mischievously. 'Me? Hard? I'm an old softy and you know it.'

She didn't confide – not even to Danny – that her unfortunate experience at the school in Lincoln had left her with a sliver of ice in her heart. Never again would she allow herself to be treated as she had been then. Whilst outwardly she was friendly with everyone she met, only with a very few people would she ever drop her guard completely; maybe only with Danny and Rosie Maine.

'Will it mean more money?' he was saying.

'Danny Eland!' She pretended indignation. 'Is that all you can say? Here I am with news of a promotion and all you can think of is money!'

During the four years at Reynolds' Kate had been a quick and eager junior under Miss Davenport's kindly tutelage. Now, at only seventeen, she was in charge of the haberdashery department with a young, gauche school-leaver under her wing. Kate still rode between work and home on her bicycle along the Point road and, just as she had planned, by attending evening classes in Lynthorpe, she was learning dressmaking and tailoring.

It seemed that she possessed a natural talent and before

long she had begun to bring home tiny garments for Lilian, and blouses and skirts for herself and her mother from her classes.

'I can see I'll soon be handing over me sewing machine to you,' her mother had laughed, but there had been pride in her voice. Esther was a fine seamstress, but all her knowledge had come from the aunt who had brought her up. Now she watched with interest as Kate tried out all that she was learning from a professional tailoress. The front parlour at Brumbys' Farm was becoming cluttered with paper patterns and pins and lengths of material.

'Just like home,' Jonathan would tease her fondly, and Kate was reminded once more that it had been the sight of Mrs Godfrey's front room that had sown the seed of ambition in her.

Now Danny was grinning at her, quite unabashed by her pique. 'I was thinking of you being able to save for your bottom drawer.'

'Me – me bottom drawer?'

'Yeah – isn't that what girls call it when they're going to get married?'

'Going to – to get – married?'

He leaned towards her over the handle-bars of her bicycle. Gently he rubbed his nose against hers. 'Well, we'll be getting married one of these fine days, won't we?'

'Well, really!' Kate said, feigning exasperation, but she could not prevent her generous mouth widening into a broad grin. 'If that dun't beat all for a romantic proposal, Danny Eland.'

Suddenly his face was serious and there was a fleeting flash of passion in his dark brown eyes. He reached up and touched her face with strong fingers that were suddenly gentle. 'I've always loved you, Katie Hilton, and I always will. You must know that.'

'Oh Danny,' she breathed, knowing her own green eyes were glowing, mirroring his emotion with the same depth of love and longing.

Their faces were inches apart, coming slowly towards each other, until they could each feel the other's breath on their faces. Their lips met tentatively, trembling on the brink of the unknown; a soft, sweet kiss of innocence.

'Danny – I do love you so,' she murmured. As they drew back, they both heard the distant clip-clopping of a pony's hooves.

'Oh heck! That's me mam coming along the Grange road. Where's she been?'

'It's rent day.'

'Oh – so it is.'

'Quick – give us ya bike . . .'

Danny seized hold of her bicycle and pushed it up the bank and down the other side. Kate scrambled up after him. They crouched down out of sight of her mother who drove past in the pony and trap. Giggling like a couple of children, they parted the grass and watched as she passed within a few feet of them.

'So,' he asked, as they walked down the lane hand-in-hand when Esther was safely out of sight, 'do ya reckon they'll let us get wed soon, or d'ya think we'll have to wait till we're twenty-one?'

'I dun't reckon my mam'll ever agree to it,' Kate said. 'What about yours?'

'Oh, she'll be pleased as punch. She loves you.'

'My mam is fond of you – at least she used to be when we were little, but . . .'

'Aye – aye, she was.'

There was silence between them, then they both spoke at once.

'It's this thing between them . . .'

'I remember . . .'

'Sorry – you go first.'

'I was going to say,' Danny said slowly, 'I remember at ya dad's funeral. It's all a bit vague . . .'

Kate nodded but did not interrupt.

'I can remember sitting in the pew in church and watching the coffin in the front of the altar and then when the vicar had finished and ya ma and you and Will Benson came out of the front pew and down the aisle following the coffin as it was taken out . . .'

'Go on,' Kate whispered, prompting.

They had stopped walking and turned to face each other. 'Ya mam stopped – right in front of us. She didn't speak but sort of gestured with her hand that we should walk out behind the three of you. Just as if we were – well – family almost, or at the very least, close friends. And yet now . . .'

'And yet now,' Kate finished for him, 'they don't even speak to each other.'

Danny nodded and they resumed walking hand-in-hand until they came near to Brumbys' Farm.

By silent, mutual consent, they let go of each other's hand. As they reached the farm gate, Danny said, 'We won't tell 'em yet.'

'No, let's keep it our secret for a while.'

They looked at each other, seeing one another in a new way, a different way. Kate felt the thrill of excitement just below her ribs.

Danny loved her.

'I'd best be off,' he murmured, but made no move. 'It is a bit late to go out on the boat now.'

'Yes.' But she too remained exactly where she was. 'We got talking about other things, didn't we?'

They were standing very still, just looking at each other.

'How about Sunday afternoon then?'

'Sunday?' Kate murmured, absently.

'The boat. We'll go out on the boat on Sunday afternoon.'

'Oh yes,' Kate's eyes glowed. 'Sunday afternoon.'

'Me want to come wiv you.'

On the Sunday afternoon after dinner, Lilian stood in front of Kate as she pulled on her boots.

Kate sighed but said levelly, 'Not today. Another time, maybe.'

'Where you goin'?' the child persisted. At four years old, Lilian was an unattractive child with grey, expressionless eyes, mousey, straight hair and a sullen mouth that seemed always to be pouting. She was proving to be a sickly child – totally unlike her robust half-sister. Lilian was always catching cold and Esther was for ever fussing over her youngest chick; something Kate would never have believed possible.

To be fair, though, Kate thought, her mother had hardly ever needed to fuss over her, and on the only occasion when she had been really ill, well, she couldn't fault her mother for the attention she had given her then. Even if it was guilt-based, Kate often thought, remembering the days following her return from the Lincoln school.

'Yes – just where are you going?' her mother asked now.

'We're going to try out the new engine in Danny's boat – well, Mester Eland's boat.'

'Oh, that. I've heard enough about that these past weeks from ya father.'

Her stepfather's face appeared from behind his newspaper. 'Let me know how you get on. Get Danny to show you how to start it and how to steer . . .'

'Now, why would I want to know how to start an engine, or how to steer it, Dad? It was bad enough having to row

131

till we could get the sails up. Now there's a motor in it, I'm just going to lie back and . . .'

'If you ever get stranded out at sea, you might well be glad to know a little about how it works. You should learn, Kate. Any knowledge is useful. You never know when you might . . .'

'Well, it's unlikely I'll ever be out at sea without Danny, and he'll know.'

'Haven't you got some sewing you ought to finish before your class tomorrow night?' Esther put in.

'It's Sunday, Mother, the Lord's day,' Kate answered pertly, mimicking the words Esther herself used so often, but taking the sarcasm out of her tone with a cheeky, infectious grin. 'The Sabbath's not for work. Sunday's for rest and for meeting my – my friends.'

She bit her lip. She would have to be more careful; she had been about to let slip a hint of the change in the relationship between herself and Danny.

Esther's normally generous mouth tightened visibly until it was a hard, straight line. Kate saw her open it to speak, but before the words came, she was out of the kitchen, through the scullery and banging the back door shut behind her. Yet it was not until she had crested the Hump and was running across the stretch of grass between the cottages and the river bank that she was able to forget the disapproval on her mother's face, nor the lonely figure of her little sister, standing staring forlornly after her.

'Kate! Kate!' The sound of her name came bouncing across the breeze and she turned to see Rosie, a long-legged, coltish nine-year-old, galloping across the grass towards her. 'Danny's taking us both out in his dad's boat to try out the engine.'

Kate was disappointed. She would not have Danny to herself. Then, as Rosie linked her arm through hers, Kate felt a stab of guilt. It was impossible to feel irritated with Rosie for many minutes. She was so pretty with her white-gold curls and merry laughter. She was their friend – hers and Danny's. She mustn't be selfish, Kate told herself sharply, wanting to exclude Rosie from their outing just because now there was something extra special between herself and Danny.

After all, she and Danny had the rest of their lives to be alone together. Kate felt an excited flutter just below her ribs. The mere thought filled her with happiness.

Fourteen

She was cycling home along the coast road, singing softly beneath her breath, when she heard a familiar chugging noise behind her. Smiling to herself, Kate braked and jumped off her bicycle, wheeling it on to the grass verge. There was only one person around here who owned a motor car; Squire Marshall. And with his erratic driving on the narrow lane, it was much safer to dismount.

But it was not Squire Marshall at the wheel of a brand-new Austin Twelve; it was Danny. He drew to a halt beside Kate and leaned out through the window, grinning, as she gaped open-mouthed at him.

'Whatever are you doing driving that?'

'You not the only one who's been promoted.' His grin widened.

For the past two weeks Kate had been working as supervisor in the workroom. She even had three girls working under her and, with the added responsibility for their work being properly done as well as her own increased workload, there had been a substantial increase in her pay.

Kate laid her bicycle down in the long grass on the verge and went across the lane to stand beside the vehicle. 'What d'ya mean?'

'Mester Marshall's made me his chauffeur. I'm to look after his car and drive him and his missus wherever they want to go.'

Kate shook her head wonderingly. 'Won't you be working on the land any more?'

'Oh yes, but I've always liked motors. He's talking about getting a tractor and a new reaper and 'ee ses he'll put me in charge of all the machinery. It's the sort of job I've allus wanted.'

'Oh, Danny – that's wonderful.' She touched his arm as he leaned through the open window. Then she grinned archly at him. 'Will it mean more money?'

He gaped at her for a moment and then, as he realized she was mocking his own question to her a few weeks back, he poked his head further out of the window and kissed her on the tip of her nose. "Spect so. If we go on like this we'll be able to afford to get wed soon.'

Kate threw back her head, her laughter bouncing on the breeze. 'I dun't reckon a bit of promotion and a few shillings a week more is going to mek us millionaires!'

'Dun't reckon I'd want to be. Mind you, I wouldn't mind a car like this of me own one day.' He ran his hands lovingly round the steering-wheel. 'Would ya like to come for a ride?'

'Did we ought to?' she asked doubtfully.

'Squire wouldn't mind.'

Moments later they were driving towards the town, but when they reached the first houses, Danny turned the motor round and headed back along the coast road. 'Best not be seen.'

'Oh, do let me have a go, Danny. Let me drive it.'

'Well, I aren't sure about that.' Now it was Danny's turn to be doubtful.

'Oh, go on,' she pleaded with her most winning smile. 'I'll be ever so careful and do just what you say. Squire wouldn't mind,' she added coyly echoing Danny's own words.

'Well . . .'

135

Minutes later she was sitting behind the wheel as Danny was telling her which foot to put on which pedal. 'Press on the clutch-pedal – the left one.' Danny put the gear lever into first gear. 'Now, let it off slowly and at the same time press on the accelerator.' The engine spluttered and the car hopped forward.

'Slowly, I said,' Danny bellowed in her ear.

Kate grinned at him. 'Sorry.'

'Try again . . .'

They moved forward along the lane in a series of jumps and engine stalls, with Kate laughing and Danny shouting at her. At last she seemed to get the hang of it and they were crawling along in first gear, but at least smoothly. 'Now try second gear – press the clutch . . . into neutral . . . rev the accelerator . . . press the clutch again . . .' and he pushed the gear lever into second gear.

The speed was increasing as they approached a gentle bend in the road, the sand-dunes on the left-hand side and on the right a grass verge and then a dyke.

Kate careered across the road towards the verge.

'Turn your wheel. Brake!' Danny shouted.

'Which is the brake?' Kate shouted back, unconsciously pressing down harder on the accelerator. The front wheels bounced on to the grass and the car headed towards the dyke. Danny grabbed the wheel and wrenched it round, but too late. The nearside wheels were on the slope of the dyke bank and the car slid, in slow motion, into the dyke, tipping over on to its side against the opposite bank.

As the car settled itself there was a ghastly silence until Danny, thrown against her and pinning her against the door of the car, said, 'Now look what you've done. I'll get the sack for this.'

Kate was shaking but not too shocked to reply with

asperity, 'Oh, wonderful! Not a word of "Are you all right, Kate?" or "Have you hurt yourself?" '

Danny levered himself off her and started to clamber up out of the car. He glanced back down at her. 'Well – have you?'

There was a slight pause before Kate answered morosely, 'No.'

Danny pushed at the door, now opening at a tilting angle, and heaved himself out. Then he thrust his head and shoulders back inside and held out his hand to her. 'Come on, I'll give you a pull.'

They stood side by side on the bank looking down disconsolately at the car nestling forlornly on its side in the dyke bottom.

'D'ya think our horses could pull it out?' Kate suggested.

'They might.' Danny didn't sound too hopeful.

'I'll bike home and get me dad to come back.'

'What am I going to tell Squire Marshall?'

'*I'll* go and see him,' Kate said airily. 'He likes me – he'll not shout at me.'

'Oh no you won't,' Danny said swiftly. 'I aren't hiding behind a woman's skirts – not even to save me job!'

It was two hours before the Squire's motor car was standing upright on the road once more. The two horses had pulled it from the dyke once Kate's stepfather had attached ropes to the front axle. Now they were all standing in the lane viewing the damage while the two horses champed lazily on the grass verge.

'Whatever were you doing, Danny?' Jonathan was asking.

Kate and Danny exchanged a glance and Kate opened her mouth to explain, but before she could speak Danny said, 'I wasn't concentrating – me nearside wheels hit the verge and

I couldn't seem to steer back on to the lane and afore I knew it – I was in the dyke.'

'Perhaps the steering's gone.' Jonathan was on his knees in front of the vehicle, bending down to look underneath, his head almost touching the ground as he peered between the front wheels. 'If that's the case, then it's not your fault.'

'No such luck,' Danny muttered, but only loud enough for Kate to hear and understand.

Jonathan was reaching underneath the car. 'Looks to me like the axle's bent, that's all.'

'That's all!' Danny echoed wryly. 'It's bad enough.'

Her stepfather was levering himself to his feet. 'See the Squire, Danny, and explain what happened. Tell him I can put it right if he likes.'

Kate saw the hope in Danny's eyes. 'Can you really, Mester?'

She watched the exchange between Danny and her stepfather. The latter was nodding. 'I should be able to – I may need to get some parts, but it shouldn't be too big a job. Come on now, Danny, you get in and steer, and we'll pull it back to Brumbys' Farm.'

As dusk crept over the flat fields, Kate was still waiting for Danny to come back from the Grange. Watching from a bedroom window which faced westwards, she could see the tall chimneys of the Squire's home surrounded by trees. At last she saw a figure walking along the road leading from the Grange back towards the coast road. Lightly she ran down stairs, through the living room and into the kitchen. She paused in the doorway and held her breath. Her mother was bending over the range. Quietly, Kate edged her way towards the door leading into the back scullery, but her mother glanced up and saw her.

'And where do you think you're off to at this time of night, Missy?'

'Danny's just coming back from the Grange. I want to know what the Squire said.' And without waiting for her mother's permission she ran out of the back door.

Really, she thought to herself, I'm almost eighteen and yet I still can't hardly move without her wanting to know what I'm doing.

She hung over the farmyard gate and Danny's shadowy shape loomed up in the dusk. ''Ave ya still got ya job then?' she called merrily, confident that the worst Danny would receive from the kindly Squire was a telling off.

'It's all right for you to joke!' Danny muttered morosely. He was walking towards her, but his hands were thrust deep into the pockets of his trousers. Suddenly, he kicked viciously at some loose stones on the road side, sending them pattering on to the grass verge.

A sudden fear clutched at her. 'He didn't – oh, he wouldn't – sack you. Did he?'

'He did! The old bugger bloody well sacked me!'

Kate gasped. Danny rarely resorted to bad language; that he was doing so now, and being so disrespectful to the Squire, shocked her.

And what made it worse – it was all her fault.

Very early the following morning, before going to work, Kate cycled to the Grange. Standing in front of the Squire's huge polished desk, she felt the familiar fluttering just below her ribs that she got when she was nervous.

'What's so urgent, young lady, that I have to be dragged away from my breakfast?'

He was sitting on the opposite side of his desk now, glowering at her. When she had been shown into the book-lined study, he had been sitting in a wing-chair near the long window overlooking the smooth expanse of front lawn, his right foot propped up on a footstool, and a plate of bacon and eggs on a small table to one side. Leaving his meal, he had levered himself up from his chair and hobbled across the room, wincing with every step.

Kate had always liked the Squire, with his bristly white whiskers and red face. As a child, she had thought of him as a jolly Father Christmas and in her sudden concern for him, her nervousness was forgotten for a moment.

'Have you hurt your foot, Squire?'

'Gout,' he said testily. 'That's why I wanted a driver till that silly young fool put my new car in the ditch!'

Her stomach lurched afresh. 'That's what I've come to see you about – Danny Eland.'

The old man grunted and glared up at her. 'Well? What about him?'

Kate took a deep breath. She was taking a big gamble and she knew it. He couldn't hurt Danny any more – he'd already dismissed him. But the Squire was her mother's landlord. He owned the home they all lived in. If she, Kate, angered him even more ...

'Well, get on with it.'

'It was all my fault, Squire.' The words came tumbling out in a rush. 'About your motor car, I mean. I was driving it, not Danny. I begged him to let me have a go and – I know he shouldn't have. Oh, Squire – I'm so sorry. Please don't sack Danny. And me dad – he can make it good as new. He's ever so clever with motors and ...' She was babbling now in her agitation.

'Well, I'll be damned!' The look on the Squire's face was so comical that Kate gave a nervous little laugh.

He was shaking his head and staring at her. 'You're so like your mother, Kate, do you know that?'

140

Now it was Kate's turn to blink in surprise.

'She was only about your age when old Sam Brumby died and she came to see me, standing exactly where you're standing now . . .' His eyes clouded over as if he was seeing not Kate, but her mother, Esther. 'No more than a slip of a girl, she was, but there she stood almost demanding that I grant her the tenancy of Brumbys' Farm. The Brumbys had the tenancy for generations, but there was no family to carry on after Sam.' There was a pause, then the Squire said quietly, 'I always admired your mother for her honesty and it seems you too have that same virtue.'

He smiled at her now, and it was once more the Squire she knew and liked. His eyes twinkled with mischief. 'All right, young lady, I'll see young Danny doesn't lose his job. Mind you, he shouldn't have let you drive it.'

'I know, but . . .'

He held up his hand, palm outwards. 'All right, all right. Just so long as you get your stepfather to fix it up, we'll say no more about it.'

'Oh, thank you, Squire, thank you. But, just one more thing . . .'

'What is it?' he asked resignedly, but his anger was gone now and his eyes were twinkling.

'You – you won't ever let Danny know I came to see you, will you? He'd be cross. He's got his pride, you see.'

The Squire's whiskers twitched. 'All right my dear. It'll be our little secret.'

And as the Squire was rewarded with one of Kate's beaming smiles, he in turn gave her a broad wink.

Fifteen

The following evening Danny was waiting for her in the lane outside Brumbys' Farm when she arrived home from work. It was almost dusk for Kate had been obliged to stay late to finish hemming some velvet curtains by hand with her tiny, neat stitching.

'Guess what?' He came and stood astride the front wheel of her cycle, resting his arms on the handle-bars. He leaned forward and planted a kiss on her mouth. Something had pleased him, Kate thought. He was grinning from ear to ear and forgetting to be cautious right outside the yard gate.

Carefully Kate said, 'You haven't found another job already?'

'Nope – but I've got me old one back.'

Kate gave an exaggerated squeal of delight and hoped it sounded convincing. She flung her arms around Danny's neck and hugged him. He grasped her arms and they were scuffling playfully when a sharp voice rang out in the still night air.

'Kate! Kate – I want you in. Now!'

Danny let go of her as if he had been burned, and sprang away, but Kate merely called back over her shoulder, 'I won't be a minute, Mam.' She leaned her cycle against the gate post and turned back to Danny. Lowering her voice, she said, 'Now, tell me quickly. What happened?'

'Squire sent a message I was to go up to the Grange. I

142

was quaking in me boots, I can tell you, when I went into his study,' Danny said.

So was I! thought Kate, but she said nothing, listening as Danny continued. ' "I was a bit hasty yesterday," ' he ses. "If you can get the motor put right, Eland, you can have your job back." So I told him that ya stepdad reckoned he could fix it, and Squire said, "Godfrey's word is good enough for me. He's a good mechanic." '

Kate's heart warmed to the Squire for his praise of her stepfather.

'Squire said,' Danny's even teeth shone white in the darkness as he grinned, 'ya dad's so clever with mechanical things he's wasted on a farm, even though he comes in handy when we get a problem with the machinery. He put his hand on me shoulder as I was coming out and said, "You could do a lot worse than learn from Jonathan Godfrey." Oh, Katie, I'm that glad to get me job back, I can tell you.'

Kate let out a long sigh too. 'Well, that's all right then.' She moved closer to him, her mouth curving into a smile. 'So when do I get another drive?'

'You don't!' he replied shortly and then, obviously hearing the mischief in her tone, he reached out to grab her arms. 'Oh, you tease, you . . .'

Kate dodged his grasp and squealing with glee, she began to run, across the lane and into the trees on the dunes, glancing back over her shoulder, inviting him to chase her.

Danny was not one to refuse such an invitation. Underfoot, twigs cracked whilst overhead, roosting birds fluttered from their resting place as the two youngsters, their laughter echoing in the stillness of the night, chased each other up and down the dunes like a couple of young puppies.

'Sssh,' Danny said, stopping suddenly. 'What was that?' They stood listening.

Distantly, they heard Esther's voice, 'Kate – Kate!'

Grabbing Danny's hand, Kate whispered, 'Come on, let's go to the beach.'

'You sure, Katie? You'll only mek ya mam madder than ever.'

But Kate was already dragging him up the slope and down on to the marsh. Then they were running towards the easterly dunes, splashing through the creeks in the darkness, skirting the deeper streams. They knew every inch of the marsh and could quite literally find their way in the dark.

Laughing, they flopped down at last in the sandy hollow in the dunes that was their special place. They lay on their backs, close together, just staring up at the vast expanse of darkening sky above them, listening to the musical lap-lap of the waves, somehow louder in the darkness.

Danny raised himself on one elbow and leaned over her. She could feel his breath, soft upon her face. 'When are we going to get married, Katie?'

She touched his face and, with gentle fingers, traced the outline of the features she knew – and loved – so well. She had always loved him. He had been part of her life always, and that was the way she wanted it. It was what they both wanted; to be part of each other's lives for ever.

'As soon as you like, Danny. But I'll have to leave me job. Mr Reynolds dun't – doesn't . . .' she corrected herself. Since her recent promotion she was more than ever conscious of the strong dialect in her speech and was making a determined effort to correct it. She had never felt her speech to be a defect until she had been ridiculed for it at the school in Lincoln. Sometimes, in the dead of night, she still shuddered at the memories of that time and her private humiliations were locked away in the depths of her soul.

'Mr Reynolds', she was saying now, 'doesn't employ married women. I'd have to leave if we got married.'

144

'Well, I'd want you to anyway.' His head came lower until his mouth brushed her lips. 'You'll have plenty to do looking after me – and the kids!'

Kate giggled and then was lost as his butterfly kiss became more demanding. His arms were around her and he was pressing his strong, muscular body against her. Now she felt his urgency; felt the heat and desire in his kiss.

'No, Danny, no. We mustn't.' Kate pulled away from him suddenly and sat up. She sat with her arms wrapped around her knees drawn up to her chest – a chest that was no longer childishly thin; now her breasts were firm and rounded – and desirable! And Danny wanted her, she knew.

Miserably she buried her face in her skirt. Now Danny would be angry with her, might even hate her, she was thinking. All young men got angry if you didn't let them – well, do things! At least that was what Sheila, one of the young girls in the workroom, said. Sheila was a pert, petite blonde, who wore make-up and high-heeled shoes and short skirts; she seemed to have a different boyfriend every week.

But Esther's warning sounded in Kate's ears so clearly, she might have been standing over them. 'Dun't let him touch you – promise me!'

'I'm sorry,' she muttered. 'But I dun't want to – to . . .'

She felt Danny's touch on her arm and he sat up at the side of her. ''Tis me who should be saying sorry. You're right. We mun't spoil it. We should wait till we're wed.'

She reached out to him in the darkness. 'Oh, Danny,' she breathed. 'I was afraid you'd be cross, that you wouldn't understand . . .'

'Kate – I love you, really love you. I wouldn't do anything to hurt you, or – or upset you.' The grin widened, cheekily, 'But I dun't reckon I can wait for ever.'

'Oh Danny, nor me. Nor me.'

145

She held his beloved face between her hands and gently kissed his lips.

'Just where do you think you've been, Miss? Do you know what time it is? It's half-past ten.' Her mother was waiting at the open back door as Kate came across the yard. Silhouetted against the light from within, Esther stood with her feet set apart and hands on hips. It was a stance that meant trouble.

'Hello, Mam,' Kate said happily. Not even Esther's anger was going to be allowed to spoil things. Danny loved her – and he had got his job back. The Squire had kept his promise. Danny didn't know she had a hand in it – but that was the way she wanted it. She loved him too much to belittle him. She would always let him think that he had regained his job because the Squire valued him and not because she had pleaded his cause.

In her joy, Kate grasped her mother round her slim waist and drew her outside. In the darkness she whirled her mother round the back yard in a merry jig.

'Stop it, Kate . . .' but Esther was laughing in spite of herself. 'Do stop – I'm getting a stitch in me side.' Kate stopped and let go of her. Esther leaned against the pump in the yard, holding her side. 'What's got into you, girl? You're as daft as a brush.'

Kate stretched her arms skywards and threw back her head. 'I'm happy, Mam, that's all. Danny's not going to get the sack and me dad's going to get the job of repairing the Squire's motor. So he'll be happy with his head stuck under a motor car.'

Esther snorted. 'Aye, I might have known – just when harvest is upon us.'

Kate smiled, ''Night, Mam.' And before Esther had a chance to berate her daughter further for her lateness, Kate

146

gave her a peck on the cheek and ran indoors. She was up the stairs, through the nursery where Lilian now slept, and into her own small back room before her mother had got her breath back.

Harvest was upon them. Every evening and on her time off from work, Kate hurried into her outdoor work clothes and ran to the fields. Here, the old traditions survived. Neighbour helped neighbour at harvest and the horses from Brumbys' Farm were in demand.

'I'm not having them new-fangled tractor things in my fields.' Esther vowed, and Kate would see her stepfather smile fondly and hide his disappointment. 'It's bad enough at threshing with the steam engine . . .'

Kate listened to the conversations that were repeated every year and smiled, winking at her stepfather behind her mother's back, knowing he looked forward to the winter days when the huge machine would come into their yard to start the threshing.

'Why don't you persuade Mam to get a tractor?' Kate encouraged her stepfather as they walked out to the fields. 'She would if she knew it would make you happy.'

Jonathan smiled. 'Maybe I will when the horses get too old . . .'

'Oh, there's Danny,' Kate said suddenly, feeling the familiar ripple of pleasure as she saw him standing high on top of the wagon, spreading the sheaves as they were passed up to him by the men below. In the early evening sun, his muscular body, stripped to the waist, glistened with sweat. She began to run, and then, remembering suddenly, glanced back over her shoulder. 'Don't you forget, Dad, when the horses go – it's a tractor we want.' She wagged her finger at him and grinned.

Jonathan smiled too, but then he glanced at Danny and back at her, and she saw the smile fade from his face. 'Kate . . .' he began, but, filled with the desire to be with Danny, she waved and said, 'See you later, Dad,' and was gone.

Through the bright days of late summer, the two young people were filled with happiness, revelling in the secret they shared, planning their future.

'Mebbe Squire would let us rent a farm of our own one day.'

The look in her eyes softened lovingly. 'Is that what you really want, Danny?'

He wrinkled his forehead. 'I reckon. Would that suit the new Mrs Eland?'

He was teasing yet there was an underlying seriousness. They were deciding their future and he cared about her happiness.

She nodded. 'Oh yes, it'd suit me. I could still do dress-making at home if I wanted.'

'We'd only be tenants, mind. Mebbe he'd let us have Rookery Farm. Tom Willoughby's getting on a bit now and he's no family to carry on after him.'

Kate was doubtful. 'It's more acreage than our farm. Wouldn't you be better staying on the Squire's estate? Maybe one day you could be. bailiff.'

She leaned her head against his shoulder as they sat beside a stook, nestling against the sweet-smelling corn and hidden from the inquisitive eyes of the other workers. Danny slipped his arm around her.

'I suppose it wouldn't be a bad job, though I'd sooner have a place of me own. It's not easy to be put in charge of other folk, specially people ya've known all ya life. Ya can soon lose friends.'

She twisted her head to look up at him. 'No ambition,

that's your trouble,' but she took any criticism out of her words by planting a kiss on his cheek.

He rested his cheek against her hair. 'I've only one ambition,' he said softly. 'To marry you and live happily ever after . . .'

They sat quietly, watching the sun sink slowly behind the horizon, streaking the sky golden-red.

'It's ya birthday in a couple of days, in't it? Ya eighteenth.'

'Yes. Why?'

'Shall we get engaged on ya birthday?'

Kate sat up and looked at him, her eyes shining. 'Yes, oh yes!'

'Then,' Danny said slowly, 'we'll have to tell them.'

Some of the joy left Kate's face as they regarded each other solemnly. 'Right,' she said firmly, for it was she who had the most difficult task and they both knew it. 'I'll do it tomorrow night when I get home from work.'

'I'll tell my folks, too, then they'll all know at the same time. Okay?'

Kate nodded, feeling the churning of apprehension in her stomach.

'No. No! *No!*' Esther Godfrey's voice rose to an hysterical scream. Kate gaped at her mother, while four-year-old Lilian ran to her father and climbed on to his knee as he sat in the wooden Windsor chair at the side of the range in the kitchen. She flung her arms around his neck and buried her face against his shoulder. Automatically, Jonathan patted the child's back comfortingly, but his attention was not on his young daughter.

'Esther, love, steady on.' To Kate's ears his concerned tone also held a kind of warning. But her mother was in no mood to listen to the voice of reason.

149

'Steady on? Steady on, you say?' Esther leaned on the kitchen table, her palms flat down on the scrubbed surface, her green eyes flashing fire, but there was a stillness about her body that was ominous. 'You will never, never marry Danny Eland.'

'I will. You can't stop me.'

'Oh yes I can, my girl.' Her mother's voice was quiet now, but that very quietness was more menacing than the screaming.

'Esther . . .' came Jonathan's deep voice, but now the two women – mother and daughter – were locked in their private battle of wills and scarcely heard him.

Esther moved suddenly and swiftly towards the door. 'I'll put a stop to this once and for all.'

'Esther – no! You can't. You mustn't!'

She whirled to face her husband. 'Keep out of this, Jonathan. It's nowt to do wi' you.'

She could not have hurt him more if she had slapped him physically. Kate saw her stepfather wince, but his voice was calm as he rose from his chair, still cradling Lilian in his arms. 'Esther – I'm warning you. You'll hurt too many people and do something that can never – ever – be undone.'

Esther flung out her arm, gesturing towards Kate. 'And what do you suggest I do? Let her get on with it, eh?'

'No, but . . .'

'It's got to be stopped, Jonathan. You know it has.' And with that she almost ran from the house.

Kate stared at her stepfather in anguish. 'Dad – what's going on? What *is* it?'

Jonathan sighed and sat down heavily in his chair, shaking his head. 'It looks as if you'll find out very soon now, love.'

'You tell me, Dad.'

'No. It's not my place to do so.'

Kate left the house and ran towards the Point. She crested

the Hump and stood staring at the scene below her. In the distance she could see Danny and his father, Robert Eland, walking away from the cottages up towards the headland where the river joined the sea. The older man had his arm across Danny's shoulders and their heads were slightly inclined towards each other as if they were talking earnestly. At least, as if one were talking and the other listening.

Kate's gaze swivelled and came back to the cottages. She drew in a breath of surprise. Her mother stood outside the Elands' cottage and Beth Eland was in the open doorway, standing quietly while Esther Godfrey flung her arm out in the direction of Danny's departing figure, and then pointed at Beth, stabbing her finger towards the woman's breast to emphasize whatever it was she was saying.

Then Kate felt her heart go out to Danny's mother for suddenly Beth Eland covered her face with her hands and sagged against the door-frame for support. With a shock, Kate noticed that her mother made no move to help Beth, did not even put out her hand to steady her, but appeared only to bend towards her to press home her point even more forcefully.

Kate wanted to run forward, wanted to shout to Danny, wanted to stop whatever it was that was happening.

For all of a sudden, the most dreadful feeling of foreboding flooded through her.

She waited for what seemed an age and yet it could only have been minutes in reality until her mother turned away abruptly, leaving Beth still standing in the doorway, clutching at the door-jamb for support. And although she could not see the woman's face clearly from this distance, Kate knew instinctively that Beth Eland was weeping.

Danny and his father were at the headland, standing side by side, close, yet not touching now. They stood outlined against the sky, just staring out to sea. They did not seem to be speaking now.

Esther was coming towards Kate, her stride swift and purposeful, anger in every movement. Her head was bent and it was not until she began to climb the Hump that Kate saw her glance up and notice her daughter.

They stared at each other for a long moment until Kate burst out, 'You won't stop us, Mam. We love each other, and . . .'

'I warned you, Kate. For years I've been trying to keep you apart. I even tried to get you away from here.'

Kate gasped. 'You mean – you mean – that was why you sent me away to that school? Because of *Danny*?'

Esther nodded. She was quieter now, and strangely there was sadness in her tone as she said, 'I'm sorry, Kate, but you can never marry Danny Eland.'

Tears sprang to Kate's eyes. 'Why, Mam? Please tell me why.'

Kate saw her mother take a deep, unsteady breath. 'Because – he's your half-brother!'

Sixteen

The world revolved. The scene before her danced and blurred. It was like a knife being thrust in just below her ribs. Her heart seemed to stop and then begin to thud painfully. Fear prickled her scalp. She gasped for breath, clutching a hand to her chest, while with trembling fingers she reached out. 'Mam . . .?'

But her mother was walking away, striding down the Hump back towards Brumbys' Farm.

Kate cast a despairing glance towards Danny, still standing on the very point of the land, motionless, just staring out to sea. Matching his stillness, Robert Eland stood silently by his side.

Kate gave a sob, drew in a shuddering breath and ran down the Hump. 'Mam – Mam . . .' She caught up with Esther and grasped her arm roughly, pulling her mother round to face her. 'What do you mean – he's my half-brother? I don't understand.'

Esther's jaw was clenched, her eyes angry, defiant.

'Ya father – Matthew Hilton – got Beth pregnant before he married me.'

Kate gasped and stared at her, eyes wide. 'Didn't – didn't he *know*?'

Esther twisted her arm from Kate's grasp, turned and began to walk swiftly away again. 'No,' she said shortly.

Kate took little running steps to keep up with her. 'But Mam . . .'

Esther put up her hand as if to fend Kate off physically. 'I dun't want to talk of it. You can't marry Danny. Not ever. I've tried to warn you, all these years. But you wouldn't listen. Now you know and there's an end to it.'

Kate stopped and stood watching the slim figure of her mother walking towards the farm, her back rigid, her face turned away from her daughter.

Kate bit down hard upon her lower lip, drawing blood. The pain she caused herself was almost a relief. Then, tears blinding her, she turned towards the dunes and began to run.

'I want to die. I don't want to live any more. Just let me die!'

She was standing at the end of the Spit, at the very tip of the promontory of land that jutted out into the Wash. It was the place where the land, the sea and the sky all seemed to meet. Like the end of the world . . .

The water of a high tide was swirling around her. Dropping to her knees on the shingle, she wrapped her arms around herself. She closed her eyes, screwing up her face in an agony that was a real pain in the pit of her stomach.

'Kate – Kate, don't.'

He was there, picking her up, turning her unresisting body towards him and enveloping her in a fierce embrace. Danny was stroking her hair and murmuring words which made no sense to her, for she was crying hysterically, sobs shaking her body.

'I – don't want – to live – any more.'

'Shush, shush. You must live – for me. What would I do if you were no longer in the same world as me?'

Her arms slipped around his waist and she buried her face against his chest. Beneath his shirt she could feel the rapid beating of his heart. It matched her own.

Her sobs lessened and, muffled against him, she said, 'It isn't true, is it? Tell me it isn't true.'

His hand stroked her hair gently. 'I – can't, Katie. But – oh, how I wish I could!'

She raised her head then and looked up into his troubled face. Tears glistened in his eyes too and he pressed his lips together as if to prevent their trembling. For a long moment they gazed at each other whilst the water lapped at their feet and seagulls screeched mournfully overhead.

Haltingly, she began, 'Me mam won't tell me much, but she said my dad – me real dad – and your mam . . .'

Danny nodded. 'This is going to kill her!' he murmured and then added bitterly, 'Your mam has got a lot to answer for.'

Kate pulled back a little. 'My mam? Why, what has my mam got to do with it?' Her voice became harsher in her frustration at still not being able to understand fully. 'Danny, what do you mean?'

'Me dad ses . . . ' he began and then hesitated, as if suddenly realizing the enormity of the revelation. Robert Eland, the man who had loved him, reared him, been everything to him that anyone could wish for in a father, was not his natural father; was not, in fact, even a blood relative.

In his agitation, Danny ran his strong fingers into his hair and grasped a handful, as if he would pull it out by the roots. He took a deep breath to steady himself and yet, when he spoke, his voice still shook. 'It seems,' he said slowly, as if he still couldn't – or wouldn't – believe what he was telling Kate, 'Your dad – Matthew – and my mam were walking out together when your mother arrived here to work for old Sam Brumby on the farm. Matthew was after anything in skirts, me dad ses.' Still Danny could not break the habit of a lifetime. Robert Eland was, to him, his father. He cleared his throat and went on. 'Matthew chased after Esther and when Sam Brumby died, they got married and he moved into the farm with her – and left me mam pregnant with me.'

Kate gasped. 'Oh, how could he?'

'Evidently – very easily,' Danny said bitterly.

'But yar mam wouldn't ... I mean ...' Kate began, then stopped.

They stared at each other. 'I suppose,' he said slowly, 'she was young and – and in love.' His voice dropped to a hoarse whisper. 'Just like us, Katie.'

Kate's eyes widened and she gasped. 'We almost did, didn't we?'

He nodded. 'Thank goodness we stopped in time.'

Kate shivered suddenly as a chill wind blew in from the sea. Her voice broke on a sob. 'I – wish we *had* done it!'

He held her close again, resting his cheek against her ruffled hair. 'Now – we can't – ever.' His arms tightened around her as if he would never let her go.

'I still don't understand it all,' she murmured.

'Nor me. All I know is,' he added grimly, 'what they did has wrecked *our* lives even all this time after.'

'You're only a few months older than me. It can't be true. I won't let it be!'

His tone was flat with misery. 'I – think it is, Katie. If you think about it – looking back – it explains a lot of things.'

'What?'

'Why your mam and mine never speak to each other; why she sent you away to school and why, when that went wrong and you came home, she still tried to keep us apart.'

Kate was silent now. He was right. About everything. And there was something else that even Danny didn't know. The solemn promise which her mother had extracted from her that she would never – ever – let Danny touch her. Behind

156

that promise had been the awful truth her mother had known.

'God, how I hate her!' she muttered through her teeth. 'It's all my mother's fault. If she hadn't come here – if she hadn't married Matthew, then – then . . .'

'Then,' Danny said softly, 'you wouldn't have been born.'

Gently, he cupped her face in his hands. 'Oh, Kate,' he said, his voice deep with emotion, 'we can't ever marry, or be lovers . . .'

'Why? Why not? We could go away where no one knows us. We have different names. We're not related in the eyes of the law.' She was clutching at straws.

'You know we can't!'

She drew back from him suddenly, pushing him away. 'You don't care. You don't love me. Not as I love you. You can't, or you wouldn't be giving in so – so easily.'

He flinched as if her words were physical blows. He caught her by the arms and held her fast so that she could not turn away from him, held her so tightly that she was forced to listen to him. 'Katie, don't say that to me. Not to me. Me dad wouldn't lie to me. He must know . . .'

'Mr Eland, ya mean,' she said cuttingly. 'He's not ya dad, is he? Any more than Mester Godfrey's mine. We've both got *step*dads – now.'

Danny winced and Kate was immediately contrite. She was lashing out blindly in her pain, and hurting the one who was already suffering along with her.

She closed her eyes but fresh tears forced themselves from under her eyelids and coursed down her cheeks. 'Oh, Danny, Danny. I can't bear it. It – hurts so much.' She flung herself against him, wrapping her arms around his waist, burying her head against him again.

'I've always loved you, Katie, and I always will,' he said gently.

'But – but can't we be together? Somehow?' She raised her head to look into his face, her mouth slightly open, hanging on to his words like a drowning woman reaching for the hand of her rescuer, willing him to make it come right.

But Danny could not make it come right; there was only one thing he could promise her and it was all they had left to cling to. With dreadful finality, he said again, 'We can't marry, but they can't stop us loving each other. Not ever, Katie, not *ever!*'

'Oh, lovey, do you hate me?'

The back door of the Elands' cottage had opened to Kate's knock. Beth stood there, her eyes red and swollen. Kate threw herself against the older woman, her arms clasped around Beth's thickening waist, and buried her head against the comforting bosom. She could feel Beth trembling.

'Oh Katie, Katie, can you ever forgive me?'

Kate lifted her head and looked into the older woman's face. She didn't know what to say.

Gently, Beth steered Kate towards the range. She sat down in the chair while Kate sank down on to the rug, her head resting against the older woman's knees. For a long moment Beth stared into the flames and then, in her soft voice, she began, haltingly, to explain. As the memories, both happy and sad, came flooding back, her voice became stronger.

'I loved Matthew,' Beth began simply, 'I think I always had – right from a child . . .'

Like me and Danny, Kate thought bitterly, but she remained silent.

' . . . Even though he was a bit of a flirt . . .' A fond smile curved Beth's mouth. It was a kinder judgment than Robert Eland had given to Danny, and despite all the unhappiness that flirting had caused, Beth still loved Matthew enough to forgive him.

'When Esther arrived at Sam Brumby's farm – well – it was in his nature to try his luck with her. She was a very pretty girl and so fiery, she was a challenge to him. He could never resist a challenge.'

Kate looked up. 'How d'you mean?'

'For a time, Esther would have none of him, but the more she held him off, the more he wanted her.' Beth's voice dropped to a whisper as she admitted, 'That's where I made my mistake . . .'

Kate pressed her cheek closer to Beth's knee but could think of nothing to say.

'She wouldn't give in to him, told him she wouldn't give in to him – nor to any man – till she was wed.'

Kate was silent, knowing all this must have been true. It was her mother's strict code of life – it still was! 'Ya don't give ya'sen to a man till you've a wedding ring on ya finger, girl,' she'd told Kate repeatedly. 'Dun't ever bring a bastard into the world!'

Beth was sighing softly, but continuing. 'Then Sam Brumby died and – to be fair – I don't think ya mam had anywhere else to go.'

'What about me grandad? Why couldn't she go to him?'

Beth looked down at Kate's upturned face. 'Ya'll have to ask ya mam about that, lovey . . .'

'She won't tell me anything.'

'Well, perhaps ya grandad, then. Maybe – maybe he's the one to ask.'

Yes, Kate thought grimly, she would certainly have some questions to ask her grandfather. Intuitively she knew that there was more to all this than even Beth Eland was telling her.

'The Squire would only let her stay on the farm if she

were married – so that the tenancy agreement could be in a man's name. So – she and Matthew were married all quick-like. I dun't know to this day how they managed it without any of us knowing.'

'You – you didn't *know*!' Kate was appalled.

'No. I didn't know till Matthew moved his things from – from this very house.'

'He lived here? In this cottage?'

Beth smiled sadly. 'Yes,' she said softly. 'He was born here and lived here with his parents till they both died. Then, for a while, he lived on his own. Of course, Grannie Harris next door and me saw he was all right for food and his washing . . .'

'Where did you live?'

'Next door.' Beth indicated the adjacent cottage on the other side, where her father, Dan Hanley, the coastguard, still lived.

'And Mester Eland?'

Beth's eyes filled with sudden tears. 'On – on a boat on the river bank.' She glanced out of the cottage window to the place on the river bank where the huge hulk of a boat had once rested, shored up on poles and sleepers, half-in, half-out of the water.

Vague pictures, fleeting and disjointed, were flitting through Kate's mind. Memories from childhood that she could glimpse in her mind but not quite hold on to and understand.

'Did Matthew marry her to get the farm, then?'

Beth shook her head. 'No – no, I don't believe he understood what – what ya mam was up to.'

Kate's head jerked up. She felt the coolness of Beth's deep sigh brush her cheek. 'He wanted her – lusted after her and she – she took advantage of that to get him to marry her so she could get the farm.'

'You – you mean it was her fault?'

'In a way but – but try not to be too hard on her, Katie. It's very difficult for us to understand how someone – a young girl of eighteen or so – must have felt with no family, no home. Ask yourself what you would have done in the same circumstances.'

Kate stared up at Beth in surprise. 'You're – you're taking her side.'

'I'm – trying to tell you it fairly. But it's not easy for me.'

'So – all this – all that happened – that's why you never speak to each other. You – you must be very bitter?'

'Oh yes, I'm bitter all right.' Beth's mouth tightened and for a moment there was a flash of fire in her dark brown eyes, but it was gone in a moment as she sighed and added, 'It's funny though, if things had been different – we might have been friends, yar mam and me.' A wry smile twisted the corner of her mouth. 'And despite everything, we always seem to come together if one of us has trouble.'

'How – how d'ya mean?'

'Matthew went off to the war and was reported killed. Ya mam brought me a photograph of him. I – I still have it. It was a kind gesture. I've never forgotten that.'

Kate frowned. 'But I – I thought me dad drowned. Here – at the Point?'

'Matthew came back from the war a broken wreck of a man. Pitiful to see him, it was. Ya mam was wonderful then. She devoted herself to caring for him and he improved beyond what any of us ever thought possible. And that was down to Esther; with her strength and determination, she pulled him through. But she – she sacrificed her own chance of happiness to look after Matthew. I thought then, that somehow, in her own way, she must have loved him to do that.'

'What do you mean, "her own chance of happiness"?'

161

Beth avoided Kate's direct gaze, reluctant to answer. 'She – she'd met Jonathan in the war – when ya dad was away.'

'Oh – I see.' Kate said flatly. She didn't see it all, at least not clearly, but she could sense that Beth would not be drawn on that part any further. 'And me dad – me real dad? *Did* he drown?'

Beth's voice was a hoarse whisper. 'There was a dreadful storm in the winter of nineteen-twenty. Matthew knew the boat we lived on wouldn't stand up to the gales and the surging tide. He – drowned trying to rescue us – his son and – and me.' Beth bowed her head and covered her face with her hands.

Kate gasped. This woman's love for Matthew Hilton was still, even now, as strong as ever. Tentatively Kate put out her hand and touched Beth's arm.

'What about Mester Eland? Where – how does he fit into all this?'

Now there was a tender, loving smile on Beth's mouth, a smile tinged with gratitude. 'He loved me, he'd always loved me. As great a love as any man could have for a woman, Kate. When he knew I was expecting Matthew's child, he married me to give Danny a name.'

Kate's own voice broke. 'He must have loved you very much to do that.'

Beth nodded. 'Oh, he did. He still does. And I have loved him, truly I have, but in – in a very different way to the way I loved Matthew.'

She sighed deeply. 'Robert's been a good husband and a wonderful father to Danny, but he's always been very resentful towards Matthew – and towards your mam. That's why I'm glad to have been able to tell you about it mesen.'

Kate nodded. She was glad too, for the version Danny had heard from Robert Eland treated her mother and father far more harshly than did Beth – the woman who had been hurt most of all. Yet, it was understandable, Robert Eland, too, had suffered.

So it was told – the whole sorry tale. And now Kate understood, if not every little detail, then enough to know that what they said was true.

She and Danny were indeed half-brother and sister.

'Has *she* told you it all, then? What's she said about me, eh? 'Spect I'm the bad woman in it all . . .'

'Why . . .?' Kate's voice was a whisper, but her eyes held her mother's gaze relentlessly. 'Why didn't you all just tell us the truth? If we'd grown up with it – knowing – we'd have accepted it. Been just friends, been,' the bitterness crept into her tone, 'been brother and sister!'

She was standing facing her mother across the kitchen table.

Esther, hands on hips, her mouth a grim line, said, 'There'd have been no need for you to know, if you'd done as I'd told you . . .'

'You didn't want us to know 'cos it was your fault . . .'

'Oh aye, I thought as much! Trying to set you against ya own mother . . .'

'Who? Danny's mam? Oh no, dun't blame her. She even told me not to think badly of you; said I should understand how it must have been for you with no family and nowhere to go . . .'

'She had no right to tell you anything about me . . .'

'She stuck up for you, Mother! Her, of all people!'

Esther blinked.

'Yes, that's shocked you, ain't it? And she wouldn't tell me much about you, either. Said I'd to ask you or me grandad.'

'Ya'll do no such thing. Ya'll not say anything to ya grandad. It'll upset him.'

163

'Then you tell me. Go on, *you* tell me.'

'No,' Esther said through gritted teeth. 'It dun't concern you. You know now all ya need to know, an' that's too much! Ya'll learn no more from me.'

'Well, I'll find out. One day I'll find out everything. As for now – I'm going away. You wanted me gone four years ago, so now you'll get your wish. I'm going!'

Suddenly the fight seemed to drain out of her mother and she sat down heavily on a chair, leaned her elbows on the kitchen table and dropped her head into her hands. 'You don't have to go, Katie. Not now.'

'Oh yes, I do,' Kate leaned towards her mother as if to drive the hurtful shaft in harder. 'I can't stay here – seeing him every day. Not the way we feel about each other. Mother – we're in love. We want – wanted . . .' her voice broke a little as deliberately she changed the tense, 'to get married.'

Esther gave a soft groan. 'I wouldn't have had this happen to you – or Danny – for the world. I tried, really I did, in the only way I could think of to keep you apart. But the harder I tried, the more you seemed drawn to each other . . .' She broke off, raised her head and looked straight at Kate, a sudden urgency in her tone. 'He – he hasn't – touched you, has he?'

There was silence in the kitchen except for the ticking clock and the hissing of the red-hot wood in the grate as Esther waited for the answer that was so important to her, meant everything to her.

Kate stared back at her mother, holding her breath. She had it in her power at this moment to wound her mother deeply; to plunge a knife into her heart in retaliation for the hurt she and Danny were feeling; to punish Esther for the actions of her youth which had brought about this tragedy.

She opened her mouth to speak, to say, 'Yes, yes, yes, he's touched me! We've lain together. We're man and wife in all but name . . .' But she couldn't do it. All the years of love that lay between Kate and her mother, all the values that Esther had instilled into her daughter and Kate's own natural, inborn honesty, would not allow her to tell such a dreadful lie. Slowly, Kate let out the breath she was holding and, with it, some of the resentment against her mother. After all, she had not been solely responsible either for what had happened years ago or for keeping it secret. Danny had been kept in ignorance too. Yet Kate could not blame Beth Eland so much; she had more to risk by telling her son the true circumstances of his birth. She must have feared losing his respect, perhaps even his love.

So, although shreds of resentment against her mother still remained for she believed Esther could, and should, have told her the truth years ago, now Kate said heavily, 'No, Mam. We haven't – done anything.'

'Thank the Lord!' Esther murmured.

Then, as Kate added, 'But I have to go away, Mam. At least, for a while,' all Esther could reply sadly, was, 'Kate, oh, Katie.'

That night as Kate lay in bed, her knees pulled up to her chin, she cradled the whelk shell in her hand.

It was all she had left of Danny; and all she would ever have.

She gave a sob into the darkness as she remembered suddenly, and tears trickled down her cheeks.

Tomorrow was her birthday.

Part Two

Seventeen

SEPTEMBER, 1939

'War! Oh no! Not again. Not another one.'

Kate watched in amazement as her mother stood in the middle of the yard, staring at her husband and wringing her hands in agitation. She could not remember having ever seen her so distressed. Angry, yes, many times, but the sight of tears in her mother's green eyes shocked Kate.

Then, at Esther's next words, Kate understood. Her mother had rushed towards Jonathan and was grasping his shoulders, looking up into his face, her eyes wide and afraid. 'You won't go this time, will you?'

Of course! That was it. Kate felt a moment's pity for her mother, usually so strong and sure. For her to be so obviously frightened spoke volumes about the seriousness of the situation.

Jonathan put his arms about his wife and held her close. 'I shouldn't think so, my dear. I'll probably be too old now.'

Esther was clinging to him. 'You can't go – not again. I couldn't bear it. It'll be bad enough all the young fellers having to go . . .'

Now fear clutched at Kate. Feeling sick, she turned away and walked out of the yard and across the lane to the dunes. Under the elder trees it was shady, the breeze rustling the leaves above her. She slipped off her shoes; the sand was cool beneath her feet. The prickly buckthorn bushes were laden with orange berries, bright splashes of colour against the silvery green leaves.

169

Kate climbed the dune and came out on the top above the trees. She stood and looked about her, her glance sweeping the land all around. It was so peaceful; the whispering of the leaves, the trilling song of a soaring skylark, the sudden cry of a gull and the soft splash of the sea were the only sounds to break an absolute quiet.

It seemed strange to be home again. She had been away for almost nine years; nine long years in which so much had happened and yet, perversely, nothing had changed. She had come home frequently; not so much at first when she had been trying to put time and distance between herself and Danny. But recently she had come back to Fleethaven Point more and more until, with war seeming inevitable, she had made the decision to come home.

When she and Danny had learnt why they could never marry, Kate had gone to Lincoln. It seemed ironic, and yet somehow fitting, that she should go back to the place where her mother had tried to send her once before, and where she had been so miserable. She was wretchedly unhappy again, though it was not, she acknowledged, the fault of the beautiful city where she tried to make her home and build a new life. She found comfort in the vast interior of the cathedral and a melancholy catharsis in wandering the streets throbbing with people; yet she felt she was entirely alone. Nor was it the fault of the kindly people who gave her a home; the Godfreys.

At first, Kate had intended to stay only briefly in the small room that had once been her stepfather's in their terraced family home. But an affinity and a friendship sprang up between Peggy Godfrey and the young, unhappy Kate, despite the sixteen years or so between them. Whether her stepfather had told them the circumstances, Kate never knew, but the Godfreys never pried into what had caused Kate's sadness and were gently considerate and made her welcome;

indeed they treated her as another daughter. The weeks grew into months and although at first she made tentative efforts to find herself other lodgings, she could see that the Godfreys' desire for her to stay with them was genuine. She found work in the sewing room of the store where Peggy worked and during the first two years, she returned to Fleethaven Point only twice. She did not see Danny then, but on her third visit, they met accidentally in the lane.

In two years they had changed little in outward appearance, but in their eyes was the sadness they shared.

'You're thinner, Katie,' he had said softly, his brown eyes searching her face.

'You're – not laughing so much,' she'd said.

There had been silence between them as they had stared at one another, each reliving the last time they had been together; that dreadful day.

Then Danny had taken a deep breath. 'We've got to come to terms with it, Katie. Learn to live with it. I dun't want you staying away from here just to avoid seeing me.'

'I don't know which is worse, Danny,' she murmured, 'seeing you – or *not* seeing you.'

'I know. I've done a lot of thinking while you've been away. We can't ever marry . . .' Although there was a wealth of sadness in his tone, there was also a new strength as if the cruel blow had toughened him into manhood. 'But, you know, maybe we have a love far greater even than that. The ties of brother and sister, blood ties, can be even stronger and deeper.'

She listened in silence to his reasoned words, knowing instinctively what torment, what heart-searching, had gone into reaching this sensible acceptance. The hurt was still as deep, but the pain was not so intense. In the two years, Danny had not stopped loving her, but had wrestled with how they might salvage a different kind of love from the wreckage.

So Kate had taken her lead from him, and although she had stayed in Lincoln, she had come home to Fleethaven more often. Little by little the agony eased as they drew strength from each other.

And down the years, Danny's words to her on that fateful day at the end of the Spit were locked within her heart: 'They can't stop us loving each other. Not ever, Katie, not *ever*!'

Now, nine years on, standing on top of the sand-dune, drinking in the sight of the marsh spread before her, Kate was a very different young woman from the distraught girl of eighteen. She had held a responsible position in her work and from that had gained self-confidence. In the Godfreys' home, she had been as happy as it was possible for her to be and she had grown to love their city. But always her heart lay at Fleethaven Point.

How could she ever have thought she could leave this place for good, she thought now. She took a deep, satisfying breath of the fresh, clean air, closed her eyes for a moment and held her face up to the breeze as it ruffled her carefully styled, city hairstyle. Opening her eyes again, she gave a little laugh of exultation and ran down the grassy slope and across the marsh to the beach. She walked at the water's edge, scuffing her toes through the shingle, paddling in the frothy edges of the encroaching waves and gazing across the wide expanse of grey water half expecting to see enemy ships already lying off shore.

This place was in her blood. Its tranquillity enveloped her and welcomed her home. How can we possibly be at war, she thought.

Then, distantly, she heard the rising wail of a siren.

*

'Danny, you won't have to go, will you?'

She had been waiting for him that evening at the junction where the lane leading westwards to the Grange joined the coast road. He came pedalling towards her on his bicycle, the sound of his whistling reaching her long before he did. When he saw her, he took his feet off the pedals and scuffed his boots along the road to slow down.

'Haven't you got those brakes mended yet?' she scolded as he wobbled to a halt, speaking to him as easily and as naturally as if they had seen each other earlier that day and not several weeks ago.

He grinned sheepishly at her. 'Nope – it dun't matter round here. No hills, a' there?' He paused and then added, 'You home for the weekend?'

She shook her head. 'No – I'm back for good.'

'Not afore time neither. You're not a city lass. You dress nice, I'll grant you that . . .'

'Oh thank you, kind sir.' She bobbed a mocking curtsy.

'But you're too pale – and too thin.'

Now she laughed. 'Well, if I can't get my old job back in town, I'll be working on the land, so I'll soon end up as leathery-looking as you.'

Then the teasing stopped; the look that passed between them saying that they both knew what the other was thinking. Without the need for explanation, it was then she asked, 'Danny, you won't have to go, will you?'

His face sobered, the grin fading. 'Farming's what they call a reserved occupation . . .' He hesitated. She held her breath, knowing very well what was coming. 'But I – I might *want* to go, Katie.'

She let out her breath slowly in a deep sigh. She might have known. Someone like Danny wouldn't want to be thought a coward. Not Danny.

She was watching him, seeing, suddenly, the changes the

last nine years had wrought in him. He, too, was thinner in the face, yet his shoulders and chest were if anything even broader and more muscular than ever. Men of his age, she thought, were usually married with two or three little ones. But then, she thought wryly, so were young women of her age!

Neither of them had found a partner. There had been one or two young men in Lincoln who had asked Kate out and sometimes she had gone. But there had never been a second meeting. Either she had politely refused, or a further invitation had not been forthcoming. Perhaps the young men were vaguely aware that they were being compared with the ghost of a love from the past.

As for Danny, he didn't seem interested in any of the young women in the district. He was now Squire Marshall's farm bailiff, well liked and well respected by all those under him, and he still acted as the ailing Squire's personal chauffeur when the old man needed to go anywhere, though gout and increasing infirmity confined the Squire more and more to his home. Mrs Marshall had died in the winter of 1932 and the Squire lived alone with only a few servants to care for him. His son, Arthur, lived in London, taking no interest in the affairs of the small estate and visiting only rarely.

'He's doing very well,' the Squire would tell anyone who would listen. 'Something in the City, you know. A wonderful career . . .' Then the old man's eyes would cloud over and he would sigh, 'I don't know what's to become of the estate, though, when I'm gone.'

'It'll be sold or broken up, you'll see,' Kate's mother would say resentfully to her family in the privacy of their home. 'Young Arthur's for the high life and no mistake! He doesn't want to know what hard work is!'

Jonathan and Kate would exchange a fond smile. Esther could not understand anyone who did not share her love of the land. Her prediction was right, although not quite in the way she would have expected.

The thirties brought their own particular problems for the nation. The Depression hit hard but for Esther Godfrey it brought good fortune. The Squire, rather than see his land go to strangers, decided to offer the three farms which made up the bulk of his estate – Brumbys' Farm, Rookery Farm and Souters' Farm – to the sitting tenants.

'I'd rather see you have the land, Esther, my dear,' he had told Kate's mother, blowing his nose vigorously on a huge handkerchief. 'I know you love Brumbys' Farm.'

Esther's eyes had glowed and the wooden box that held all her savings had been pulled from under her bed and the coins and notes carefully counted. With land at the lowest price anyone could remember, there was just enough for Brumbys' Farm to become Esther's.

Kate still smiled every time she thought of that Sunday morning on one of her visits. Her mother had been as excited as a young girl.

'It'll be mine – really mine – I mean,' she had added swiftly, glancing at Jonathan, 'ours!'

Kate had watched as Jonathan had put his arms around his wife. 'No, my love,' he had said quietly but firmly. 'The papers will be in your name and your name alone.'

'But—'

'But nothing. I won't hear of it being otherwise. You *are* Brumbys' Farm.' He had smoothed back the tendrils of hair from her forehead. 'Your name shall be the first one on the deeds after the Marshalls. There now, won't that be something?'

Esther had nodded, her eyes brimming with tears. 'Yes,' she had whispered. 'Yes, it will.'

Esther had been the only one to take up the Squire's offer. Tom Willoughby, with no family to carry on after him, decided to remain as a tenant for the last few years of his working life.

'I can't see the point of me buying, Esther lass, though I'm glad for you,' the big man had boomed, his red cheeks wobbling with laughter. 'No one deserves it more 'n you. But I only want to work a few more years and what bit o' savings we've got, I want to enjoy. See a bit o' how the other half lives afore I die.' His laughter had boomed out and he had winked saucily at Esther. She had smiled indulgently, trying to understand how anyone could even think of leaving Fleethaven Point. Less than six months after their conversation, Tom's wife, Martha, had died. So now only Tom and his sister-in-law lived at Rookery Farm.

The Souters, whom Kate didn't know very well, for their farm lay to the west of the Squire's estate and was the farthest away from Brumbys', were known to be spendthrifts and had neither the ready money nor the collateral to raise a loan.

So Esther was the only one to buy. At last, she had her reward for all her years of hard work. And now, Kate thought, all that might be snatched away from her mother if their country were plunged once more into war.

But perhaps, Kate thought, our little corner of England will hardly notice the war.

How wrong she was!

Kate walked down the lane towards home, with Danny riding his bike at the side of her, wobbling precariously as he tried to slow his pace to match her walking speed.

'So what are you going to do, now you're back? Get your old job back at old man Reynolds'?'

'I might. Miss Davenport was telling Mam only last week that the workroom supervisor's leaving to get married.'

'Your old job, eh?'

'Maybe, but I might be needed to do something a little bit more important.' She glanced at him and added, impishly. 'I could always join up.'

Danny's eyes twinkled with mischief. 'What d'you reckon women could do, eh?'

'Plenty!' she flashed back, just as he had known she would. 'It was the last war that set us free from the kitchen sink. Women worked as VAD nurses, in factories, all sorts . . .'

'Remember it, do you?' He was grinning at her indignation, teasing her fondly.

'No. One of my clients in Lincoln, Mrs Clarkson, was a VAD nurse in the last lot. She loved to talk about it when she came for a fitting. We'll play an even bigger part this time – you'll see!'

'It'll not come to much, I don't reckon. It'll all be over by Christmas.'

Ominously, Kate reminded him, 'That's what they said last time!'

Eighteen

Of course it was not over by Christmas, nor even by well into 1940. The news was not good and as it got worse, Kate began to fear that any day, Danny would say he was volunteering.

The rationing of certain foods sent Esther into a fury. 'What are we supposed to do then? Us that produce the butter and bacon? Ration oursens? Answer me that?'

'They'll tell us, Esther love, just as they'll tell us what crops they want us to plant.'

'Aye, potatoes!' Esther said scathingly. 'Whoever heard of beautiful fields of waving wheat and oats being replaced by 'tates?'

'We must do what we can to help the war effort, love,' Jonathan replied gently.

Then Esther's wonderful smile, like the sun appearing once more, lit up her face. She put her arms about her husband and rested her head against his chest. 'I'll do whatever they want, as long as they don't take you away from me this time.'

Jonathan chuckled softly. 'We'll be in a bad way if they have to call up men of fifty!'

Watching them, Kate smiled fondly, but in her heart she feared for Danny. Conscription had been extended now to include men up to the age of twenty-seven – Danny's age. Would he be called up, Kate anguished, or was he safe as an agricultural worker?

At the beginning of April the enemy invaded Denmark

and Norway and in May they swept through Belgium and also into Holland. Then northern France came under attack.

The menace was coming closer.

'Danny? Where are you going?'

The late May morning was bright, the sun glistening on the water as Kate stood on the river bank, looking down into Robert Eland's fishing boat moored at the end of the wooden jetty. Danny was packing blankets, boxes of food and tins of diesel into the stern.

'Sheerness.'

'*Sheerness*! Whatever for?'

'Me dad had to register the boat because it's just over thirty foot and now it's been commandeered, so I'm takin' it down there mesen.'

'What for?' she repeated.

'I – dunno.'

'Yes, you do. I can tell.'

He continued carrying boxes from the jetty on to the boat. 'There's trouble across the Channel.'

'Is your dad going with you?'

'No, he's got to man the lifeboat. I'm going on me own.'

'Then I'm coming with you.'

'No, you're not . . .'

But she was scrambling down the bank and marching along the wooden planking. He barred her way. ''Tis no place for a woman.'

Kate laughed in his face. 'Oh no? Do you really think I'm going to let you go without *me*!'

'Kate, yar mam . . .'

'Me mam's got nowt to do with it. I'm of age, aren't I?' The dialect, which she had made valiant efforts to smooth out in her working life, came back strongly when she was angry. And she was angry now.

'Well, ya not dressed right.'

'Then I'll go home and get mesen dressed in trousers and warm clothes.'

'Ya'll need oilskins . . .'

She pointed beyond him at the boat bobbing gently on the swell of the river. 'You've always got a spare pair on board. I've seen 'em.'

'Oh, *you*!' Danny said, half exasperated, half amused. 'Ya know too much for ya own good. Go on, then.'

'You'll wait for me? You'll not go without me?'

Now he was grinning broadly. 'I wouldn't dare!'

She was away and running across the turf. At twenty-seven she could still run as fast as she had at fourteen. And for the moment, any dignity which her advancing years and her position as workroom supervisor in the department store in Lynthorpe had brought her, was forgotten.

'Bring more blankets and some food, if you can,' he shouted after her. She did not pause but lifted her hand in acknowledgement that she had heard him.

'And don't forget your . . .'

' . . . gas mask,' she finished for him.

Breathless, she reached Brumbys' Farm to meet Lilian pushing her doll's pram around the yard.

'Shouldn't you be doing something more useful than playing with dolls at your age?' Kate snapped. Lilian, a gawky thirteen-year-old, never failed to irritate Kate. From a whining child she had grown into a sulky, solitary girl who seemed deliberately to shun the company of friends of her own age. To Kate's idea, their mother pampered Lilian, who was never asked to help with the housework or farmwork as Kate had been from a very early age.

'It was different then,' Esther would say when Kate grumbled. 'I was on me own and there was a war on.'

'There's a war on now, for heaven's sake!' Kate would argue.

'But none of our family's involved this time, thank the Lord!'

So what would her mother say, Kate thought now as she raced upstairs to find her warmest clothes, if she knew Kate was about to involve herself deliberately in something to do with the war – even though at the moment she didn't know exactly what?

Dressed in slacks, a thick woollen jumper and grey knitted socks, Kate ran down the narrow stairs carrying three blankets. Swiftly, she packed some bread and cheese into a bag. Sitting in her father's Windsor chair to pull on her wellingtons, she looked up to see Lilian standing in the door watching her. 'Tell Mam I've gone out in the boat with Danny. I don't know how long we'll be gone, but tell her she's not to worry.' Snatching a warm coat from the hook behind the door and stuffing a headscarf and a wool beret into her pocket, Kate turned back to look at her young sister. The girl looked so forlorn standing there, awkward and, even in her own home, somehow lost. Strangely moved to a feeling of tenderness, Kate planted a swift kiss on the girl's forehead. 'You hear, Lilian?'

The girl nodded and then suddenly flung her arms around Kate's waist and buried her head against her. Just as suddenly, she let go and stood back, her face flaming red. Kate wasn't sure which of them was the more embarrassed. She gave the girl a quick grin, said, 'Take care, Lilian,' and was gone.

Funny child, Kate thought as she hurried back to the Point. At her age I'd have been begging to go along too. Lilian hadn't even asked where they were going. Perhaps that was just as well, though, Kate thought shrewdly. But the sudden display of emotion from her sister had surprised Kate.

Danny was standing on the edge of the jetty, the mooring rope already unfastened.

'Hop in and start her up, will ya, Kate?' He grinned suddenly. 'Thank goodness for ya dad and his engines!'

Kate knew the boat and its workings almost as well as Danny did, for she had often gone out to sea with him on her visits home. Good job too, she thought, Mam'll think nothing about it when Lilian tells her.

But she would when Kate did not arrive home that night, she thought with a stab of guilt. Well, she reflected with wry humour, me mam'll just have to break years of silence and go and ask Danny's mother where we are if she's that bothered!

Kate smiled to herself as she guided the boat into the centre of the river and made for the channel which led out through the intertidal marsh and into the North Sea. She doubted very much that even a war would make Esther Godfrey speak to Beth Eland!

They chugged steadily out to sea and turned southwards, following the coastline. It was a long way and would take them a long time to get there.

'I just hope we're in time for whatever it is they want,' Danny said, as they settled themselves for the hours ahead.

'Just look at all them boats!' Danny was standing up in the prow of his boat. It looked as if hundreds of small craft of all shapes and sizes were heading for Sheerness. He turned and looked back at Kate. 'This looks like something big, Kate, I dun't reckon you ought to have come . . .'

Kate gave him one of her looks and he raised his hand, palm outwards, as if to fend off an impending attack. 'All right, all right . . .'

She grinned at him but kept her hand firmly on the tiller. 'I never said a word,' she shouted across the breeze.

'No – but ya looked it!'

Somehow they found a place to moor and joined the rest of the boatmen on the quay.

As they walked towards the building where they had to report their arrival, Kate took a beret from her coat pocket and pulled it over her thick hair, tucking stray strands beneath it. In trousers, a bulky jumper and jacket, she could pass for a young boy. Only her luxurious auburn hair gave her away!

Very soon they found out why their boats were needed. The British Expeditionary Forces were virtually trapped on the coast of France at a place called Dunkirk and had to be rescued. Enemy planes were strafing the beaches, and the opposing army was closing in around them. Every available boat was needed to bring the soldiers off the beaches.

One of the boat owners proposed that he should take his own boat across and suddenly there was a chorus of offers. After a brief consultation among the senior officers, they agreed to the suggestion.

Silently the boatmen listened as they heard what their mission was to be; to bring the men off the beaches to ships anchored offshore. Larger boats could bring as many as they were able to carry safely back across the Channel if they wished. It seemed that off the beaches where the soldiers waited, the water was very shallow and some of the larger vessels could get nowhere near the shore.

'It's dangerous,' they were warned. 'The enemy are shelling from inland and there's the Luftwaffe to contend with too . . .'

'Kate . . .' She felt Danny's grasp upon her arm. 'I really don't think . . .'

She looked into his brown eyes, her own almost on a level

with his. 'Danny, ya can't possibly man the boat on ya own *and* rescue people.'

'No, Katie. It'll be dangerous. You're not coming. I won't let you.' His fingers tightened on her arm. 'What if – what if something were to happen to you?'

'Something might happen to you,' she whispered.

They stared at each other and his sigh was cool on her cheek. 'Please, Katie, stay here where it's safe.'

She shook her head. 'No, Danny,' she said with quiet firmness. 'I'm coming. I can't stay here – just waiting – while you're out there. Besides,' she added grinning cheekily, trying to lighten what was a very desperate situation. 'Think I'd let you out alone in France?'

'All right,' he said heavily. 'But if it's really bad I'll put you on one of the big ships.'

Kate grinned. She'd argue that when they got there, she thought, but said nothing.

Pulling her beret down well over her hair, she hovered behind Danny as they formed a queue to sign a form. In the mêlée she managed to scribble her signature and was out and following Danny back to the boat before anyone had realized she was a girl.

The sea was amazingly calm and the weather smiling benignly on their venture. Yet as they drew near the French coast, towed by one of the large vessels to save their precious fuel, the breeze whipped across the water, making the seas choppy.

Ahead now Kate saw a black pall of smoke rising above the town, and heard the thud of gunfire from the shore. Four black lines snaked out into the water. She squinted through the drifting smoke, there was something odd . . .

'Danny!' she clutched his arms. 'Look, those are men standing in the water!'

Lines of soldiers, standing three abreast up to their chests in the freezing water, formed disciplined queues stretching from the shore out towards the boats.

'Poor buggers!' Danny muttered, and Kate knew the sight had affected him deeply for she hardly ever heard Danny swear.

They were released from their tow and Danny started up the engine and steered the boat towards the nearest line of men. From the west came the steady hum of aircraft, growing louder and louder, nearer and nearer. Then they heard the sound of gunfire from three planes coming in low.

'Get down, Kate!' Danny yelled and pushed her into the bottom of the boat. She felt a jagged splinter from the planking dig into her hand.

'Ouch, I've got . . .' But the rest of her words were drowned as a plane passed overhead close to the prow of the boat, bullets splashing into the water directly in front of them. The planes flew off to the east and Kate raised her head. ' . . . a splinter in me hand.'

Danny ran his tongue nervously over his lips and made a valiant attempt to smile, 'If that's all ya get on this little trip, Kate, ya'll be bloody lucky! Come on, they'll be back in a minute. Let's see if we can get a few on board. You steer and I'll help 'em climb in.'

All along the coast the little ships pulled the men from the water, loading their small craft almost to sinking point before they chugged precariously back to the large vessels standing offshore.

Kate steered the boat while Danny helped the soldiers in. When one put his hands on the side, glanced at Kate and then hesitated, Danny said, 'Come on, mate, up with ya.'

'I can't . . .' He nodded towards Kate. 'She's a woman . . .'

'So?'

'I've – lost me trousers, mate. I've nothin' on.'

Danny grinned down at him. 'Born and bred on a farm, mate. You ain't got nothing she's not seen afore.'

There was a ripple of laughter, even amidst all the horror.

'Come on, Bashful Bert,' shouted another soldier waiting in line behind him. 'Get a move on.'

Smiling, Kate averted her gaze to save the poor man's embarrassment and when she looked again, he was wrapping a blanket around himself and grinning sheepishly at her.

'That's all for this time,' Danny shouted. 'We can only take fifteen at a time.'

'Can't we hang on to the side, mate?' one of the soldiers still waiting shouted.

'Sorry,' Danny said firmly. 'We'll capsize and then we'll get no one off. We'll be back as soon as we can...' he promised, but the look on the faces of those still waiting up to their necks in the water tore at Kate's heart.

Those they had taken on board sat hunched and silent. Their faces were streaked with oil and many had at least four days' growth of beard on their chins. One had a dirty handkerchief tied around one eye, another was only in his vest and underpants and all were wet through and shivering.

Kate opened one of the boxes and passed some bread and cheese and apples round. 'I'm sorry we've nothing hot,' she apologized.

A young soldier – no more than a boy, he seemed to Kate – wolfed the food, stuffing the bread into his mouth.

'How – how long have you been without food?'

'Three days, Miss. We've been on the beach for two, wading out into the water when it looked like a ship was coming, then back to the dunes again when the enemy planes came over...'

Suddenly Kate's hand seemed frozen on the tiller as a dreadful fear clutched her. This could happen on our beaches! The thought terrified her.

She shuddered, thinking of the peaceful tranquillity of the beach at home; she couldn't imagine Fleethaven Point becoming a place of death with guns blasting and soldiers fleeing for their lives into the dunes and bodies floating in the sea . . .

We can't let it happen, she thought suddenly. We have to help stop it happening – Danny and I. We must.

Until this moment the war had seemed far away; unreal. Oh, they'd read the papers, but it hadn't really affected their small community.

Now – off the beaches of Dunkirk – it was very real.

On their fourth trip back to the lines of waiting men, Danny shouted. 'Give us a hand here, Kate, this one can't help himself. He's about had it.'

'Here – hold this,' she asked one of the soldiers already in the boat.

'Anything you say, Cap'n.' The soldier's face was black with oil, and his clothes were saturated, but he still managed a grin as she handed the tiller over to him and moved down the boat to help Danny.

The man Danny was trying to bring aboard was in a semi-conscious state, almost sinking under the water. 'Give him a shove up, will ya, mate?' Danny asked the man waiting next to him.

'Shouldn't bother,' put in one of the soldiers already in the boat. 'He's only RAF. Where are they, that's what I'd like to know? Ain't seen one of *our* planes all day.'

'Shut up!' said the man next to him. 'He's here, ain't he? He must have been doing something. There's a lot of sky up there. Here, Miss, let me give you a hand.'

The men carefully shuffled position in the boat so that

the friendly soldier moved to Kate's side. 'Come on, mate, let's be having you back to good old Blighty.'

They hauled him into the bottom of the boat where he lay with his eyes closed. The sleeve of his pilot's jacket was ripped open and blood oozed out, mixing with the sea water. Kate took off her scarf and wrapped it round the man's arm, tying it at the back of his neck in a makeshift sling.

'Danny, are there any blankets left?'

'No – we've used 'em all.'

'Here, Miss, take mine,' said the soldier who had helped pull the airman aboard.

'The glamour boys get all the attention,' grumbled the soldier who had already moaned about the RAF.

'Shut it, will you?' muttered the friendly one. 'Else I'll shut it for you.'

The other sniffed. 'All the same – the women . . .'

The other man put his mouth close to the grumbling soldier's ear, but Kate still caught his words. 'This lass had no need to come and save your miserable hide. Risking her life, she is. So shut it!'

Danny turned the boat around and headed out to sea, the small craft low in the water with the weight. Kate bent over the airman and was relieved to hear a low moan escape his lips. She tapped his face with the flat of her hand, not exactly a slap but sharp enough to try and rouse him.

'That's right, Miss,' the friendly one encouraged. 'Don't let 'im go to sleep. The cold will kill him, else.'

Kate put her mouth close to the airman's ear, her whole attention now on the injured man. 'Come on, try to wake up. What's your name?'

She continued to talk to him, gently tapping his cheek to try to rouse him, while in the sky above, enemy aircraft swooped in again from the west, strafing the beaches and sending the waiting soldiers diving for cover in the dunes.

The planes shot off to the east but turned and came back over the water, this time aiming for the small boats loaded with soldiers. Further out to sea, two more planes dropped bombs close to the larger ships waiting for the retreating British Army.

Kate hardly noticed the noise now; she was trying to wrap an already sodden blanket around the airman. She sat down in the bottom of the boat and cradled the man in her lap, wrapping her arms around him and holding him close, rubbing his back to try to warm him.

'I tell you, them glamour boys get all the blooming luck,' the grumbling soldier said again. Kate glanced up at him and opened her mouth to speak, but her words were drowned by a terrific explosion and all heads turned to see the very ship they were making for receive a direct hit. Flames engulfed the bow and black smoke drifted skywards.

'Oh no!' Kate muttered, while the soldiers stared at the rescue ship in grim silence.

Wordlessly, Danny changed course slightly and headed for a smaller boat some distance further out to sea, skirting round the stricken vessel which was now burning fiercely. They could see men jumping back into the sea from which they had just been rescued, but with the present load they carried, Danny could do nothing to help. He steered away, thinking that if they went closer, panic-stricken men would grab their little fishing boat and capsize it.

'We'll see if we can pick some up when we've dropped you lot off,' Danny promised, but no one on board answered him. They just continued to stare at their comrades struggling in the water. As they watched, a figure, his clothes alight, jumped from the vessel into the water. Even above the turmoil they could hear his screams.

'Looks like every man for himself now,' muttered the friendly soldier.

They neared the smaller ship but already they could see that the decks were lined with soldiers.

A ship's officer hung over the side. He cupped his hands and shouted down to Danny as the small boat bobbed against the side, 'We can only take ten maximum.'

In the small boat, heads turned, counting their number. There were eleven soldiers and the airman besides Danny and Kate. The soldiers began to haul themselves up the nets hanging over the side of the ship.

'What about him?' Kate indicated the airman. 'He ought to be taken on board first. He needs medical attention urgently.'

The soldier who had been so scathing about the RAF glanced down as he began to climb. 'Shouldn't bother, miss, he's a gonner anyway.' And with that parting shot, he hauled himself up to safety.

Ten were on board, leaving the airman and the soldier who had been friendly. 'Reckon I'll stay and give you a hand, Miss, if we're to save this lad's life, eh?'

Kate gazed into his craggy face. He was older than the rest – a regular soldier, she thought, rather that a conscript.

'Reckon it's time we introduced ourselves.' He held out a large hand that was blue with cold. 'Gordon Stratford, pleased to meet you, Miss, though I could have wished for better circumstances.'

Kate grinned at him and put her own cold hand briefly into his. 'Kate Hilton, and he's Danny Eland.' She nodded towards Danny, who was manoeuvring the boat around to head back towards the soldiers from the sinking ship.

'We ought to get him roused if we can,' Gordon said. 'He'll slip away if we don't keep him awake.'

Together they struggled with the dead weight of the unconscious airman, trying to get him into a sitting position in the prow of the boat.

The airman's face was gaunt and pale, his eyes closed.

'I've got some rum stowed in that locker,' Kate said. 'Let's try that.'

She held the neck of the bottle to the airman's blue lips and gently tried to ease some of the reviving liquid into his mouth.

'He's a squadron leader,' Gordon said, suddenly. 'Wonder where the rest of his chaps are?'

'Now don't you start, Gordon!' Kate said, but she was smiling, teasing the friendly man who had so generously given up his own chance of immediate rescue to stay to help her and Danny.

Gordon's teeth shone white out of his oil-streaked face. 'No – I'm not like our friend back there.' He jerked his head back towards the ship they had just left. 'The RAF is here all right – I know that – but they've a hell of an area to cover and they won't have a lot of flying time from a fuel point of view when they do get here.'

'Talking about fuel . . .' Kate looked around at the cans Danny had brought. There was only one remaining tin. She glanced at Gordon. 'You go aboard with him the next trip back to a ship,' she said firmly, nodding towards the airman.

Gordon gave her a mock salute. 'Yes, Ma'am.'

While Danny steered the boat back towards the ship that had been hit, Kate chafed the airman's hands, though her own were now as cold as his. Then she rubbed his back again. 'Come on, feller, do wake up,' she murmured as his head lolled against her breast. She wrapped her arms around him again, rocking him as she might a child.

Above the airman's unconscious form, she met Danny's glance as he sat with his hand on the tiller. There was a fleeting look of pain in his eyes. Intuitively, she knew that he had felt a sudden stab of jealousy seeing her with her arms around another man. It was the first time, but it might not be the last, and she could see his inner struggle to come to terms with it. She smiled at Danny, understanding and commiserating. For a brief moment amidst all the chaos, they gazed at each other, and then he gave her a small smile and lifted his shoulders fractionally in a tiny shrug of helpless, reluctant acceptance. Even now, she thought, after all this time, for Danny as well as for her, the pain was never very far away.

'What's all that smoke?' she asked Gordon, watching the huge pall of black smoke ahead of them on the shore billowing and spreading, clouding the coastline for miles until it seemed like dusk, in stark contrast to the bright blue sky over the sea behind them.

'Oil storage tanks. They've been bombed. And the whole town's on fire.'

From out of the smoke hurtled three enemy planes, diving down towards the boats, the rattle of their machine-guns audible even above the engines. Ships' guns were turned on them and those soldiers on the decks who still had rifles pointed them skywards. Even though it was perhaps a futile gesture, nevertheless it was a display of defiance.

Defenceless, Danny, Kate and Gordon watched as the planes swooped directly towards them. Instinctively, Kate's arms tightened around the airman.

It was then that she felt him move. He gave a spluttering cough, then a groan, and opened his eyes.

The planes shot past them, spattering bullets into the water only two feet from the boat, and Kate felt the cold splash of sea water on her cheek. Then they banked away and were gone.

Gordon winked at Kate and said, 'Well now, young feller, back in the land of the living.'

They propped him upright and from the bag, Kate brought out more bread and cheese. 'See if you can get him to eat something – and have some yourself. We're getting close to the men in the water now. I'd better take the tiller for Danny.'

As she turned away to move along the boat, Gordon, his mouth full, said, 'By, this cheese is good. Long time since I tasted proper cheese. You *do* live on a farm, then? Where?'

'Fleethaven Point. It's on the Lincolnshire coast, near the Wash.'

'Good Lord! You come all that way down here?'

'Yes, Danny's boat was commandeered, so he decided to bring it himself. I came too – so here we are.'

'And thank the good Lord for you, lass. For you both – you and your man.'

Yes, she thought wryly, Danny was her man. Still, despite the knowledge of their true relationship, deep in a corner of her heart, locked away, he was still 'her man'.

Nineteen

The little fishing boat all the way from the Wash went back towards the sinking ship, now listing heavily to port and obviously beyond salvage. The men in the water were exhausted. After days and nights on the exposed beaches, under fire from the enemy, then standing in human piers stretching into the cold water of the Channel, they had dared to believe themselves rescued. To be thrown back into the water had sapped the strength and resolve of even these brave men.

Still the enemy aircraft swooped and dived above them. Every three-quarters of an hour or so they were back, splattering bullets across the water and dive-bombing the ships laden with soldiers.

While the men struggled to keep afloat in the water, Danny and Kate went back and forth between the sinking vessel and another rescue ship farther out to sea; so many times that Kate lost count. On the first trip out to the bigger ship, Danny sided with Kate and insisted that Gordon take the young airman aboard and stay with him.

'Ya've done your bit, mate,' Danny said, putting his hand on the older man's arm.

'I don't like leaving you and the young lass to cope.'

'Just stay with him,' Kate said, nodding down at the airman, 'Get him some proper help as soon as you can.'

'I'll do that, Miss, I promise. But you take care, mind.' He shook Danny's hand warmly and, without a trace of embarrassment, kissed Kate's cold cheek. 'I hope we meet again . . .'

They watched Gordon climb a swaying rope ladder, while alongside him, the RAF officer was hoisted aboard on a swinging stretcher. When he was half-way up, they saw Gordon swing round and look out across the water towards the soldiers on the beach running towards the dunes as yet again, enemy aircraft swooped low overhead. For a moment Gordon released one hand-hold, leaned back and looked up at the planes. He shook his fist at them. 'We'll be back, you buggers!' he shouted. 'We'll be back.' Then he turned and continued his climb.

Danny laughed. 'He's a character, in't he?'

'He's a great chap to have around in a crisis,' Kate murmured, half sorry to see Gordon leave them. 'Danny, do you reckon the airman'll make it?'

'I dunno, Kate. He looks bad to me. Come on, let's not stay here – we're sitting ducks!'

Each time they returned to the same ship, Gordon was there, hanging over the ship's rail.

'Your young airman's below,' he shouted down. 'We're in luck – this is a hospital ship. There's a doc on board – and even nurses! He's in good hands now.'

Kate smiled up at him and waved.

Then later, Gordon was still there. 'Come on, mate, come aboard yourselves now. The Captain says we can't take any more and we ought to be on our way before we get hit.'

Danny shook his head. 'There's still men on the beach.'

Gordon shaded his eyes. 'Not so many now – and there's still boats picking them up. Come on board, man. That lass is exhausted.'

Kate felt Danny's eyes on her. 'You go, Kate. I'll manage . . .'

'No!' she said with far more strength than she felt. She

was bone-weary, wet, cold and hungry. Her mind kept wandering so that she imagined herself fourteen again and walking across the Wolds in the pouring rain to find her grandfather. Only will-power was keeping her going – as it had then – only sheer determination made her drag her frozen mind back to the present.

But the decision was taken from them, for as Danny revved the engine to head back once more towards the beach, it spluttered twice and died.

'We're out of fuel' he said flatly, as their boat bobbed silently up and down on the waves.

'We'll – get the oars out, then,' Kate said and dragged herself to where they were stowed at the side of the boat.

They were just drifting away from the side of the larger boat, struggling to get the oars in position and aware that Gordon was still watching them anxiously from the deck, when they heard the sound of an enemy plane screaming towards them, a dive-bomber aiming for the laden ship.

'Row, Kate, for God's sake – row!'

Frantically, they pulled on the oars, trying to put distance between themselves and the target. Kate panted and strained at the oars, sobbing with fear and frustration. After all their efforts, all the men they had saved – especially Gordon and the airman – were going to be bombed. Killed or, at best, thrown back into the water.

The Stuka screamed towards them in a steep dive, its black crosses on the top of each wing clearly visible.

One bomb left the aircraft, hurtling down towards them. Then from under the wings, four smaller bombs were released. One landed on the far side of the ship, sending up a plume of water. Another fell between the hospital ship and the little boat trying desperately to escape. It hit the water and exploded, causing such an eruption that the larger ship rocked, sending men slithering about the deck. Only Gordon hung on to the deck rail, fearful for the fate of the little boat.

The vibration thudded through Kate and the surge of water bore their fishing boat aloft, held it suspended for a timeless moment and then plunged it downwards, capsizing it and throwing both Danny and Kate into the sea.

The last thing she remembered hearing was Danny's desperate cry of 'Kate! *Kate!*'

Someone was holding her head above the water. Someone was shouting at her but she could not hear properly for the rushing sound in her ears. Then some kind of strap was being put around her under her armpits and she felt herself being hoisted clear of the water, her legs dangling limply. Then willing hands were reaching out for her, pulling her on to the comparative safety of the deck of the ship. Blankets were wrapped around her and she was being carried.

'Danny?' she croaked. 'Where's Danny?'

'What's she say?' A voice spoke above her.

'Never mind,' said another. 'Get her below – to the doc.'

She was carried below and found herself being placed, with surprising gentleness, on a narrow bed. But no sooner did they set her down than Kate began to struggle. 'No, no. Danny – I must find Danny. He's in the sea. He can't swim.'

'Now, now, young lady.' A man was bending over her. 'I'm a doctor. You just lie still.'

'But Danny – is he safe? Please, I must . . .'

The doctor jerked his head at one of the soldiers who had carried her down, 'See what you can find out. She's obviously very distressed.'

The soldier gave Kate's arm a swift pat. 'Don't worry, Miss. One of our lot dived in when your boat capsized. He got to you first, but he's still looking for – who is it? Danny?'

Weakly, Kate nodded. She sank back against the pillow as exhaustion claimed her.

'That's better. Leave it to the lads. They'll find him.'

Kate closed her eyes and sent up a silent prayer. 'Oh please, dear Lord, please let them find him!'

Later, warm and dry and placed in a bed alongside other casualties aboard the hospital ship, Kate still fretted for news of Danny. The ship was so crowded that the beds in the ward had been pushed close together and men lay on the floor on stretchers or just on blankets.

'It's bloody murder up top,' one of the stretcher bearers said, as they struggled to find a clear space to put down their burden. 'The deck's that crammed, fellers are lying on top of each other.'

It wasn't much better down here, Kate thought ruefully, glancing round. There was scarcely a clear foot of floor space between the soldiers. The nursing sisters of the Queen Alexandra's Nursing Service had to step carefully over patients to tend the wounded. The ward was filled with the sounds of groaning and coughing, and now and then a scream of agony.

Kate raised herself a little. 'Please – do you know if the young man from the little fishing boat has been rescued?'

The stretcher-bearer shrugged his shoulders. 'Sorry, Miss . . .' He turned away and bent over a soldier whose whole face seemed to be a mass of congealed blood, a filthy bandage round his head.

Kate bit her lip. No one seemed to know down here what had happened to Danny and no one had time to go and find out for her.

She became aware that someone in the next bed was watching her. Kate turned her head to find herself looking into the bluest eyes she had ever seen in a man. His fair hair was short and curly, brushed straight back from his broad forehead. His face was lightly tanned yet there were rings of exhaustion around his eyes. His left arm was freshly bandaged, but instead of a proper white sling, his arm was still supported by her scarf.

It was the airman she had cradled in her arms and willed to live.

He was older than she had thought him to be, but he had looked young and vulnerable lying unconscious in the bottom of the fishing boat. Yet, even then, Gordon had said the insignia on his jacket was quite a high rank. What was it he had said? Squadron Leader?

She smiled weakly at him. At least now, clean and dry, he looked more like a member of – what was it the disgruntled soldier had called the RAF? Oh yes, that was it – the glamour boys.

Kate felt her eyelids close, but she opened them again as he spoke. His voice was deep, yet a little croaky from his recent ordeal.

'I want to . . .' he began, but Kate said, 'Don't, please don't. I just want to know what's happened to Danny . . .' Her voice broke and she turned her head away towards the wall so that he should not see her tears. She knew he was going to start thanking her, maybe telling her how brave she had been. She didn't want that, because she didn't feel she had been particularly courageous. She had only come to be with Danny. How could she explain to the airman that for some reason she had not even felt afraid, at least, not for her own safety. The only fear she felt was to think that all this carnage could happen in England; that had made her angry.

Now, however, her terror was very real. She was desperately frightened for Danny.

Hearing the airman move, she looked back at him again.

He was struggling to rise from the bed. 'I'll go – and see – what I can find out.'

She put out her hand to stop him. 'No, no, you mustn't. You'll . . .'

'And just what do you think you're up to, young feller?' Gordon's cheerful face appeared round the door. Carefully he stepped between the soldiers on the floor and came towards them. He was soaking wet, his hair plastered down, and rivulets of water were running down his face. The airman sank back on to the bed as Gordon grinned broadly at Kate and said, 'He's okay – we've got him. He's taken in a lot of water. They're pumping him out now. But he'll be all right.'

'Oh, thank God!' she whispered. 'It was you, Gordon, wasn't it?'

'Me – what do you mean? What have I done?' He drew the back of his hand across his eyes and blinked.

'It was you found him, wasn't it? Did you pull me out too?'

The grin widened as he turned away to go and dry off. 'Well, you know what they say? One good turn deserves another . . .'

With that, he was gone.

Gordon appointed himself personal nurse to the three of them – Kate, Danny and Squadron Leader Philip Trent. 'Just don't let on I'm looking after one of the boys in blue,' he grinned, 'or me life won't be worth living.' The nurses, overwhelmed by the numbers, welcomed Gordon's help. Moving among the wounded and exhausted men, the cheerful soldier was as good as a tonic.

An hour or so later, he brought Danny into the cabin, his strong arm under the younger man's shoulder. 'Here you are, girl. He's all safe and sound. And we're nearly half-way home. Just let's hope that Luftwaffe don't find us!'

Danny grinned sheepishly at Kate. 'I really ought to learn to swim, didn't I?'

'I've been telling you that for years, but do you ever take notice of me?' She was smiling at him, so thankful that he was safe. But she knew if she were to fling her arms around him, as she felt like doing, it would only embarrass him. So her mock admonishment covered their deeper emotions.

He sat down carefully on the bed beside her.

'Are you hurt?' she asked anxiously.

'No – just bruised. How about you?'

'I'm fine. I ought to get off this bed, really. There are far worse than me . . .'

'You lie still, girl,' Gordon ordered, 'You took in a lot of water. 'Sides, you've earned a bed, if anyone has!'

One or two soldiers nearby, less injured than some, heard Gordon and raised a cheer of agreement. Kate felt herself blushing.

Danny grinned at her and then, sobering suddenly, looked up at Gordon. 'Do you know what happened to me boat?'

'Sorry, mate, blown to smithereens.'

Danny closed his eyes and groaned. Kate watched him anxiously. What would Robert Eland say when they returned home? That boat was his livelihood.

As if catching some of their anxiety, Philip Trent asked, 'Is it a great loss to you?'

When Danny didn't answer, Kate explained quietly, 'It's his dad's. He's a fisherman.'

Danny opened his eyes. 'Oh, he'd have come himself, if he could have done, only he had to stay. He's coxswain of our lifeboat . . .'

'Oh, so this rescuing business runs in the family, does it?' Gordon laughed and Danny and Kate smiled. The loss of the boat – even though a big loss to Danny's father – was nothing in comparison to the many lives they had saved.

Robert Eland would understand.

Their homecoming to Fleethaven Point was greeted in differing ways.

'Thoughtless, irresponsible, selfish . . .' Esther Godfrey's tirade went on. 'Fancy just telling our Lilian you were going out in the boat with *him* and then disappearing for nearly a week. We thought you'd been drowned.'

Calmly, Kate said, 'Him? His name's Danny, Mother. And if you'd taken the trouble to ask Mrs Eland – she knew where we were. Well, sort of . . .'

Obviously her private thoughts had been right, Kate realized. Not even the safety of her own daughter had been enough to make Esther Godfrey speak to Beth Eland.

Reluctantly, Esther muttered, 'Ya dad did speak to Mester. He said you'd both gone off down south. We thought it was a pleasure trip and then I find out you've been getting yarsen into *this*!' Esther rattled a daily newspaper under Kate's nose. Plastered all over the front page were dramatic accounts of how an armada of ships of all shapes and sizes had brought back thousands of men from the beaches of Dunkirk.

Kate grinned. 'What – no picture of us on the front page? Well, I'd have thought we warranted that at the very least!'

'I'll have none of your sarcasm, Miss,' her mother snapped, and flung the paper away from her in disgust.

'I suppose you'll be wanting to join up next.'

There was a long silence between them; a waiting silence.

Kate met her mother's fierce gaze. 'I'm thinking about it – yes.'

She saw the colour drain swiftly from her mother's face and Esther put out her hand to steady herself against the table. A small gasp escaped her open lips and her green eyes – so like Kate's own – stared at her daughter.

Kate felt a stab of remorse. She hadn't meant to be quite so blunt, and yet, she had to make her mother understand. She turned and began to pace up and down the kitchen, spreading her hands. 'You don't understand, Mam. It was awful over there. All those soldiers trapped on the beach and in the water – thousands of them. There were bodies too . . .' She gulped and closed her eyes for a moment, then she went on strongly, 'We've all got to do our bit – even the women this time, Mam. We can't let Hitler just walk into our country and take it over. And he will – if we don't stop him. You don't understand, Mam . . .' she said again and then stopped.

Her mother had sunk down into a chair on the opposite side of the kitchen table and was resting her arms on the scrubbed surface. Wearily, she said, 'Yes, I do, Kate. It was the same for me when I went to France after the last war.'

'What? You – you went to France?' Kate could not hide the surprise in her voice, and hearing it, her mother smiled. 'Yes – can you imagine me leaving Fleethaven Point to go all the way to France?'

Kate lowered herself into a chair and faced her mother across the table. 'Tell me about it, Mam?' she asked softly.

There was silence in the kitchen, the only sounds the ticking of the clock and the singing of the kettle on the hob.

'I went out there with the Squire. His eldest son had been killed and he was trying to find his grave. I – went to try to . . .' She stopped, glanced swiftly at Kate and then dropped her gaze again. She took a deep breath and continued. 'When I saw their land . . .' Esther's eyes took on a faraway look, as if she were not here in her warm kitchen in 1940 but out on the battlefields of France in 1919, 'absolutely devastated, gouged with trenches as far as you could see. Not a living thing for mile after mile – not a blade of grass; trees, blackened and dead; no birds – only rotting bodies and rats!' She shook her head, murmuring, 'Those poor folk, they can only just have recovered from all that, and now it's happening to them again.' She raised her eyes and met Kate's gaze steadily. 'Oh, I understand all right, Kate, just how you feel. I saw for myself what all our men fought for – and died for – last time. It's just that —' She reached out with fingers that shook slightly to clasp Kate's hands. 'You're my daughter and I – I don't want you to be in danger . . .'

Into Kate's mind came the words 'you'd still have Lilian' but they remained unspoken.

Already, Kate thought, she had said more than enough to hurt her mother.

Esther levered herself up from the table. 'Well, I'spose ya'll do what ya like, whatever I say. But ya'd best go in an' tell ya grandad what you intend.'

'Oh heck!'

The two women looked at each other and the comical expression upon Kate's face at the thought of having to tell her grandfather what she intended, made them both burst out laughing.

Twenty

'Grandad?' Kate opened the door of the front room quietly. Are you awake?' she asked softly.

'Aye, lass. Ah'm allus awake for you. Come in, come in, dun't stand there dithering in the doorway. There's a draught!'

Kate smiled, stepped into the room and closed the door behind her. She sat on a footstool at her grandfather's feet and smiled up at him.

Will Benson now lived at Brumbys' Farm. In the winter of 1936 he had caught influenza and had developed severe bronchitis. Kate smiled as she remembered how it had happened. All the time Will had been really ill, Esther or Jonathan, often with Kate along too when she had been at home, had driven in the pony and trap every day to the village of Suddaby, some thirteen miles inland.

'You're too old to be going about on the front of that carrier's cart any longer,' Esther had railed. 'You're just a stubborn old man who won't realize it's more than time he retired.'

'Shall you retire from the farm, girl, specially now you own it, just 'cos you get old?'

'That's different . . .'

'No, it ain't. What'll I do shut up in me cottage all day with only Minnie Raby and her gossiping tongue for company?'

The next day Esther had returned hands on hips, ready

205

to do battle. 'Me and Jonathan have talked it over. You're coming to live with us at Brumbys' Farm. I'll turn the front parlour into a bed-sitting room for ya. And dun't think I'll let you be idle, 'cos I shan't. Ya can mek ya'sen useful about the farm. And I won't have no argument, it's only right you should come to us. We're yar only family. I won't tek no . . .'

She had stopped as she had heard Will Benson's wheezy laughter. 'I aren't arguing, lass. It's what I want to do.'

'What? Well! Well – I never!' Esther's face had been a picture while Kate had clapped her hand over her mouth to stifle her laughter. But it had gurgled out until she was leaning weakly against the wall. The crafty old devil, Kate had thought, he'd engineered that very cleverly.

So here he was now, installed in the front room that was scarcely ever used anyway; a single bed in one corner and an armchair set in front of the window overlooking the front garden and the flat fields stretching to the setting sun. He had his privacy, yet his family were only a step away, and a little work about the farm when he felt like it kept him feeling useful and needed.

Will Benson was a contented man, it was written on his face for all to see. Yet he was still a force to be reckoned with within the family, which was why Kate found herself sitting at his feet and taking a deep breath before telling him of her plans.

Before she could begin, he said, 'You had us worried, girl. Whatever did you go off for like that with young Danny?'

Kate told him – in far more detail than she had described to her mother – all that had happened to her and Danny since they had set off from Fleethaven Point. She omitted nothing. She told him all about Gordon and the airman and how at the end of it all they'd lost Robert Eland's boat.

When at last she fell silent, she felt Will Benson's gnarled fingers touch her hair. With a catch in his voice he said, 'I'm proud of you, girl. I wish I'd bin there mesen.'

She looked up at him again, holding his gaze with her steady green eyes. 'Grandad, I'm thinking of – of joining up.'

His fingers, still against her hair, trembled slightly. 'Aw, lass. Are ya sure?'

'Oh, Grandad, if you'd seen it out there. Seen our soldiers coming back bedraggled and beaten. And yet,' she added with the ghost of a smile as she thought about Gordon Stratford, 'they didn't act like they were beaten. They were still shaking their fists at the enemy planes and promising to go back.'

'And you reckon you want to lend a hand, eh, lass?'

'I want to "do my bit" as they say.' She smiled up at him, trying to be light-hearted about it, but there was no deceiving the old man.

His face was sober as he asked quietly, 'Danny going too, is he, lass?'

She looked squarely into the watery, faded old eyes. 'I – think so, Grandad.'

Slowly, the old man nodded.

'What did your dad say about the boat?'

'He was very good about it,' Danny answered her. He grinned at her. 'Said he wished he'd been with us.'

She smiled back. 'That's just what me grandad said. Oh, but your dad's so good. He never says much, does he? But he's a wonderful person.'

'Aye,' Danny murmured. 'An' he's been good to me.' There was silence and Kate knew they were both thinking about the same thing; that he wasn't really Danny's father.

'He loves your mam so much. You can see it in his eyes when he looks at her, even now, after all these years.'

'Aye, an' it can't have been easy for him.'

'But she loves him,' Kate reassured him. 'I know she does.'

'Aye, well . . .' They were getting into dangerous waters, touching on a subject that they had not openly discussed for years. Yet always it lay between them.

As if deliberately to change tack, Danny said, 'By the way, can you have a word with Rosie?'

'Rosie?' Kate was surprised. 'What about?'

'She'll be getting herself into trouble if she dun't watch it.' When Kate still looked puzzled, he went on, 'It's them Army lads that's billeted with me grandad.'

Beth Eland's father, Dan Hanley, was the coastguard at Fleethaven Point and, living alone, was the only one with room to spare for the soldiers who manned the gun emplacement on the dunes facing the North Sea.

'Oh.' Now Kate understood. 'What about her mam or Grannie Harris? I'd have thought she could make young Rosie toe the line.'

'She's grown into such a pretty little thing,' Danny murmured.

'All those blonde curls and big blue eyes,' Kate laughed. And Rosie's figure too, she was thinking, all curvey in the right places.

'She's so innocent, though,' Danny was saying. 'Living here at the Point all her life, she ain't had much to do with men. She just won't know . . .'

Kate stifled a snort of laughter. It was Danny who was the innocent one, she thought. If what she had heard was true, then young Rosie Maine knew exactly what she was doing.

When Rosie had turned fifteen, she had found a job in Reynolds' store in Lynthorpe. She was still the same bright chatterbox and, as Danny rightly said, had now blossomed into a very pretty young woman. She was always smiling and friendly and was liked by customers and the other staff as well. It was impossible not to like Rosie Maine, and strangely, even though she was so pretty, she did not seem to cause jealousy. Now, at nineteen, Rosie still had no steady boyfriend but seemed to run a string of them, carefully balancing the attentions of several, never deliberately hurting anyone. When she went dancing in the town on a Saturday night, she was never short of partners. And now her partners were in uniform.

'I'll have a word with her,' Kate promised.

'Aw, thanks, Kate,' Danny said.

It was more than likely, Kate thought wryly, that young Rosie could teach her a thing or two instead of the other way round.

'You're getting yourself a bad name, our Rosie,' Kate said, with some of her mother's bluntness coming to the fore.

The girl fluffed her blonde hair and then smoothed down her skirt with the palms of her hands. 'Oh, Kate, I'm only having a little fun. I'm not doing any harm.'

'It's the harm that might come to you, Rosie, that we're worried about.'

Kate heard the girl draw in her breath sharply. Rosie whirled about to face her. 'We? Who's we?' Suddenly, her eyes were shining with an extra brightness.

'Danny and me.'

'Danny? Danny said something about me? What did he say?'

'He's worried about you – and the soldiers billeted at the Point.'

'Who – Taffy and Don? Don't be daft, our Kate. I'm only friendly with them. They're a nice couple of boys and a long way from home. They're lonely.'

'That's the whole point, Rosie . . .' Kate persisted.

'What else did Danny say about me, Kate?'

'Nothing – he just said he was worried about you. We both are.'

Rosie pulled a face and turned away. 'Well, you've no need. I can tek care of mesen, ta. Tell Danny he – he's no need to worry himself about me.'

If she hadn't known her better, Kate could have sworn there was a tearful catch in Rosie's voice.

When Kate reported her talk with Rosie to Danny, far from being reassured, he frowned. 'She's too flirty for her own good, Kate. I've tried having a word with her brothers, Mick and Jimmy, but all Mick can think about is joining up in December when he's eighteen. Not even going to wait for his call-up papers, he ain't.'

There was a deep silence between them as they walked side by side along the beach, close by the water's edge.

'Kate . . .' Danny began, stopped and let out a deep sigh as if he had been holding his breath.

She linked her arm through his. 'Come on, out with it.'

'I – I'm going to volunteer.'

'I know.' She stopped and turned to face him. Checked by her hold on him, he too stopped. Slowly they turned to face each other. She smiled at him and was amused by the look of surprise on his face.

'I guessed you would,' she whispered.

'You – you did?'

She nodded. 'After Dunkirk – I guessed . . . No, that's not quite right, I *knew* you'd want to go.'

His grin was sheepish. 'I thought you'd throw a ducky fit.'

Kate laughed softly. 'Not really, Danny, because I am going to join up too.'

They looked at each other and Danny said quietly, 'Just like our dad did the last time, eh?'

Kate smiled and pressed his arm. Rarely did they speak

of the father they shared, and yet now at this moment, it seemed right to think of him.

They walked on together in silence. A silence that was companionable and yet now held an added poignancy. Not for the first time, they were to be parted. But this time it might mean they never saw each other again. Hardly realizing it, Kate tightened her hold on Danny's arm, and he placed his hand over hers.

At last he said, 'Shall we go and join up – together?'

'Of course – don't you dare go without me!' She aimed a playful punch at his shoulder. 'Where is the nearest recruiting office, by the way? Is it Lincoln?'

'I'm not sure – I'll find out, though.'

'Well, wherever it is, we'll go together,' she said, softly now.

'I reckon it'd be only fair to get hay-making and the harvest over first. I owe the Squire that much. What d'you say?'

Kate nodded. 'Yes, you're right. It looks like being a good one and we're all short-handed as it is. We'll go after harvest.'

They walked back across the marsh and stood on the top of the western dunes to watch the sun set behind Brumbys' Farm, silhouetting the farmhouse and the buildings against the bright orange sky.

The peace of the place they both loved so much wrapped itself around them in its cloak of serenity.

It was difficult to believe at that moment that there was a war going on; that together they had already taken part in it and that in a few months' time they would be caught up in it completely.

She felt an overwhelming sadness. With a certainty she could not explain, Kate knew in that moment that their lives would never be the same again.

Twenty-One

By the end of August, even at Fleethaven Point, the news-paper headlines were beginning to dominate their lives, pushing even the long, exhausting days of harvest into second place.

'Have you seen this?' Danny waved the daily paper under Kate's nose. 'They're getting closer; bombing Midlands towns now, though they're still concentrating on the south-east.'

'Really.' Kate grabbed the paper and scanned the news-print. She jabbed her finger at the picture of a crashed Hein-kel on a British beach. 'They're not getting it all their own way, though.'

'Far from it! The RAF are really coming into their own now.' Danny rubbed his hands together gleefully. 'They reckon there are dog-fights going on over the Kentish coast most of the day.' He ran the tip of his tongue over his lips in excitement. 'I've made up my mind, Katie. It's the RAF for me an' no mistake.'

A picture of the injured airman they had pulled from the sea came into her mind. She shuddered inwardly at the thought that Danny could so easily end up like Philip Trent; baling out over enemy territory, injured and totally depen-dent on the good-will of complete strangers to rescue him. Resolutely, she pushed such morbid thoughts from her mind. No doubt Philip Trent was back in the air by now, maybe even involved in these dog-fights Danny spoke of. She wondered what had happened to him. Was he still alive?

She hoped so.

Aloud she said, 'Good! Then it's the WAAFs for me.'

'Well, that's it then. We've been an' gone an' done it now,' Danny said as they emerged from the recruiting centre. 'Me in the RAF and you in the WAAFs.' He grinned saucily. 'I hope they know what they're letting themselves in for.'

Playfully, she punched his arm. She felt better now that it was done. There was no going back and her family would just have to accept it.

As if reading her thoughts, Danny said, 'Still thinking about yar mam?'

Kate nodded.

'She had a rough time in the last lot,' he reminded her. 'First Ernie Harris getting killed; yar mother thought a lot about him.'

'I can't remember him. Can you?'

Danny shook his head. 'He was Grannie Harris's eldest. Joined up when he was only sixteen.'

'Me mam never talks about anything to do with the last war. It's as if she wants to forget it all.'

They sauntered back towards the railway station, walking close beside one another but not quite touching, and reminiscing about their childhood, piecing together the snippets they knew of a time they could scarcely remember, yet knowing that what had happened then had shaped their own lives.

'And now we have to do it all again,' Danny said. 'It's sad for the older folk, when you think about it. They called it the "war to end all wars" and yet here we are only twenty odd years later into another. All those families who lost folk in the last war risk losing loved ones this time around. Like Grannie Harris – she easy might, and there'll be plenty of families like her. Ya can understand 'em feeling bitter.'

It was not quite as Kate had imagined. When their papers arrived on the same day about three weeks later, she and Danny were told to report to training camps miles away from each other. Some romantic notion had led her to imagine them arriving together, being kitted out together, training together, working together.

Reality was entirely different.

As she packed a small suitcase – so different from the huge trunk that had been filled with 'three of everything' when she had been leaving home to go to school – she glanced around her bedroom. On the window-sill was the whelk shell. Smiling wryly at her own sentimental foolishness, she popped it into the corner of her suitcase and snapped the lid shut.

They were able to travel as far as Lincoln together but then they had to catch different trains, one going north, one going south.

'Seems as if they're hell-bent on separating us,' Kate grumbled.

'How – was it when ya came to leave?' Danny asked. They had said their goodbyes separately to each set of parents. 'I got the shock of me life when ya mam put her arms round me and gave me a real bear-hug. I reckon there were tears in her eyes.'

Kate stared at him. 'Really?' She shook her head wonderingly. 'She's a strange woman, my mother. I think she's fond of you, deep down, but it takes a war to make her to show it!'

'What about you?' he persisted.

Kate shrugged. 'Almost off-hand really. She just said, "Well, ya off then – tek care of ya'sen" and that was it. Of course,' she added wryly, 'she still has Lilian.'

'Oh, come on, Kate. You're not *still* jealous of that poor kid, are you?'

Kate pulled a grimace. 'No – no, I'm not. If anything, I feel sorry for her. She seems such a lonely child.'

'Not so much a child now. What is she – fourteen?'

'Almost.'

'Well, there you are then. She'll be leaving school in another year.'

Kate shook her head and, mocking her mother's voice, she said, 'Oh no. Our Lilian's clever. Our Lilian's going to university.' She smiled then and added, 'To be fair, the kid is clever and she's happy at the Grammar School – well, as happy as she'd be anywhere. She's so serious all the time – no wonder she hasn't any friends.'

There was a silence, then Kate asked softly, 'What about your mam? Was she all right when you left?'

Danny's eyes were troubled. He nodded, 'She was very brave, but I suppose it must bring back a lot of memories of the last time – seeing the young men off to war, not knowing if they'd ever come back.' He looked at her steadily. 'And young women too, this time. Oh, Katie, do be careful, won't you?'

She nodded. 'You, too, Danny. You too,' she whispered.

There was half an hour before the train Kate had to catch left. In the café they sat across the table from each other, hardly speaking. They'd said everything and yet they'd said nothing. There was so much they could say, so much that still lay between them.

They sat together in an oasis of silence while all around them was the bustle of imminent departure. Most of the men were in uniform, while their families clustered around them; proud, tearful, apprehensive.

They heard the sound of a train approaching the station.

'Come on,' Danny said, getting up. 'That'll be yours.'

Now there was no time left to say anything and suddenly there was so much to say.

'I had so hoped we'd be on the same camp,' She raised her voice to him as they weaved their way through the crowded platform.

'We might be – eventually. They shift people about quite a bit and I think you can apply for – what do they call it – remustering, I think it is. Here, let me put those on the rack for you.'

'What on earth is remustering?' she asked as he heaved her baggage up and then stepped off the train again. They stood on the platform, close but not touching, facing each other.

'It's when you apply to go into a new type of job.'

'You'll write?' Kate said with sudden urgency.

Danny smiled lopsidedly. 'I aren't much of a letter-writer, Katie.'

'That doesn't matter. I just want to hear from you some-times; just to know you're . . . safe.'

He nodded. 'All right.'

'And when you get a posting, be sure to let me have your new address?'

Again he nodded.

'And we could try to get leave at the same time, so we can be at home together.' She was babbling now, desperate to put off the moment of parting.

'That might be difficult.'

'Oh, but we could try. Promise me you'll try, Danny . . .?' The shrill whistle sounded and doors banged. 'Oh no, not yet . . .'

'You must get on the train, Katie . . .'

Then suddenly she was in his arms, being held in a fierce hug. 'Katie – take care,' he whispered huskily against her hair. Then he released her suddenly and pushed her towards the train.

Tears blurred her vision so that she stumbled as she stepped into the carriage. The door slammed behind her and by the time she had wrenched open the window, the train was already moving.

She waved frantically, leaning out of the window until billowing smoke hid him from her view.

The moment she entered the sleeping-quarters at the recruitment depot, time seemed to tilt. Kate shuddered. For a moment it was like catapulting back in time into the cheerless dormitory at the boarding school. But then the image faded, for coming towards her, almost bouncing towards her would have been a more apt description, was a plump, jolly-faced girl with short brown hair and laughing hazel eyes.

'Hello, come on in and make yourself at home. We've all just arrived today, so we're still getting to know one another.' Like Kate they were all still in civvies, some dressed in high-heeled shoes and summer dresses, their hair carefully curled, whilst others wore plain, flat-heeled shoes and skirts and cardigans.

'I'm Mavis Nuttall,' the friendly girl was saying, 'and this is Jill Porter, but that's as far as I go, I'm afraid . . .'

The faces in front of her began to introduce themselves one by one but there were so many that after the first few, Kate gave up trying to remember them and merely smiled and nodded.

'What's yours?' asked Mavis.

'Kate. Kate Hilton.'

'You can have this bed between me and Mavis,' Jill offered.

'Shall we all leave our stuff here and go in search of food?' Mavis suggested. 'My stomach says it's tea-time!'

There was general laughter and agreement and a sudden flurry of activity as everyone prepared to leave.

'We'll get settled in later,' Mavis promised cheerily. 'I hear they're pretty strict on tidiness.' She pulled a face. 'And I'm the world's worst. Me mother says my bedroom's like a pig-sty.'

At the mention of pig-sties, Kate felt a sudden surge of longing for home sweep through her. The farm, the Point and all the people there. And Danny – especially Danny. Where was he now, she wondered? What was he doing? Was he feeling as lost and mesmerized by everything as she was at this moment?

The first day seemed to be taken up with various intelligence tests.

'That'll be me on my way out before I've been in a day,' Mavis moaned. 'It's like being back at school.'

Inwardly, Kate shuddered, although she thought she had coped quite well with the tests.

The following day, when they were given their six-digit number, poor Mavis was flustered again. 'Thick as pea soup, me. I'll never remember this.'

Kate laughed. 'Well, you'll have to, else evidently you'll get nothing. No pay, no leave and – no food! You know what the sergeant said – your number's more important than your *name* now.'

'I know,' her new friend wailed, and bent her head over the piece of paper with her number written on it.

The next few days passed in a blur. Form-filling, medical

checks and inoculations, drill and uniform issue. Having queued for their kit of about sixty different items, they staggered back to their quarters.

'Feels like a hundred and sixty when you try to carry it all,' Mavis laughed as she dumped it on her bed and began to sort through it. 'How are we supposed to get all this stuff in this kit-bag?'

'Wear most of it, probably,' Kate suggested.

Mavis gave a shriek of laughter and held up a large pair of navy-blue knickers. 'Have you seen these? Passion-killers, if ever I saw 'em. My *gran* wouldn't be seen dead in a pair like this!'

Kate giggled. 'We'd call them "apple-catchers".'

Mavis blinked. 'Eh?'

Kate sat on the side of the bed and rocked with laughter. 'A pair like that could hold quite a lot . . .'

Puzzled, Mavis looked at the item of underwear again and then, understanding, 'You mean when you're apple-*scrumping*. I've never heard that one before. I see what you mean.' She gave another hoot of laughter. 'I don't reckon you could run very fast with the farmer after you and these full of apples.'

'What on earth are you two laughing about? Share the joke,' Jill called.

In moments, all the girls in the room were convulsed in laughter and, minutes later when their NCO came to give them a demonstration as to how to make their beds in the required manner and how to lay out their kit for inspection, there were still stifled giggles when it came to the folding and laying out of a particular garment!

'Kit inspection first thing tomorrow morning,' the NCO said as she left the room.

Kate surveyed her belongings on her bed. 'What did she say we have to do with our civvies, Mavis?'

Her friend was again studying the scrap of paper in her hand. ' . . . Six-five-nine. Er – parcel 'em up to be sent home.'

'Oh yes.' Kate began to fold her clothes. 'Can you remember how to lay out all this kit? I've forgotten what she said already.'

' . . . Five-nine. Nope. Jill's good at that,' Mavis said, nodding towards the girl bending over the bed on the other side of Kate. 'She's promised to go through it again with me tonight.'

'Great! Can I watch too?'

' . . . nine. Got it! At least – I think I have. Yeah, 'course you can. Come on, let go and find the mess.'

'Oh my,' Kate teased, 'we're learning all the names, even if we can't memorize our number!'

Mavis grinned good-naturedly. 'Anything to do with food, Kate, and I can be absolutely *relied* upon to remember it! Come on . . .'

Jill stood at the end of Kate's bed, scrutinizing the kit laid out on it. 'I should refold all your sheets and blankets for a start – they're not very neat. Your greatcoat goes on top of them and your cap on top of that.' She took a side-step and stood at the foot of Mavis's bed. 'Shoes go on the front row – soles uppermost.'

'Oh, I'll never get the hang of it,' Mavis muttered.

'Don't worry, Mave,' Jill said cheerfully, 'neither will Kate by the way she's juggling with her irons and toothbrush. Other way round, Kate. That's it. Where's your button stick? Oh, there it is. It should be on that same row.'

'Seems okay now,' Jill said when the two girls had reshuffled everything to her direction. 'Can you both remember it for tomorrow morning?'

Mavis sighed. 'Not a chance. What about you, Kate?'

'I can remember all the main items, it's the little fiddly things I can't remember where they go.'

'Well, if we do okay with the inspection we get the rest of the morning off,' Jill told them and then spoilt the promise of some free time by adding, 'to finish marking *every* item of kit!'

There were groans all round. 'How do you know all about the lay-out then?' Mavis asked. 'Not that I'm not jolly thankful you do,' she added, anxious not to offend.

Jill shrugged. 'Older brother in the RAF,' she explained. 'He used to practise when he came home. I used to watch him and when the NCO was showing us earlier – well, it was a bit different naturally, but the basic idea seems to be the same.'

'Right,' Mavis said, shuffling all her items of kit into a big heap at the end of her bed. 'Now I'll have a go on my own.'

She began to lay everything out on the bed once more, from the sheets, blankets and bolster at the head of the bed, right down to the shoes – 'Soles uppermost,' Mavis muttered as she worked – at the foot.

Two hours later, just before lights out, Kate and even Mavis could finally lay out their kit perfectly.

After the first three days, it all seemed to get easier. The girls were so friendly; they had so much to talk about because they all came from different places. It was nothing like that awful school, Kate thought. How could she have even thought it the same?

There had been only one occasion when she had been sharply reminded of Miss Denham. The NCO had suddenly said one day, 'Hilton, your hair is too long . . .'

Kate had drawn in her breath sharply and held it, waiting

for the dreadful sound of snipping scissors being brandished. She almost winced in anticipation.

'But as long as you tie it back and keep it firmly under your cap . . .'

Kate let out her breath with relief. School, and all its horrors, faded once more.

On the sixth morning, Mavis, who always seemed to be first with news of any sort, burst into the hut, the buttons on her jacket heaving up and down in her breathlessness. 'Guess where we're all going?'

The other girls turned blank expressions towards her.

'Home,' said one girl with a heartfelt sigh.

'Abroad,' suggested another hopefully.

'Don't be daft – we're not trained yet.'

'My feet think they've had quite enough training,' muttered someone else.

'No idea,' Jill smiled, sensing Mavis's desire to be the bearer of what looked like good news. 'You tell us, Mave.'

'Harrogate!'

'Harrogate?' chorused a dozen voices.

'Why?'

'Whatever for?'

'To finish our training. It seems this recruitment camp is bursting at the seams and we're being shipped off to Harrogate.'

'Wonderful!' said a voice heavy with sarcasm. 'It's a spa town, for heaven's sakes. All the smart folks go there. There are some bee-oo-tiful hotels. Can you imagine us lot red-faced and sweating running along the streets of Harrogate in our passion-killers and gym-shoes?'

'Well, there's a war on,' Mavis countered stoutly. 'They'll have to put up with us.'

'Old biddies tut-tutting and dirty old men leering at us in our WAAF issue underwear.'

'It won't be like that, w-will it?' one girl asked nervously.

'You'll see,' said Winifred, the self-appointed Job's comforter.

It wasn't so bad after all, Kate thought. It was quite a laugh doing drill in the Valley Gardens and learning to march in neat formation up one of the steepest hills. It reminded her of the hill in Lincoln, she mused, leading up to the cathedral. She had *run* up that one, and now, out of all of them, only Kate Hilton arrived at the top with enough breath to say, 'Race you back to the billet . . .'

She and Mavis were lucky in their landlady, who fussed over them like a mother hen. Others could be a bit grim, from the accounts of some of the girls.

Kate smiled as she thought of Winifred's dire warnings. They did have to run along the streets jacketless and in gym-shoes with their lisle stockings rolled down to the ankles, and it caused a bit of a stir among the locals, but their waving was friendly and the children running alongside were joining in rather than mocking.

But on a Sunday, for Church Parade, well, there was a real sense of pride in being seen marching smartly along the wide roads, each wing vying with the others to be the best turned out.

'*It's all lectures, drill and PT,*' Kate wrote in her letter to Danny. '*Then more lectures, drill and PT. Sometimes there's gas mask drill, clothing parades and then more lectures, PT and more drill! Is it the same for you?*' she wanted to know.

'*Yesterday we had a second inoculation and more than half the girls fainted. I have to admit I felt a bit sick but*

223

managed not to be.' Thank goodness, she thought to herself as she wrote the words. She didn't want to give anyone the chance to bestow that awful nickname on her again.

A few days before they were due to leave Harrogate, Kate received a much-delayed letter from home. It was from her stepfather telling her that his father, the kindly Mr Godfrey, had died suddenly in his sleep. *'The funeral is in Lincoln on Friday. Would you be able to come . . .?'* Oh, poor Mrs Godfrey – and Peggy! Her heart went out to them. Friday, her stepfather wrote. Today was Thursday. Could she . . .? She turned the letter over again to read the date at the top and saw that it was dated over ten days earlier. The funeral must have taken place on the previous Friday. Kate immediately sat down to write letters to her stepfather and to Mrs Godfrey and Peggy. Then, with an hour of free time left before tea, she went out to post them.

Needing to be alone, she walked to the edge of the town overlooking the Stray, a vast expanse of smooth parkland. She missed the beach and the sea but the expanse of green before her was a comfort. She sat down on the grass, her chin resting on her knees drawn up to her chest, her arms wrapped around her legs, and watched two children running and chasing each other. They reminded her sharply of herself and Danny at the same age.

The news in her stepfather's letter had saddened her, and suddenly she felt incredibly homesick. It washed over her in waves. She longed for the bite of the east wind off the North Sea, the flat landscape behind, the cries of gulls overhead. Back home they'd be threshing now; the scene was so vivid she could almost smell the dusty chaff and hear the steady throb of the steam engine. Her stepfather would be finding solace up to his elbows in oil and grease, whilst her mother would be teasing him gently, helping to ease his recent loss; 'Great noisy, lumbering thing!' she'd be saying of the engines Jonathan loved.

Oh, why aren't I there, Kate thought suddenly, with Danny feeding the drum and me holding the sacks ready at the other end for the corn . . . ?'

She heard footsteps close by and Mavis's cheerful voice. 'There you are.'

Kate sighed, her moment of solitude – so hard to snatch these days – gone. She stood up, shook the bits of grass from her skirt and smiled at Mavis coming towards her. The plump girl was so extrovert and friendly, never taking offence. It was impossible to feel irritated with Mavis for many minutes.

She linked her arm through Kate's as they walked back towards the town. 'Pay Parade tomorrow and Posting Parade the day after. What have you put in for?'

'Motor Transport.' Kate grinned inwardly remembering her tongue-in-cheek lie when she had been asked if she could drive, especially recalling that the only time she had been behind a wheel she had ended up driving the Squire's motor car into the dyke and had nearly cost Danny his job.

'What about you?'

'R/T operator on an operational station,' the girl replied promptly.

Kate nodded. 'You'll be good at that. A friendly voice over the airwaves is just what the pilots need when they're up there.'

The two friends were lucky; they were posted for further training to the same place, but they had to part from all the other girls they had come to know.

'We might never see any of them again, you know,' Mavis said, unusually sober as they stood together in the train. It was crowded with soldiers and the carriages were stuffy and smoke-filled. The two girls didn't even bother to try to find a seat.

Kate said nothing. Her thoughts were once more with Danny. With all this moving about to different camps to complete her training, she had heard nothing from him, and even anxious letters home to Beth Eland had brought no reply.

The weeks that followed were exhausting but Kate enjoyed the intensive Motor Transport training. She found the lessons in the mornings when they had to learn theory hard – it reminded her too much of school; but in the practical sessions – the driving, the maintenance work and even learning to do minor repairs – Kate was in her element. She became the instructor's star pupil and passed out with the highest marks in all the practical tests. During one of the final tests – driving a convoy at night through the country side where the signposts had been removed and with headlamps dimmed to only a slit of light – Kate was placed at the head of the column of huge lorries.

'You've got three hours,' their instructor told her. 'If you're not back to camp by dawn, we'll send out a spotter plane!' He was grinning as he said it and she knew he was pinning his hopes, and possibly his reputation, on his recruits being first back to the camp. 'Don't forget, only you and the last vehicle have their lights on, everyone else follows the diff-light.'

Kate nodded. At the rear of the vehicles a small light had been fitted to shine down on to the white-painted differential. All the following vehicles would follow her lead. If she went wrong . . .

'Don't forget – I'm relying on you.'

Kate glanced at the clear night sky. She was in luck! Every star shone bright and true for her. Smiling, she revved the noisy engine and pressed her foot down on to the clutch-pedal. She had memorized the route from the map and she set off at a steady speed, glancing frequently into the wing mirror to check that the following vehicles were still there.

In the darkness, she grinned to herself. Oh, Danny, I wish you could see me now driving this great lorry. I wouldn't drive the Squire's new motor into the dyke now!

Two hours and forty-three minutes later, Kate pulled up at the guard-house, every lorry in her convoy following suit.

'Halt! Who goes there?' came the routine inquiry.

'WAAF.' Kate smiled in the darkness.

'Good Lord!' The guard on duty peered at her. 'You back already? We didn't expect you back till first light.' He grinned, stood back and waved them all through. As Kate pulled to a halt in the MT yard, the instructor appeared as she jumped down from the cab.

'Well done! You're first back.' He said no more but the man who had shouted at them, bullied them, despaired of them over the past few weeks, finally put his hand on her shoulder and squeezed it.

That was better than a medal, Kate thought. Later she was to find that the instructor had specially recommended her for promotion and she was immediately upgraded to Aircraftswoman First Class.

Mavis was not so fortunate.

'They keep telling me that I'm too friendly over the radio. That I get too excited when there's a flap on,' she moaned to Kate. 'They say I've got to be calm and efficient at all times. I know they're right. A pilot in trouble doesn't want to hear some hysterical female on the other end of his radio link . . .' She sighed. 'But it's awfully difficult not to yell at a pilot to get out of his burning aircraft instead of trying to find out objectively if it's feasible for him to bring it in to land.'

'You'll get the hang of it, Mave,' Kate encouraged. 'I still think you're just the right sort of person. It's no good having some cold fish who doesn't give a damn.'

'Mmm,' Mavis said doubtfully.

But in the end, Mavis too passed out, not quite at the top of the class like Kate, but well enough to make her ecstatic at becoming a fully-fledged Aircraftswoman Second Class.

'Now keep calm,' Kate teased her. 'You know what they told you.'

'I know, but it's the first time I've passed *anything*!'

'Me too. First time I've ever been good at anything – except perhaps sewing.'

'Sewing? Crikey – not much difference, is there?' Mavis laughed.

Kate laughed too and spread her hands, looking down at them. 'I suppose I'm just practical,' she murmured, 'rather than brainy.' Unbidden, into her mind came a picture of her studious young sister, poring over her school books.

When they heard their postings, she and Mavis were still together.

'Oh, isn't that wonderful? By the way, where is Suddaby? I've never heard of it, have you?'

Kate nodded. 'It's where me grandad used to live before he came to live with us.'

'Really? Evidently it's a new station – an operational bomber station – just being built. Oh, I can't wait! We'll be there from the beginning.' Mavis rubbed her hands together, her face wreathed in smiles. 'Oh, isn't it exciting? Where's the nearest hot spot for night life there, then?'

Kate grinned. 'Suddaby is out in the wilds, miles from anywhere with only birds and the cattle in the fields for company.'

Her friend's face was a picture until she spotted Kate's mischievous smile. 'Oh, you, you're teasing me.'

'Well, a bit maybe. There are one or two market towns within easy reach, but it isn't near a big city.'

'Is it near where you live?'

'Yes, it's about thirteen miles inland from the sea.'

'Oh goody, I've never seen the sea.'

Now it was Kate's turn for her face to register surprise. 'Never seen the sea! You're joking.'

'Nope. I was born, brought up and lived all my life in Leicester. We never had holidays when I was a kid.' Her merry face brightened. 'Why do you think I joined the WAAFs? Thought I'd see the world.'

Kate smiled ruefully on her friend's behalf. 'And the nearest you get is Lincolnshire!'

Mavis shrugged philosophically. 'I don't mind. I'm loving every minute.' She paused, then asked again, 'Well, where is the nearest big city, then?'

'Lincoln,' Kate said quietly and saw Mavis looking at her quizzically.

'You don't look very pleased,' Mavis said, linking her arm through Kate's and pulling her away from the excited chatter of the other girls comparing their postings. 'I'd have thought you'd have been pleased if it's nearer your home.'

Kate made an effort to smile. There were so many memories attached to that city, Kate thought; her childhood and then later, when she and Danny . . . Her mind shied away from that dreadful time. 'Just – a few ghosts, Mave,' she murmured.

'Oh, we'll lay those to rest good and proper, Kate, when we get whooping it up in the town. Poor old Lincoln won't know what's hit it when we get there! You mark my words.'

'See you in Suddaby in a week's time, then,' Mavis was shouting, leaning precariously out of the train as it began to move. A cloud of smoke enveloped her and she was obliged to draw her head into the carriage.

Kate smiled. What a character! She'd been lucky to pal up with Mavis, she thought, as she heaved her kit-bag on to her back and made for another platform to catch her connection to Lynthorpe.

Seven whole days, she thought, with Christmas in the middle. And Danny is sure to be getting leave at the same time, she told herself.

She couldn't wait to get home to see him.

Twenty-Two

'He's not here, lovey.'

'Not – not here? But – he – he must be. He must be getting leave at the end of his training like me, surely? And it's Christmas too!'

Sadly, Beth shook her head as she pulled open the back door wider, silently inviting Kate in. Although it was warm in the kitchen, Kate pushed her hands deeper still into the pockets of her greatcoat, hunching her shoulders.

Suddenly, she felt very cold.

The train journey home had seemed interminable. Standing on draughty platforms, waiting for connections, and then the train had chugged along at what seemed to Kate an inordinately slow pace.

And now Danny was not here.

'Do you know when he's coming?'

Beth shook her head, laying out cups on the table and mashing a pot of tea. 'All I know is he's having extra training so he can fly.'

'Fly! Oh no. He's not going to be a pilot, is he?'

A frown creased Beth's brow. 'No – but he's going to be part of the crew on – on bombers. He said he was going to be – now, what was it? "A tail-end Charlie", that was it.'

Kate sat down suddenly as her legs gave way. 'A rear-gunner – and on bombers!' Kate whispered, then her voice rose shrilly. 'He – he'll be flying over enemy territory. He'll – he'll . . .'

The sight of Beth's white face stilled Kate's outburst and she swallowed hard. She stood up suddenly and went to the older woman, putting her arms about her. Beth laid her head against Kate's shoulder. 'Oh, Kate, I couldn't bear it if – if . . .'

The two women clung together in their mutual fear for Danny's safety.

A little later when she left the Elands' cottage, Kate felt too restless to return home. She set off across the marsh towards the Spit, walking the full length of the promontory of land. She stood at its tip, letting her gaze travel around the expanse of water. The wind whipped across the sea, making the waves choppy, the surface like a huge sheet of corrugated iron. It was grey and cold and so lonely, especially without Danny.

She turned away and retraced her steps towards the beach, wanting to find their hollow in the dunes. But her path was barred by coils of barbed wire, bouncing and rocking in the breeze, stretching along the edge of the dunes. And a huge notice in red lettering proclaimed 'DANGER – MINES'. Kate gasped. They'd blocked off the beach and mined the sand-dunes too.

Thinking back longingly to the days when she and Danny had run barefoot across the smooth, unspoilt sands, for the first time she felt a spurt of hatred for this war.

Close by the concrete pillbox which the army had built for their observers stationed at the Point, she was about to turn away when she heard the unexpected sound of girlish giggles.

Kate's mouth set in a grim line as she marched towards the entrance and peered into the gloomy interior. On a groundsheet, wrapped together in a passionate embrace, were a young man in khaki army uniform and a girl with blonde hair and shapely legs.

'Rosie!' Kate's startled gasp escaped her lips before she could prevent it.

The couple shot apart, the girl pulling down her dress and scrambling to her feet.

Kate turned and stumbled away through the tufts of thick grass.

'Kate! Kate! Wait – please!' There was such desperation in Rosie's voice that Kate stopped. She did not turn around but stood still until Rosie reached her.

Grasping Kate's arm, Rosie begged, 'Please don't tell me dad, Katie. He'd kill me. But it's not what you think. Honest. It's – it's only a bit of fun.'

'It looked like it!' Kate snorted. 'Danny was right about you . . .'

Rosie's eyes widened and in them now was a look of sheer terror. 'Danny? Oh, no – please don't tell Danny. *Please*, Kate. I couldn't bear it if he – if he . . .'

'If he – what?' Kate asked quietly.

Rosie's gaze fell away and her grasp on Kate's arm loosened. 'Nothing. I just don't want you to tell – anyone.'

Kate regarded her thoughtfully. That was understandable she thought reasonably. Yet the thought of Danny knowing of her romping in the sand-dunes had positively terrified Rosie. Kate sighed. 'All right, I won't tell anyone, but as long as you promise me you'll be careful. These lads are lonely and a long way from home, Rosie. They – they might want too much from a pretty girl like you.'

'It's only a kiss and a cuddle, Katie, honest,' Rosie promised.

'Well – just mind it is.'

As she turned away and left Rosie to go back to her young man, Kate couldn't help thinking to herself, 'I sound just like my mother!'

'Please, Kate,' Rosie's plea followed her. 'Please don't tell Danny.'

Kate tried to put on a brave front over Christmas for the sake of her family. They were all so pleased to see her – even Lilian hugged her enthusiastically when she opened the page-to-a-day diary Kate had given her as a Christmas gift.

'It's lovely, Kate. I always keep a diary and never have enough room to write everything in those little ones . . .'

Kate smiled kindly at her sister; the round, childish glasses gave the young girl an owlish look. Her straight hair was cut short to just below her ears. Lilian would have been the perfect pupil for Miss Denham. Kate couldn't imagine what Lilian could possibly have to write about that would fill half a page, let alone a whole one. Overcome with a feeling of pity for the lonely young girl, Kate gave her a swift hug.

'We've invited the two Land Army girls for Christmas dinner,' Esther told Kate. 'Poor things! They're sisters – from Coventry.

'Oh heck!' Kate said at once, staring at her mother, the unspoken question in her eyes.

Her mother nodded. 'Yes, their home was bombed in that awful raid in November. Their parents were safe, thank God, but the lasses have no home to go back to.'

'How awful!' Kate said. 'Where are they billeted?'

'At the Grange. The Squire's turned it over for the duration. He's taken a small house in the town.' She shook her head, murmuring. 'Poor old Squire – he's not well.'

'Do the girls help here?'

Her mother's impish smile was back. 'Oh, yes. They're surprisingly good too – for townies.'

Kate hid her smile at her mother's innocent tone of condescension.

234

'But I have to watch 'em with ya dad,' Esther added and touched her husband's cheek tenderly.

Kate exchanged an amused glance with her stepfather. As if the idea would even cross his mind, she thought.

So Christmas passed pleasantly enough, but it was not the same without Danny.

Her pen was poised above the white page of the writing pad. Should she tell Danny about Rosie? Kate bit her lip with indecision and then decided to keep her promise to the girl. She sighed. She just hoped young Rosie did know what she was doing else it could all end in tears, as Grannie Harris was fond of saying.

She was sitting in front of the window in the sitting room, her legs curled up in a chair, the writing pad resting on her knee. From time to time she paused, looking up to stare out of the window across the smooth fields towards the Grange, the straight brown furrows white-tipped with the morning frost. In an hour's time, her stepfather would take her to Suddaby in the pony and trap.

'Who needs petrol?' her mother had snorted in contempt, when the rationing had hit so many folks' mode of transport. Jonathan, whose love for motors and engines seemed never to be catered for, at least on Brumbys' Farm, had winked at Kate who had smiled back sympathetically.

A shadow fell across the page of her half-written letter and she looked up to see her grandfather.

'Writing to Danny, lass?' he asked without preamble, and eased his stiff limbs down to sit in the chair beside her. 'You leaving this morning?'

She nodded.

'Ah've got you a little something extra to what I gave ya on Christmas Day, lass,' he said and dropped a package into her lap. 'I expect ya'll be making a lot of new friends and maybe seeing new places and I thought this might come in handy.'

Carefully, Kate unwrapped the square-shaped parcel. It was a Box Brownie camera. 'Oh, Grandad, that's a lovely present. And yes, it will be very nice to have. You make friends with people and then get posted to different places and maybe never see them again.'

Will Benson sniffed. 'That's what Ah thought. Ah got 'em at the shop to put a film in it, lass, so if ya wanted to take a few pictures 'afore ya leave ... And Ah'd like to take one of you in yar smart uniform. Ya'd send it back to me when ya get it developed, would ya?'

'Of course. Thank you, Grandad.' She leaned forward and planted a kiss on his stubbly face.

He sniffed and grunted with embarrassment. Changing the subject, he asked again. 'A' ya writing to Danny?'

'Yes – just to let him know my new address. I haven't heard from him in ages. I expect it's all this moving about. Maybe his letters have got lost. Maybe one day I'll get a bundle arrive all together.'

'Kate . . .' the old man began, paused, and then continued haltingly. 'Katie, it's time to – to let go, lass.'

She avoided looking at him. 'What – what do you mean, Grandad?' The question was unnecessary. In her heart she knew what he meant only too well.

'Don't live ya life hankering after summat – or rather someone – ya can never have.'

'I'm not,' she snapped, and then, feeling guilty for her sharpness, put her hand on his arm. 'Truly I'm not. We're – we're . . .' She took a deep shuddering breath and said the words she had always found so difficult to voice: 'Brother and sister. We know we are. It's just that . . .'

Now she could not put their feelings into words. How

236

could she explain to her grandfather the love which still lay between her and Danny, a love which she believed would never go away or even be replaced?

Maybe the old man understood, at least in part, for he covered her hand with his wrinkled one. 'I know, lass, I know. But mebbe ya've the chance now to meet other fellers. It's time you were married and settled down and having bairns.'

'Yes, Grandad,' she said dutifully, and forced a smile on to her mouth. She knew her grandfather meant well, but she could not imagine meeting anyone who could take Danny's place in her heart. Not ever.

'ACW Hilton. Ah yes, you're the new driver for the CO, aren't you?'

Kate gasped in surprise. The officer looked up. 'Well? Doesn't that suit?' There was sarcasm in the woman's tone that told Kate immediately that whatever she felt, it would have to suit.

'Oh yes, Ma'am. It – it was just a surprise, that's all. I hadn't been told. I mean—' She floundered, feeling herself going red. 'I mean, I knew I'd be in Motor Transport but I didn't know exactly what I'd be doing.'

'You'll still be in the MT Section and will have to carry out other duties when the CO doesn't need you. The officer in charge of the MT Section is Flying Officer Cooper, but you'll take your day-to-day orders from Flight Sergeant Martin. It seems, however,' the officer added drily, 'that our new Commanding Officer has asked especially for your services.'

'Oh!' This was an even bigger surprise. She could not imagine why.

The officer was looking at her keenly. 'It's a very good

posting, particularly for a new recruit. Just mind you are up to it.'

Kate saluted smartly, some of her confidence returning. 'I'll do my best, Ma'am.'

She was dismissed.

As she left the orderly room, Kate stood for a moment to get her bearings. The airfield was in fact divided by the main road; on one side were all the quarters for the officers and airmen – and the WAAFs – and the administration offices were also sited there. On the opposite side, spread out before her, flat and windswept, was the operational site; the runways, the hangars and control tower and all sorts of buildings whose use Kate had yet to learn.

She drew in a deep breath and held it, revelling in the feel of the wind upon her face and the panorama before her. A small smile curved her mouth as she looked about her. She was so happy to be back in her home county. Before her, beyond the perimeter of the airfield, lay the gently rolling fields of the Wolds. Nearer, she watched a tractor, driven by a WAAF, hauling a bomb-train from the ammunitions dump towards the waiting aircraft. That was a job she might have done. But it seemed as if her new Station Commander had other plans. Now, her main duty would be to familiarize herself with the MT yard and the CO's staff car in particular. Crossing her fingers that it would be a Humber Super Snipe, the same type on which she had done her training, she went in search of the MT Section office.

Flight Sergeant Martin was a kindly, fatherly figure, affectionately known by all in the section as 'Chiefy'. He was bald, apart from tufts of grey, bushy hair which sprouted on either side of his head just above his ears. His eyes twinkled at her from behind round, steel-rimmed spectacles. 'CO wants to see you the minute you arrive. Leave your gear here . . .' He took her outside and pointed in the direction of the building which housed the CO's office. 'Now, you be careful. He's a handsome devil, if ever I saw one,' Chiefy chuckled, a deep, rumbling sound from his round belly.

Waiting in the outer office for her interview with the CO, Kate's confidence ebbed away again and her stomach was churning with nervousness. She was uncomfortably aware of the eyes of the Adjutant upon her.

Then for some reason she suddenly thought about her mother. A picture of Esther Godfrey was in her mind's eye, standing with hands on hips, feet planted firmly a little apart, her strong jawline jutting out resolutely. A small smile twitched at Kate's mouth. No one, as far as she could remember, had ever intimidated her mother; not the Squire, not a headmistress, not authority of any kind. And were she in Kate's place at this very moment, the man beyond that door would hold no fears for Esther Godfrey either. Some of the fluttering under Kate's ribs settled a little.

Something buzzed on the man's desk and he lifted a telephone receiver and listened. 'Sir,' was all he said into the instrument. Replacing the receiver, he looked up at Kate. 'You may go in now.'

Kate stood and marched through the door. As it closed behind her she came to attention in front of the CO's desk and rattled out her rank, name and number.

Then her hand fell away from her forehead in an untidy end to her salute and her lips parted in a gasp.

She was staring straight into the blue eyes of Philip Trent.

Having returned her salute, he at once seemed to relax and become completely 'unofficial'. He came round the desk and held out both his hands to her.

'Kate – it's so good to see you again. You look wonderful.'

Hesitating only a moment, but then taking the lead from him, she smiled warmly. 'And you. How are you? How's your arm?'

'Fine. It wasn't broken, thank goodness, only dislocated and a small flesh wound just here.' He indicated a point just below his collarbone. 'It's healed well now.'

They stared at each other, smiling, genuinely pleased to be meeting again.

'Well, this is a coincidence,' she said.

Philip's smile broadened and he shook his head. 'No coincidence, Kate.'

A slight frown furrowed her forehead. 'Why? What do you mean?'

'Do sit down.' He indicated a wooden chair in front of his desk. 'I'll get us some tea.' He leaned forward conspiratorially. 'If anyone asks, we're discussing details of your job as my driver.'

He went towards the door, opened it, issued orders for two teas, closed the door and returned to his desk. Sitting behind it, he smiled across at her again. 'I'd better look all official when the corporal comes in with the tea. Actually, joking apart, we will have to discuss your – er – position as my driver. But first, I want to catch up on what's been happening to you since we last met.'

They looked at each other, remembering Dunkirk, and their faces sobered. 'I'm so glad you're safe,' he said softly. His gaze held hers and for a long moment they just sat staring at each other. Then Philip Trent cleared his throat and seemed to shake himself. His glance fell away and he shuffled some papers on his desk in front of him. 'How's Danny?' he asked softly.

'Fine. He's joined the RAF.'

Philip nodded. 'I know.'

'You do?' This was getting more mysterious by the minute.

'I can't believe this is happening.' She shook her head in disbelief. 'What did you mean when you said it wasn't a coincidence?'

He was smiling again, though looking a little sheepish.

'When we get to this exalted position,' he cleared his throat as if poking gentle fun at himself. On looking more carefully, she could see by the four half-inch stripes on his sleeve that he was now a Group Captain. 'It does have its perks,' he was saying. 'We have colleagues in all sorts of posts. And if necessary, we can pull rank to get information.'

Kate still looked puzzled.

'I was pretty sure you – and Danny – would join up after Dunkirk. Not only did I find out that you had, but also where you went for your training and that you'd ended up as an MT driver *and* with a special recommendation for promotion from your instructor,' he added, teasing gently. 'So – I made the right contacts and got you posted here as my personal driver.'

Kate gasped aloud. 'Goodness. Just like that.'

He pulled a face. 'Not really. I had to do a lot of string-pulling. But it worked.' His face clouded momentarily and he leaned towards her. 'You don't – mind?' he asked, suddenly boyish in his anxiety.

Before she could answer, there was a knock at the door and a corporal entered carrying a tray with two cups of tea on it, a small milk jug and sugar bowl. He set it down on the desk and retreated.

The very new station commander was still looking anxiously at his even newer driver. 'Do you mind?' he repeated the moment the door had closed behind the corporal.

'Of course not,' Kate reassured him swiftly. 'I'm really very grateful.' She smiled mischievously as she added, 'I've

241

already been told by a WAAF officer that it is a very important posting and she hopes I'm up to it!'

Now he laughed aloud as he handed her a cup of tea. 'Oh, you'll be up to it all right, Kate Hilton. There's no doubt about that, and I'm recommending you be made up to Leading Aircraftswoman with immediate effect.' His smile broadened. 'Promotion can come amazingly quickly sometimes!'

'Thank you,' she whispered, touched by his faith in her.

Then his face sobered. 'There is just something we must get straight, though . . .'

Kate nodded and, trying to lessen any embarrassment he might feel considering the debt of gratitude he owed her, she said, 'I know – this is the last time we can talk like this. In future we must be – well – official.'

A look of surprise flitted across his face. 'Oh, I hope not, Kate. No, what I was going to say was that on duty and in front of others, yes, we must be "official" as you put it.' The smile lit his face again, 'But I hope that in private we can still continue to be friends.'

'Well, if you're sure it won't compromise your position in any way.'

'It won't trouble me. After all,' he puffed out his chest with mock pride, '*I* am the new Station Commander. My word is law!'

Kate laughed, but he said quietly and more seriously now, 'No, Kate, all joking apart, it's you who could be compromised, and I wouldn't want that.'

He stood up and Kate followed suit, placing her empty cup back on the tray. He was moving towards the door and opening it for her. 'And this is the last time I'll be able do this for you. I'm afraid you'll have to open it for me in future.'

She smiled and then, deliberately adopting a bland

expression before leaving his office, she saluted smartly and said, 'Sir!'

Kate threw her kit-bag on to the end bed nearest the big grey stove – Mavis already having laid claim to the bed opposite – and surveyed the rest of the hut. 'Did you have a good Christmas, Mave? There doesn't seem to be many here yet.'

There appeared to be only three other beds occupied besides the one she was now claiming.

'Yes, thanks. There's more arriving later today.' Mavis bounced down on the unoccupied bed next to Kate and lay back with her hands behind her head. 'Two more R/T operators and a meteorologist. You and me are lucky to know each other. I guess for a while we shan't know anyone else. They'll be coming from all over.'

'Mmm,' Kate agreed absently, and sighed. All she hoped was that her recent letter to Danny got delivered to him all right and that he knew where she was. Wouldn't he be surprised that she'd met up again with Philip Trent and that from now on she'd be seeing him every day? She must write at once and tell him . . .

Almost as if reading her thoughts, Mavis said, 'I hear you're the envy of the camp. Landing a job as driver to the dishy CO. Lucky old you!'

Kate just smiled.

'Mind you,' Mavis went on, 'there's a rather nice Flight Sergeant in the Ops Room . . .'

'Oh, Mavis, you're impossible!'

Kate sat down on her bed and pulled out her writing pad.

'Oh, you're not writing to him *again*, are you?' Mavis cast her eyes to the rafters in mock exasperation. 'And you try to tell me he's not your boyfriend!'

Kate said nothing, but bent her head over the page and began to write, 'Dear Danny . . .'

The door of the long hut opened and two newcomers entered. Mavis twisted her head to look towards the door but made no effort to move from the bed.

'Hello there,' she called cheerily. 'Welcome to your new home.' Now she levered herself up on her elbow, swung her legs off the bed and sat up. 'I'm Mavis and this is Kate.'

The two arrivals walked down the length of the hut, a tall, slender girl with sleek blonde hair leading the way with confidence in every stride, while behind her came a smaller, thin girl.

Ignoring Mavis's greeting, the tall girl was complaining loudly in affected tones, 'If I have to endure another Free From Infection inspection just once more . . . it's so humiliating!'

Kate looked up, glancing over the newcomers. Her gaze rested briefly on the thin girl and then was drawn to the other girl. There was something vaguely familiar about her. Kate frowned. The girl nodded stiffly towards Mavis, her only acknowledgement of the friendly greeting.

There was something about the sulky mouth, the tilt of her head as if she were looking down her nose at everything and everyone . . .

Even before the newcomer opened her mouth to speak again, Kate recognized her.

'How do you do?' Her tones were affected and cold. 'This is Edith Brownlow and my name's Isobel Cartwright.'

Twenty-Three

Kate knew she was staring at Isobel Cartwright, but she could not stop herself.

Her stomach was churning. Of all the people she had hoped never to meet again in her life, this girl was top of the list, apart, perhaps, from Miss Denham. Any moment, she expected the girl's petulant mouth to twist into a sneer and hear herself called that dreadful name. 'Why, if it isn't Sicky!'

But Isobel's cool glance flickered over Kate without recognition and she turned her attention to the bed next to Mavis. 'I'll take this one. I see you two have already bagged the ones nearest the stove.'

'First come, first served,' Mavis said airily. She waved her hand towards Kate, making the introductions.

Kate held her breath. Would Isobel remember the name, if not the young girl who had grown up?

Isobel nodded briefly and glanced around, more concerned with her surroundings. 'Well, I don't like being under a window. They're *always* draughty.' She prodded the three-sectioned mattress with her fingers. 'Ugh! I shall have to get Mummy to bring my own bed over from Lincoln. This is disgusting!'

Kate heard Mavis's splutter of laughter which she tried to turn into a cough, but failed.

By contrast, Edith Brownlow was standing uncertainly in the centre of the floor. Kate noticed now, with a stab of pity, that the girl's hair was plastered with an evil-smelling concoction, proclaiming to all that in the medical inspection, Edith must have been found to have head lice.

Kate watched as Isobel glanced coolly towards Edith. 'You'd better take a bed on that side of the hut, Brownlow. *I* don't want to catch nits!'

Obediently and without a word of complaint, Edith took the bed on the opposite side under the window next to Kate and began to unpack her belongings. Kate had a shrewd idea that the girl's bent head was hiding tears. She remembered how she had felt under Isobel Cartwright's scathing jibes.

She went over to Edith. 'Here, let me give you a hand,' Kate said, smiling at the younger girl who was obviously feeling very embarrassed. 'Our corporal's not a bad old stick, actually,' Kate continued, trying to open up a conversation. 'We're lucky – the girls in the next hut have got a battle-axe!'

She kept up a bright chatter while helping the girl to sort out her kit. 'Where are you from?'

'Nottingham.' Edith's voice was no more than a whisper.

'Oh, that's not too far away. You should be able to get home on leave quite easily.'

The girl bent her head again and did not reply. Kate had the feeling that perhaps she had said the wrong thing.

Isobel's complaining voice rose again. 'Where's the bathroom?'

Now Mavis did laugh outright. 'Where on earth did you do your basic training – the Ritz?'

Isobel shot her a vitriolic glance, sat down on her bed and crossed her shapely legs. She was wearing silk stockings, Kate noticed. She doubted if even their easy-going corporal would let Isobel get away with that! From her pocket, Isobel pulled out what looked like a silver cigarette case, opened it, extracted a cigarette and lit it, inhaling deeply.

'Actually,' she drawled, 'we were in an hotel – in Harrogate. At least it was civilized. When we went to the place for our R/T training it was very basic – to say the least! But I thought this would be different. I mean, it's a newly built station.'

Kate couldn't stop herself trotting out the well-worn phrase that was used as an excuse for every short-coming. 'There is a war on, you know...' She paused and then added with delicious delight, 'Cartwright!'

Isobel glared at her and instantly Kate regretted drawing her old enemy's attention to her. But Mavis took up the cudgels. 'New it may be, but I suppose they had to get the place banged up and operational as quickly as possible. The new squadron arrives tomorrow complete with Manchesters.'

Kate's interest sharpened. 'Really?' According to something her stepfather had said at Christmas, Danny could be on Manchesters. 'Where are they coming from? What squadron is it?'

'How should I know?' Mavis laughed and added teasingly. '*You* should be able to get all the info – after all, you're closest to the CO.'

'That's true,' she murmured, her mind racing.

'Close to the CO? How come?' Isobel was watching her with renewed interest.

'She's the CO's personal driver,' Mavis told them with a tinge of reflected importance. 'Hand-picked, she was.'

'Really?'

Kate glanced up to see Isobel watching her. On the girl's face there was a rather calculating expression and something else too. Could there possibly be a tinge of respect, Kate thought in surprise. But then, she reminded herself, Isobel Cartwright hasn't realized just who I am – yet!

*

More WAAFs arrived over the next two days and soon their hut was fully occupied, with the corporal in charge of them sleeping in the small single room just off the entrance into the hut. After a couple of days they were gradually getting used to being with girls from different parts of the country – from all walks of life.

'God, that woman's useless!' Mavis moaned to Kate as they cut across the grass to the ablutions at six-thirty one morning.

'Who – Edith?'

'Edith? Oh no, not Edith. She's very clever, actually, with the met reports. Seems it's a special interest of hers. No, no, me Lady Isobel Cartwright! I would get lumbered with her on my shift, wouldn't I? Thick as cloud at forty thousand feet, she is!'

Kate felt a moment of sneaking glee to hear Isobel criticized. She bent her head forward so that Mavis should not see the smile on her lips.

'Still,' Mavis added, mellowing a little as her normal generous nature surfaced again, 'she does try, I'll give her that.'

Kate's head shot up. 'Really?' she said, without thinking. 'You do surprise me. I'd have thought she'd think it all beneath her.'

'How on earth she passed out as an R/T operator I don't know. Dave's getting fed up with her already. She comes in for some flak from him, I can tell you.'

'And does she take it?'

'Oh, yes. Hasn't much choice, really, now has she?'

'Suppose not.' Kate paused a moment then asked, 'Who's this Dave?' As they pushed their way into the wash-room, Kate glanced at her friend and saw Mavis's cheeks were a faint shade of pink that had nothing to do with the walk through the frosty morning air. Teasing, she added, 'Do I detect a romance blossoming?'

248

'Don't be daft, Kate,' Mavis countered, but the pink tinge deepened. 'I've only just met him.'

'Mmm. I can see I shall have to keep my eye on you. Anyway, tell me more about Isobel.'

Mavis launched into a list of mistakes and inefficiencies of which Isobel Cartwright had managed to be guilty in just two shifts. The catalogue was secretly gratifying to Kate, but she hugged the knowledge to herself. She didn't want anyone – not even dear old Mavis – to have the slightest inkling that she knew Isobel.

'How are you getting on with the CO? Is he as nice as he looks?'

'Every bit,' Kate said. Again she made no reference to the fact that she and Group Captain Philip Trent had met before, or that he owed his life to her. It was a secret best kept between the two of them. He had done her an enormous favour in arranging for her to be his driver, but neither of them wanted it common knowledge that he had singled her out for biased treatment.

'Of course, he's a bit old for you, isn't he?'

'Oh, Mavis, really!' Kate laughed. 'The thought never even crossed my mind . . .' But then she remembered his intense gaze across the desk on the day of her arrival. It was more than just a 'thank you for saving my life' look.

'How old do you reckon he is, then?'

'Forty-ish, I should think.'

'Is he married?'

'Oh Mavis, really. I just drive him about – I don't get to know his life history. It's – all very official,' she added, hesitating over the lie.

'I'll find out,' Mavis said confidently and Kate knew she would.

In the seclusion of the staff car, the CO's attitude towards his driver was anything but 'official'.

'Is everything okay in the WAAF quarters? Are you quite comfortable? You can tell me, you know, Kate, quite unofficially. I could try to find you a room in my office block, if you would prefer it.'

She was surprised to hear herself saying. 'Oh no, thank you. I like being with the other girls.' Who would have believed it, she thought, that I could ever come to terms with sleeping in a dormitory of sorts again? 'The only thing is, when you don't need me – there's not much for me to do.' She smiled. 'I can only polish and tinker with this car for so many hours in a day.'

'Well, my demands on your time will no doubt get heavier when we get fully operational, which should be by next week. We shall have two squadrons of bombers here by then. But the station will be very stretched for staff and you may well find yourself being detailed to do other jobs, such as driving the crewbus taking the chaps out to the aircraft when there's an op on. I shall be around myself then anyway.' There was an expression of regret on his face as he met her glance in the rear-view mirror. 'It's the nearest I shall be able to get to flying with them.'

Kate was not surprised; she had known instinctively that Philip would be a fully committed and caring Commanding Officer, nor was she surprised to hear he lamented the fact that his senior post had virtually grounded him.

As she pulled up outside the Control Tower, and was about to jump out of the car to open the rear door for him, he leaned forward and touched her shoulder. 'Are you sure there's nothing you want?'

'Well . . .' she hesitated.

'Go on,' he prompted.

'I – I don't suppose it would be possible to get Danny posted to this station, would it?'

She thought she heard him sigh softly. 'Are you sure it's

what you really want, Kate? Wouldn't it be worse for you knowing when he was flying, waiting for his plane to come back?'

She gripped the steering-wheel, her knuckles showing white. 'I – don't know. All I know is that not knowing where he is, or what he's doing, or if he's safe, is unbearable.'

There was a flatness to his voice as he said, 'I'll see what I can do, Kate. But I can't promise anything.'

Before she could move, he had opened the door himself and got out of the car, his long strides taking him towards the building without looking back at her.

Kate bit her lip. Now she did not know whether to wait here for him or go back to the MT yard. Sighing, she got out of the car and followed him. It would be better to hang about waiting for him even if he didn't want her, than to disappear and be missing when he did!

He was in the Met Office on the ground floor talking to Edith who was standing, not exactly to attention, but rigidly upright, answering his questions with a clipped 'Yes, sir,' 'No, sir'.

Kate saw Philip's glance flicker over her but he looked away and concentrated again upon Edith.

Kate went up the concrete stairs to the upper floor. The walls were freshly painted, the top half cream with bottle-green at the bottom. The smell of the paint still lingered. She passed the Signals Room and peeked round the door of the Control Room. Directly in front of her sat Mavis with headphones over her short, springy brown hair. Beside her sat Isobel, leaning forward and listening intently to what Mavis was telling her. There were all sorts of instruments and telephones on the long desk in front of them and on the walls were maps and clocks and blackboards giving local weather conditions and target information. Most interesting of all to Kate was the large operations blackboard with

251

'SUDDABY' painted in white at the top followed by its call sign, then the squadron numbers and their call signs. In the middle was the word 'RAID' with a blank space for the name to be chalked in each time. Below that was a blank white-painted grid where a WAAF would stand to fill in all the details of each aircraft as it took off on a raid giving the pilot's name, the take-off time and the column everyone watched anxiously: 'RETURN'.

To Kate's left as she stood in the doorway, sat a man at a table. This must be the famous Dave, she thought.

As if feeling her gaze upon him, the Flight Sergeant looked up and grinned at her.

'Hello. Come to see what we get up to here?'

'I'm with the CO,' Kate said. 'He's downstairs.'

Dave winked. 'Thanks for the tip-off.'

At the sound of Kate's voice, Mavis looked around. 'Hello, Kate.' But immediately she turned back to the instruments on her desk.

Dave nodded towards her. 'She's good, is our Mavis. Friend of yours, is she?'

Kate nodded.

At that moment, hearing footsteps on the stairs and seeing Philip appear in the passage behind her, she moved aside to allow him to come into the Control Room.

Standing in the background, she watched while Philip spoke to each person there. As he paused behind Mavis, Kate saw Isobel look up at him, tilting her head coyly, her blue eyes shining and a smile curving her mouth. He spoke briefly to her and then bent over Mavis to talk to her. Kate was amused to see that Isobel bent forward with a semblance of keen concentration. She heard Philip's deep laugh, Mavis's giggle and Isobel's tinkling, affected laughter. As Philip straightened up and turned away to speak to another WAAF on the other side of the room, Isobel glanced at Kate. There was a look of triumph on her face and then, as she continued to stare at Kate, a slight frown creased her smooth forehead as if she were trying to draw something out that was nudging at the depths of her memory, something she could not quite catch and hold on to. Kate felt the old fluttering just beneath her ribs.

One of these days, Isobel was going to remember . . .

At that moment they all heard the distinctive sound of the air-raid siren.

'Right, everybody to the shelters,' Philip said calmly, and waited until everyone had preceded him out of the room.

'Come on, Mavis, don't hang about,' Dave's voice was sharp but Kate noticed he made no move himself until Mavis had pulled off her earphones, pushed on her tin hat, grabbed her gas mask and followed Isobel who was already heading for the stairs. Kate felt Philip grasp her arm firmly and propel her out and across the grass to the trench shelter. The winter sky hummed and, fascinated, Kate looked up to see two fighter planes wheeling and diving around each other, guns spurting death.

'They'll crash into each other,' she gasped.

Beside her, Philip said grimly, 'It happens.'

As it became obvious that the warning had not been for a bombing raid on the airfield, personnel began to emerge from the shelters again to stand watching the fight taking place above them. The aircraft with the circular red, white and blue emblem of the RAF had the black plane in its sights. The enemy aircraft twisted and dived, but to no avail; the British pilot followed his every move as if an invisible cord tied them together. Suddenly, they saw black smoke trailing from the enemy plane. Forgetting where they were, Kate gripped Philip's arm, her horrified gaze watching the aircraft screaming towards the ground, the smoke slashing the grey sky. As the plane hit the ground and burst into flames, around her there came the sound of cheering and against the clouds the Spitfire rolled victoriously.

Philip was silent.

'There – there was no parachute, was there?'

'No, Kate,' he answered quietly as they stood together watching the pall of smoke on the far side of the airfield marking wreckage. As fire engines set off across the grass towards it, the all-clear sounded.

Around them there was laughter and congratulation, but Kate could not join in. Despite the fact that she had joined the battle and knew they must fight to the bitter end, nevertheless she could feel no elation at witnessing the death of another human being.

The dead enemy pilot was somebody's son, somebody's brother.

The thought pushed its unwelcome way into her mind; it could so easily have been Danny.

Twenty-Four

The following morning, Kate received a letter from Danny. It was enclosed in a letter from her stepfather. Kate tossed that aside and ripped open the letter from Danny. It was short and didn't tell her very much, but he gave her an address she could write to and he told her he was well and that he would be going home on leave in just over a week. Was there any chance she could get leave at the same time, he asked.

Any chance? Oh, she'd get it if she had to beg on bended knee. Of course, although it wasn't normal procedure, with her unusual relationship with the CO, she could ask Philip personally.

She glanced at her watch. She was due to drive him into Lincoln in about half an hour to catch a train north.

The expression on Philip's face, when he got into the back of the car, was not encouraging. He seemed preoccupied and his eyes were tired. His face looked drawn and strained and the smile, which so altered his expression, was missing. He nodded briefly at her, but sat back in his seat, his shoulders rigid. In the rear mirror she saw him remove his cap and run his hand through his springy, short-cut hair. She could feel the tension in him. Kate bit her lip. She desperately wanted to ask him to approve at least a forty-eight-hour pass for her to coincide with Danny's leave, but above the noise of the large car's engine, it would mean shouting back to him.

She drew into the station and jumped out to open the

255

door for him. As he bent his head to climb out, she saluted smartly as always, but said softly, 'Sir?'

He straightened up and looked down at her, frowning. 'What is it?' he almost barked at her.

'I – I was wondering how long you w-will be away, sir,' she stammered, deciding instantly that he was in no mood to grant favours, and floundering to think of something – anything – to ask.

'I'll be gone about five days. If you can meet me off the train on Tuesday evening – it gets in about six – I'd be grateful.'

He turned and strode away and Kate found herself saluting to no one in particular.

'Damn!' she muttered to herself as she got back into the car and wove her way out of Lincoln and back towards the station.

'Oh, I can't grant you leave. There's no knowing this far ahead what "Sir" will be doing. You took the job as his driver,' the WAAF officer said sarcastically. 'It's a cushy number, Hilton, so you take the rough with the smooth. You knew you would have to be on call virtually all the time. You'll have to apply through the usual channels.'

So Kate was obliged to reply to Danny's letter explaining the situation. She finished off on a hopeful note. 'I'll do my best though – perhaps I could even ask the CO when he comes back on Tuesday.'

That night as they lay in bed after lights out, Kate was still trying to work out how she was going to wangle some leave to coincide with Danny's. She lay in her narrow bed, feeling the ridges of the three-section 'biscuit' mattress beneath her and staring up with sleepless eyes into the blackness of the rafters. She listened to the steady breathing of the other girls; a cough here, a gentle snore, a murmur there.

Then, above her head she heard a scuffling noise. A noise that was familiar to her and reminded her sharply of home.

In the darkness, Kate smiled.

She didn't remember falling asleep, but she awoke with a start to a piercing scream.

Immediately, pandemonium broke out.

'What's the matter?'

'Is it an air-raid?'

'There's a feller in here – must be!'

The door opened and the corporal flashed her torch around the hut. Isobel was standing on her bed shrieking, clutching her nightdress to her.

'Cartwright. Stop that noise at once.'

But the noise did not stop, if anything, the pitch heightened. Isobel was clearly genuinely terrified.

Kate swung her legs out of bed. On bare feet she padded across the wooden floor. Calmly she said, 'May I borrow your torch a mo, Corp?'

Handing it over, the officer said, 'Do you know what's the matter with her, Hilton?'

'I've a good idea.'

Kate left the room for a moment to delve in the cupboard outside the corporal's room. Now some of the other girls were getting decidedly nervous. 'Kate, bring the light back.'

'Won't be a minute. Hang on. Ah, here it is.'

She returned brandishing a broom. 'Now then, mester, let's be 'aving ya.'

'Heavens! Is it a man?' Mavis's voice broke in comically. 'I was only joking – at least I thought I was! '

'Let's just say it's an unwelcome visitor.'

257

'Something – fell – on my bed and,' Isobel stuttered 'and – ran across my legs!'

Kate turned the torch beam to the roof and ran the beam of light along the rafters. 'Ah,' she smiled her triumph. 'There you are, Mester Rat!'

The whole room erupted in screams. All the girls were now standing on their beds, pressing themselves back against the wall, staring with horrified eyes at the little creature crouching on one of the rafters, its bright eyes shining in the light from the torch. To Kate's amusement, even the corporal took a flying leap on to the nearest bed, nearly knocking the occupant off the other side.

Kate marched towards it and banged the rafter with the broom. The rat scuttled along the beam to the edge of the room, and the girl on the bed beneath squealed, jumped to the floor and leapt on to her neighbour's where bed they clung together, turning frightened eyes upwards.

'He's far more frightened of us than we are of him,' Kate said.

Mavis snorted. 'Wouldn't bank on that, Kate. Get rid of the bloody thing.'

Kate grinned. Mavis rarely swore. In fact few of the girls ever used bad language; the use of it now showed just how terrified they were.

The rat dropped to the floor and ran under the nearest bed. Kate pushed her broom underneath and the animal ran out the other side. Then it ran the full length of the hut.

'Open the door, Corp. It'll run out.'

'Not likely. I'm staying here.'

'Well, if I come down there,' Kate said reasonably, 'it'll run back this way.'

'Well, where is it now?' the corporal asked quaveringly.

'Under the bed opposite where you are.'

'But it might come out when I get on the floor.'

'It won't come for you. They don't come for you unless they're really cornered.'

'Well, for heaven's sake don't corner the bloody thing!' put in Mavis.

The corporal was stepping gingerly off the bed, clutching her nightclothes closely to her. 'J-just bring that broom up here, Hilton.'

'I've told you, if I come any nearer it'll start to run again. Look, Corp, just do it, will you?'

On bare feet the corporal tiptoed towards the door, her eyes fixed on the point where the rat might emerge from under the bed. The occupant of the bed was standing on it, peering with terrified eyes over the edge, convinced the animal would take a flying leap at her.

'Where is it?' she quavered.

'Keep quiet,' Kate ordered, 'else you'll frighten it.'

Mavis smothered an hysterical giggle. '*We'll* frighten *it*! That's a laugh.'

'Ssh!' The rest of the girls hissed.

The door was open and the corporal had never moved so fast in her life back to the safety of the nearest bed.

'And the outer one, Corp.'

'Oh, I can't, Hilton,' she wailed. 'Really I can't.'

Kate sighed. 'Is the door to your room open?'

'Oh Lor'!' the corporal squeaked. 'Yes. I left it open when I came flying in here to find out what all the racket was about.'

'That's why I want you to open the outer door,' Kate said reasonably. 'Oh, never mind, I'll do it myself.'

But as she moved down the room the rat ran out from under the bed. It came to the middle of the floor, stopped and turned wicked eyes upon Kate. It was a huge, brown mangy-looking creature. The frightened girls were whimpering, but clapping their hands over their mouths to keep from screaming out loud. Out of the corner of her eye, Kate saw Isobel slither down the wall on to her bed. 'Mavis – see to Cartwright. She's about to pass out,' Kate said in a matter-of-fact tone.

The rat was on the move again.

It ran first to the right, then to the left, and then seemed to become aware of the open door and went towards it.

'It's gone into your room, Corp. I thought it would.'

There was another wail from the corporal.

'It's all right, we'll soon have him out now.'

And she did. Having opened the outer door, it was a comparatively simple task to shoo the offending animal out into the night.

It took some time for them all to settle back to try to sleep, for they all insisted that Kate should scour the hut with her torch light to ensure there were no more unwelcome visitors.

By morning Isobel had regained her composure and was on the defensive. 'You enjoyed that last night, Hilton, didn't you? You actually enjoyed seeing us all squirm.'

Slowly Kate straightened up from bending over to make her bed to meet Isobel's resentful gaze. She was standing at the foot of the bed glaring at Kate.

Time seemed to take a tilt and, for a fleeting moment, Kate was once more the child in the cold, unfriendly dormitory facing the scathing expression of Isobel Cartwright.

Not this time, you don't, Kate thought. 'Yes, Cartwright,' she said quietly. 'There are people in this world who enjoy teasing others, seeing them squirm, as you put it.' As she was speaking, Kate opened the top drawer of her locker at the side of the bed and reached in. Her fingers closed over the wrinkled roundness of the whelk shell. Without taking her eyes off Isobel's face, she lifted it out and placed it in full view on top of the locker. 'Normally,' she went on softly, 'I'm not one of them.'

Kate saw Isobel's glance flicker towards the shell and become fixed upon it. She watched as a deep red flush crept up the girl's neck and suffused her face.

Isobel's voice was a strangled whisper. 'It *is* you!' They stared at each other, then Isobel said slowly. 'You said you'd get your own back one day, didn't you?'

Kate nodded, her gaze holding the other girl's relentlessly.

'Do . . .' Isobel began and then bit her lip. They were both aware that their conversation was being listened to with interest now by one or two of the others. ' . . . I mean . . .' Isobel was still struggling, but Kate waited, saying nothing. She was not a vindictive girl, but Isobel's taunts had cut deeply all those years ago and in the few days they'd been together again, Kate could see that Isobel had hardly changed. Her unkind attitude towards poor Edith had proved that.

She saw Isobel take in a deep breath. 'Would you agree to call it quits and – and make a fresh start . . .' Again she hesitated and then added, deliberately, ' . . . Kate?'

Kate picked up the shell, put it back in its place and closed the drawer. 'Suits me . . . Isobel.'

She guessed that Isobel found it hard to apologize or even to admit she had been in the wrong, but the expression in the girl's eyes and her muttered 'Thanks,' were enough for Kate. For her, one of the ghosts from the past had been confronted and laid to rest.

Two days later, Mavis said, 'D'you know, Kate, I think m'Lady Isobel is really starting to get the hang of things. She's *really* trying.'

'Very trying, I should think,' Kate laughed.

As they stacked their beds ready for kit inspection, Mavis asked, 'Er, what was all that about the other morning between you and her?'

'Oh, just a – a misunderstanding we had a while back. Best forgotten now.'

At that moment, saving Kate from having to answer more awkward questions, the door opened and the subject of their conversation came in, rubbing her hands together. 'Does this awful place have to be so cold? It must be freezing point in these huts.'

She walked the length of the hut, flapping her arms around herself, and came to stand close to the stove. 'How you can bear to sleep under that window, Kate, beats me.'

'I always liked to be able to see out,' Kate murmured, remembering the high, barred windows of the school dormitory. She glanced at Isobel, but the girl was touching the grey stove. 'It's cold!' she accused. 'Isn't it even lit?'

'Nope,' Mavis said. 'Not allowed to light it till five o'clock tonight.'

Isobel clicked her tongue against her teeth in exasperation and wrapped her arms around herself, tucking her hands under her armpits.

'We could go out and drill,' Mavis suggested impishly.

'No thanks,' Isobel replied shortly. She seemed about to move away and then hesitated and stopped. Her head dropped forward, her eyes downcast, she traced an imaginary pattern on the floor with the toe of her shoe. Without looking up and in a tone quite unlike her normal complaining voice, Isobel said, 'Mavis, I'm very grateful for your help in the Control Room.'

'Eh?" Mavis gawped at the bent head.

'Don't make me repeat it,' Isobel snapped, her tone returning to normal almost immediately. 'It's embarrassing enough for me to say it once!'

'Oh – er – yes.' Mavis was floundering, her plump cheeks turning pink. 'Well – you don't need to say anything, Isobel. We all help each other.'

'Well,' Isobel said, slightly mollified. 'I just wanted you to know I appreciate it, that's all.'

Kate listened to the interchange in amazement. Was Isobel Cartwright actually beginning to behave like a human being?

Mavis, still embarrassed, glanced towards the door as it opened and several girls came in, Edith amongst them. With relief at being given the chance to change the subject, Mavis called, 'What's the weather like, Edith? Is this fog going to lift?'

Edith came towards them, shaking her head. 'No. It looks like it's here for a couple of days at least. All aircraft are grounded. There won't be any operations and,' she smiled and Kate thought immediately how pretty Edith was when she lost her frightened-mouse look, ' . . . there shouldn't be any air-raids from the other side either.'

'Oh, Edith – you clever old thing!' Kate clapped her hands. Edith's cheeks were pink with pleasure as if she were being given the credit for having personally arranged the blanket of fog that lay over the strangely silent airfield. During the last few weeks, the girl had blossomed. Her short hair now gleamed glossily and curled prettily around her face which was not so white and pinched. She was still shy, but thanks to the efforts of Kate and Mavis, she was now included in all the activities and the humiliation surrounding her arrival was forgotten.

'She's not the only one to get nits!' Mavis had said in her blunt, matter-of-fact manner. 'My mother travelled home from London once in a filthy railway carriage and somehow, she got 'em. She nearly went mad! You should have seen us – she had us washing our hair every day for a fortnight – the whole family. Me dad threatened to shave his all off, if she carried on.' Mavis guffawed at the memory.

Isobel had said nothing, but even she made no more sarcastic remarks to Edith, and whilst she made no effort to befriend the girl, she made no objections when Mavis and Kate included Edith in what was fast becoming a foursome.

'So are we all getting a forty-eight-hour?' Isobel drawled now at the news.

'No – but almost as good as.' Mavis's eyes sparkled.

'Come on, Mave,' Kate said, 'we can see you're dying to tell us something.'

'The lads said if the fog didn't lift, they'd put on a dance in the Officers' Mess tomorrow night and we're all invited.'

There were whoops of delight and even Isobel's eyes gleamed.

'Back to earth, girls,' someone shouted from the end of the hut near the door. 'Stand by your beds. They're coming – kit inspection!'

As Isobel moved across to her own bed, she murmured, so that only Kate could hear, 'Have they got their rulers and scissors at the ready? Should we kneel down, do you think?'

Kate spluttered with laughter and Isobel gave her a rare, wide smile. Kate was still trying to stifle her giggles as the NCO and corporal entered the hut, but Isobel stood at the end of her bed, cool, calm and in complete control of her features.

'Shut up, Kate,' Mavis hissed. 'You'll get us all on a fizzer and then there'll be no dance in the Officers' Mess for any of us!'

She would never have believed it possible, Kate thought later, that she could have been laughing so uncontrollably over memories of St Mary's School for Young Ladies! And with – of all people – Isobel Cartwright!

*

As the four of them entered the Mess the following evening, Mavis gasped. 'It's like Christmas!'

The large room had been decorated with trimmings and balloons and at one end, on a raised dais, seven officers were setting up their musical instruments.

Mavis nudged Kate. 'Dave was telling me about them trying to get a band together. I say, he's a bit of all right on the drums, isn't he?'

'Really, Mavis – what about Dave?'

Mavis smiled. 'Oh, he'll do for me all right, but I was thinking about you.'

'Thanks very much – I can find me own fellers, ta!'

The newly formed band struck up, slightly hesitant at first, and then from the floor a young fair-haired Pilot Officer jumped up on to the dais and began to conduct. With more confidence, the players swung into 'We're going to hang out the washing . . .' The room began to fill and soon couples were moving on to the area cleared as a dance-floor.

Soon the girls, outnumbered by the men, were never without a partner. Kate found herself dancing with a tall, dark-haired man who danced woodenly round the floor, not speaking and holding her almost at arm's length. As they danced close to the dais, the fair-haired conductor jumped down and cut in. ''Scuse me, mate . . .' and Kate found herself looking up into his eyes as he took her hand and put his arm around her waist. 'Hello, there. My name's Sandy. What's yours, pretty WAAF?'

'K-Kate,' she gasped from surprise and now breathlessness too, for they were jigging round the floor at twice the speed of her previous pedestrian partner. 'What – what about the band?'

'Oh, they'll survive ten minutes without going to pieces completely.'

'Are you their conductor?'

'Not officially. I've done a bit in my time and I could see they needed a hand.' He grinned as he added, 'Literally!'

Kate laughed and shook back her hair which tonight she had left long.

'Has anyone ever told you you've got the most beautiful hair?' Sandy said.

'Oh, frequently,' she responded lightly, and although she did not resist when the band began to play 'Over the Rainbow' and Sandy pulled her into his arms again and rested his cheek against her hair, she could not help thinking, 'If only Danny could hold me like this'.

Then resolutely she pushed the thought of Danny Eland from her mind. Sandy seemed a nice boy with his open, honest face and laughing eyes. She'd seen him once or twice around camp when he'd given her a cheeky wink. Perhaps he could be the one to help her forget? Deliberately, she snuggled closer into his arms, closed her eyes and tried to let the soft, dreamy music engulf her.

On Tuesday evening when Kate parked the staff car and went into the station to meet Philip Trent, she found that his train from York had been delayed by an air-raid warning.

'I haven't a clue when it'll get here, Miss,' the ticket-office clerk told her, shrugging indifferently. 'It's getting harder and harder to keep to any sort of timetable these days. Trains come and trains go, Miss, that's all I can promise. But *when* – now that's a different matter.'

Kate pulled a face and then smiled at him. It wasn't this poor man's fault that the war was disrupting all his carefully planned timetables. It must be a nightmare for the railway staff at times, she thought. 'Well, thanks anyway. I'd better hang around. I wouldn't like to be missing when it does get here.'

The man pointed. 'There's a waiting room there and you might just wangle a cup of tea from the ladies over there.'

Kate turned to see that a train had just pulled into the station and a tidal wave of khaki was flowing on to the platform as troops spilled off the train. Set against the wall at the rear of the platform was a long trestle-table on which were numerous cups and a huge tea-urn. Behind the table two women in WVS uniform dispensed tea to the soldiers.

Kate nodded to the clerk. 'Thanks. I'll let the rush subside a little and then I'll see if they've any left.'

Half an hour later, Kate approached the two women. She had been standing a little way off watching them while they handed out cups of tea, always smiling, a cheery word for each soldier, and although the queue stretched right down the platform, they appeared calm and unhurried. But by the time Kate felt she could join the queue the two middle-aged ladies were red-faced and flustered and beads of sweat stood on their foreheads. Kate glanced up the track. There was no sign of the train she awaited, so she left the queue and pushed her way to the end of the table.

'Could you use another pair of hands?' she volunteered. The older of the two women turned to face her and Kate drew in a sharp breath.

She was staring straight into a face she knew. An older, more lined face, but there was no mistaking the gentle features of Miss Ogden.

Twenty-Five

Was she never to be free of that dreadful place, was her first shocked reaction, but when the initial surprise had subsided, Kate realized she was actually quite pleased to see Miss Ogden again.

'You don't remember me, do you?'

Miss Ogden was smiling apologetically. 'I expect you're one of our girls, but you do change so much . . .'

Kate took off her cap and her glorious auburn hair tumbled down to her shoulders.

Miss Ogden gasped. 'Oh! Oh – now I know.' She reached out with hands that trembled slightly. 'My dear Kate. How are you? Oh, I *am* pleased to see you.'

''Ow about a cuppa, darlin'?' a rough voice broke in and, distracted, Miss Ogden's hands fluttered without purpose. 'Oh, yes – er – of course. I'm sorry.'

Behind Kate another group of soldiers had joined the queue, swelling the demand for tea. She slipped behind the table and stood next to Miss Ogden. 'Here, let me help.' Immediately her hands deftly caught up a cup and held it under the tap of the urn. 'Where are you heading, soldier?'

The man grinned at her, showing yellow and misshapen teeth. He tapped the side of his nose. 'Can't tell you that, darlin'. You might be a bloomin' spy!'

Kate laughed gaily. 'Ya think this uniform'd be a good cover, do ya?' Without thinking, she had lapsed into her native dialect.

The man guffawed. 'I take it back. With an accent like that, you're one of us, all right.'

'Thanks.' Kate grinned back, knowing he meant it as a genuine compliment.

For the next ten minutes the three women worked side by side, and when at last the flood had subsided to a trickle, the other helper handed Kate a cup of tea. 'Here you are, me duck, you've earned that.'

Kate accepted it gratefully.

'You go and 'ave a sit down with yer friend, Elsie. I can manage the rest of 'em.'

'Well, if you're sure, Mabel...' Miss Ogden said tentatively.

''Course I'm sure – and take yerself a cuppa as well.'

'Oh, I'm so pleased to see you,' Miss Ogden said again, as they sat down in the waiting room together, their hands round the cups and sipping the hot tea. 'You look wonderful and that uniform suits you a treat. I've often thought of you over the years and wondered ... You had such a rotten time. I've often felt guilty I didn't do more.'

Kate smiled. 'You did as much as you could in the circumstances, I realize that now, and a lot more than anyone else there. Tell me,' she added suddenly. 'Was it you who put the sugar on the second helping of gooseberries that day?'

Shyly, Miss Ogden nodded. 'I couldn't believe she did that to you. I was horrified. I should have said more – done something ...'

Swiftly, Kate patted the older woman's knee. 'Please, don't worry any more about it. It might have made things even worse if you had.'

Miss Ogden sighed. 'That's true.' She paused, then added, 'I didn't blame you for running away, but I was so worried about you.'

'You went to see my relatives, didn't you?'

269

'Mrs – er – Godfrey, was it?' When Kate nodded, Miss Ogden continued, 'I didn't know if I'd done the right thing, because the poor woman flew into a panic. She said she'd just posted a letter to your people only half an hour beforehand . . .'

'Yes,' Kate murmured, remembering vividly the woman's kind and concerned letter.

'And the next day she sent a telegram and received a reply that you had arrived home.'

Kate grinned ruefully. 'I was wrong to do what I did – I realize that now – but at the time, I didn't think anyone would even care that I had gone.'

Miss Ogden gave a nervous laugh. 'Oh, there was pandemonium that night. But I suspect Miss Denham was more worried about the precious reputation of the school than about your welfare.'

Kate did a swift calculation in her head. Although obviously in the intervening years Miss Ogden had aged, she was nowhere near retirement age. 'Are you still there – at the school?'

Miss Ogden nodded and smiled ruefully. 'No doubt I shall finish my days there.'

They fell silent. Deliberately, Kate refused to ask about Miss Denham. There was nothing she wanted to know about that woman.

She opened her mouth to tell Miss Ogden that she had met up with Isobel Cartwright again too, but then she closed it. If Miss Ogden still felt so guilty even after all this time about the treatment Kate had received at the school, then hearing that she was once again in a kind of dormitory with one of her tormentors might fuel the woman's remorse.

Now Miss Ogden was asking Kate about herself, about her life in the WAAF. Relieved, Kate launched into telling her

270

about driving for the CO and why she came to be waiting on the station.

'And what did you do before joining up...?' Miss Ogden's question was drowned by the arrival of a train.

Kate jumped up. 'I'm sorry, I'd better go. That must be the one I'm waiting for.' Swiftly she took Miss Ogden's hands in hers and squeezed them. 'I'm so glad we've met. Perhaps I'll see you again some time. I often have to bring the CO here.'

'I hope so. Oh, I do hope so, Kate...' were Miss Ogden's final words.

When Philip Trent finally stepped off the train which was running over an hour and a half late, climbed into the car and flopped back against the leather seat, Kate did not have the heart to ask him to grant her leave. He looked exhausted. His eyes were dull, with dark shadows beneath them as if he had not slept since leaving five days earlier.

As if to confirm this he said, 'Just get me to my bed, Kate, will you?'

She glanced at him in the rear-view mirror. He was leaning his head back against the leather of the car seat, his eyes closed, his face gaunt with tiredness.

Kate sighed and pressed the starter. The noisy engine burst into life, cutting off any further chance of conversation.

As she drew up outside the CO's quarters, the sirens began to wail and almost immediately they saw enemy aircraft swooping in from the east, low and deadly.

'Out the car, Kate. Quick!'

Kate grabbed her tin hat, opened the door and launched herself from the car.

'I hope you can run – come on.' Philip grasped her arm and began to haul her along, but then Kate began to run –

really run – and he let go of her. When they reached the brick-lined trenches that served as an open-topped shelter, he was a couple of yards behind her. He was grinning as he joined her in the shelter, already crowded with airmen and WAAFs. 'Remind me never to ask you again if you can run!' he said. But his smile faded as, from the comparative safety of the shelter, they watched the enemy aircraft trying to destroy their station. Some aircraft were making a valiant effort to get into the sky, to escape being bombed where they stood on the ground. But the attack had been swift and sudden and the warning had come too late to allow evasive action.

Four planes managed to get into the air, but three on the ground were already in flames. Anti-aircraft guns pumped bullets at the enemy aircraft as they swooped and dived overhead. One enemy plane was hit and came down in a field just off the airfield's limits, bursting into flames on impact.

Horrified, Kate watched as a plane came in low, its black swastika clearly visible. It flew straight towards the control tower. She saw the bomb leave the belly of the aircraft, whistling down towards the tower, where Mavis and Isobel were on duty.

'Oh no!' Kate screamed and jumped up.

'Get down!' Philip shouted at her above the noise, grabbing her arm roughly and pulling her down again.

'But Mavis – and Isobel – they're in there. I know they are.'

Philip got up and pushed his way out of the trench. In an instant, Kate was right behind him.

'Stay there,' he commanded.

'No – I'm coming too . . .'

'Hilton – that's an order.'

Kate hesitated. It was a serious matter to disobey a direct order from her CO. Philip had turned away and began to run across the stretch of grass between the shelter and the control tower. Fire crews and medics were already running in the same direction. She saw Philip raise his arm to direct a crew towards the tower, one corner of which was badly damaged. Another enemy plane swooped low, aiming its nose directly at Philip as he ran. In his urgency to reach the control tower personnel, it was clear he had not even noticed the plane coming directly for him.

Kate screamed at him, 'Philip – look out!' but above the noise and confusion, she knew he could not hear her. She was up and out of the shelter and running after him before she knew what she was doing. The plane, directly in front of him, was coming closer, but the space between herself and Philip was narrowing too. She saw him glance up, see the aircraft, realize that its blazing guns were heading straight for him. He slowed his pace and hesitated, staring up at the plane. In that split second, Kate reached him, grasped his arm and pulled him a yard to the right. They fell to the ground together as the hail of bullets spattered the ground, pitting the earth exactly where he had been standing.

They lay there panting.

'I thought I told you – to – stay there,' he gasped, lying flat on his back.

Kate raised her head to look at him, disbelief on her face.

He got up and held out his hand to haul her to her feet. 'Looks like they're clearing off now. Out of ammo, I expect,' he said grimly.

He stood there for a brief moment amidst all the chaos, still holding her hand, looking down into her eyes. 'Kate Hilton,' he said softly, his voice a caress now, 'are you going to make a habit of saving my life?' Then he squeezed her hand. 'Come on, we'd better find your friends . . .'

The bomb had fallen on one corner of the control tower, demolishing the Signals Room and, below it, the Met Office.

There could easily have been as many as five people in the two rooms at the time, Kate knew. The Control Room, where Mavis and Isobel worked, looked, at first glance, comparatively unscathed, although the glass observation room on the roof was completely shattered and fragments were scattered everywhere.

Figures were staggering from the building, their faces grey with dust and hardly recognizable. Kate saw a tall, plump figure emerge, her arm about a girl whose sleek blonde hair was dishevelled. She had never seen Isobel Cartwright look such a mess.

Kate rushed forward. 'Mavis, are you all right? Isobel?'

'I'm okay,' Mavis gasped, 'but Isobel's got a cut on her face.'

Philip's deep voice spoke suddenly close by. 'Is everybody out of the place?'

'No,' Mavis said. 'We can't find Edith.'

'Where was she?'

'In the Met Room,' Mavis said.

Already people were digging at the rubble. 'Go carefully,' Philip shouted. 'There may be people still alive but trapped.' He turned back to the three girls and, nodding towards the wilting Isobel, said, 'Look after her. I'll have to get back to my office – if it's still standing – and see if I can organize some help. Kate – you stay here. I want you to act as my runner . . .' He paused briefly, and looked at her. Even in the midst of all the devastation, a small smile quirked the corner of his mouth at the aptness of the task he was giving her. No one else he knew could run as fast as Kate Hilton. 'Keep me informed of everything that's going on, will you?'

Kate nodded. 'Yes, sir.'

*

Two hours later they found the bodies; there were three. An airman and two WAAFs. One was Edith.

'She wouldn't have known what hit her, Kate,' Philip said gently, when she burst, breathless, into his office, her eyes wide, her cap stuffed into her pocket and her hair flying free, all protocol forgotten in her agitation.

'Here, sit down . . .' He pushed her firmly into a chair and closed the door between them and the outer office. 'You could do with a drink.' From the drawer of his desk he took a bottle and two glasses.

'Oh, I didn't ought . . .'

'I know, I know,' he said impatiently. 'You're on duty and you didn't ought to drink, specially not with your CO. But this is for medicinal purposes only.' Holding out the glass to her, he added, 'And it's an order. Perhaps it's one you won't mind obeying – for once.'

Kate was still shaking, her hands felt cold and clammy. Seeing Edith's lifeless body, covered in dust, being dragged from the wreckage, had made her feel physically sick.

'No – I mean – I didn't ought to because – because it goes to my head a bit quick.'

'My dear girl, I'm not suggesting you should get roaring drunk.'

'No, but I – I tend to talk too much even when I've only had a little.'

He came and sat on the corner of the desk, just above her. Gently he picked up her hand and put the glass into it, making sure she was gripping it before he let go.

'Well, I'm listening,' he said softly. 'It's no bad thing to talk.' He sighed. 'I wish I had someone to talk to sometimes. I'm finding command is a very lonely occupation.'

She looked up at him, meeting his gaze. Deep in his eyes there was anxiety. Suddenly, she understood the loneliness of his position and all its responsibilities. No wonder he often looked tired and seemed withdrawn.

She had lost a friend in Edith, for whom she would grieve, but Philip had lost several personnel in his charge and at least three aircraft, and his airfield had been shot to pieces. It was his responsibility to get his station operational as soon as possible. And there would undoubtedly be questions asked about whether correct procedures had been observed before and during the raid and, worst of all to face, whether anything could have been done that hadn't been to minimize the damage.

She gulped the liquid in the glass. 'I'm sorry, you must have lots to do, I'll . . .'

He smiled, but it was a sad, forlorn smile. 'That's the better side of being in command. One can delegate, you know. I've done everything I can for the moment.' His eyes clouded. 'I need a few moments myself. Soon I shall have to write some very difficult letters.'

Of course, now there was no question of anyone on the station having any leave, except perhaps on compassionate grounds. And in all truthfulness, Kate could not say that going home to meet Danny fell into that category. But how she longed to lean her head against his shoulder and feel the comfort of his arms around her and tell him just how she felt, knowing he would understand completely.

Philip Trent, in his capacity as Station Commander, decided to attend the funerals of those who had been killed. Clearance was given for Edith's body to be transported home to Nottingham, and the day before her funeral, Philip called Kate into his office.

'I know it's maybe not usual, but you've probably guessed I don't always go by the rule-book.' He grinned at her, and, at ease, she smiled back. 'I want you to drive me to ACW Brownlow's funeral tomorrow, so I was wondering if you'd like to attend the service too?'

'Yes, I would. Thank you.'

He nodded. 'This is where the – er – rule-book gets thrown out of the window. If your two friends would like to come along too, you have my permission to ask them. I can arrange for them to alter their shifts if necessary.'

'Oh, thank you. I'm sure they would like to. The four of us had got quite close.' She was almost surprised to hear herself voicing the fact that she looked upon Isobel Cartwright as a friend. But it was true – now.

Philip nodded again, his face serious. 'I know.' He sighed. 'You make a lot of good friends in this kind of life, all thrown together. But – when something like this happens, well, being close makes it extra painful.'

He really is an understanding man, Kate thought, marvelling as she ran towards the WAAF site and her hut.

'Did he really say that?' Mavis asked incredulously when Kate repeated Philip's offer to her two friends.

Isobel sat on her bed and blew smoke rings into the air, savouring her new packet of cigarettes; it had been pay day the previous day. 'He's different – I'll say that for him,' she observed.

'All the chaps like him too,' Mavis put in. 'Dave says . . .'

Kate and Isobel gave a mocking groan, but Mavis only grinned and went on, 'Dave says they really admire him 'cos he can keep authority and yet be human at the same time.'

Isobel glanced at Kate, sharing the past for a moment. 'Not an easy thing to do,' Isobel murmured.

'So I take it you'll come.'

They both nodded. 'Poor old Edith – it's the least we can do.'

Sadly, Kate sighed. 'It's *all* we can do.'

The car journey to Nottingham was a little strained. Philip, sitting beside Kate in the front, said little, and, taking their cue from him, the two WAAFs in the back seat were silent.

They stood in the rain awaiting the funeral cortège which was already late. Then, as it appeared around the corner, they saw a strange procession walking behind the slow-moving vehicle. A man led the way, lurching from side to side, with a tiny, bird-like woman walking behind him carrying a child of eighteen months or so. Behind her straggled five more children of various ages and sizes. A tall, lanky youth, incongruously still in short trousers; a girl in a coat which was far too big for her, the hem flapping round her ankles; and three smaller children, one with jam smeared across his mouth, another with his nose running and grey socks wrinkled around his ankles. Kate glanced at Isobel, but she was staring fixedly ahead, deliberately ignoring the family.

The man came and stood in front of them. 'You 'ere for our Edie's funeral?' The smell of alcohol wafted into their faces.

'That's right, sir. My name's Trent – your daughter's Commanding Officer.'

The man wiped the back of his hand across his mouth and then proffered it to be shaken. Without a flicker, Philip took it and shook it firmly.

''Ow do?' the man said gruffly, then he jerked his thumb over his shoulder. 'The wife and kids,' he added, rather unnecessarily, Kate thought.

Philip inclined his head towards Mrs Brownlow and her brood. Standing a pace or so behind their CO, the three WAAFs were able to avoid shaking hands with Mr Brownlow, as the party, now complete it seemed, moved towards the church porch. As they fell in behind the coffin, Isobel muttered, 'Now we know why she had nits!'

'Shut up, Iso!' Kate hissed between her teeth as they passed through the porch and into the musty interior of the church.

The service was conducted in a swift, unfeeling monotone. It was obvious that the vicar knew neither Edith nor any member of her family and Kate felt a surge of pity for the girl as her coffin was lowered into the grave. As the party moved away, Edith's father said loudly, 'I told 'er she'd come to no good, joining up. She had a good job – a safe job – in a factory. What did she 'ave to go and join up for? Officers' groundsheets, that's all them WAAFs are. I told 'er.' He glared accusingly at the three girls in uniform as if he held them personally responsible for his daughter's death.

'She wanted to make something of herself, Bert.' The woman looked up at Philip, appealing for support. 'She was a good girl, sir. Not like 'ee's makin' out.'

Philip nodded at the woman, his voice gently sympathetic. 'She was a clever girl, Mrs Brownlow, and well thought of, I promise you. We shall all miss her.'

The woman's eyes filled with tears and she nodded, a swift, pecking movement, hitched up the child in her arms and turned away. The children followed her while Edith's father, with a last baleful glare at the officer and three girls in uniform, sniffed, wiped his hand across his mouth once more, turned away without a glance at his departing family and shuffled off down the road in the opposite direction towards the swinging sign of a pub.

'Good grief! What a family!' Isobel could contain herself no longer as they got back into the car. 'Ooh, sorry, sir.'

'That's all right.' Philip took off his peaked cap and ran his hand through his springy hair. 'Thank goodness that's over. Let's get going, Kate.'

As Kate started the car she heard the gasp of surprise from the back seat at Philip's use of her Christian name. Once out of the city, Philip relaxed and leaned back in the corner of the front seat, half-turned towards the two girls in the back, his arm along the back of the bench seat.

'In the confines of this car, we're unofficial,' he grinned. 'My name's Philip and you're . . .?'

'C-Cartwright and Nuttall,' Mavis stuttered.

In the rear-view mirror, Kate could see Mavis's eyes were nearly popping out of their sockets.

'No, no, Christian names, please.'

'Isobel – and I'm Mavis.'

'Well, Mavis and Isobel, just so long as we're very official when we get back to the station, eh?'

'Oh yes, sir.' Mavis gasped. 'Of course.'

'Now, Kate, if you can find us a quiet, out-of-the-way pub on the way back I'll treat you girls to a spot of lunch.'

The atmosphere relaxed at once and soon Mavis had them in fits of laughter with stories about the antics her young brother had got up to in his efforts to join up at fifteen. 'My mother wanted Dad to leather him, but Dad just smiled and said he wished he could join up again himself. He was in the last lot and got gassed . . .'

Kate was silent, but vague memories of her own father flickered through her mind; hazy pictures of an emaciated figure shaking uncontrollably. In her memories Danny was there and they were walking down the lane at home, one on either side holding the hands of the man they now knew had been the father of the them both.

Over lunch, Kate was amused to notice that Isobel positioned herself next to Philip, engaging him in conversation, tilting her head to one side coyly as she listened, intensely interested in whatever he was saying.

'Well, ladies,' he said at last, 'I'm sorry to break this up, but we must be getting back . . .'

'Oh, isn't he *nice*?' Mavis said later, when they had returned to camp.

'Is he married?' Isobel asked, and when Kate glanced at her, she saw a cool, calculating look in Isobel's eyes.

'I can't find out anything,' Mavis said in disgust. 'Even Dave doesn't know, and normally what he *doesn't* know isn't worth knowing! I know he comes from the York area, but honestly, that seems to be all anyone can find out about him.'

'Mmm,' Isobel said and her eyes took on a faraway look.

A week later a letter came from Danny containing anxious inquiries as to Kate's safety. Although he was avoiding putting anything in writing directly, it was obvious he knew about the terrible raid on Suddaby airfield.

'*Please write back at once and let me know you're safe.*' His concern gave her a warm glow, but in contrast the rest of his letter left her with the cold chill of being excluded from a happy event.

'*It was a shame,*' he wrote, '*that you couldn't get leave the same time as me. We had a great time.*'

We, who was 'we'? The next line made it clear.

'*I took Rosie dancing in town, or rather – if I'm truthful – Rosie took me! She really is a great kid and fun to be with. All the fellers are around her like bees round a honeypot, but she danced with me all evening and made an old man feel young again!*'

Kate smiled as she read the letter. Fool! she thought, he's only nine years older than Rosie and yet he talks as if she's still a child. Then her smile faded and her glance went to the window. Her hands, still holding the letter, lay in her lap. She looked out across the gently rolling landscape. But

Rosie was no longer a child. She was a young woman who liked to flirt and have a good time. And she had spent a weekend with Danny.

For the first time in her life, Kate felt a tinge of jealousy towards Rosie Maine.

In her reply posted the same day, Kate promised she would get leave the very next time he did. *'Then we can go home together. I do miss you so, and I've so much to tell you.'* She paused, her pen wavering above the page, knowing that what she was going to write next was unfair, possessive when she had no right to be, and yet she could not help herself.

'And if it doesn't work out and I can't get leave, maybe you could come and stay somewhere near here instead of going home.'

Kate ignored her conscience and posted the letter quickly.

A whole month went by and she did not hear from Danny. Now it was her turn to worry that something might have happened to him.

Twenty-Six

'I know what we ought to do,' Mavis said in her best organizing voice. 'We ought to go to a dance in Lincoln.'

Kate gasped and Isobel looked disdainful. 'Do you think that's appropriate in the circumstances?' Her glance flickered over the empty bed that had been Edith's. No one had arrived yet to fill it.

'Edith wouldn't have wanted us to mope about it. What matters is that we should remember her.'

'I suppose you're right,' Kate said, and even Isobel shrugged.

'If I can fix it up with some of the lads, we'll go into Lincoln next Saturday night. There's bound to be a dance going on somewhere. Dave'll know.' With that Mavis whirled about and was gone from the hut, banging the door behind her, without giving Kate or Isobel any time to argue further.

Kate shook her head, smiling fondly after her friend. Then she reached into her locker for her writing pad.

'*Dear Danny,*' she began. '*My new friend Mavis – you'd like her, she's so jolly – has bullied us into going to a dance in Lincoln on Saturday night. How I wish you were nearer and could go too!*'

Isobel eased her last pair of silk stockings over her shapely legs with tender care. 'If anyone ladders these tonight at the dance, I'll get them put on a charge.' She turned to look at

Kate who was still sitting on her bed. 'Are you getting ready or what?'

'I – I don't think I'll come,' Kate faltered. Most of the girls not on duty were going to the dance in Lincoln, but Kate wasn't in the mood. She'd had no reply from Danny to her last two letters and was just beginning to feel a little uneasy about his safety.

Mavis, hands on hips, came and stood over her. 'Oh yes, you are, my girl, so you'd better look slippy and get ready.'

Adopting that stance, Mavis reminded Kate so sharply of her mother that she burst into laughter. 'Oh, all right then. I'll come.'

She levered herself off the bed, gathered her things together to get washed, put on a clean shirt and brush her uniform.

Mavis had not moved away but was still hovering near Kate's bed. 'I hope you're not going to bawl me out,' she said, chewing the side of her thumb.

'Now what have you done?' Kate said in mild exasperation.

'I've fixed the three of us up with Dave and a couple of his mates.'

'Oh, I'll take Dave, then,' Isobel said airily.

'Keep off, Cartwright. He's mine, and you too, Kate Hilton, with those green eyes of yours.'

'Sounds like you've got the "green eye" over him yourself,' Isobel drawled, and Kate said, 'Oh, I get it! We get the pimply friends, do we? I'd sooner go with Sandy.'

'Eh?'

'You know, the navigator in T-Tommy.'

'Oh yes, I know him. Sorry – he's on leave, evidently.'

Kate pulled a face. 'On second thoughts, then, I reckon I will give it a miss . . .'

'Oh no you won't, when I've spent the last couple of days running round like a headless chicken fixing it all up.'

'Nobody asked you to,' Isobel put in tartly, but Mavis ignored her.

'There's the three of them,' she went on. 'My Dave, Johnny and Brian. Johnny's a bit of a lad, but Iso will handle him. And Brian's nice. Besides, he's – er – married.'

'I see – I get lumbered with the nice safe ones, do I?' Kate pretended huffiness.

'Well, to be honest,' Mavis wriggled her shoulders with embarrassment, not realizing, for once, that Kate was teasing her, 'the way you talk – I thought you'd want it that way. I mean—' she was floundering now. 'The way you talk about this Danny, I thought he was your boyfriend – someone special.'

'He's very special,' Kate said softly, 'but he's not my boyfriend.'

Mavis looked puzzled. 'Oh. Then . . .?'

'That's enough questions for one night,' Kate laughed, and linking arms, the friends ducked out into the night to dash across to the ablutions through the drizzle.

Kate was wishing heartily that she had not come. She had never learned to dance properly, and the local girls in their pretty dresses with their hair curled into the latest styles, made her think of Rosie. Thinking of Rosie made her think of home and, of course, thinking of Fleethaven Point made her think of Danny.

Brian – her blind date for the evening – proved to be not spotty and shy, but overweight, extremely loud and far too familiar for such a short acquaintance.

'Oh Kate, do let yourself go a bit, for heaven's sake,' Mavis hissed, snuggling closer to Dave, who sat with one arm draped around her, leaving the other free for lifting his beer glass with frequent regularity.

'You seem to be doing enough "letting go" for all of us,' Kate snapped back.

'Don't be such a prude!' the good-natured Mavis laughed. Morosely, Kate wondered if it was even possible to offend Mavis.

'I quite agree with Kate,' Isobel put in, crossing her legs and puffing elegantly on a cigarette which she had inserted into a long ebony holder. Her blonde hair was smoothed back into a neat pleat and, despite the uniform, she looked like a model off the front of a pre-war fashion magazine. She had taken an instant dislike to her date and had despatched him with icy politeness to try his luck elsewhere. Isobel looked so incongruous sitting there amidst the smoke and the spilled beer, coolly fending off any young man who dared to approach her with an invitation to dance, that watching her, Kate was suddenly overcome by a fit of the giggles.

'That's better.' Mavis leaned forward and whispered in her ear, jerking her head in Isobel's direction. 'We can only cope with one killjoy at a time.'

To her surprise, Kate began to enjoy the evening. It was not the local girls in their pretty, feminine dresses who attracted the attentions of the young men but the girls in uniform, and, once she decided to join in, Kate found herself never without a partner. Without causing any offence, she skilfully managed to steer clear of Brian for most of the evening. Before long, her feet were aching and she was sure she had left a few bruised toes where she had trodden on her partners' feet. It hardly mattered that she couldn't dance well, because there was scarcely room to do so anyway. But the atmosphere was wonderful; she had never known anything like it before. Everyone seemed so happy, so carefree. It was hard to believe that some of those young men singing heartily, their arms draped casually around a couple of WAAFs, might be flying over enemy territory dropping bombs by this time tomorrow night.

And some would not be coming back.

Kate shuddered. Suddenly, amidst all the jollity, she felt lonely. It was all false, a forced gaiety to hide their fear, their terror of tomorrow. But what else could these brave young men do? Sit around moping, waiting for death in the morning? No, this was their way of being courageous; it was the only way they knew.

The music seemed to grow louder, the laughter became strident; Brian's arm around her was suddenly too tight, the smoky atmosphere oppressive, cloying and stifling. She wanted to push her way through the crowd and escape into the fresh air. A sudden longing for the peace and tranquillity of the end of the Spit overwhelmed her. The desire would not be wholly denied. Kate gave a little sob and thrust herself away from Brian's clutch.

'Hey, what did I do?' he asked, bemused.

'Nothing, nothing,' she mouthed above the noise. She put a hand to her head. 'I must get some – air.'

He grinned stupidly at her, misinterpreting her reasons. Lurching towards her, he grabbed her arm again. 'What a good idea,' he leered.

Kate twisted herself from his grasp. 'No!' She pulled away from him, knocking against the couple dancing nearby. The whole dance-floor was crowded now, there was scarcely room to move.

'Aw, now don't be a spoilsport . . .' he began. Blindly, Kate turned away, but found her face pressed against another blue uniform, the buttons digging into her cheek. Two arms were around her holding her tightly. She gave a cry and began to struggle.

'Kate – it's me . . .'

With a gasp of surprise, she pulled her head back to find herself looking directly into a pair of laughing brown eyes.

'Danny, oh Danny!' And she flung her arms around him.

Behind her, her former dance partner shrugged philosophically. 'Oh well, I know when I'm beaten. Hope you have better luck than I did, mate.'

Danny pushed his way through the throng, with Kate in his wake. When they reached the edge of the floor, he said, 'Come on, let's get out of here,' and together they almost burst through the doors of the hall and out into the open air.

'Whew! I don't think I could have stood another minute!' Danny took great gulps of air. 'It's worse than being in the belly of a Manchester!'

'What are you doing here? How did you know where to find me? How did you get here?'

'Rescuing you, in answer to your first question. And not a moment too soon, by the look of it. As for your second question, you told me in your letter. Forgotten already?' he teased gently. 'And your last question – by truck, like you, I expect.'

'But I thought you were miles away.'

His grin broadened. 'My squadron's just been moved to East Markham.' In the darkness she could not see his face, but she could hear the excitement in his voice. He made no effort to conceal it.

'East Markham! Why, that's only a few miles from Suddaby.'

'I know.' He put his arm casually around her shoulders as they walked along the street. The pavements were wet now with a fine drizzle. 'We'd best get out of this, else we'll end up soaked. There's a pub over there. It might not be too crowded. Let's try it.'

Pushing open the door to the bar, they were met by that unmistakable pub smell, a mixture of beer and smoke. Four old men sat in one corner playing dominoes and the barmaid leaned against the bar examining her long painted nails in close detail. She straightened up as Danny approached the bar, and smiled.

'I was beginning to think I'd 'ave to close up an' go home. All our regulars is at the dance.' She pulled a face and it was obvious the girl wished she were there too. 'What'll it be, love?'

Danny ordered a beer for himself and a shandy for Kate. As he carried them across to her and placed them on a small round table, he jerked his head towards the opposite corner. 'Reminds you of me dad and old Tom Willoughby playing dominoes in their usual corner in the Seagull, dun't it?'

The barmaid had gone back to leaning against the bar and had resumed her nail examination.

Kate smiled as she sipped her drink. 'And you – given half a chance.'

He grinned and then sighed. 'What I'd give sometimes to be safely back at Fleethaven Point playing dominoes with the old 'uns! I had a game with 'em last time I was home.'

'Have – you flown any missions yet?'

He twisted the glass round and round as it stood on the table, staring at it but not really seeing it. The frothy beer slopped from side to side in the glass. 'Yup,' he answered shortly.

'Is it very bad?'

There was silence for a moment. 'Varies.'

She leaned forward. 'Danny. It's me – Kate. You can talk to me about it.'

He sighed deeply. 'It's not that, Katie, you know I'd tell you. But – well – we all like to try to forget about it for a while when we're out. Y'know.'

'Oh, I see,' she said, but her tone indicated the opposite. He was leading a different life now, a life in which she had no part and he was reluctant to tell her about it. She felt resentful.

Sensing her mood, he grinned. 'Come on, Katie. Let's go for a walk up the hill, eh? It's stopped raining.'

Mollified a little, she agreed.

They climbed Steep Hill, their arms linked casually, talking when they felt like it, or just in companionable silence.

'Tell me how things are at home. Have you managed any leave recently?' he asked her.

'No – not since you were there. It was difficult – after the air-raid.' She was silent for a moment, thinking about Rosie, seeing in her mind's eye the girl in the shadows of the pillbox with a soldier.

'You were right about Rosie,' she murmured.

She felt his arm stiffen under hers. 'Rosie? What about Rosie?'

She couldn't see his face in the blackness, but there was a strange note in his tone, almost like a defensiveness.

Kate was silent. She was remembering now Rosie begging her not to tell Danny. Of all people, she didn't want Danny to know. Kate felt guilty, wishing she had kept quiet. She'd had a little too much to drink, that was the trouble; her mouth was apt to say what it liked.

'Kate?' he prompted. He was not going to let it rest there.

'Oh, it's nothing. She just flirts about a bit. You know.'

He stopped and turned to face her, taking hold of her shoulders, peering at her through the darkness. 'No, I don't know. You tell me.'

I – I caught her in that pillbox the army has built at the Point – with one of the soldiers.'

For a moment, his fingers dug into her arms. Then he let go.

'Well, I'm not having that. Next time I go home, I'll sort her out – an' him, if need be.'

'Oh Danny, don't be stupid. I wish I hadn't told you.'

'I'm glad you did. I wouldn't want to see young Rosie getting 'ersen into trouble.'

'And how are we going to stop her? We're not there.'

'I'll think of something,' Danny muttered.

They walked along in silence, Kate wishing she hadn't let her unruly tongue run away with itself.

'We'd better be getting back to the dance hall. It must be getting late.'

They turned and walked back down the hill, their footsteps echoing hollowly on the cobbles.

When they arrived back at the hall, the caretakers were clearing up. There was no sign of any of their friends.

And worse still – all the transport trucks had disappeared.

Twenty-Seven

'Oh heck! Now what are we going to do?' Danny muttered, while Kate stared in horror at the spot where the trucks had been parked. There was not a vehicle of any sort to be seen.

'Come on,' Danny said. 'We'll start walking and see if we can hitch a lift.'

'Not likely,' she argued, finding her voice. 'I've tried that once before. I'm not walking all that way . . .'

'What do you mean, you've done it before?' he asked, a belligerent note in his voice. 'When?'

'When I ran away from school – remember? I walked for miles, got soaking wet – and lost! There'll be nothing come along at this time of night to give us a lift. Shouldn't think that carrier of mine's out at this hour – even if he's still around.'

'Don't be daft, Kate. That's years ago. It's a fine night – no rain. You're not a fourteen-year-old kid any more, and besides . . .'

She could hear the amusement in his voice and although she couldn't actually see it, knew he was smiling. 'What?'

'You've got *me* with you this time!'

'Ah well,' she said, laughing and linking her arm through his again. 'That makes all the difference!'

'I don't know what we're laughing for, 'cos there's going to be hell to pay when we get back – it'll be jankers at the very least for both of us.'

292

'Oh, I'll be all right,' Kate said confidently. 'I'm the CO's pet driver.'

You wouldn't think so, Kate was thinking to herself the next morning as she faced a livid Philip Trent across his desk, or that I'd saved his life – twice!

She was standing to attention, so rigidly that her back began to ache. It was like waiting for sentence to be passed. In this mood he was going to throw the book at her and, most likely, at her section commander too. She and Danny had walked up Steep Hill and out on to the Wragby Road. They'd only had to walk a couple of miles before they had hitched a lift to within two miles of Suddaby camp. Danny left her at the gate and disappeared into the night to get back to his own station. She wondered how he was faring now, up before his own CO!

Kate had reported to the guardroom, praying that it was Isobel's friend on duty. But her luck had run out; the man was a stranger to her and one who obviously stuck rigidly to the rule book.

She had been reported to Chiefy for being half an hour late.

'Oh Kate,' Martin moaned at her, running his hand across his bald pate. 'You would make life difficult. I can hardly confine you to barracks for a couple of days when you're the CO's driver.' He'd sighed and fiddled with his pen on the desk. 'Look, I'll let it go this time. But we'll have to hope the CO doesn't hear about it, or we're both in trouble.'

And now she was standing facing Group Captain Trent and wondering how on earth he had heard about her escapade.

'Everyone else got back on time. Where were you?' Philip barked, his handsome face creased with angry lines.

'We took a walk, sir.'

'We? Who's we?'

'Danny Eland, sir.'

'Oh!' For a moment he seemed nonplussed. 'That's – er – Danny from home?'

'Yes, sir.'

'I – didn't realize he was stationed nearby.'

Kate remained silent, her gaze fixed on the top button of his jacket. Philip ran his hand distractedly through his short, springy hair. 'I was worried sick, Kate. Don't ever do that to me again.'

'What?' she could not prevent the surprise in her tone. His remark – nor the tone in his voice now – was not that of a commanding officer. Then she recollected herself. 'No, sir.'

He stood up and came round the desk. 'You can stop standing there like you're on parade now.'

She relaxed and, for the first time, met his eyes. The anger had gone, but the anxiety still lingered. 'A girl was injured last week walking back to camp in the night. It was an accident, of course, but in the blackout, the driver didn't see her,' he explained softly. 'I couldn't get it out of my mind when I knew you weren't back.'

'How did you know I wasn't back?' she asked in a small voice.

He smiled now, a little sheepishly, Kate thought. 'Oh, I – er – sent for you. Your friends tried to cover for you valiantly, but it was obvious you weren't there and that they didn't know where you were.'

'I'm sorry. Did you want driving somewhere?'

'No,' he said, but did not offer any further explanation.

Kate was thankful that Philip took no further action against her or Flight Sergeant Martin, although it rather surprised her. He had been so very angry at first, yet his fury seemed to stem from anxiety about her safety rather than that she had broken the rules.

She doubted Danny had been so fortunate and she waited anxiously for a letter. But the days went by, a week and then two, and no word came from Danny.

'The Adj has just rung through,' Chiefy bent his head under the raised bonnet of the Humber where Kate was changing the plugs. 'CO's been summoned to a high level meeting at Group HQ. You're likely to be very late back . . .' He grinned at her. '*Officially*, this time!'

'Sir!' Kate smiled and connected the final plug. She packed up her tool kit, wiped her hands on a rag and then sprinted to the wash-room.

Seven hours later she was dozing fitfully in the car parked in the sweeping driveway of Group Headquarters when the sudden sound of someone opening the passenger door and climbing in made her jump.

'Oh, I'm sorry, sir . . .'

'Don't apologize, Kate,' Philip said gently, his voice heavy with tiredness. 'I hope you haven't been sitting here all this time. Have you had something to eat?'

'Oh yes, I've been fine. I only came back to the car about an hour ago when I heard the meeting was breaking up.'

'Yes. Sorry about that, I got caught up with the CO from East Markham. I'm afraid he needs a lift back, Kate. His car broke down on the way here. He'll be here in a minute.'

Wearily, Philip removed his hat and ran his fingers through his thick hair that curled so tightly each curl was like a coiled spring. He leaned his head back against the seat and closed his eyes.

'Er, shouldn't you really sit in the back, sir?' Kate said

hesitantly, reluctant to disturb him, but if they were to have company in the car . . .

His head snapped up and his eyes opened. 'Oh Lord, yes.' As he opened the door and swung his legs out, Kate was sure she heard him mutter, ' . . . and I was so looking forward to sitting in front with you.'

By the time Group Captain Sellick appeared and Kate hopped out to open the door for him, Philip was sitting sedately in the back seat.

'This is very decent of you, Trent.'

'Not at all,' she heard Philip reply as they left Grantham and headed out into the black country road. The moonlight was only fitful as heavy clouds scudded across it. One moment the landscape was bathed in silvery light, the next plunged into pitch blackness. Thank goodness for all that rigorous night driving during training, Kate thought.

Suddenly she slammed both her feet down hard on the brake and the clutch pedal as a black shape loomed up directly in front. The heavy car slithered to the right, throwing the occupants sliding about the back seat.

'What the devil?' she heard one of them mutter as the car came to a halt on the grass verge. Kate half turned her head to see the sorrowful faces of several cows pressed close to the car windows.

'Ahem – it seems they have us surrounded,' Group Captain Sellick said, making no effort to move.

Kate was out of the car and closing the door behind her. 'Come on, cush, cush. Now where have you lot come from, I wonder?' Out in the night air, her eyes became more accustomed to the darkness. She moved among the cows, gently pushing them. 'There, there, girl . . . Ah, now I see.' Dimly, in the fitful moonlight, she could see that the hedge into a nearby field had been trampled down. 'And I see you've brought Dobbin with you too, have you?' she added, laughing softly to herself as she saw a cart-horse amongst the herd.

Slapping the rump of the nearest cow, she turned it and shooed it back towards the opening, all the time murmuring soothing encouragement. Thankfully, she saw the rest of the herd turn and follow the lead of the first cow.

'Want any help?' she heard Philip call.

'Can you get hold of the horse and bring him along?' she called back. 'They've got out of a hole in the hedge here. He must have been in the same field.'

He seemed to hesitate a moment before he said, 'Right.'

It took a good twenty minutes to get all the cows back into the field and lastly the horse, who seemed the most reluctant of all to return.

'Come on, boy,' Kate said, letting him nuzzle her hand. 'I'd have brought a sugar lump if I'd known we were going to meet like this.'

Philip's voice came out of the blackness. 'Oh, I don't mind about the sugar.'

Kate giggled. 'Careful, he might hear you . . .'

'Not him! He's staying safely in the car. You'd never think he was a DFC and yet daren't get in amongst a herd of cows.'

'Can you grab hold of his mane on your side? Come on, boy.' There was a pause while they struggled to get the horse to move. Suddenly it shot forward, through the hole and into the field.

'Thank goodness,' Kate breathed relief. Together they turned to walk back towards the car.

Philip sneezed three times in quick succession. 'Maybe he's getting ready to award *you* the DFC.' Through the darkness she heard his deep chuckle. 'Not the Distinguished Flying Cross, of course. I was thinking more of something like . . . Dispersing Frightening Cows.'

Reaching the car, Kate stifled her laughter. As she started

the engine, Group Captain Sellick asked casually, 'Brought up on a farm, were you, driver?'

'Yes, sir.'

'Ah – that explains it then.'

Beside him, Philip sneezed again – three times.

When they delivered their passenger to East Markham, Kate thought fleetingly that maybe Danny was quite close . . . Then, in the dim light, Kate's attention was caught by the sight of a dark patch on the right side of Philip's face. And he was still sneezing every few minutes. As they pulled away from the gate, she asked with concern, 'Are you all right, sir?'

'Kate – we're on our own now. Drop all this "sir" nonsense. Yes, thanks, I'm fine.' He didn't sound it, she thought. He sounded as if he had suddenly developed a dreadful head cold.

'But – your face . . .?'

'It's only a rash. It was the horse.'

Mystified, she repeated, 'The horse?'

'I get a kind of hay-fever when I get near horses and dogs.'

'Really? Oh, I am sorry. I wouldn't have asked you to help if I'd known.'

'It's nothing. It'll wear off after a time.'

'And the rash on your face . . .?'

'I touched the horse and then my face. It's all part of the allergy.' He grinned. 'Pull over a minute. I think I'll sit up front with you – at least until we get back near camp. I rather like sitting next to you, *Corporal* Hilton.'

'Pardon?'

'Oh yes,' Philip said airily as he got in beside her. 'I've recommended you for promotion. You'll be made up to corporal next week.'

Kate was thankful for the darkness for she knew her face was pink with pleasure.

*

'You should have seen the East Markham CO sitting rigidly in the middle of the back seat, hardly daring to move!' Kate regaled the others with her story later that night. 'And then poor old Ph . . .' Quickly she corrected herself. 'Our poor old CO, when he got out to help me, started sneezing his head off. Seems he gets a type of hay-fever from horses and dogs.'

Mavis was nodding. 'My dad does and so does my younger brother. It can be hereditary, evidently.'

'Really?' Kate said. 'I can't say I've ever heard of it before. I know about ordinary hay-fever of course, but not from animals.'

'Good job you don't get it, Kate, brought up among all the moo-moos and gee-gees, you'd never stop sneezing!' Isobel drawled.

Kate glanced across at Isobel lying languidly on her bed blowing smoke rings into the air. Isobel would never change completely, she thought. The odd snide remark slipped out occasionally. Right now she was probably feeling miffed at the news of Kate's promotion.

Kate smiled to herself. There was a vast difference in one way, though; now Kate was strong enough not to be hurt by anything Isobel said.

The early months of 1941 had been gripped with wintry weather and operations were often cancelled. But with the coming of spring, activity at Suddaby increased. Almost nightly there were bombing raids over enemy territory and Philip never left the station when 'his boys' were away on a raid. Kate was kept busy driving him around the huge air-field; to briefing sessions, watching the ground crews bombing-up, and then later out to dispersal. Often he would ask Kate to drive the bus taking the crews out to the waiting aircraft, climbing aboard the vehicle himself and staying with the airmen until the last moment.

Kate's admiration for the pilots and the other members of the crews grew. They laughed and joked on the bus, as if they were on a jolly works outing, flirting a little with her as they clattered down the steps in their bulky flying jackets and boots.

'See you later, sweetheart.'

'How about a date on Saturday night, gorgeous?'

On one such trip, she met Sandy Petersen again when she drove him and the rest of the crew of T-Tommy out to their aircraft. Sandy, with hair the colour to match his nickname, was a little more persistent in his approach. 'There's a good film on in Lincoln on Friday. If we're not flying would you like to go?'

Kate smiled. 'Yes, thanks, Sandy. I would.'

The smile he gave her as he waved goodbye stayed with her through the long night. She waved as he crossed the tarmac towards the huge bulk of the waiting aircraft. In the dusk she saw him raise his right arm in farewell.

Kate turned the bus around to drive Philip back to the control tower where they went up on to the roof to watch take-off. On clear, fine nights they would stay out in the open, only sheltering in the glass observation room if it were cold or wet.

As the engines of the sixteen Avro Manchesters burst into life and taxied out on to the runways, the ground seemed to vibrate with their throbbing; the whole world seemed filled with noise. They took off, labouring into the night sky, cumbersome with their weight of bombs. Then, for those left behind, came the long hours of dreadful waiting.

'Take me back to my office, would you, Kate? I'll try to get an hour or so shut-eye.'

As she pulled up outside the door of the building housing

the CO's office and was about to open her car door, she felt his hand on her arm.

'Kate . . .' he began, strangely hesitant. 'Would it – would it compromise you too much if I were to ask you to come in and have a drink with me?'

She looked at him through the gloom. 'No – of course not.'

She saw the gleam of his teeth as he smiled. 'Come on, then,' he whispered, gleefully conspiratorial.

'Sit down,' he invited, closing the door of his office and moving to the cabinet where he had a bottle and glasses stowed away. 'I hate these hours when they're away,' he murmured. 'And yet, it's almost worse when they come back and you're counting the aircraft, willing them all back safely and yet knowing . . .'

He left the rest of his sentence unsaid. Placing a drink before her, he sat down in his chair, taking off his cap and running his hand across his forehead, up and through his hair. He let out a deep sigh. 'Oh, Kate, my dear girl, don't get too involved with any of them, will you?'

Kate looked up, a sharp reply on her lips. What business was it of his what she did in her off-duty time? What right had he to give her such advice?

Her mouth set in a rebellious line, she said shortly, 'I won't.'

He sat twirling the glass, watching the swirling liquid. She heard him sigh deeply and then, deliberately changing the subject, he began to ask her about her home, the farm, her family; anything to steer their thoughts away from the squadron at this moment facing flak as they crossed the enemy coast. But not once during the hours they sat together through the long night did he mention his own life or family.

As a pale, watery dawn stretched itself across the flat

fields, they went back to the control tower to await the returning aircraft.

'I'll be on the roof, Kate,' he told her, 'but do you mind taking one of the buses out to meet the crews? One of the other drivers has gone off sick.'

'Of course,' she agreed.

She had often driven the airmen out to their aircraft, but this was the first time she had met their return. When the first plane landed and she drove the bus as near as she could to pick up the crew she was shocked by the sight of them. The laughing, joking boys who had departed now returned exhausted, dirty and silent. Their faces were streaked with grime, their eyes wide with tiredness and they climbed unsteadily into the bus as if every bone in their bodies ached to lie down and rest. Now there was no laughter, no joking, no flirting. They didn't speak to her, didn't even look at her.

Silently she drove them straight to de-briefing and returned to meet another aircraft. By the time the day was fully light, the sky was silent. All the aircraft were back; all, except one.

T-Tommy did not return.

Later that day she drove Philip to Group HQ. As they pulled up outside, he leaned forward from the back seat.

'Kate, I'm sorry about Sandy. I know I have no right to tell you how to run your life but . . .'

'No, you haven't . . .' she began and then, turning to look at him, she saw the tender expression in his eyes, his forehead furrowed with anxiety for her, and her retort died.

His voice was low and hoarse as he added, 'I just don't want to see you get hurt, Kate.'

His concern for her brought a lump to her throat. All she could do was nod.

'Was – was there anything between you and Sandy? I – I overheard him ask you out.'

She shook her head and said flatly, 'No, no there wasn't.' Silently, in her own mind she added sadly, 'There wasn't time.'

She was surprised to see the look of relief that crossed her Commanding Officer's face at her denial of an involvement with the young airman. Thoughtfully, she watched him stride into the building with almost a spring in his step.

Weeks had gone by and she had heard nothing from Danny. Since the loss of Sandy Petersen's aircraft, Kate had become even more aware of just how vulnerable Danny was. Their own aircraft were on ops night after night; East Markham would be no different.

'I'm going to ring East Markham and find out if he's all right!'

Mavis gasped. 'You can't do that, Kate.'

'Why not?'

'They won't like it,' Isobel put in. 'They don't like girls ringing about their boyfriends and if they find out you're a WAAF, they'll take a very dim view.'

'Shan't tell 'em who I am.'

'I doubt they'll tell you anything then.'

'You're allowed to ring the Mess, aren't you?'

Mavis and Isobel exchanged a glance, then Mavis shrugged. 'Don't ask me. If he's on ops they'll tell you absolutely nothing. You can bet your life on it.'

'If that's the case, then I'll know, won't I?' she said reasonably.

'You can't ring from here, you know. It means walking down to the village.'

'Well then, I'll go down to the pub when I'm off duty and ring from there.'

That evening she cajoled the telephone number out of the Adjutant and rang the Airmen's Mess at East Markham. As the receiver was lifted and a voice said 'Hello,' she could hear noisy singing and laughter in the background.

'Is Danny Eland there?'

'Who?' She repeated his name and gave his rank. 'Sorry, I've never heard of him.' He covered the mouthpiece with his hand, but she could still plainly hear him shouting above the racket. 'Anyone know a Danny Eland?'

She heard an answering shout but could not distinguish the words. The man on the other end spoke into the receiver again. 'Seems he's on leave. Got a seventy-two to go home.'

'Home?' Her voice was a strangulated squeak. 'But he – he can't have.'

'Oh – er – sorry. Have I let the cat out of the bag? You mean he's not come home?'

'No – yes – no – oh, never mind,' Kate said, and rang off.

She was seething as she walked back to the huts. How dare he go home – again – and not let her know? Was she taking it for granted that she could never get leave to coincide with his? He hadn't even written to her to give her the chance to try.

Just wait till she saw him again; she wouldn't half give him what-for!

'There's someone to see you.' Mavis cupped her hands around her mouth and yelled at Kate across the stretch of grass between the control tower to which she was headed, and the MT yard where Kate was washing down the staff car.

Kate looked up to see Mavis gesticulating towards the guard-room near the gate. 'Get a move on. It's Danny.'

'Danny!' Kate dropped her cloth into the bucket, hardly

noticing the water that splashed on to her foot, for already she was racing towards the gate.

'Danny. What are you doing here?' In her joy at seeing him her anger with him was swiftly forgotten. But in the next moment her delight turned to apprehension. He looked very solemn and somehow strangely ill at ease. 'Kate,' he said, taking her arm. 'There's something I have to tell you.'

Fear stabbed her. 'Is something wrong at home?'

He hesitated a fraction of a second, but then shook his head. 'Come on, let's go somewhere quiet.'

Having booked in at the guard-room, Danny took her arm and together they walked round the edge of the airfield. It was sultry; the only sound in the stillness was a bee buzzing along the hedgerow.

'Kate – Rosie and I – we're going to get married.'

She stood still, her mouth slightly open. The sun beat down mercilessly, so hot upon her head, that she felt dizzy.

'What? You're not serious, Danny?'

'We've spent a lot of time together lately – when I've been home on leave.'

She thrust her face close to his. 'Yes – when you've been home without me! Now I see why.'

'It's not like that, Kate. Be reasonable.'

'Reasonable, reasonable? You ask me to be reasonable when you're – you're going to get married and to – to *her*? Why are you doing it, Danny? To keep her away from the soldiers? Think she'll be safe, married to you? "Oh, I'll sort her out," you said,' she mimicked bitterly. 'Well, ya've certainly done that, bain't ya?' The dialect was strong now; she was angry. She prodded his shoulder with her forefinger. 'Ya don't have to marry the little bitch to stop her getting 'ersen into trouble, Danny.' She saw him wince and look away from her with a look of disgust on his face. A stab of fear shot through her. She was losing him.

'It's not like that, Kate,' he said quietly. 'I'm – very fond of Rosie. I *want* to marry her.'

'You wanted to marry me. Remember?' Her voice rose and she jabbed her finger into her own chest. 'Me!'

Soberly, he nodded, his voice scarcely above a whisper. 'I remember.'

They stared at each other; she, hurt and resentful, he, determined yet with an air of sorrow. In his deep brown eyes there was still a sadness for what might have been, but could never be.

'Don't pity me,' Kate spat at him.

He shook his head. 'Oh, Kate, Kate. Why are you acting like this? I thought you'd be pleased. I thought you loved Rosie . . .'

'I did,' she almost screamed. '*That's* what makes it worse. She was my friend – and she's betrayed me. If you had to get married then I'd rather it be anyone else rather than Rosie. Anyone but Rosie.'

'But – but why? She's still your friend, she loves you dearly. She's going to be so hurt that you . . .'

'I'll never speak to her again, not as long as I live, I won't. I don't even want to see her – not ever.'

'Oh Kate, don't. Please don't say that.' His brown eyes were dark pools of suffering. 'We want you to come to the wedding – you must come . . .'

Kate broke into hysterical laughter. Go to their wedding? How could he be so cruel, she thought, or so stupid? Didn't he understand what this was doing to her? Didn't he know how she felt about him; how much she loved him and always would?

At this precise moment, she wanted to kill Rosie Maine.

Twenty-Eight

Chiefy found her, sloshing water all over the Humber and soaking her feet and legs as well.

'Whatever's got into you, Hilton...?' he began, then, coming closer, he realized that she could hardly see what she was doing for the tears streaming down her face.

Kate felt him touch her arm. 'Leave it, love. Come on...'

'I can't – I must finish – the car,' she sobbed.

'It's okay. I'll get one of the lads to do it. Come with me.' There was a gentle firmness in his tone that forbade further argument. With a heavy sigh, Kate dropped the cloth into the bucket and turned away.

As they walked back towards the office, Chiefy asked gently, 'Anything I can do to help?'

She shook her head. 'No, no thanks. I'll be fine,' she replied and wondered how she could tell such a lie. She couldn't believe she would ever be 'fine' again.

'Well, go and get a lie-down in your quarters.' He glanced at his watch. 'I can give you an hour, but no more. All right?'

Grateful for his understanding, even though he didn't know what was causing her misery, Kate nodded.

It was almost as bad as before, she thought, as she lay flat on her back on her bed, gazing up at the rafters of the hut, when they had found they were half-brother and sister and that they could never marry.

Now Danny was going to marry Rosie. How could he?

How could he do this to her, Kate? Obviously, he no longer felt the same way about her, or else he wouldn't – couldn't – marry someone else. And Rosie! Why, oh why did it have to be Rosie?

The hut was hot and stuffy and now she had a blinding headache. How she longed for the cool, blissful tranquillity at the end of the Spit . . .

'What's up with you? I thought you were out with lover-boy?'

Kate groaned as she rolled over. She had not realized she had fallen asleep. 'Just let me die!' she moaned.

Mavis was bending over her bed in the half-light of evening. 'You ill, Kate?'

She laid her hand against Kate's forehead. 'You do feel a bit hot. Have you reported sick?'

Kate rolled her head from side to side on the pillow.

'Well, come on then . . .'

'Just – leave me alone!' she whimpered.

'Oh sorry, I'm sure.'

The door opened and Isobel marched down towards them, coming to stand beside Mavis to stare down at Kate. 'Oh, you've found her then?'

Mavis turned questioning eyes upon Isobel, who said, 'One of the lads from MT said some bloke came to see her . . .'

'Yes, it was Danny,' Mavis put in. 'You know, the famous Danny we're always hearing about . . .'

'Well, she came back and began throwing water all over the Humber,' Isobel went on. 'To coin his phrase, not mine, she was "bawling her eyes out and making a right pig's ear of it", until Chiefy sent her off duty.'

'Eh?' Mavis stared aghast. 'Oh, heavens! Me putting my great size sevens right in it.'

'As usual,' Isobel murmured, but now they both looked down again at Kate, then they sat either side of her on the bed.

'What's the matter?' Isobel asked.

'Come on, Kate,' Mavis coaxed. 'You can tell us.'

'He's – he's . . .' Fresh tears spurted and Mavis pushed a handkerchief into her hands. 'Getting married!' Kate wailed.

'Married? You – you mean – not to you?'

'Of course she means not to her, idiot, or she wouldn't be blubbering like this, would she?' Isobel snapped.

'Then – who?'

'My – best – friend.'

'Oh hell! That is rough,' Isobel muttered, and for once there was real sympathy in her voice.

'You don't understand . . .' Kate began, then stopped. How could she explain it all to them? It would sound very odd. She was in love with her own half-brother. No – no, she couldn't tell them; certainly not Isobel, even though they were friends now, and not even the easy-going Mavis. It would sound decidedly odd to them.

She made a determined effort and pulled herself upright. 'I'll be – okay, honest,' she sniffed and blew hard into the handkerchief. 'It was just a – a shock. But really, I'd rather not talk about it. Best to try to forget, you know.'

They regarded her seriously for a moment, then, taking their cue from her, Mavis said, 'That's the spirit, girl. Tell you what, we're off duty tonight. If his nibs doesn't want you, we're off down to the pub in the village. All right?'

Kate nodded. Anything, she thought, to blot out her own thoughts right now.

Of course, she couldn't avoid going home – not for ever. She

309

missed seeing her grandad, who wasn't too well now, and her mother and stepfather; even, to her surprise, Lilian. Since she had been away from home, she had begun to feel strangely sorry for Lilian. Detached from home, Kate could see things a little more objectively. Her young sister was a strange girl. She had proved to be clever, academically clever, and Esther's pride in her younger daughter knew no bounds. Two years before war had broken out she had passed the scholarship to go to the local Grammar School.

'University, that's where our Lilian's going when this stupid war's over,' Esther vowed.

'What's the use of a woman going to university?' Will Benson would growl. 'Ya don't need book learning to care for a husband and family?'

'Why shouldn't she go?' Esther would bristle. 'Women ought to have the same chance as men.' And under her breath she would mutter, 'Would have saved me a lot of trouble if Squire'd have thought that years ago and given me the tenancy of the farm straight off! And what about our Kate then? Doin' her bit for the war, ain't she, alongside the fellers?'

'Huh!' Beaten in the same old argument, Will would stamp off to his room slamming the door as he went, leaving Esther triumphant.

But Kate was no longer jealous of her younger sister. In fact, she felt rather sorry for her. It was difficult to live up to the high expectations of proud parents.

'Oh, Kate, it's good to have you home,' Esther said, hugging her. 'Come on in. I've a rabbit pie in the oven and ya grandad's feeling better today. We'll all sit down to dinner together. How've ya been?'

'Not bad, Mam.'

There was a moment's pause as Esther held her at arm's

length and studied her face. Then she sighed gently. 'I can see you've heard the news, then.'

Kate nodded and bit her lip. 'He came to the camp to – to tell me himself.'

'That must have taken a bit o' doing,' Esther murmured, and Kate saw the truth in her words.

'I suppose so.' She sat down in the Windsor chair by the range which still warmed the kitchen and cooked the food. Nothing had changed here at Brumbys' Farm, and in her present state of unhappiness Kate found a reassuring security in that fact. She leaned her head against the back of the chair and closed her eyes. 'Oh Mam, what am I going to do?'

When she opened her eyes, it was to see her mother standing in front of her, hands on her hips. 'Do, lass? What d'ya mean, do?' And then in answer to her own question, she added. 'Ya going to get on with ya life, lass, that's what ya going to do. Meet a nice feller, get married and give me a barrow-load of grand-bairns.'

Kate smiled. Oh, how good it was to be home!

Feigning the submissiveness of childhood, she said, 'Yes, Mam.'

She didn't see Rosie or Beth Eland. She didn't want to see Rosie, not ever. And she couldn't even face Beth – not yet.

'Ya will come home for the wedding, though, Kate, won't ya?' her mother asked.

Kate shook her head. 'I can't, Mam, I just can't.' Then she eyed her mother with amusement – the first flash of genuine humour she had felt recently. 'Don't tell me you're going, Mam? Not to an *Eland* wedding?

Esther wriggled her shoulders. 'Ya Dad ses I've got to go,'

she smiled self-consciously. 'We allus seem to come together – me an' Beth – for funerals and the like. I 'spose a wedding's as good a reason as any.'

'Well, it's an improvement on funerals!' Kate remarked drily, and her mother had the grace to smile.

'Ya ought to come, Kate. He is ya brother.'

'By heck, you've changed your tune!' Then her tone softened sadly. 'Oh, Mam, if only you'd told us that years ago.'

'I know, lass, I know. Mebbe we should have done.' She sighed. 'But it weren't all my secret, y'know.'

There was silence between them, only the ticking of the clock and the crackling of the wood on the fire in the range.

'I can't come to the wedding, Mam. Really I can't.'

On the day she knew Danny and Rosie were getting married, Kate was safely back at camp, although her mind was anywhere but on her job.

'What is the matter with you today, Kate?' Philip asked her as she took a corner too sharply and the offside wheels bounced on to the grass verge. Even that reminded her sharply of Danny, she thought wryly, and the time they had landed up in a ditch in the Squire's car. Aloud she said, 'Sorry, sir.'

'Is there something the matter?'

'No – no, sir.'

'I've told you not to call me "sir" when we're on our own.'

'No – Philip.'

They fell silent and didn't speak again until she drew up a little way from the camp to allow him to get into the back as had become their habit.

'I shan't need you again today. Get yourself down to the pub in the village with some of your mates and relax a little.'

She forced a weak smile and met his gaze in the rear-view mirror. 'Is that an order – sir?'

She watched the serious expression on his face lighten as he smiled. 'Yes, Corporal Hilton. It's an order.'

'Yes, sir!'

Twenty-Nine

'Shut up, Kate, do,' Mavis hissed.

As if from a great distance, Kate heard them arguing over her head as she felt herself being dragged along between them, her stumbling feet seeming to have a will of their own.

'Silly cow'll get us on a fizzer,' Isobel muttered, forgetting her lady-like manner for once. 'Whatever did you let her drink so much for?'

'Don't blame me, you were there too. Or were you too busy chatting up Ron?' Mavis countered.

'We should have known – we should have watched her.'

'He doesn't love me,' Kate wailed. 'He's gone and married . . .'

'Has he got married then?' Isobel hissed at Mavis above Kate's lolling head.

'Yes – today. He rang up again last night to try to get her to go to the wedding. I ask you! Must be a heartless bastard!'

'No – no,' Kate's head came up. 'You've got it wrong, Mave. He does love me, really. He can't marry me, so he's got to marry Rosie. But I didn't want him to get married. 'Specially not – not *Rosie*!'

'What *is* she on about?' Isobel asked.

'Search me,' Mavis said. 'Got this Rosie up the stick by the sound of it.'

'No – no! I – will explain it all,' Kate enunciated carefully. 'Because you're my – my friends now. But you weren't always my friend, were you, Isobel? You – were – very unkind to

314

me at sh-chool, Is-o-bel.' Kate wagged her forefinger in the air at no one in particular seeing as both her arms were being held tightly by the girls on either side of her. 'You used to – call – me Sicky . . . '

As if the memory again prompted the action, she felt the bile rise in her throat. 'I'm gonner be sick!' was all she could mumble before the quantities of beer she had consumed came spewing up into the road.

'Seems I wasn't far wrong either,' Isobel said brutally, but she put her hand on Kate's forehead and held back her long hair while she heaved and retched on to the grass verge.

'Where's her cap?' Isobel asked.

'In my pocket,' Mavis said grimly. 'Oh, heavens! There's something coming!'

Mavis and Isobel looked back over their shoulders as the noise of a vehicle and the pin-pricks of light from its shrouded headlights came towards them.

'Quick, there's a ditch here. Come on, they might not see us.'

'Ugh! There's water in the bottom,' exclaimed the fastidious Isobel.

'Better than being in the guard-room,' Mavis said tartly, shuddering as the cold water covered her ankles.

Kate groaned and slipped from their grasp, splashing on to her knees in the bottom of the ditch.

At that moment the moon, which had been hidden by the clouds, chose to appear, lighting up the countryside with its silver glow.

'Oh hell!' Mavis muttered. 'Now we're for it . . . '

The vehicle slowed as it drew level with the three girls cowering in the ditch and then stopped. As the engine was cut, silence bathed the countryside. Mavis and Isobel held their breath, but Kate, oblivious to what was happening, began to sing.

'There was I waiting at the church, waiting at the church . . .'

Footsteps sounded on the road and then whispered across the grass verge.

'Can't get away to marry you today,' Kate yodelled tunelessly, 'my wife won't – let me!' The final words ended on a high-pitched wail. She threw back her head and looked up into the shadowy face of a tall man standing on the bank directly above them.

'What on earth is going on?'

Kate giggled. 'Why, if it isn't the handsome Groupie!'

Beside her, Isobel groaned, but Mavis was scrambling up out of the ditch. 'Sir – could you just forget you've seen us, please?' She was standing on the bank beside him now. 'Kate's had an awful shock – some sort of family trouble. This isn't like her – really it isn't.'

The silence was all around them again. 'Please, sir, couldn't you – just this once . . .?' Mavis pleaded softly.

Philip Trent's deep voice came gently out of the darkness. 'It's all right, I won't be taking any action over this. I just want to help.' He bent down and stretched out his hand. 'Come on, Kate Hilton. Let's get you back to camp. Maybe I can get her past the guard easier than you two could.'

They couldn't see his face in the darkness, but they could hear the genuine concern in his voice. With him pulling and Isobel pushing, they heaved Kate out of the ditch and between them half-dragged, half-carried her to the jeep he was driving.

'Put her in the back with my coat over her. It's on the back seat. One of you sit with her. The other, come in front with me.'

Hardly able to believe this was actually happening, they obeyed meekly and a few moments later they were heading along the lane back towards camp. Kate was no longer singing – now she was crying. 'I'm sorry. I'm sorry. I didn't mean to . . .'

Her voice faded away and she was quiet.

Isobel leaned forward from the back seat. 'I think she's asleep.'

Philip Trent nodded.

A few yards from the camp gate, he stopped the jeep. 'Look, I hate to do this to you, but if you two get out here and come into camp as normal, I think I can get her past the guards better than if I've got you on board as well.' His deep chuckle made them both smile. As they slid out of the jeep, Mavis said. 'Thank you, sir – for everything.'

'Yes, thank you, sir,' Isobel echoed, 'you've been jolly decent about this.'

'Think nothing of it. But not a word to a soul, mind.'

'No, sir,' they chorused with heartfelt agreement.

Kate was not asleep. Through the mists of alcohol, she had heard everything that was going on, but she couldn't seem to get her mind to work properly. She was muddled and confused. She had never in her life felt like this before; but then never before had she been drunk.

Fortunately for them both, she lay quietly while Philip drove through the gates, pausing to prove his identity to the guard. 'My driver's in the back. We've had a long day . . .'

The soldier on duty glanced into the back of the jeep, then stepped back and saluted smartly. 'Sir!' he barked and the barrier was raised for the vehicle to pass into camp.

It was as if she was waking up in a fog. Her head throbbed abominably when she tried to raise it. She groaned and dropped back against the pillow and a sharp stab of pain shot up the back of her neck and gripped the top of her head.

Somewhere above her a deep voice spoke. 'Oh, surfacing at last, are we?'

Kate opened her eyes and tried to focus on the face bending over her. She blinked rapidly and recognized the face of her commanding officer.

'Oh bloody 'ell!' she muttered and closed her eyes again.

'Such language, young lady!'

'Where am I? What are you doing here?'

'You're in my bed where you've been all night – at least, what was left of it.'

Her eyes flew open. 'Your – *your* bed?'

'Don't look so shocked. I wasn't in it. Taking advantage of a young woman in that state isn't in my line. It's the room behind my office. I like to stay here when there's an op on, so I got it fitted out with the basic necessities. Good job I did. I could hardly have taken you to the CO's house, now could I?'

He sat down carefully on the edge of the bed and leaned over her, resting on his hands placed either side of her. 'Want to talk about it, Kate?' he asked gently.

Kate was just beginning to realize what he had done for her this past night, and at the kindness in his tone easy tears filled her eyes. 'I'm so sorry.'

'It's okay,' he said softly. 'No harm done, as it happens. Your two friends got safely back into camp and – er, Mavis, is it . . .?'

She nodded and he continued. 'Well, Mavis came early this morning and collected your uniform to get it cleaned up. She's just brought it back so you can get up when you like, use my bathroom and then, when you're ready, you can go out through the front office as if you've just been to get your orders for the day. And hopefully . . .' He raised one hand and crossed his fingers, 'No one will be any the wiser for your little escapade.'

She closed her eyes and groaned, imagining what a fool she must have made of herself the previous night. And Philip was being so good about it, even conspiring to sneak her back into camp. She wondered just how many other COs would have done that. No wonder he had said he threw away the rule-book when he felt like it.

'I don't think,' he said slowly, 'you'd better drive today.'

Kate smiled ruefully and put her hand up to her head. 'No, I don't think I better had,' she murmured ungrammatically.

As he got up and turned away, she said, 'You've been very kind. I – don't know how to thank you . . .'

He turned and stood looking down at her. Although his expression was grave, there was a gentle look in his eyes.

'If you remember, Kate Hilton, there have been two occasions when *I* didn't know how to thank *you*. I haven't forgotten, you know.' Then, as if to save them both any further embarrassment, he turned and left the room.

After washing her hair and taking a bath, Kate felt much better, though a little fragile. Dressed in her clean uniform, she waited nervously in Philip's bedroom.

The door opened. 'All clear!' he said in a stage whisper and she went through into his office. 'Parkes has nipped out for lunch so the outer office is empty at the moment. Right now,' he sat down in his chair and steepled his fingers, 'I have to go to East Markham. If you could just drive us out the gate and then in at the other end, I'll drive in between.'

Kate bit her lip and nodded.

'Bring the car round in about an hour. Try to get a bit of lunch . . .' He began, but noticing her turn paler, added, 'If you can face it.'

She smiled thinly and nodded again.

*

319

'Oh, so you are still in the land of the living,' Isobel greeted her as Kate stepped into their hut.

Mavis was hurrying towards her. 'Are you all right? Did he put you on a charge?'

Kate shook her head – and then wished she had not done so for the throbbing increased. She looked at Mavis's troubled face. 'He said you two got back okay. Is that right? You – you didn't get caught?'

Mavis glanced across at Isobel. 'No, he was marvellous. Dropped us off a few yards from the gate and we walked in cool as you like. Oh, wasn't he terrific about it, though?' Mavis said again, a dreamy expression in her eyes.

Kate was relieved. 'That's all right, then.'

'I must say he was jolly decent,' Isobel agreed magnanimously. 'Is he sweet on you or something, Kate?' she added bluntly.

Before Kate could refute such a suggestion, Mavis burst out, 'I jolly well hope not. He's married!' Kate and Isobel stared at her.

'Is he now?' Isobel said softly, but Kate said nothing.

She was surprised at the shaft of disappointment that shot through her. 'How – how do you know?'

'Dave says . . .'

'Ah well, there we have it, then,' Isobel mocked. 'If the fountain of all knowledge says he's married, then married he must be.'

'Shut up, Iso. Dave told me,' Mavis continued patiently. 'He's mates with the Adjutant in the CO's office – Parkes. His *wife* often rings up. Says she's got an aw'fly posh voice. Quite la-di-da.'

Isobel smoothed her blonde hair. 'I'm absolutely devastated,' she said, looking anything but. 'I'd begun to think our lovely CO would be quite a catch. But married – oh dear me no. There's no future in that. Only a lot of heartache.'

Kate glanced at her. How coldly calculating Isobel Cart-wright was. There were times when Kate thought the girl had not really changed that much since their school days.

'Excuse me, I've got to go out again. The CO wants driving to East Markham.' She saw the other two exchange a worried glance.

'Will you be all right?' Isobel asked, and there was no mistaking the genuine concern in her tone now. 'I mean — *he's* there, isn't he?'

Instantly Kate regretted her uncharitable thoughts about Isobel.

She managed to give them a wan smile. 'I'll be fine. Danny — Danny won't be there. Don't you remember? He's on honeymoon!'

Safely out of sight of the guard-room, Kate stopped the car and slid from the driver's seat. Philip took her place. 'Don't stand there dithering, get in the front.'

He drove fast but expertly and after a mile or so, she began to relax and some of the guilt for her foolish behaviour began to ebb away. About midway between the two camps, he pulled over on to a wide grass verge on the top of a hill and cut the engine. They sat looking at the scene before them.

She felt his gaze upon her and turned to meet his eyes. They were full of compassion and tenderness. 'Last night wasn't like you, Kate. Not a bit. I know that. Something awful must have happened.'

She looked down at her hands, twisting together in her lap. Tears welled in her eyes and spilled down her cheeks, splashing on to her hands.

'Tell me,' he urged her gently.

So she told him. Everything. From the very beginning, as

far back as she could remember and even before that; about her mother, and Danny's mother; about her father, who was also Danny's father. And about Danny – oh, she told him all about Danny. She cried as she told him, but there was laughter too as she remembered everything. It was like reliving her life again. All the happiness – and then all the sadness.

When she had finished, she found she was lying with her cheek against the rough fabric of his jacket and became aware that his hand was stroking her hair. 'You poor kids,' he murmured.

She became aware of his nearness and sat up, suddenly embarrassed. 'I'm sorry.' She tried to smile, but her mouth quivered. 'I seem to be saying that a lot today.'

His smile was sympathetic. 'Has it helped?'

She nodded, and said, surprise in her tone. 'Yes, yes, I think it has.'

'They say it's good to talk your troubles out. I sometimes wish . . .' He leaned forward and pressed the starter. The engine leapt into life and whatever he had been going to say was drowned in the noise.

'*My dear Kate*,' her stepfather wrote.

I was grieved you could not find it in your heart to attend Danny and Rosie's marriage. On what should have been a happy day for her, the dear girl was heartbroken that you were not there. I know how you feel – and even though these words may deny it – I do understand. But years have passed since you learned the truth and you should by now have come to terms with it. Try to understand, my dear, that life must go forward. You and Danny cannot remain in the safe cocoon of childhood, all in all to each other to the exclusion of all other relationships. It is unhealthy and damaging to you both. A man needs a wife, and you, my dear, should have a husband and children. Danny has done the right thing in breaking free of those bonds. It does not mean he loves you any the less – only, perhaps, differently.

Tears blurred the rest of the words before her eyes. But this time they were not tears of bitterness over Danny. Kate was surprised to find how much her gentle stepfather's rebuke hurt her, made her feel small and petty-minded. She sniffed and, like a small child, scrubbed the tears away with the back of her hand.

'They are away on a short honeymoon – please try to come home to see your grandfather. He is not too well . . .' The letter continued with news about her mother and Lilian and the farm, but no further mention was made of Danny or Rosie.

Slowly Kate got up from her bed, biting her lip. She knew she had hurt Rosie, but until this moment she had not stopped to think how her absence from their wedding had hurt so many people. Beth Eland and Enid Maine, Rosie's mother, too. But more than anything she could not bear to think that her stepfather was disappointed in her.

She would apply for leave. She was sure that Philip, understanding and kind, and now knowing the full circumstances, would grant her compassionate leave to go home . . .

'Get down, Grandad, get down! Do you want to be killed?'

The old man was dancing up and down in front of the window, waving his arms, his bare legs, thin and white, sticking out from under the flapping tails of his night-shirt. 'You dirty swine! You . . .' But his expletives were drowned by the roaring of engines as another enemy plane, its swastika plainly visible, swooped by, low and vicious, strafing the front of the farmhouse with a shower of bullets. Kate threw herself at the old man, pushing him to the floor and landing on top of him, knocking the breath out of him. He lay there gasping, but still found the strength to swear volubly. As the plane roared past, there was a rat-a-tat-tat of bullets against the brickwork. Just above them the glass of the window shattered and bullets whistled over their heads to embed themselves in the far wall of the room.

'There, are you satisfied now?' she panted. 'You nearly got us both killed . . .' Her words were drowned by a loud 'crump' which rattled the very foundations of the farmhouse. Every door and window rattled and more glass shattered. Soot billowed from the chimney stack like a black shroud, enveloping them both.

'Oh my God! That's a bomb and it's bloody close.' Now she was scrambling up, oblivious to further danger.

'Kate, don't . . .' he wheezed, struggling to his feet, but she was out of his room and running through the house. There was glass everywhere. It looked as if every window was shattered. As she passed through the living room, soot covered everything. In the kitchen, pots lay smashed on the floor where they'd been vibrated from the shelf and the door stood drunkenly, half off its hinges.

Kate rushed out into the yard. 'Mam! *Mam*!' She looked wildly about her. Hens were rushing to and fro squawking loudly and flapping their wings in the pretence of flight. From the stable came the whinnying of the frightened horses and hooves struck repeatedly at the door.

'Mam – Dad! Where are you?' she yelled. Now there was silence – a deathly silence. The planes, having wrought their havoc, had gone, streaking away across the North Sea to safety.

She ran to the gate and looked up and down the lane. To her right, beyond the Hump, rose a cloud of dust and smoke.

'Oh no!' she cried. 'Not the cottages – please, not the cottages.'

Then she was running, running like the wind, her heart pounding, desperately afraid of what she would find.

She had arrived at Brumbys' Farm only half an hour before and hadn't even seen her mother and stepfather. Only her grandfather had been at home, sitting in the chair by the window in his room, still in his night-shirt.

'Ya mam wants me to stay in bed. Me chest is bad, but I 'ate lying in bed. Me elbows get sore. 'Sides, I like to see out the window, across the fields . . .' His old eyes had watered and she knew he must miss being out in the open air when illness confined him to his room. Then he was smiling at her, but the old eyes were still regarding her shrewdly. 'This is a surprise. Couldn't make it for the wedding, I s'pose?'

Kate returned his gaze steadily. Then, finding she was holding her breath, she let it out in a deep sigh. There was no point in even trying to deceive Will Benson. 'I – I couldn't face it, Grandad, but I've been feeling bad about it ever since.'

'Aye, well, lass. I can understand, but I can't excuse ya, 'cos it upset poor Rosie. And Danny.'

'I – just need a bit of time, Grandad. It was such a shock when he – he came to the camp to tell me. I thought I was over it – beginning to lead my own life, but then when Danny came and said he – he was getting married and – and to Rosie . . .'

The gnarled old hand reached out and covered hers, twisting in her lap. 'I know, lass, I know,' he said hoarsely.

'I – I came home to see his mam and Enid . . .'

It was then they had heard the drone of the aircraft coming nearer and nearer . . .

Kate arrived at the top of the Hump and stopped. Before her was a scene of devastation. It was not the cottages, although they had suffered damage. It was the Seagull, which had taken a direct hit. A small incendiary bomb had fallen on one end of the building, slicing rooms in half so that Kate could see the interior, like her own dolls' house when the whole of the front was opened. She could even see the wallpaper on the remaining inner wall of the bedroom. A bed hung precariously half-on, half-off the portion of floor left, teetering on the edge. The bomb had buried itself in the soft earth, making a crater the size of the pond at Brumbys' Farm, and now flames licked at the already half-destroyed building.

Kate absorbed all this in a brief second's pause, then she was flying down the slope towards the building. It was lunchtime opening; there must have been people in the pub. Others were emerging from the cottages and hurrying towards the scene. Kate could see Grannie Harris watching through the broken window of her kitchen, her hand to her mouth. Then two of the soldiers who had been on duty through the previous night and sleeping in Dan Hanley's cottage when the bomb fell, appeared. They were bare-chested, their trousers pulled on hastily. Enid Maine appeared in her doorway, clutching at the door post for support, staring wide-eyed.

Then, suddenly, there was Beth Eland. She came out of her cottage, wrapped a black shawl over her head and walked slowly towards the pub. She didn't run, didn't even hurry. It was as if she were drawn to the scene but was reluctant to reach it.

'Get some water!' Kate shouted to the two soldiers. 'Let's get this fire out first. Get buckets, anything. Form a chain.'

Without realizing it, she was taking charge. All her young life, she had seen how farmers dealt with stack fires and then she had witnessed the calm efficiency on Suddaby Station after an air-raid.

Kate ran to the nearest cottage – Enid's home. 'Look sharp, our Enid, get working the pump in your kitchen filling buckets. Where's the boys? They can help too . . .'

Soon everyone there was helping to transport water to the base of the fire – all except Beth. She stood, a lonely, lost figure, a little way off, just staring at the ravaged building.

Kate grasped her arm. 'Where's Mester Eland? We could do with his help. Is he out fishing?'

Slowly Beth shook her head.

'Where is he, then?'

Beth's gaze was fixed upon the building, mesmerized. Kate shook her arm, trying to bring her out of her stupor. 'Where is he?' she repeated.

Beth's voice was a strangulated whisper. 'In – in the pub.'

'Oh, no!' Kate breathed, then, grasping at straws, she added, 'Maybe he'll be all right. Perhaps he was in the other end of the pub that wasn't hit. Maybe he's just – trapped.'

'He – he'd have been playing dominoes with Tom Willoughby,' Beth whispered.

Kate put her arm around Beth but she could think of nothing more to say now for she knew as well as Beth that the men played dominoes in the corner of the main bar; the end of the building where the bomb had fallen. Kate felt sick in the pit of her stomach. Her stepfather, Jonathan, sometimes played with them too.

'I must go and help,' she whispered. Beth nodded but remained standing where she was; a still, silent, watchful figure, her arms clasped about her body, hugging the shawl closely around her.

I wish I hadn't come home, Kate was thinking. I wish I was anywhere but here.

It was like the time the station had been bombed and Edith's lifeless body had been dragged from the rubble. But this was worse, much worse. This time there were going to be the bodies of people she had known all her life; and among them Robert Eland, the man Danny had called Father all his life.

The fire was out and now they started to move the rubble carefully, praying – but without real hope – that they might find Tom and Robert alive. An air-raid warden and a police constable arrived from Lynthorpe.

'We saw the planes swooping over here and then the bombs.'

'Bombs?' Kate looked up sharply. 'Was there more than this one?'

'Oh aye,' the warden said. 'One fell into a field not far from Souters' Farm. It's not done much damage as the soft ground took the impact and another fell in the lane on the way to town from here – that's why we've been a long time getting here. We had to come right round by the Grange.'

'You – you haven't seen my mother and father, have you?'

'No, love, sorry, I ain't. They missing?'

'I don't know. I've only just got home. I'd only just got into the house and was talking to me grandad when the planes came.'

'The old man all right, is he?'

'Just!' Kate replied wryly. They stood looking at the ruins that had been the pub. The warden sighed. 'I aren't looking forward to this, lass.'

'No.' Kate glanced back over her shoulder and saw that Beth was still standing in the same place, her arms wrapped around herself, just waiting.

At that moment, a figure appeared at the top of the Hump and came plunging down the slope towards them, her hair dishevelled and flying free, her eyes wide with fear, her hand outstretched.

'Oh, Mam!' Kate breathed, and ran to meet her.

Esther gripped her arms, not pausing to express surprise at Kate being there; there was only one thought on her mind. 'Where is he? Where's ya dad? Where's Jonathan?'

Thirty

'Isn't he with you?' Kate realized it was a stupid question immediately she'd spoken.

Her mother shook her head wildly. 'No – no. I've been into town – in the trap. I saw the bombs. I – I thought it was the farm . . .' She gulped painfully. 'I came tearing home – a bomb had landed in the lane – I had to go right round by the Grange to get back.'

'Where is me dad, then?'

Esther was staring with terrified eyes at the ruins of the pub and clinging to Kate, her grip so intense that her fingers dug into Kate's arms. 'He – he said he would tek the cows up to North Marsh Field and then when he came back he – he might walk down the road and have a – game of dominoes at the pub.'

'Esther.' Beth's voice came gently, flat and unemotional. Kate turned and saw her standing just behind them. 'Leave her to me, Katie love. You go and – help.'

Kate eased herself from her mother's grasp and Beth took her place, putting her arm about Esther and holding her close. Never taking her gaze from the heap of rubble, Esther clung to Beth and the two women stood together in silence watching and waiting . . .

They found the landlord first. He had been standing behind the bar when the bomb had come whistling down. With seconds to spare, he had dived under the counter of the bar and, though cut and bruised, he was still alive when the rescuers dug their way to him. The workers continued and more helpers arrived from town. Gently they removed the rubble brick by brick.

'There's someone here. Oh, no . . .'

Kate glanced back towards her mother and Beth. She saw Esther start forward, saw Beth hold her back. Kate saw Beth's lips moving and knew she was talking softly, soothingly to Esther. 'Wait, just wait, Esther. They'll – tell us.'

They had found Tom Willoughby – and Robert Eland.

'They wouldn't have known much about it.' The doctor, who had been one of those to arrive from town, tried to comfort them. 'It would have been very – quick.'

Esther had her arms about Beth, who stood looking down at the lifeless form of her husband. 'Poor Robert,' Beth murmured. 'He didn't deserve that.'

'No – no, he didn't. He was a good man.' Esther patted her arm. Now it was she who must comfort Beth.

The search was continuing and Esther was leading Beth away to her own cottage, while still glancing back anxiously over her shoulder at the devastated building.

Something made Kate glance towards the Hump. 'Mam!' she shouted, and pointed.

Jonathan was standing on the Hump gazing at the horror before him. Esther gave a sob and ran towards him, her arms outstretched. She flew into his arms and clung to him, babbling her relief.

Then, as she told him what had happened, Kate saw her stepfather and her mother go back towards Beth. Jonathan put his arm about Beth and kissed her cheek. Together he and Esther took her to her home.

331

Kate found that tears were running down her cheeks. 'Here, love, you tek a rest – now ya dad's okay, I shouldn't think there's anyone else in here, is there?'

Kate shook her head. Everyone was accounted for now. The police constable mounted his bicycle. He had the unenviable task of going to Rookery Farm to inform Tom's sister-in-law, Flo Jenkins, of his death.

And Danny, Kate thought. How would they tell Danny? No one knew where he and Rosie had gone on their brief honeymoon. What a dreadful homecoming! Then another thought struck her; a thought that left her sweating with fear for what might have happened.

If Danny had not been on honeymoon with Rosie, he might well have been sitting in the corner of the pub playing dominoes with his stepfather and Tom Willoughby.

'You must come to the funerals, Kate, if you can get leave,' her stepfather said firmly.

Kate bit her lip. 'Dad – I feel so awful now that I didn't come to Danny and Rosie's wedding.'

'What's done is done. But don't make it worse by staying away again.'

It was the worst moment in her life when she stood in the church and looked across at Danny; worse even than when they had found out the truth of their relationship, and that had been bad enough.

She felt sick and wanted to run out, away from them all, out to the end of the Spit. But she was obliged to stand there and watch Beth's white, strained face and see Rosie being the one to take hold of Danny's arm; Rosie comforting Danny when it should have been her, Kate. The longing to step across the aisle and put her arms about him was so strong that she swayed for a moment and had to grip the back of the pew in front of her to stop herself moving towards him. She felt her stepfather's anxious eyes upon her, and she bent her head in the pretence of prayer so that he should not read the expression in her eyes, for she knew her feelings must be plain for all to see.

The congregation knelt in the final prayer and when they rose and began to move out of the church, Kate remained where she was, on her knees, her head bowed, her hands covering her face. She sensed the coffin being carried out first, and knew that the Eland family were following, Beth, Danny – and Rosie, for now she was Mrs Eland.

She felt a light touch on her shoulder and Jonathan's whisper, 'We must go, Kate.'

Slowly she stood up and turned to see Danny going out of the church, one arm around his mother, the other around Rosie.

He did not even glance back at her, and in that moment, Kate had never felt so lonely in her life.

'Will Beth want us at the graveside?' Kate heard her mother whisper to Jonathan as they hesitated outside the porch, their glances going towards where the three figures stood near the freshly dug hole in the churchyard.

'Yes,' Jonathan said firmly and took Esther's arm. 'Come along. You too, Kate.'

The coffin was lowered into the ground and Danny bent to scoop up a handful of earth and scatter it on to the lid. As he straightened up, across the grave his glance met Kate's.

For an instant, the years fell away and they were again two children standing beside Matthew Hilton's grave, the man they now knew had fathered them both. Yet the man they were burying this day had been more of a father to Danny. Poor Danny, she thought, he must have so many conflicting emotions churning inside him, and she wasn't making it any easier. This was not a day for bearing grudges.

The interment ended, and as they began to move away, Kate saw her mother go to Beth's side and take her arm. Together, the two women walked away down the path. Jonathan was speaking to Rosie and, taking her chance, Kate went up to Danny and laid her hand gently on his arm.

He turned swiftly and gripped her hands. 'Kate,' was all he said, but it was enough.

They walked together down the footpath, following the others. She heard him sigh and looked up to see his gaze upon the black-coated figures of his mother and Esther Godfrey ahead of them.

'Strange, isn't it, how those two come together in times of sorrow and yet they can't bring themselves to speak to one another ordinarily?'

Kate was silent. She could have said, 'I know how they feel!' She had made a tentative gesture of reconciliation towards Danny, but even now, Kate admitted guiltily to herself, she could not bring herself to speak to Rosie Eland.

Back at camp it was a little easier, but letters from home renewed the pain.

'*Rosie's living with Beth until after the war and when Danny comes home, the Good Lord willing, the Squire has promised him the tenancy of Rookery Farm, now that poor old Tom has gone. Miss Jenkins has moved into the town – she didn't want to try to run the farm on her own . . .*'

So Kate was kept informed of all the gossip and news from home by her stepfather. Her mother was no letter-writer, but always sent messages via Jonathan. '*Your mother says . . .*' littered every page and Kate would smile fondly as she read the latest instruction from home.

She sat with the letter in her lap and stared out of the window of the hut. So Danny and Rosie would one day live at Rookery Farm, God willing, as her stepfather said, that Danny came through the war. He would work the land he had once dreamed of farming. He would live there with his wife and he would raise his children; all just as he had planned, just as they had planned together so long ago. Only now, his wife was Rosie and not Kate.

She sighed and got up from her bed. It was time to drive one of the lorries taking the crews out to dispersal. The camp had been buzzing with anticipation all day, and Mavis and Isobel expected to be on duty through the night.

'It's something big,' Mavis had told her. 'They're concentrating on the ports and the Rhineland. Night after night, they'll go on – as long as the weather holds.'

At East Markham, they'd be getting ready too. Maybe at this very moment, Danny was climbing into his aircraft, squeezing himself into the rear-gunner's turret.

Kate closed her eyes for a brief moment and groaned aloud. Tears squeezed themselves from beneath her eyelids. Despite everything, she loved him still. 'Dear Father in Heaven, keep him safe,' she prayed. 'Bring him back, just bring him back.'

Thirty-One

'CO wants you – and the car – his office – two minutes.'

'I'm on my way.' Kate scrambled off the bed, pulled her skirt straight and rammed her cap over her long hair, tucking up the stray strands as she ran towards the CO's office.

As she came breathlessly to attention in front of his desk, she noticed at once that Philip's handsome face looked almost grey with fatigue – and something more. His jawline seemed hard, clenched almost, as if he were trying to conceal an anger, and yet at the same time there was an infinite sadness in his blue eyes; today there was no sparkle, no hint of mischief in them.

'I have to go home urgently. Er – family illness,' he said, his voice tight. 'Can you drive me to Lincoln to catch the train?' Suddenly, he leaned forward, resting his elbows on his desk, dropping his head into his hands, his shoulders slumped. 'Oh Kate – Kate! How I wish . . .'

For a long moment there was silence in the room. Kate bit her lip uncertainly. An overwhelming longing to comfort him made her start forward, her hand fluttering towards him to touch him, but in that instant she remembered just who he was and where they were.

'Sir,' she prompted gently. 'Your – your train?'

He lifted his head and looked up at her and, for a long moment, their gaze held. Then he sighed deeply and rose slowly as if his limbs were leaden. 'Let's go,' he said flatly, without a shred of enthusiasm in his voice.

As she saw him on to the train, he said. 'I don't know when I'll be back, Kate, but I'll try to send word for you to meet me.' He looked at her oddly for a moment, opened his mouth as if to say something, then closed it again. Suddenly he clasped her hand briefly. 'Take care of yourself while I'm gone . . .' Then he turned swiftly away from her, leaped on to the train and slammed the door behind him.

Kate was thoughtful as she walked out of the station. His behaviour was puzzling. Mavis had said he was married and yet Philip seemed to avoid mentioning his wife and children – if, indeed, he had any. But if he had been called home on compassionate leave – a man in his position – then someone close to him must be seriously ill.

As she walked along the platform, she saw two women in WVS uniform setting up a trestle-table with a tea-urn, cups and saucers. She looked closely at them but they were strangers; Miss Ogden was not one of them this time.

Outside the station, heavily protected by sandbags piled up either side of the entrance, she moved towards where the staff car was parked. She hesitated. There was no need for her to rush back to camp. Officially, she was off-duty now that she had driven Philip to the city to catch his train. She wouldn't be missed for an hour or so. Kate bit her lip and glanced up the hill towards the cathedral standing sentinel over the city sprawling down the hill beneath it. Almost without her making a conscious decision, her steps took her up High Street and through the Stonebow. As the road began to rise she took a turning to the left in the direction where she believed the school was. All the time she'd lived in Lincoln she had never ventured anywhere near.

It was time to lay to rest a few more ghosts from her childhood.

She stood before the place where the school had been and gazed at the ruins before her. On either side the buildings, though damaged, were still standing. It looked as if the school had received a direct hit.

A woman came trudging up the hill, carrying a heavy shopping basket, a child dragging at her skirt.

'Excuse me . . .' Kate began.

The woman looked at her with tired, defeated eyes.

'Do – do you know what happened to the school?' Kate nodded towards the demolished building. The woman glanced in the same direction. 'Bomb fell on it,' she explained, rather unnecessarily, Kate thought. 'Awful, it were. My old man's an air-raid warden. Several girls and three teachers were buried. He 'ad to dig 'em out.'

'Were they . . .?'

'Dead? Oh, no – only the headmistress was killed. T'others were hurt, like, but they've got over it.'

'How dreadful!' Kate murmured automatically, but she was thinking, 'Miss Denham is dead.'

'Oh yes,' the tired woman was finding new vigour in her recounting of the event, now she had an interested listener. 'A lovely woman, she was, the headmistress. All the girls loved her . . .'

'Loved her? Miss Denham?'

The woman's gaze was mystified. 'Who? Who did you say? Don't know no Miss Denham. No, the headmistress was called Miss Ogden!'

Kate gasped. 'Oh, no!'

'Knew her, did you?'

Kate nodded, sick at heart. Immediately she felt contrite, ashamed of her moment's fleeting glee at the thought that Miss Denham had been killed. Now she was being punished for her uncharitable thought for unkind Fate had taken the woman who had shown her genuine kindness.

Kate continued up towards the cathedral. In the peaceful atmosphere she knelt in prayer for Miss Ogden. Outside again, she walked back down Lindum Hill in a daze, hardly knowing where she was going. Then she found herself in a street she knew very well. In the nine years she had lived in the city she had walked along it hundreds of times to and from work. Kate smiled and quickened her pace.

The door opened upon Peggy. She stared at Kate for a moment and then gave a squeal of delight.

'Kate! I hardly recognized you in your uniform . . .' Peggy flung her arms round her and gave her a swift hug, then stood back, holding Kate by the arms. 'Let me look at you. Oh, you do look smart.' Excited as a young girl, Peggy almost dragged the laughing Kate through into the back room. 'Mother, look who's here!'

Although she ·passed hurriedly through the front room, there was still time enough for Kate to notice its tidiness with a stab of disappointment; not a paper pattern nor a length of fabric to be seen – not even a stray pin. When she stepped through into the back room, she saw why. Mrs Godfrey was sitting near the fire hunched in her chair.

'Mother's not so well these days, Kate, since we lost Father,' Peggy explained softly, and Kate nodded, understanding. The whole family had mourned the kind and gentle man. 'But she keeps cheerful,' Peggy was saying, 'and she loves visitors.'

Indeed, it seemed to be true, for at the sight of her, Mrs Godfrey's wrinkled face seemed to light up. 'Why, my lovely Kate. Come in and sit down. Make a cup of tea, Peg, there's a dear. I can't get about now, it's my legs. What I'd do without our Peg, I don't know,' and her gaze went fondly to her daughter.

The time flew by as they chatted. Mrs Godfrey wanted to know all about the family at Fleethaven Point and Kate found herself telling the two women all about the bombs, and even, though haltingly at first, about Danny's marriage to Rosie. As she talked she was surprised to find it became easier.

'I've just been up the hill – to look at the school.'

'Really?' Peggy could not hide the surprise in her voice.

'I met Miss Ogden on the station a while back, handing out cups of tea to the soldiers. She was kind to me when I was there—' Kate gave a wry laugh. 'She was the only one who was, mind you.'

'Ah yes, poor Miss Ogden. She took over as Principal seven or eight years ago now.'

'What – what happened to Miss Denham?'

'She retired. Went to live in the country with her sister who'd also been a headmistress somewhere.'

So Miss Denham was living somewhere comfortably in retirement, whilst poor Miss Ogden was dead.

Sometimes, Kate thought bitterly, Fate really got it wrong!

'Drive the long way round, Kate,' Philip said as he got in beside her on his return. 'If everything's all right, I'm in no hurry to get back. I seem to have been away a lot longer than a week.'

'Everything's fine. There was an op on last night and everyone got back safely. Well – more or less,' she grinned. 'B-Baker's undercarriage jammed and he had to do a belly-landing. Honestly, Jeff landed that kite as if it were a glider.'

'He's a great pilot.' There was a pause and then he added softly, 'And how about you? Are *you* all right?'

'Yes, thanks, I'm fine.'

It was already dark as she drove up the hill and out on to the Wragby road. About five miles from Suddaby, in open country, Philip said, 'Pull in over there, Kate. Let's take a breather.'

She drew the car to a halt on the wide grass verge. Below them the ground sloped away across fields of ripening corn, almost ready for harvesting, yet in the light from the full, bright moon in a clear sky the countryside seemed different shades of grey. With a shock, Kate realized it was almost a year since she and Danny had joined up.

'A bomber's moon, Kate,' Philip murmured, interrupting her thoughts. 'I wonder where they're headed for tonight?'

'Who? Us – or them?'

He gave a wry laugh. 'Both! It's mad, isn't it? It's all absolutely mad. A waste of young lives.'

'But, sir . . .'

'Oh, don't get me wrong. I'm as patriotic as the next man and I know full well what we have to do. But – oh, dear Lord – just sometimes I get so sick and tired, so desperately tired, of seeing all those fine young men flying off into the sky and knowing that by the law of averages some aren't going to come back.'

'I know – I feel exactly the same sometimes.'

'I thought you did,' he said, so quietly that she almost didn't catch his words. In the car, side by side, there was an intimacy between them that had nothing to do with a commanding officer and his driver.

Kate was emboldened to ask softly, the use of his Christian name coming naturally at this moment, 'And how about you, Philip? How are things with your family?'

He gave a long, deep sigh. 'So-so,' he replied, his tone non-committal.

Kate stared at him but his face was in heavy shadow and she could not read his expression. Questions buzzed around her brain, but Philip volunteered no more and she could hardly pursue the matter.

He pulled a pipe from his pocket and began to pack it, more, it seemed, to give his hands something to do, rather than because he needed to smoke it. 'You don't mind, do you?' he asked her, indicating the pipe.

'No – no, of course not.'

'I suppose,' he said in staccato clauses between puffs, 'we had – better be – getting back.'

As she started the engine and eased the car off the grass verge and down the incline, Philip said suddenly, 'Am I imagining things, or is that aircraft?'

Kate opened her mouth to answer, but at that moment a small bomb fell into the road about two hundred yards in front of them. The whole world seemed to explode in a flash and Kate gave a cry and swerved. The car bounced across the grass verge and settled, nose-first, into a ditch. Kate groaned and thought, irrationally at such a moment, there I go again falling back into my bad ways!

'Out the car, quick!' Philip was out of his side and scrambling round to the driver's side. He tugged at the door. 'Open the door, Kate.'

'I can't – it's stuck.'

'Slide across to the other side,' he shouted, and struggled back round the car again. He bent and reached in to grasp her hand and pull her out. She fell out of the car into his arms.

'You're not hurt, are you?'

'No – no . . .'

'Come on then, we must get away from this car. If a bomb drops on this, we'll be toast.'

He grabbed her hand and pulled her after him, thrusting a way through the hedge and into the cornfield. They waded through the waist-high corn until they were almost in the centre of the field and well away from the car. Above them, the sound of an aircraft came steadily nearer.

'Down, Kate, down!' Even as he spoke, Philip pushed her to the ground and flung himself on top of her, his body shielding hers, his hands covering her head protectively.

The bomb fell a hundred yards from them, and the earth shook beneath them. Soil erupted and spattered down all around, and they could smell the burning cordite. Kate gave a shriek and put her arms round Philip's back, burying her face into his neck. The noise of the plane was growing fainter, yet they lay there tense and waiting for the sound of more bombers.

'I think,' Philip murmured, 'they've gone.' They could smell the burning crater but now there was a beautiful silence, the whispering wind rippling through the corn and the pitiful cries of birds, disturbed from sleep and flying in disorientated circles above them, the only sounds. Philip shifted his weight a little, but made no effort to get up. He put his right arm under her neck and the other around her waist and bent his face towards her. 'Oh, Kate, Kate . . .' Then he was kissing her, gently at first and then with increasing urgency.

Her arms were about his neck and she twisted her body towards him. She felt him unbutton her jacket and suddenly his hand was warm and gentle on her breast. His fingertips, trembling slightly, caressed her nipple which hardened immediately under his touch. Her lips parted and his kiss became deeper, probing, yet tender.

'Oh, Kate, I love you, I need you . . .'

She was returning his kisses with matching ardour, drowning in the new sensations her body was experiencing, lost to all sense and reason, awakened from innocence to the sensations of passion . . .

'Oh, I wish we could stay here for ever,' he murmured,

cradling her head against his chest as he lay on his back looking up at the moon and stars. She was quiet, a gentle smile playing on her lips, savouring the tumult of emotions, enjoying the aftermath of an ecstasy she had never even guessed existed between a man and a woman. His fingers were stroking her hair, touching her cheek, and then he lifted his head to kiss the top of hers, nuzzling his face against her hair. 'My dearest Kate.' Then as her silence lengthened, there was an anxious question in his voice. 'Kate?'

She did not speak but lifted her head, seeking his mouth. She heard him groan deep in his throat. It was the answer he sought. His arms came strongly about her, pulling her on top of him.

They made love again, slowly, savouring every moment, every touch, until desire claimed them once more.

'I suppose we shall have to go,' he said reluctantly, some time later. He got up and held out his hands to help her up. Standing, he pulled her close to him, searching her face, pale in the moonlight. Gently he bent down and kissed her forehead and then her mouth. Kate put her arms about his waist, hugging him to her. It had happened so suddenly, and yet so naturally; she had no regrets.

They had begun to walk across the field, their arms about each other, when they heard the sound of an approaching vehicle.

'Come on, we'd better hurry. If they spot the car, they might stop.'

They reached the edge of the field as the RAF policeman got out of his jeep and slid down the sloping grass verge towards the staff car, nose first in the ditch.

'It's okay, we're here,' Philip called, holding aside the hedge for Kate to squeeze through.

A torch was shone in their faces and then flicked off quickly. 'Oh, sorry, sir. Are either of you hurt?'

'No, we're fine. There was an air-raid. A bomb fell on the road in front of us and we landed up in the ditch and then took cover in the field. We thought it safest to get right away from the car.'

'Of course, sir. Can I give you a lift back?'

'Yes, please. I just want my bag out of the car . . .'

'I'll get it, sir.'

He held open the door of his jeep for Kate and Philip to climb in, closed the door, retrieved Philip's bag and returned to his own vehicle. 'If you say there's been a bomb up ahead, sir, I'd better go another way. Is that all right, sir?'

'Fine.' The jeep's engine burst into life and under cover of its noise, Philip whispered, 'Take as long as you like.' In the darkness, he reached for Kate's hand and held it until they had passed through the gates of Suddaby Station.

The next morning, with a fresh staff car, Kate drew up outside the CO's office. Before she could get out of the car to open the rear door for him, Philip came bounding out and got into the front seat of the car, slamming the door and grinning at her. For one dreadful moment she thought he was going to kiss her there and then in front of the whole station, but instead, he leaned back against the leather seat, stretched his long legs, and gave a self-satisfied sigh.

'Drive.'

'Sir – shouldn't you – er – sit in the back?'

'Drive! Into the country.'

An impish smile curved her mouth. 'Where?' she asked in an innocent tone. 'To the nearest cornfield?'

'Shameless hussy!' But he was smiling fondly at her as he said it.

Confused now, she bent to touch the starter button. 'Sir – you really shouldn't look at me like that.'

'Can't help it,' he said, never taking his gaze from her. 'I don't know when I last felt so happy.'

She gave a little gasp of surprise and turned to look back at him, but the look on his face told her that his words were genuine.

She had never seen him looking so relaxed and contented. His face looked years younger and, with the lines of worry smoothed from his forehead and a sparkle in his eyes, he was even more handsome than ever.

'Go back to where we parked last night and, no, I don't mean the cornfield. The top of the hill, you know where I mean?'

Kate nodded.

'We can sit and talk there, yet I think we can see the road in both directions if anyone comes along.'

She pulled carefully on to the wide grass verge, bringing the car to a halt and pulled on the brake. As she switched off the engine, Philip reached for her hand, raised it to his lips and kissed each one of her fingers slowly and deliberately. A thrill of pleasure ran through her and she knew she was blushing.

'Kate – I want you to know that this is not just a wartime fling. I've been falling in love with you for ages, oh, maybe ever since that first moment I opened my eyes and saw you bending over me in the little boat off the beach at Dunkirk. I don't know. I wanted to see you again and all the time I was making inquiries to see if you'd joined up and then pulling strings to have you posted as my driver. Well . . .' He shrugged his wide shoulders. 'All I know is I had the strangest – compulsion – to see you, to be with you, even though I also had the feeling that it might be – well, dangerous.'

'Dangerous?'

A cloud came over his new-found happiness. His eyes were filled with sadness as he said hoarsely, 'I want to be honest with you . . . I don't want to hurt you . . .'

'What is it, Philip?' she encouraged, guessing what he was trying to say.

'I'm – married.'

'I know,' she said, and the look on his face was so comical that she laughed, leaned across and kissed his cheek.

'You know?' he said incredulously.

'Mmm – Mavis!'

'Oh – Mavis,' he echoed, and a wry smile curved his mouth briefly.

'Yes. What Mavis doesn't know, Mavis will make it her business to find out,' she smiled, and added, so that he would not get the wrong idea about her friend, 'but it's not malicious nosiness. Not with her, anyway.'

'No, I know that.' He sighed. 'I'm glad you do know. I spent half last night reliving . . .' he looked at her and his eyes darkened with desire at the mere memory, 'the cornfield – and the rest of the night feeling a real heel because it had happened.'

'Well, there's no need to feel a heel. I'm a big girl. I knew you were married but it doesn't take a genius to see you're not exactly happy, or presumably your wife – and children if you have any – would be here with you, living in the CO's house.'

'You – don't know it all then? You don't know about my – daughter?'

'No, I don't know anything other than that you are married.'

He looked down at her hand, still resting quietly in his, then he raised it again and held it against his cheek.

'I must tell you . . .'

'You don't have to,' she cut in quickly.

'I – want to,' he said firmly. He was thoughtful for a long moment and then he began to tell her about his life before he had known her.

'I'm from a Forces family and so is my wife. My father was a Brigadier in the last war. Of course, he wanted me to join his old regiment and he was rather cut up when I opted for the youngest service, even though I decided to make a career in the RAF. My wife too was from a long line of serving officers and our parents were friends – still are, which makes it all the more difficult. Grace and I were thrown together and soon it became expected that we should marry. I think both of us got caught up in it and carried along without making any conscious decision for ourselves. I was – still am – very fond of Grace and never wanted to hurt her . . .' He hesitated and then began again on a different tack. 'We have a daughter, Lizzie. She – she was born with serious physical handicaps and the prognosis is that she won't reach her teens.'

'Oh, Philip!' Kate whispered, and tears filled her eyes.

'Grace has devoted her life to the child, whereas I – well – I can't do very much, not unless I leave the RAF and devote myself to her in the same way. But Grace's devotion has become almost an obsession. I think her own mother has filled her mind with the thought that the abnormalities must come from my side, when in truth I don't think there's blame to be attached to either of us. It just – happened.'

The words came unbidden to Kate's lips and were voiced before she really realized she was saying them. 'Some people find it easier to deal with life's cruelties if they can find someone to blame.' She heard the words almost as if someone else were speaking them.

'I suppose so,' Philip said heavily. 'Grace's mother moved in with us and sort of – took over.'

'And pushed you out and the more distant you became, the more they blamed you.'

He looked at her wonderingly. 'You *do* understand, don't you?'

She said nothing but gave his hand a little squeeze.

'Oh, Kate, what am I going to do? What are we going to do?'

Sensibly, she said, 'We'll take it day by day, just like everyone else is having to do in this war, and when it's all over – well, we'll see then, won't we?'

She smiled at him as he leaned forward to kiss her mouth. As his lips touched hers, desire ran through her like a shock wave.

When she went back to her hut in the early evening, the letter was lying on her bed. At once she recognized Danny's sloping handwriting on the envelope.

With a jolt Kate realized that during the last twenty-four hours she had not once thought of Danny Eland.

Thirty-Two

So, Rosie was to have Danny's child.

Kate sat on the bed, waiting for the hurt to come. Rosie is having Danny's baby, she told herself, and tightened the muscles in her stomach, waiting.

She felt nothing. All she could see in her mind's eye was Rosie's happy face, her dancing golden curls, and Danny's proud grin stretching from ear to ear. And just fancy, Beth a grandma! How pleased she would be.

Kate had the strangest feeling that she was gripping Danny's hand tightly, hanging on to it like someone drowning. Then gradually, she felt as if she were loosening her hold, not completely, but just starting to let go; beginning to let Danny go.

She stood up, folded his letter and put it back into the envelope, opened the drawer of her locker and tucked it behind the whelk shell.

Slowly she closed the drawer.

'Do you know,' Philip said, a comical expression on his face, 'I'm running out of excuses for us to drive out of camp.'

Kate giggled, then her face sobered. 'We shall have to be careful. I wouldn't want to see your career damaged.'

'What about you? I don't want to see you hurt.' He sighed heavily. 'Oh, Kate, I love you so but I wish things could be different.'

'They couldn't be so very different, even if you weren't married,' she said directly, but the gentleness of her tone took away the bluntness of her words. 'We still wouldn't be able to meet openly. Me a lowly corporal and you a Group Captain!'

'Yes. Isn't it ridiculous?'

'It seems so, but the powers-that-be must have had their reasons for setting such rules. I suppose they had the undermining of discipline in mind.'

He nodded. 'Well, not all girls would be as understanding as you, Kate. Some would try to take advantage.'

She giggled again. 'Oh, I take advantage of you – whenever I get the chance.'

'Kate!' he exclaimed, pretending to be shocked, but in truth enjoying her admission that she enjoyed their love-making as much as he did. He put his arm along the back of the seat and caressed her neck. The tingling sensation his touch caused made her swerve slightly.

'I think you'd better stop that unless you want to end up in the ditch again,' she said.

They laughed together.

Their love affair continued through the winter months of 1941. As its intensity grew, it was inevitable that they could not hide it from everyone. Though they tried to be circumspect in public, strove valiantly to be strictly CO and driver in front of others, there was the light of love in their eyes when they looked at each other, such a spring in their steps as they hurried to drive away from the camp to be alone for a few snatched moments, that soon, someone must notice and the tongues would start wagging.

At the Christmas dance in the Officers' Mess, Philip came towards Kate and she went into his arms as if it were the most natural thing in the world. They danced together the whole evening. He did not dance with any other girl – not even the senior WAAF officer there – and when he led Kate to a table, brought her a drink and sat down with her, all the other airmen and officers shrugged their shoulders and turned their thoughts away from even thinking of asking the CO's beautiful driver for a dance.

But for some, the sight of Group Captain Philip Trent monopolizing the company of Corporal Kate Hilton was not so easily forgotten.

'Kate – you'll get yourself into bother.' Mavis, with Isobel one pace behind as if to back her, was standing at the foot of her bed the following morning.

'Eh?' Kate glanced up from the letter she was writing home, and could see at once by their faces that they had guessed. 'I don't know what you're talking about.'

'Oh yes, you do. You don't usually tell lies, Kate Hilton.'

Kate felt herself colouring. No, she didn't. She had always been a very truthful person, but this time it was not just herself she was trying to protect.

As if reading her thoughts, Isobel murmured, 'You see, Mave, her trouble is that she's not a tell-tale. I can vouch for that.'

'And don't say it's none of our business . . .' Mavis began, as they came and sat on her bed, one either side of her.

' . . . Because it is,' finished Isobel.

'You'd make a good double act,' Kate said, trying to steer them off the topic. 'Ever thought of applying to ENSA?'

'It's got to stop, Kate,' Isobel said. 'You'll get into awful trouble – and so will he. He might lose his whole career and he's a nice bloke.'

'Too nice,' Mavis said.

'You've got it wrong. We're just good friends . . .'

Isobel snorted. 'Now, where have I heard that before?'

352

Mavis leaned closer, whispering even though there was no one else in the hut to overhear. 'I told you before, Kate, he's married. If there is anything going on, you're both running a terrible risk.'

'It's not as if he is a flier,' Isobel resorted to shock tactics, 'and any day might be his last.'

'We're trying to make you see sense,' Mavis said. 'We both know how upset you were over Danny and no one more than us wanted you to meet a nice feller and fall in love, but did you *have* to pick the CO *and* a married man?'

'Not very sensible, was it?' Isobel added.

'I've told you,' Kate tried to insist. 'There's nothing . . .'

'Well, it ought to stop – now!' Isobel said ruthlessly, totally disbelieving Kate's protests, and Mavis added, 'Don't say we didn't warn you.'

'Kate – come in.' Philip moved to pull down the blackout blinds on his office window, then came and locked the door behind her. He took her in his arms.

'Darling, there's something I have to tell you.'

Fear clutched her stomach. What had happened? Was it something awful?

'You know, don't you, that the two squadrons on this station are switching to the new Lancaster bomber?'

She nodded.

'Well,' he went on slowly, his blue gaze never leaving her face, 'so are East Markham.'

Kate stared at him, running her tongue over lips that were suddenly dry.

'The Lanc is too heavy for Markham's grass runways. So they're closing East Markham temporarily to lay new concrete runways . . .'

'And?' Kate prompted, although now she was beginning to guess what was coming.

' . . . and their squadrons are being moved elsewhere – again only temporarily. Kate,' his fingers gently traced the outline of her face, 'Danny's squadron is coming here.'

She found she had been holding her breath. Now she let it out slowly and smiled. 'That's all right,' she said.

He searched her face. 'I didn't know how you would feel. I mean, I know you once asked me to see if I could wangle a posting here for him, but – well – that was before he got married and before – us.'

'I'll be fine,' she promised him softly, and some of the anxiety was smoothed from Philip's face.

Kate was pleased Danny was coming to Suddaby. She would have the chance to talk to him, to explain why she had not attended the wedding. If she could talk to him – alone – she knew she could make him understand. Soon, everything between them would be all right again; it would be as it had always been.

But she could not go home. Even yet, she could not face Rosie – especially a heavily pregnant Rosie.

The day the Lancasters arrived at Suddaby, there was great excitement.

'Heavens! They're big!' Mavis gasped, as, along with Kate and Isobel, they stood on the peritrack watching.

'Who? The Lancs – or the fellers?' Kate grinned.

Mavis's laughter bounced on the breeze. She rubbed her hands together, 'Well, if the crews are as good as their aircraft – wheel 'em out!'

'Mavis, really! What about the wonderful Dave?'

Mavis turned pink. 'I can still look, can't I?'

'Is it serious with you two, then?' Isobel asked, but Mavis

only grinned and said, 'Can't hear you above the racket, Iso, old thing.'

The aircraft taxied past them, several with symbols and pictures painted on them just below the cockpit. A shapely female proclaimed M-Mother and the three girls pointed and laughed.

'Well, if that's someone's mother, I'm a Dutchman.'

'Look, there's P-Pluto,' Mavis pointed. Behind it came another, D-Doggo, depicting a bulldog with an enemy plane – the swastika plainly visible – crushed in its massive jaw.

'Aren't they wonderful?' Mavis said, her admiring glance following the aircraft. 'Four Rolls Royce Merlin engines and they can carry over twenty thousand pounds of bombs.'

'I don't know how they get 'em into the air. They're massive!'

'Well, you just watch, sunshine. They will – and tonight if this weather holds.'

Kate gasped. 'So soon? But they've only just got here.'

'War won't wait for them to be pampered. That reminds me, Iso, we might have to do double shift tonight. With all these extra kites here, we're going to be a bit busy. And if it's long-range, they're going to be very low on fuel by the time they get back.'

Isobel groaned. 'Then I'm off to get a bit of shut-eye now.'

Mavis and Isobel turned and walked back across the grass towards the camp gate and the road leading to the WAAF site, leaving Kate staring at the new arrivals and wondering just which aircraft was Danny's.

Throughout the day the airfield hummed with activity. The arrival of an additional squadron and all its attendant personnel put an additional strain on the new airfield's resources. And now, with the rumour spreading that the night's op was to be 'a big one', there was an air of tension and scarcely concealed excitement.

'I must go to Group HQ,' Philip told her, 'for a meeting with the AOC.'

'Sir,' Kate responded dutifully, but beneath her breath she muttered a frustrated 'Damn!' She was so anxious to see Danny before he flew that night, but now she was to be away from the station for most of the day.

At Group Headquarters, Kate found herself with little to do while she waited for Philip. It was always the same, she thought. He was involved in lengthy conferences and meetings whilst she wandered from room to room, feeling in the way, on the edge of all the activity yet unable to take part.

Kate sat watching a WAAF Flight Officer who was analysing the photographs from the previous night's raid ready for the meeting called by the Air Officer Commanding.

'Do you know what tonight's target is?' Kate asked her.

The WAAF officer looked up and smiled. 'Not yet. We should be getting the signal from Bomber Command any time. The weather's exceptionally good just now, so it'll probably be something big.'

Kate nodded, but her thoughts were back at Suddaby. She just had to see Danny before take-off that night.

As the WAAF officer had predicted, when the signal came through it was a 'maximum effort raid'; the Ruhr.

Back on station, Kate drove Philip immediately to briefing.

'Would it be all right if – if I came in? I'll sit right at the back out of the way.'

He looked at her. 'Danny?' he asked softly.

She smiled tremulously and whispered, 'You're far too observant, Group Captain Trent.'

He smiled, but there was still a sadness in his eyes, though whether it was for her or for himself, she couldn't be sure.

'You'll have to pretend you're dispensing tea or something, Kate. I really can't get you admitted to the briefing. I'm sorry.' His apology was genuine; she realized at once that she had put him in a very difficult position by even asking for such a favour.

She forced a smile on to her mouth and said brightly, 'I understand. I'll go and help Christine.'

He nodded and at the doorway, they parted; he strode into the briefing room whilst Kate slipped into a tiny room at the side where a WAAF was pouring out cups of tea from a huge urn. Christine glanced up, but seeing that it was the CO's WAAF driver she made no demur about Kate's presence. Almost everyone on the camp now allowed her admittance even to the most sensitive of areas, recognizing that the CO trusted the discretion of his driver implicitly. The knowledge warmed her.

Outside the aircraft were being fuelled from the huge tankers and the armourers would be loading up the bomb trains; twelve 500-pounders and one 4000-pound bomb for each Lancaster. It was a physically demanding and sometimes dangerous job.

By the time the aircrews were filing into briefing, their aircraft would be standing ready at dispersal, fuelled, tested and bombed up.

As the crews trooped in, Kate scanned their faces eagerly through the hatch from the tiny kitchen. No one even glanced in her direction; their eyes went immediately to the large wall map showing their target. By the time most of the chairs were filled and the men came to attention as the Station and Squadron Commanders entered, Kate had still not spotted Danny. As the briefing began, she searched among the heads, trying to pick out his black hair, but then as the man from the

Met Office opened the proceedings, Kate found her attention captivated. Unobserved, she was able to eavesdrop on the whole procedure. It was impossible to be oblivious to the tension in the room, the feeling of a peculiar excitement. In front of her the airmen were making notes, their whole attention focused on the man pointing at the weather map, transferring all the information in front of them to their own maps and charts.

'Over the target, conditions should be fair . . . over base on return, clear . . .'

The Met man stepped down and the Flying Control Officer stepped up to give details of the runway to be used and take off times. The intelligence officer fascinated Kate and she found herself gripping the edge of the hatch as she leaned forward to listen to him giving route details, where the aircraft, once over enemy territory, might encounter flak and where they might expect to be intercepted by enemy night fighters.

Then came the Squadron Commander and lastly she watched Philip as he addressed his men, emphasizing the importance of accurate navigation and time-keeping. There were to be a great number of aircraft all heading in the same direction . . . Everyone in the room synchronized their watches and finally Philip wished them all good luck.

As the CO left the dais and marched between the ranks of men, Kate scuttled out of the building. By the time Philip emerged she was standing with the car door open in readiness. Only when they were in the staff car did he ask, 'Did you manage to see him?'

'No,' she said, unable to keep the tremor from her voice. He leaned forward from the back seat as she added, 'But I've only just realized, he'll be at the other briefing, won't he? He's a rear-gunner.'

The radio operators and gunners had a separate briefing.

'Oh Kate, I'm sorry. I hadn't realized he was a gunner. I haven't had chance to meet everyone yet. Tell you what – drop me off at my office. You might just catch them drawing their flying kit. But can you be sure to be back to pick me up in time to take me out to dispersal?'

'Oh, thank you. Yes, of course I will.'

Minutes later, Kate was hovering outside Parachute Section waiting for the crews to emerge.

If only she could just see him, talk to him . . .

'Kate! Kate!' Suddenly there he was, coming towards her, a bulky figure in his sheepskin flying jacket and leather boots, his parachute slung carelessly over one shoulder. But the cheeky grin was the same as ever.

'Danny, oh Danny . . .' For a moment her vision blurred as tears filled her eyes. Then she was reaching out and he was taking her hands in his.

'I had to see you, I want to tell you . . .'

'Eland,' came a deep voice behind them and they both glanced round. 'Time to go.'

'Sir,' Danny responded and turning back, squeezed Kate's hands quickly. 'I'm sorry, Katie . . .'

'But, Danny, I have to talk to you, I have to explain . . .'

'Later, Katie, when I get back.'

For a desperate moment she clung to his hands, but he pulled himself free, smiled a rueful apology and hurried after the rest of his crew.

'Danny, Danny . . .' she called, running after him. 'Which – which is your plane, please tell me?'

She had to know which aircraft he was in; she had to be able to watch for it coming back.

He turned back briefly, raised his hand in a wave, and called, 'D-Doggo . . . I'll see you when I get back.'

Thirty-Three

Kate watched him walk away from her. There was still an hour to take-off, but the crews needed to go out to their aircraft, for all the cockpit checks and starting the engines of forty aircraft – more now a third squadron had arrived – would take up every minute of that time.

As she saw Danny climb into the back of a covered lorry, Kate turned towards the staff car. It was time to pick up Philip.

She watched take-off from the roof of the control tower as she had done so many times before alongside Philip. This time it was different; this time Danny was out there somewhere, hunched in his lonely rear turret, the most vulnerable position in the whole aircraft to enemy night fighters. The huge aircraft, cumbersome with their weight of bombs and fuel, taxied from the various dispersal points, forming up to take off in orderly, timed intervals. At the end of the runway, each aircraft waited for the controller's red light to switch to green before revving its engines and beginning its lumbering, heart-stopping take-off. The noise of over two hundred Merlin engines filled the night air, as one by one they trundled down the runway, gathering speed, faster and faster, till Kate found she was holding her breath, willing each one into the air. The end of the runway came nearer and nearer until it seemed impossible they would make it. Then, just as her knuckles were turning white as she gripped the rail, the aircraft would lift unwillingly into the air, its undercarriage immediately raised. Silhouetted against the darkening sky, the bombers were like a flock of predatory birds carrying death and destruction in their bellies.

From this distance, she could not see which was D-Doggo, but it did not stop her praying, 'Oh, please let him come back safely – let them all come back safely . . .'

Soon they'd be flying over the coast, maybe over Flee-thaven Point. Would Danny be thinking of Rosie far below, blissfully ignorant of the danger he was in, when she, Kate, knew only too well?

In the control tower, in a pool of light, the personnel on duty – Mavis and Isobel among them – began to plot the movement of the aircraft.

As the sound of the last aircraft faded into the distance, Kate felt a light touch on her shoulder and turned to see Philip's concerned face. 'Come on, Kate,' he said gently. 'We'll go back to my office.'

She nodded. 'I'll drop you off and then – then I want to go back to my hut . . .'

She hesitated as she saw the pain flit across his face, and added swiftly, 'I need my coat, but I'll come back if – if you want me to.'

His voice was husky as he said, 'Of course I want you to.'

She took Philip to his office, leaving the staff car parked outside, for they would need it once more in the cold light of dawn as the Lancasters struggled home. She walked out of the airfield's main gate and across the road to the WAAF site. Inside the hut she pulled on her greatcoat, feeling suddenly cold. About to turn away, she paused and, with fingers which trembled slightly, pulled open the drawer of her locker. The whelk shell nestled against her pile of clean handkerchiefs. Hesitating only a moment, she picked it up and slipped it into the pocket of her coat. It was their talisman and during the long night ahead she was going to need it. There was nothing to do now but wait!

When the first aircraft were due back the airfield beacon was switched on. How glad the crews would be to see it flashing the signal SB; Suddaby, home and safety. As the first planes began to land, Kate and Philip were back in the Control Room. While Philip stood quietly behind the R/T operator, Kate sat in the shadows in one corner, listening and watching in fascination as the personnel worked. There was an air of deliberate calm, and yet the atmosphere crackled with tension. A WAAF began to fill in the landing times of the returning aircraft on the huge board. Kate's glance kept coming back time and again to D-Doggo.

There was no need for radio silence now the raid was over, and Mavis and Isobel began calling up the aircraft. One by one the planes landed. There were anxious moments when one aircraft had to do an emergency landing because its undercarriage was damaged, and another limped in on only two engines. As always, the fire crews stood ready and raced towards the aircraft as it slewed off the runway and on to the grass. There was another crisis when two planes wanted to come in at the same time because they were dangerously low on fuel and were given permission to land, one immediately after the other.

Kate felt the sweat prickle the back of her neck and marvelled at her two friends for their composed efficiency and the way they kept their voices calm and professional when giving directions to the aircrew. Long gone were any criticisms that Mavis was too excitable. Now, she nursed down a lame aircraft, soothed the momentary panic of a young pilot on his first op and juggled expertly with the extra aircraft stacking above the airfield, all demanding runway space at once, it seemed to Kate.

Now, there were only three Suddaby aircraft and four from the visiting East Markham squadron to come in.

Philip was bending down in front of her. 'I must go across to de-briefing . . .' he began, and as she made to rise to take him across in the car, he put his hand briefly on hers. 'You stay here, if you want to,' he whispered.

'If you're sure . . .?' She looked up into his eyes, but in the dim light, his expression was difficult to read. He gave her hand a swift squeeze, straightened up, turned away and was gone.

Huddled in the corner, she watched and waited, feeling even more alone now that Philip had left.

The radio fell silent, yet Mavis and Isobel were still vigilant. They would not relax until all the aircraft were in, or . . . Kate shuddered, suddenly realizing what her two friends dealt with every day. Waiting and listening for the planes to come back. Sometimes, waiting in vain.

The waiting was becoming unbearable. Quietly, Kate slipped out of the Control Room.

The vehicles were drawing up outside de-briefing and she watched the young airmen walking towards the building, their young faces lined with tension and grey with exhaustion. It was so hard to believe that these were the same men who laughed and drank and made merry in the pub and the dance hall. Then, they looked as if they didn't have a care in the world, whereas now . . .

Tentatively, she touched the arm of a pilot officer passing close by her. 'Excuse me, are you from the East Markham squadron?'

His glance took in her WAAF uniform. Guardedly, he nodded.

'Do you – know Danny Eland?'

'Yes,' he said briefly.

'Is – is he safe?'

The young man, his eyes glazed with tiredness, shrugged. 'Sorry – can't say. I mean – I don't know. I don't know yet who's back – and who's not,' he added significantly.

There was another aircraft approaching the runway, its engines coughing and spluttering. Any moment it would be out of fuel. Lower and lower it dropped until its huge tyres hit the runway with a squeal and it was racing along the concrete. In the darkness Kate could not see its name and she shivered in the cold morning, waiting, still waiting . . .

The crew were piling out of the crewbus and walking towards her. She moved forward a step.

'Danny?' she whispered, but the men were strangers. It was not Danny's crew.

She swallowed the fear rising in her throat and looked anxiously towards the east, willing there to be another plane in view. But the dawning sky was empty and silent.

She went into the building where de-briefing was taking place; the crews, drinking tea, were moving from one WAAF interrogator to another as they gave their various reports. Kate felt the fear in the pit of her stomach, as she glanced around the room. There was no sign of Danny, nor of any other member of his crew.

She repeated her question. 'Are you from East Markham? Do you know what's happened to D-Doggo?'

'No, sorry. Three aircraft went down over the target. Maybe . . .'

She turned away; she didn't want to hear.

Across the room, she saw Philip, moving among the crews, glance at her. Kate bit her lip. She shouldn't be here, really. But he did not look angry, only worried.

She left the building and ran, her heart thumping, back towards the control tower. Breathless, she ran up the stairs and burst into the Control Room. She paused in the doorway, her hand still holding the door-handle, her frightened eyes going at once to the blackboard.

There were two names still on the board: P-Pluto and D-Doggo. Dragging her terrified gaze from the board, she met Dave's sympathetic eyes. Instead of being annoyed with her for charging into the Control Room, he rose, came towards her and led her gently to a chair in the corner. 'Sit there, love, I'll get you a cuppa.'

The room, which only half an hour ago had seemed chaotic, a nerve centre of activity, was now silent. Only crackles and whistles emitted from the radio, no pilot's voice requesting permission to land, no voice giving the call-sign 'D-Doggo here'.

She had to face the truth; Danny was missing.

Mavis and Isobel were sitting in front of their radio control panels and Kate sensed they could not bring themselves to say anything, or even look at her.

Kate started up as footsteps sounded hollowly on the concrete stairs outside. Then Philip came into the Control Room. He glanced immediately at the board, just as she had done, and then his gaze came around slowly to rest upon her huddled miserably in the corner.

Ignoring the rule-book once more and how it would look to those in the Control Room, Philip touched her shoulder, his voice firm yet infinitely tender. 'Come on, Kate.'

Stiffly, Kate eased her aching limbs from their locked position and, with his arm about her shoulders, allowed herself to be guided down the narrow stairs.

Outside, to the east, the sky was growing lighter. Dawn would be casting its soft glow over Fleethaven, she thought, silhouetting the cottages, rousing the sleepy occupants to another day. Soon, at home, they would be rising, her mother first, then Jonathan, and the day's work would begin.

And Beth. In her cottage she would be first to rise, perhaps taking Rosie a cup of tea in bed. Perhaps they would speak of Danny. Of course they would speak of Danny. But did they know, could they guess, the agony she, Kate, was going through at this very moment? Did they, too, watch the sky night after night, hearing the aircraft droning overhead, and wonder if somewhere in the vast dark sky was Danny up there? Did they lie awake waiting, listening for the return?

Walking along beside Philip, she thrust her hands deep into her pockets and felt the whelk shell. She gripped it until the point dug into her palm. Was this really all she would have left of Danny now? She would keep it with her always, she vowed, until he was safely home . . .

In the seclusion of his office, Philip took her in his arms. She clung to him, burying her head against his smart commanding officer's uniform, her tears making mottled damp patches on his shoulder. Her held her tightly, stroking her hair, but saying nothing.

She drew back a little and looked up at him, his features blurred through her tears. 'I'll have to go home,' she stuttered. 'I must t-tell – Rosie.'

Gently he wiped the tears from her face, but could not stem the flow.

His voice was flat and heavy as he said quietly, 'Yes, my dear. I'll arrange it for you.'

Thirty-Four

'Why, Katie love!' The joy on Beth Eland's face at seeing her was unmistakable, but then she saw Kate's solemn face, the anxiety in her eyes. Beth's hand flew to cover her mouth which formed a silent 'oh'. Then she reached out and drew Kate into the kitchen.

'What is it?'

Kate looked into the older woman's face. Gently, she took hold of her hand and said, 'Is Rosie here?'

Beth nodded. 'She – she's lying down. She gets very tired. She's only a few weeks to go . . .'

'Can you fetch her?'

Beth nodded, her eyes anxious, an ill-concealed terror growing in them.

Rosie came into the kitchen, her young face flushed from sleep, her blonde curls tousled, her body swollen with child. She paused in the doorway as she met Kate's steady gaze. Kate held out her arms to Rosie, and the girl gave a little cry and with surprising swiftness covered the distance between them. They clasped each other, Kate leaning forward over Rosie's bulge. The girl drew back with a nervous laugh of embarrassment and glanced down at her stomach. 'Gets in the way a bit, dun't it?'

'Sit down, Rosie,' Kate said, and Beth stood quietly beside her daughter-in-law's chair. Instinctively, the girl put up her hand and caught hold of Beth's. Then their eyes met Kate's.

She took a deep breath, trying to still the sick feeling

that was rising in her stomach. 'You know that Danny was stationed at East Markham and I'm at Suddaby.'

They nodded, their gaze never leaving her face.

'East Markham has been closed temporarily for concrete runways to be constructed...' She paused again. 'And Danny's squadron has been moved to Suddaby.'

Rosie's face brightened. 'Oh, how lovely! You'll be together. I *am* pleased.'

Kate bit her lip. There was not a trace of jealousy in Rosie's tone. She was genuinely happy to think that Kate and Danny would be together. 'Isn't that wonderful, Mother?' Rosie smiled up at Beth, but the older woman's gaze never left Kate's face.

'Have you seen him, Katie?' Rosie chattered on brightly, her joy at thinking they had met twisting like a knife in Kate's heart. She pulled in another deep breath. This was even harder than she had imagined it would be. 'They arrived two days ago but I only saw him very briefly. I – I didn't have a chance to talk to him – not properly.' Here her voice almost quavered. She had wanted so desperately to speak to him, to explain, to make up their quarrel. Now she might never have the chance.

'That same night all the aircraft from Suddaby and the squadron from East Markham – they – they all had to go on a big operation...'

She was going round in circles, avoiding the moment when she must tell them the awful news. And they were waiting so patiently, so trustingly, not firing questions at her or demanding that she hurry up. Yet surely they must realize...

'My two friends are R/T operators and I was allowed to sit in the Control Room and – and watch for the planes to come in. Only – only – oh, Rosie...' Tears filled her eyes and their faces became blurred in front of her. 'Danny's aircraft didn't c-come back.'

There was silence in the room save for the clock ticking and the kettle humming on the hob, and outside a lone seagull cried mournfully. For a long moment the two women stared at Kate, and then Rosie's face crumpled and she let out a cry that pierced Kate's heart, for it echoed her own foreboding. She went and knelt before the girl, grasping her hands as they twisted in her lap, while Beth stood by, not moving, as if she had not really taken in the dreadful news.

'Listen, Rosie, listen. His plane has been posted missing, but that doesn't mean he's – he's dead. He could have baled out. Anything. You mustn't give up hope. None of us.' She looked up at Beth in mute appeal for help, but Beth was stunned. Woodenly, she moved to sit in the Windsor chair that had been her husband's. The husband she had lost so recently. And now perhaps she had lost her son. Beth gripped the wooden arms tightly and stared unseeingly in front of her.

Kate scrambled to her feet. Grannie Harris, next door, she'd fetch her. Then she remembered. Poor Grannie Harris could hardly walk now and spent most of her day in a bed under the kitchen window, so, as she said herself, she could 'still look out an' see what's going on'.

Kate bit her lip. Rosie was rocking backwards and forwards, wailing horribly, a high-pitched noise that went right through Kate.

There was only one person she could fetch to help; her mother, Esther Godfrey.

What was it Danny had said, she thought wryly as she ran back towards Brumbys' Farm, her feet flying across the turf. 'They never speak to one another, but when there's trouble, real trouble, they come together.' Well, Kate thought, there was 'real trouble' now right enough.

'Of course I'll come at once,' Esther said without hesitation and only paused to issue instructions to her husband.

'I'll manage the milking, Esther love, you go,' Jonathan said calmly.

'Poor Beth,' Esther murmured as she hurried along the lane beside Kate. 'To lose her husband *and* her son so close together, to say nothing of . . .'

'We don't know he's dead yet, Mam. That's what I'm trying to get them to believe.'

Her mother eyes were sharp as she looked into Kate's face. 'Do *you* believe it?'

'I've got to,' Kate muttered, 'else I'll go out me head an' all.'

They couldn't stop Rosie crying. They tried everything – comforting her, talking to her, hugging her, even, in the end, Esther being quite firm with her. But to no avail. She sat rocking, her arms around her bulging stomach, sobbing at first, then wailing loudly and then leaning back exhausted against the back of the chair, the tears just pouring silently down her cheeks.

Where they failed with Rosie, Esther succeeded with Beth. For a couple of hours she had sat in the chair on the opposite side of the range, gripping the arms until her knuckles showed white, staring ahead of her at nothing in particular.

At last, Esther, after trying soothing words of sympathy which didn't work, stood in front of Beth. Her feet set apart, hands on hips, Esther Godfrey went into action.

'Now look here, Beth Eland, this ain't no good. You've lost a good man, I know that, and you're worried sick about young Danny. But as Kate says, we've got to hope for him yet. Now you mun think on yar grand-bairn. Ya've got to help us with Rosie . . .' Esther stood a moment watching Beth for any sign of a response. There was none.

Kate saw her mother glance across at her, raising her shoulders in a gesture of helplessness. 'I'm sorry, Katie,' she murmured. 'There's nothing for it. There's one way to bring her out of it, but it's – it's a bit brutal.'

Kate watched Beth for a moment. The woman was in a kind of trance. 'Do whatever you have to, Mam.'

Esther took a deep breath and leaned forwards, her face close to Beth's. 'It's yar grand-bairn, Beth – yours and *Matthew*'s!'

Kate winced. Her mother had not been underestimating her own harsh tactics, but when Kate saw Beth blink and begin to focus her eyes upon Esther towering over her, she knew her mother had been right.

Now Beth's hands loosened their panic-stricken grip on the chair and she reached towards Esther, who clasped her hands and chafed them between her own. 'That's it, Beth. Come on, lass.'

Kate stifled a half-hysterical giggle. To hear her mother call Beth Eland 'lass' was comical and yet, she thought, perhaps they do still see each other as girls. Girls who might, once upon a time, have been friends.

'Oh, Esther.' Beth spoke for the first time since Kate had broken the news to them. 'How am I to bear it?'

Esther just patted her hand, unable, for once, to think of anything to say.

Kate's attention swivelled suddenly back to Rosie as the girl gave a gasp that was nothing to do with weeping. Rosie was bending over and clutching her stomach. 'Oh – it hurts!'

'Mam . . .' Kate began, but already Esther had turned from Beth back to Rosie.

'Where, lass?'

'Here.' Rosie smoothed her hands round her abdomen and down her groin. 'It's all right,' she sniffled, 'it's going off now.'

Esther watched her for a moment as the girl relaxed, sat

up again and leaned back in the chair. Then Esther glanced back at Beth. 'Is everything ready?' she asked quietly.

Kate watched as Beth's eyes widened, but understanding immediately, the woman nodded. 'In the other room . . .' She nodded to the door leading out of the kitchen to the only other downstairs room in the cottage. 'Rosie sleeps in there. We—' She hesitated and then corrected herself. 'I – sleep in the little room upstairs.' So fresh was Beth's widowhood that she still sometimes forgot.

'Kate – run and tell yar dad to fetch either the doctor or the midwife. It dun't matter which, but I want one of 'em to take a look at her. She's had a bad shock and with all this crying, she could be going into labour. I aren't as practised as Grannie Harris – I could use a little advice.'

Kate was off and running, and, having delivered her breathless message, was soon sprinting back towards the row of cottages at the Point.

Esther had got Rosie into the other room and had made her lie on the bed by the time Kate arrived back, just in time to hear the girl give another scream, her eyes wide with fear.

'Oh – it hurts. I dun't want it, if it's going to hurt like this.'

'There's not a lot ya can do about it now, lass. Ya can't leave it in there for ever,' Esther said briskly, but not unkindly. She turned to look at Kate hovering uncertainly in the doorway. 'Wash yar hands well, Kate, and come and help, will ya? Beth, get the kettle going. I could use a cup 'o tea, if nothing else.'

Kate hesitated for a fraction of a second, recoiling at the irony of the situation. She had hated Rosie for marrying Danny and now here she was being forced to help her bring his child into the world. Really, she thought, scrubbing her hands under the pump over the sink, life isn't fair!

When she went back into the bedroom, Rosie was rolling

from side to side on the bed, clutching her stomach and squealing.

Kate went to stand beside her, feeling helpless and inadequate.

'Let's get her clothes off and get her into her nightdress before the doc or the nurse comes,' Esther said.

'No – leave me alone,' Rosie said petulantly. 'I want Danny!' and she began wailing again.

Gradually, by alternately coaxing and being firm with her, Esther and Kate got her undressed.

'Mam, the bed's all wet.'

'Oh heck, 'er waters have broken. Go an' tell Beth . . .'

But at that moment Beth opened the door. 'Esther, Jonathan's here. He says the doctor's out on his rounds and the nurse is with a woman and can't leave her for about an hour . . .'

'Well, someone'll have to come, 'er waters have broken.'

Beth disappeared for a moment and they heard the deep rumble of Jonathan's voice, the outer door open and close, and Beth came back into the room, her worried eyes going immediately to the girl still writhing in agony on the bed.

'He – he's gone back to town to get someone to come.'

Kate saw the look that passed between her mother and Beth – a long look of shared memories from which Kate was excluded. 'Least it's not snowing this time,' Esther murmured, and the two women smiled a little sadly at each other.

'I don't want it!' Rosie was screaming. 'I don't *want* it!'

Kate, still standing beside the bed, bent over her. Something inside her snapped. ''Course you want it. It's Danny's baby. Don't you dare say you don't want Danny's baby, Rosie Eland!' she yelled back at Rosie, while out the corner of her eye she saw her mother nodding her approval.

'That's it, lass, get her good and mad, then she might do a bit o' work.'

Rosie's screams were stilled in shock. She gazed up at Kate with big round eyes, her lips parted in a gasp of surprise.

'That's better,' Esther encouraged. 'Now, just try to calm down a bit, lass, and do as I tell you. Mebbe I bain't a midwife, but I've brought plenty of calves and piglets into the world. A babby can't be that different. Prop her up against the pillows, spread your legs open, Rosie. That's it – now ya forming, lass.'

'Oh – oh!' Rosie gasped, and held out her hand to Kate. 'Katie – it – hurts!'

'It's all right, Rosie,' Kate said gently now. 'Hang on to me, grip as hard as you like if it helps, but do what me mam tells you. Please, Rosie, for – for Danny.'

Rosie pressed her lips together and nodded. 'I'll try, Katie.'

'Next time you feel a pain swelling, Rosie, try a little push,' Esther said.

Rosie nodded. 'Oh, it's – starting again.'

'Push, Rosie.'

Gripping Kate's hand, Rosie pushed, and Kate found herself straining too.

Together they were going to bring Danny's child into the world.

Thirty-Five

'I wish that midwife would come,' Esther murmured. 'The head's born, so the rest won't be long.'

'Oh – oh,' squeaked Rosie as pain engulfed her once more.

'Push, push,' said Kate and her mother in unison.

'I – *am*! Ooh . . .'

'There!' Esther was triumphant, as if she had done it all herself. 'Beth, quick, come and see! Rosie, lass, you have a son.'

Rosie was weeping with relief now and Kate found that tears were coursing down her own face as she cradled Rosie's head against her and wiped the strands of blonde hair, wet with sweat, from her forehead.

It was at that moment that the midwife walked through the door.

'Oh Kate, I'm all mixed up. I don't know whether I'm happy or – or sad.'

Rosie was sitting up in bed now, propped against pillows with her son in her arms, flushed and triumphant, yet her eyes still filled with ready tears.

'Be happy, Rosie. It's what Danny would want,' Kate said softly, and touched the soft wispy black hair on the baby's head tenderly.

'You – you don't believe he's dead, do you?'

Kate shook her head. 'No, I—' she began and then corrected herself, conscious of Rosie's feelings. 'We'd know. We'd feel it.'

Rosie shifted the baby in her arms. 'Do – do you want to hold him, Kate?'

Kate smiled and held out her arms. 'Yes, please, Rosie.'

Sitting holding Danny's son in her arms was the strangest feeling. Danny's child; a child that might – had circumstances been different – so easily have been hers. She felt a protectiveness towards the tiny baby boy, a closeness and a flood of love.

'What are you going to call him?' Kate asked.

'Robert – after Danny's father.'

Kate nodded and said softly, 'Beth will like that.' Although she knew the facts, Rosie didn't seem to remember so readily that Robert Eland had not been Danny's natural father. But then, she was that much younger than Danny and Kate and had not even the haziest memory of Matthew Hilton. It was quite natural that Rosie should always think of Robert Eland as Danny's father.

Tears glistened in Kate's own eyes as she looked up at Rosie again. 'I've just realized – I'm his aunt.'

Rosie's eyes widened as now she, too, remembered. 'Of course you are – I was forgetting. Yes – his *only* aunt.'

She was, Kate thought. Although Rosie was the eldest of five children, all the others were boys.

'Kate – er—' Rosie twisted the sheet in her fingers. 'Can I ask you something?'

'Mmm,' Kate said absently, her attention back on the baby who was beginning to stir. He whimpered and Rosie took him back into her arms and offered him her breast.

'Would you – I'd love it if you – and I know it's what Danny would – want . . .'

Kate looked up and grinned. 'Yes, of course I will.'

Rosie's eyes widened. 'Will what? I haven't asked you yet?'

'Be his godmother.'

'How did you know that was what I was going to ask?'

'Well, you were, weren't you?'

Rosie nodded and the tiny room was suddenly filled with their laughter.

For the first time, Kate was reluctant to return to Suddaby, and yet she was anxious to see Philip again. She had so much to tell him. She could talk to Philip for he knew all about her. She longed to tell him how she had made up with Rosie and how the birth of their baby had, in a strange way, helped her.

As she stepped off the train, she saw him waiting on the platform, standing tall and dignified in his uniform, a slight frown creasing his forehead. It gave her a shock to see him there. Yet a thrill of pleasure ran through her seeing him unexpectedly; it was as if her own eagerness to see him had brought him there.

As she walked towards him, she reasoned with herself. His being here is nothing to do with you, she told herself sharply. He'll have come to catch a train . . .

'Kate!' He was coming towards her, his hands outstretched, and, oblivious of onlookers, he took her in his arms and held her close. 'Oh, Kate, how I've missed you.'

She clung to him, feeling the warmth and the strength of him.

They drew apart reluctantly. She was embarrassed by his public display, but he was grinning with happiness at seeing her again and obviously didn't care what anyone else was thinking.

'Are you catching a train?'

'Eh? Oh no, just meeting one.'

'You – you mean, you came to meet me?' she gasped.

'Yes. I've missed you so much. I couldn't wait any longer. I was even rash enough to ask Mavis what train you might be on. I've only been waiting on this draughty station for two hours!'

Lost for words, Kate just stared at him, her mouth half-open.

'You don't mind, do you?' It was the same question he'd asked her when he'd engineered her posting as his driver.

'Well, of course not, but . . .'

'Then stop dithering, woman,' the grin was back, 'and let's get to the car and into the countryside where I can kiss you properly.'

They hurried out of the station and Kate drove recklessly up the hill out of the city. A few miles from Suddaby she turned the car down a bumpy track leading deep into a wooded area that had become their secret hideaway. They were hungry for each other, desperate with desire that their separation had fuelled . . .

Afterwards they sat together in the back seat of the car, cool beneath the shadows of the trees with only the sounds of the breeze whispering through the leaves and of birdsong from the high branches.

Philip glanced at his watch. 'We'd better be making a move soon.'

'Is there an operation on tonight?' she asked.

'No, we've been stood down. Widespread fog is forecast. But I have been away from the station rather a long time on unofficial business,' he chuckled. 'I ought to be getting back.'

'Has everything been all right?' she asked. 'No more air raids?'

'No – we've had a very quiet time. Some might say too quiet.' He paused and then asked, gently, 'How were things at home?'

Kate sighed. 'Poor Rosie. She was hysterical. She went into labour and I stayed with her all the time.'

His arms tightened around her. 'It must have been very difficult for you.'

'No,' she said, and there was still surprise in her voice. 'It helped – really it did. Funny, isn't it, after all the fuss I made? Although maybe it's also because I have you now,' she added realistically.

'Oh, Kate.' His voice was hoarse and he buried his face against her hair.

'There hasn't—' she began hesitantly. 'You haven't heard anything about – about Danny's aircraft?' She felt compelled to ask and yet she knew the answer. Philip would have told her at once if there had been news of any sort.

He held her close and said softly, 'No, my dear. I'm so sorry, but we've heard nothing.'

They sat quietly together in the peace of the woodland for a few moments longer, then Philip kissed her gently and sighed regretfully. 'I'm sorry, darling, but we really must go.'

Kate reached for her jacket and got out of the back seat of the car.

'Oh no!' she groaned as she noticed that the car was lurching drunkenly to one side. 'We've got a puncture.'

Philip got out of the car and stood looking down at the flat tyre. He ran his hand distractedly through his short hair. 'Oh, hell! We can hardly explain away being stuck in the middle of the wood. Now what are we going to do?'

'Do? Change the wheel, of course.'

He looked at her blankly for a moment and then shook his head and frowned. 'I'm sorry, but I can't . . .'

Mischievously, she gave him a mock salute. 'Oh, but I can – sir! What *do* you think they taught us in MT training?'

His worried expression cleared a little. 'Can you really . . .?'

'Just stand back – and watch!'

In what seemed an incredibly short space of time, Kate had whipped off the huge wheel and replaced it with the spare.

'Well, well,' Philip grinned as they got back into the car. 'You really are a young lady full of surprises. Mind you, if I'd stopped to think for a moment, I should have realized it would have been part of your training,' and he added with endearing honesty, 'I suppose part of me can't get used to the idea of a woman being able to change a huge wheel like that a darn sight quicker than I could.'

As they bounced over the rough track through the trees back towards the road, Kate giggled as he muttered, 'But thank goodness you could, else we might have had some awkward explaining to do.'

When they drove through the gates into the station, with Philip sitting circumspectly in the back seat, she could feel him taking on the mantle of Commanding Officer once more. He seemed to be two people; the serious, dedicated Group Captain who carried the awesome responsibility for the station with strength and yet compassion. And then there was the man she knew when they were alone; the man who loved her and needed her to love him.

Two days later, he called her into his office. 'Come in – close the door.'

She stood before his desk. His face was tired, the lines of weariness etched deeply. 'I've done all I can to find out about Danny.' He shook his head sadly. 'But there's nothing. His plane hasn't been found and there's no report of him being a prisoner.'

'Is there anything about any other member of the same

crew? Something that might give a clue as to what happened to their plane?'

Philip shook his head. 'Nothing. It's as if they've disappeared completely. Still, at least there's hope. Usually when this happens, it's that their aircraft has crashed in enemy territory and they're hiding out with resistance workers. I don't want you to build up false hopes, though, and I'd advise you not to say anything to his family. Living amongst it, I know you understand better.'

Kate nodded. 'Yes, you're right. And I hope you're right about Danny too.'

Philip looked at her solemnly. 'So do I, Kate. So do I.'

They spent every possible moment they could together, but it became more difficult as Philip's responsibilities increased. Now he had three squadrons under his overall command on a station purpose-built for two. Although it was only a temporary measure that one of the East Markham squadrons be housed at Suddaby, nevertheless it threw a strain on the smaller station. Frequently, Philip slept in the little room behind his office, rather than go to his official quarters. He was so committed, Kate thought. He was there at every take-off and waiting through the long night until every aircraft was back, or at least until those who had not returned were posted 'missing'. And then he would hunch his shoulders into his coat and return alone to his office to write those awful letters to the families of the missing crews.

'We have a free afternoon off, Kate,' he whispered from the back seat of the car as they drove out of the gate one morning for a routine visit to Group HQ. 'A whole four hours with nothing to do. Where shall we go?'

'I don't know. Where do you want to go?'

'How about you take me to your home? I'd love to see where you live.'

Kate gasped. 'Home! But – but do you think we should?'

Philip shrugged. 'Why not? We'll be careful. I won't hug and kiss you in front of them, though I'd like to.'

She laughed. 'But it's not quite the thing for the Commanding Officer to spend the afternoon with his driver, is it?'

'No, I suppose not.' He was thoughtful for a moment. 'Isn't Fleethaven Point a restricted area?'

'Ye-es. The Army's got men posted at the Point. There's a gun emplacement there.'

'Well, then, that's it. I've come to inspect the site officially. Something to do with balloons, if anyone asks. Yes, that's it.' The decision made, he sat back in his seat, a self-satisfied look on his face.

The rule-book out the window once more, Kate thought, and laughing, told him, 'You're impossible!'

In the rear-view mirror she saw him grinning at her.

'Mam, Dad – this is Group Captain Trent. He's the CO.'

Philip held out his hand. 'Pleased to meet you, Mrs Godfrey – Mr Godfrey. Please call me Philip. When we're away from camp, Kate and I call each other by our Christian names, but we have to be very official on duty.'

Kate sensed her mother's eyes upon her and felt the flush of embarrassment creeping up her neck. 'Careful,' Kate's glance said silently to Philip, 'me mam's no fool.' Aloud, she said, 'Please sit down, sir – I mean, Philip. I'll just go and see me grandad. Is he up, Mam?'

'Oh aye, he's up. Fighting fit, he is. He'll outlive the lot of us.' Esther busied herself laying cups and saucers on the table.

Kate turned to leave the living room to go through to the front room, but at that moment the door opened and Will Benson came in. 'Ah thought I 'eard voices,' he said, as Kate kissed the white stubble on his chin.

The introductions were made again and soon Kate began to relax as Philip chatted comfortably with her stepfather and grandfather.

'Well,' he said at last, standing up, 'we'd better take a look at the Point, Kate.'

'Ya'll spoil yar shoes, young feller, traipsing across the sand. Lend him yar boots, Jonathan.'

When Philip had squeezed his size nine feet into Jonathan's size eight boots, and Kate had put on her own pair of wellingtons, they set off down the lane towards the Point. The moment they were out of sight of the farmhouse, Philip pulled her into his arms.

'No,' she gasped. 'Someone might come along the lane . . .' But she found herself returning his kiss, unable to resist him. Once over the Hump, they walked apart again.

'Oh Kate,' he murmured. 'All this secrecy, it's driving me mad. How I wish . . .'

'Kate – Kate!'

They both looked up to see Rosie hurrying towards them. 'Have you heard something about Danny?'

Kate shook her head. 'Oh, Rosie, I'm sorry, no. This is my commanding officer. We – he's here on official business.'

Rosie's eyes widened fearfully. 'Not – about Danny?'

Philip smiled, reassuring her quickly. 'No, no. We've heard nothing. I'm sorry,' he added, gently sympathetic.

Rosie's mouth quivered, but she tried to smile bravely. 'Oh well, I suppose no news is good news. Have you time to see the baby, Kate?'

Kate glanced up at Philip, who nodded. 'May I come too?'

Shyly, Rosie nodded and led the way into Beth Eland's cottage.

As she held Danny's son, Kate felt Philip looking at her and glanced up to meet his gaze. There was a strange mixture of emotions on his face, but suddenly his jaw hardened and he turned away. 'I'm sorry, Kate, we must go. Goodbye, Mrs Eland – Rosie,' he said, courteous as ever although it was evident he wished to be gone from the cottage.

Swiftly, Kate placed the baby back in Rosie's arms, kissed her and Beth and followed Philip.

He was striding ahead of her and she had to run to catch up with him. He walked fast with long, angry strides so that every so often she was obliged to take a little running step to stay by his side.

Philip neither glanced at her nor spoke to her.

Whatever is the matter, Kate thought.

He stood on the sand-dunes, his gaze scanning the coastline and out to sea, then without a word he marched back towards the Hump. They said a brief goodbye to Esther, Jonathan and her grandfather.

As always in front of others, she opened the car door for Philip to get into the back seat, but even when they were once more driving through the countryside, he made no suggestion that she should pull over so that he could sit beside her in the front.

They drove all the way back to camp in silence.

Thirty-Six

Later that evening, Kate went to Philip's office. His strange behaviour towards her had distressed her. What *had* she done to make him ill-tempered? It was so unlike him. He was serious and preoccupied sometimes, but with all his responsibilities she could understand that. This afternoon had been different.

There was a strip of light showing under the door. Tentatively she knocked, and when bidden, she entered and closed the door behind her. Coming smartly to attention, she saluted.

'Well?' he barked.

Her courage almost failed her. 'Sir – could we – be *off* duty for a moment?'

He glared at her and then suddenly groaned and dropped his face into his hands. 'Oh, Kate, I'm sorry.'

She was round the desk and kneeling beside him. 'Whatever was the matter? I couldn't understand . . .'

'Couldn't you?' He raised his head to look at her, a half-smile on his mouth. 'Just good old-fashioned jealousy, my darling.'

'Why?'

'When you were holding the baby – his baby – you were looking down at it with such love in your eyes, as if – as if you were longing that it was yours . . .' His voice dropped to a hoarse whisper. 'Yours – and Danny's.'

Kate felt a flood of tenderness for him as she cupped his

face in her hands and gently lifted his head to make him look at her. 'Once, that would have been true. But not now, not since – you. Yes, I love that little baby – as my nephew. I still love Danny – and I always will – but in the way I should have done all along, as my brother!'

'Really?'

'Really. And that's because of you. If I hadn't known you, I would still be clinging to Danny, hating Rosie and probably bitter against a poor, innocent baby. Oh, there's a tinge of regret and sadness, I admit. You can't kill the past, obliterate it as if it had never happened. It did happen; Danny and I fell in love before we knew of our relationship and we were devastated. But time and other people – you and Rosie – have helped to heal the wounds. The scars are still there, probably always will be. But now we can, both Danny *and* me, go forward. In the last few months, I've done a lot of growing up.' She sighed and added musingly, 'It might sound daft, but – but it was as if I was locked into being a seventeen-year-old, clinging desperately to what might have been. They all tried to tell me – me mam, Dad and even *Danny*'s mother, but it wasn't until I – I found I could love someone else that I began to realize and understand that they were right.'

She sat back on her heels and said softly, 'There's only one thing I'm so sad about.'

'What's that?'

'I may never get the chance to tell Danny all this.'

Now it was his turn to reassure her. 'You will. I know you will.'

'Philip, I do love you. I don't think you'll ever really understand how much you've helped me, and come to mean to me.'

'Oh my dear – do you realize that's the first time you've actually said it?'

'Is it?' she said in surprise. 'I hadn't realized.' Then she giggled deliciously. 'But then I always did believe that actions speak louder than words.'

'You're wicked. Do you know that? Deliciously, gloriously *wicked*!'

She was glad to see he was smiling again and that their easy friendship was restored.

'The Yanks are coming, the Yanks are coming,' Mavis trilled, dancing up and down the hut. 'Now we'll show 'em just who's going to win this war. With our Lancs and their bombers, we'll really sock it to 'em!'

Since the attack on Pearl Harbor a few months earlier, Britain had no longer been alone; now she had a powerful ally and everyone was far more optimistic about the eventual outcome. Even so, they all knew the end of the war was still a long way off.

The weeks turned into months and still there was no news of Danny. As far as his squadron were concerned he became another statistic. Not forgotten, but gone, and there was no time, not yet, for indulging in mourning. There were too many to mourn.

For the WAAFs the ghosts of the young men lost still haunted the station. 'Do you remember Jim or Bill or Nick . . .?' was often whispered in the darkness of the hut. It kept the memories of the brave young men alive and the girls liked to think that their lost friends would be pleased that someone thought of them still.

'CO wants you and the car at his office now.' The corporal popped her head round the door of the hut.

'Now?' Kate echoed in surprise.

The corporal nodded and shrugged. 'Must be something important for him to be going somewhere this late. You'd better hop to it.'

Minutes later, Kate pulled up in the staff car outside Philip's office and opened the back door for him to climb in. She saluted smartly, but he waved her aside and went round and sat in the front passenger's seat.

Kate got back into the car. 'Sir . . .?'

He was sitting staring straight in front. 'It doesn't matter any more, Kate,' he said quietly. 'Just drive into the country-side, darling. I have to talk to you.'

Fear leaped in her breast as she bent and pressed the starter. As they paused at the gate to register their departure, she couldn't fail to notice the guard's glance into the car and the slight raising of his eyebrows. But Philip just sat passively beside her.

What had he meant – it didn't matter now? Had their affair been found out? Was there trouble brewing for him – and her too? Was this what he wanted to tell her?

She drove the few miles to their favourite spot. Her hands were clammy with nervousness on the steering-wheel.

She switched off the engine and half-turned to face him. Slowly he turned to look at her. He seemed to be taking in every tiny detail of her face as if to commit it to memory; as if it was important that he should know every line of it.

'You do know how very much I love you, don't you, Kate?' he said at last, his voice deep with emotion.

Her heart was thumping, beads of sweat standing out on her forehead. 'Yes,' she whispered, hoarsely. 'Whatever is it, Philip? Tell me – please!'

'I – I have to go home . . .'

'Is that all?' She almost laughed with relief but then it died immediately as she saw him shaking his head.

'I mean – I have to go home – for good.'

She was silent now, just staring at him in shock.

He took a deep breath and then let it out slowly in a sigh. 'Lizzie – my daughter – is critically ill. She – she won't live longer than a few months.'

'Oh, Philip.' At once she was all compassion. 'How dreadful! I'm so sorry.' The words seemed inadequate, but what else could she say?

'I'm – being posted to a station near home. My-in-laws have pulled strings and got it arranged. I wish they had consulted me first, but I suppose they felt they were helping. For once, Grace really seems to need me . . .'

She looked into his troubled eyes. With deep intuition she said, 'And you need to be with her – with Grace – too, don't you? And with Lizzie?'

He nodded. 'But what about you, Kate? I don't want you to think – I mean I don't want you to be hurt . . .' he said, anguished.

'It's all right,' Kate said. She heard the words come out of her mouth as if it were someone else speaking; so calm, so understanding. Yet inside, there was a fluttering of panic just below her ribs and her heart was crying out; 'Not again, oh, not again!' She wanted to throw herself against him, beg him not to leave her, not to go. But one look at the torment in Philip's face made her draw on all her reserves of strength for his sake. The poor man was being torn in two. And she did understand what he must be feeling for his daughter. Only a few weeks ago she would not have done so, but to her own amazement, holding Danny's son in her arms had wrought changes in Kate. There had still been the poignant longing that this child should have been hers – and Danny's – and yet there had been so much more. So this, she had thought, was what having children was all about. Holding a tiny, helpless, scrap of humanity in her arms, knowing it was totally dependent on its parents, well, somehow it was sobering and in one moment banished all selfishness.

And that was what Philip must feel for his child, perhaps even more so for a 'less than perfect' mite. She had only ever thought of Grace Trent as a shadowy figure, who, by her devotion to her daughter, had shut Philip out of her life. But now, Kate felt pity for Grace – and pangs of guilt thrust their way through her emotions. She couldn't let Philip shoulder all the blame or start feeling guilty about her too.

'I knew what I was doing – what I was getting into when we began our affair . . .' She tried to reassure him.

She saw him wince. 'It's not an "affair",' he said harshly. He was angry now and she was surprised how much her words had hurt him. 'It's not a sordid affair, Kate.'

'All right, all right.' She tried to placate him swiftly. 'I didn't mean it the way it sounded. Right now, your place is with your wife and little girl. But I'll wait, Philip. However, long it takes. Just remember I'm here – waiting.' She touched the back of his hand and he turned it over quickly and grasped her fingers in such a tight grip that it was painful.

'Kate . . .' he whispered hoarsely. 'I do love you so very much. Bless you for understanding.'

'I can only guess at what your wife must be going through. You must – be with her.' Though she was weeping inside, Kate kept her voice strong for Philip's sake. She wondered if he knew how much it cost her to encourage him to leave.

'Poor Grace,' he said heavily. 'It's not her fault. She's borne the brunt of looking after Lizzie. Poor little Lizzie. I was so proud and happy the night she was born. I always wanted a daughter . . .'

'It's no one's *fault*, Philip. Please don't feel so badly.'

He closed his eyes and groaned deeply. 'But I do. You've been so hurt before and here I am hurting you again.'

That, Kate thought, she could not deny. 'You're hurting too, aren't you?' she murmured.

'Oh yes. My dearest girl – you'll never know just how much.'

Gently he drew her against him and they sat together, just holding each other closely, staring out of the car window at the blackness of the night, the only light being from the stars millions of miles away, and the new moon, a curved slit of light.

'My mother would say we're unlucky – seeing the new moon through glass,' Kate said.

'At this precise moment,' Philip said sadly, 'I'd have to agree with her.'

His departure, once arranged, was swift. They only managed to snatch one brief meeting when their lovemaking was tinged with sadness and a terrible fear that this was the last time they would ever see each other.

'I'll write to you, Kate.'

'How – how can I write to you?'

'I'll send you my address at the new station. Somehow we must keep in touch. We must! After a time, I'll see if I can get you posted to where I am,' he vowed urgently. 'Oh, Kate, I'll miss you so . . .'

The whole station was sorry to see him go; he had been a kind and caring CO, maintaining authority through the strength of his personality, because people really liked him.

'May we take a photograph, sir?' Mavis rushed up with Kate's camera in her hands as Philip came out of his office for the last time. Kate, holding the car door open, bit her lip, but Philip smiled easily and nodded. As his batman put his kit-bag and briefcase into the boot of the car, Philip came and stood beside Kate. 'I'd better have one with my best driver,' he murmured so that only she could hear. 'Expert at changing wheels and driving into ditches – and positively whizzo in a cornfield.'

Instead of reducing her to helpless giggles, his words made the tears spring to her eyes.

'Thanks, sir,' Mavis chirped. 'We'll send you one when they're developed.'

'Thank you, Mavis.' With a last wave to those standing around who had come to see him off, he got into the back seat of the car. Kate bit down firmly on her lip and managed to stop the tears running down her face, at least until they were past the guard-room.

They all missed him, and none more so than Kate.

Three days after his departure, when she got up in the morning, she was sick for the first time.

Thirty-Seven

'So,' Isobel said, sitting down on the bed beside her, 'how long do you think you can keep this little secret?'

'I – don't know what you mean!'

Mavis came and stood in front of her. 'Oh, come off it, Kate. We're not daft.' There were only the three of them in the hut so they had no need to lower their voices. 'Throwing up every morning for the past fortnight. You're in the family way, aren't you?'

Kate's shoulders sagged and she nodded.

Isobel clicked her tongue against her teeth in exasperation. 'I can hardly believe you could be so daft, Kate Hilton. Born and bred on a farm and you *still* get caught! Didn't you get him to – well, you know – take precautions?'

'He did – at least . . .' She hesitated, remembering a few weeks previously when, after being separated for a few days, there had been a desperate urgency to their lovemaking, which had been wonderful. Kate felt her cheeks grow warm at the mere memory; she could not, even now, regret a moment.

'I see,' Isobel's voice was heavy with sarcasm now, 'most of the time he did, except when he got carried away in the heat of the moment, eh?'

'Something like that,' Kate murmured. Isobel was far too astute at times.

'What are you going to do about it?' she was saying.

'Do? What do you mean – do?'

'Well, are you going to get rid of it?'

'No! No – I'm not. I might have made a mistake – but I aren't going to do anything like that.' In her distress, her dialect was strong again.

'Why not?' Isobel insisted, while Mavis bit her lip. 'You'll be thrown out of the WAAFs. Look, Kate, there's places you can go. We don't mean a back street job, not now . . .'

'No!' she said with finality.

Her two friends glanced at each other. Isobel's mouth was a tight line. 'Don't be stupid, Kate. You don't want to be burdened with a kid. An *illegitimate* kid!' she added brutally. 'What'll your family say?'

Kate winced. What indeed? she thought.

'Don't be so hard on her, Iso,' Mavis put in. 'Maybe she – she wants to keep it.'

''Course she doesn't . . .'

'Will you two please stop talking about me as if I'm not here *and* trying to decide my future? I'm not getting rid of the baby. It's my baby – and I'm keeping it!'

Isobel was looking at her strangely. 'Do you think you *ought* to keep it? I mean . . .'

'What do you mean, Isobel?'

'Well, if it's Danny's . . .'

'It isn't!' Kate snapped, then, more quietly but equally firmly, she added, 'and don't go asking whose it is, because I aren't telling you. Or anyone else, for that matter.'

'You don't need to – not any more,' Isobel said pointedly, but Kate chose deliberately not to pursue it any further.

'If you're sure . . .' Mavis began tentatively.

'I am,' Kate said with far more confidence than she felt inside.

'Then,' Mavis continued, 'we'll stick by you, won't we, Iso?'

'I suppose so,' Isobel said grudgingly. 'I still think you're wrong, but it's your choice.' Getting up off the bed, she delivered a parting shot. 'Well, I wouldn't be in your shoes going home to tell your folks.'

Kate shuddered and at the thought of her mother, her insides quivered. Ever since the realization had come upon her, telling her mother was the thing she dreaded most.

'You trollop! You whore!' Esther Godfrey drew back her right hand and slapped Kate's face hard. 'How could you do that to *me*? After all I've taught you. Ain't I told you time and again – you dun't let a feller touch you till you've a wedding ring on ya finger . . .?' The tirade went on and all Kate could do was stand there and take it. It brought Jonathan running in from the yard and Will Benson hobbling through from his room. They arrived at the split second when Esther delivered her physical blow.

'Esther . . .' Jonathan was shocked and Will demanded, 'What's up? What's going on?'

Esther swung round to face her father. 'What's up? *She's* what's up. Up the stick, that's what's up. In the blood, ain't it?' she accused, so that the old man wavered slightly and grasped at the table for support.

'Esther – you've said enough . . .' Jonathan began.

'Oh no, I ain't. I ain't started yet.' She turned back to Kate, thrusting her face close to her daughter's white one, in which the only colour was two red fingermarks along Kate's jawline left by Esther's stinging blow.

'Who is it? Is he going to marry you?'

Kate, too numb to speak, shook her head.

Esther stared at her for a moment, long and hard. 'Don't tell me – it's *him*!'

Kate blinked. 'W-who?'

'Danny. It's Danny's, ain't it? Yar bastard's *his*.'

395

'No.' Kate shook her head, so violently that her hair swung from side to side. 'No – I promise you that. It's not his.'

'Then – who?'

'I can't tell you . . .'

'You little trollop . . .' Esther began again.

Jonathan caught hold of his wife, putting his arms around her. 'Esther, just calm down . . .'

But she was struggling against him, her glare never leaving Kate's face. 'Do you mean,' she spat, 'you don't know who the father is?'

Kate gasped. 'Of course I know. But – I can't tell you.'

'Why?'

'Well then – I won't.'

Now mother and daughter glared at each other, some of Kate's spirit returning. She faced the three of them and raised her head high. 'I've made a mistake, I don't deny. And I'm sorry to have caused you pain. But I won't – involve the father, nor get rid of the child . . .'

'Why won't he marry you?'

'Because he – he can't.' Her voice dropped to a whisper but the three listeners in the room heard plainly. 'He's already married.'

Suddenly the fight seemed to drain out of Esther. She sagged against Jonathan as she looked at her father. 'History repeatin' itsen',' she murmured, and then closed her eyes and groaned.

Then, for Kate, came the worst shock of all. Esther turned in her husband's arms, buried her face against his chest and began to cry, great tearing, rending sobs as if her heart would break.

Tears blurred Kate's vision and blindly, she turned and ran from the house; across the yard and the lane, under the elder trees and up the slope of the dunes, then down the other side and across the open marsh, as always seeking the sanctuary of the lonely beach.

But it was barred to her. Coils of barbed wire still blocked her way on to the east dunes. She wandered back to the westerly dunes and sat down amidst the thick spiky marram grass beneath the elder trees. Hugging her legs to her, she dropped her head to rest on her knees.

Her mind was a blank, refusing to take in the scene she had just caused. She had known her mother would be angry and upset, but Esther had been unrestrained and undignified in her wild fury. Her mother had always had a quick temper, and even as a child Kate had often felt the sharpness of her hand, though always on her legs. But never before had Esther smacked her across the face like that; not even when she had caught her with Danny. Kate could still feel her jaw smarting now.

She sat huddled in the dunes for a long time, until the cold seeped through her clothing and she shivered. She looked up to see that the sun had disappeared behind Brumbys' Farm. Stiffly, Kate stood up. She hesitated for a moment, undecided whether to go home or to go to the Point to see Beth and Rosie. She sighed. She wasn't ready to tell them yet, nor could she stay out here all night – though she wished she could!

As she crossed the yard and went towards the back door, she could hear the sounds of evening milking coming from the cowshed. She bit her lip and paused, listening. Now she could hear her father's deep tones, talking soothingly to the cows as he milked them. As she moved to the shed and opened the half-door, Jonathan straightened up and came towards her. He held out his arms to her and wordlessly, she went into them. He held her close and stroked her hair, just as he had in her childhood.

'Oh Kate, love. Don't think too harshly of your mother. She – she has reasons why she reacted so badly.'

Kate drew back and looked up at him, straining through the dimness of the shed to see his face. 'It's not what I think of her, it's what she thinks of me!'

'She'll come around. Give her time.'

Jonathan was wrong. Esther did not 'come around'. She said no more to Kate, indeed, she virtually ignored her presence. Although she laid a place for her at the table and served her meals, she refused to speak to her elder daughter and point-edly avoided even looking at her. Lilian sat silently at the table, her eyes downcast. Immediately meals were finished, the younger girl would leave the table and shut herself in her bedroom with her books, taking refuge from the storms within the household and refusing to take sides.

When Kate's seventy-two-hour pass was almost up and she had to return to camp, she had still not found the courage to see Beth and Rosie.

They'll know soon enough, she thought, as she repacked her bag for leaving.

'You ready, lass? I'm taking you back to camp.'

'Oh, Grandad, I don't think . . .'

'No, Dad,' began her mother. 'You didn't ought . . .'

'I'll have no arguments . . .' He whipped round with sur-prising agility to frown at his daughter. 'From either of you! And dun't *you* start, neither.' He wagged his finger at Jona-than sitting in his chair before the range, calmly reading the newspaper.

Jonathan glanced up. 'I wasn't going to.' He smiled. 'Do you good to get out a bit instead of sitting here all day being waited on hand and foot.' But the words were said in fun and the old man exchanged a grin with his son-in-law.

'Come on then, Kate, let's be off.'

Outside the pony and trap waited in the yard and when they were both settled in the back, Will slapped the reins and the pony moved forward. Once in the lane with the distance lengthening between them and the farm, above the rattle of the wheels, he said, 'I aren't going to ask a lot of questions, lass, and I aren't going to preach at ya. But there's one thing I've got to know. Was it true what ya told ya mam? Ya bairn's not Danny's, is it?'

Kate tucked her hand through her grandfather's arm and held it tightly. 'No, Grandad, I promise you that. It's not Danny's.' There was a note of wistfulness in her voice, almost as if she wished the baby were his, but her grandfather had no such feelings. 'Thank the Lord for that!' he muttered.

Kate sighed. Once, she had longed to be the mother of Danny's children, and even now, despite her newfound love for Philip, still not a day went by without her thinking of Danny, longing to know if he was alive and safe.

The wind whipped coolly against her face and her gaze travelled unseeingly around the vast flatness of the landscape as the trap rattled along the lanes. She was remembering Beth Eland's words – so long ago now – and yet she could still hear them on the wind. 'You and Danny will probably always love each other. No one can stop you doing that. But somewhere there will be another love for each of you, and it will be a different kind of love to the one you'll always carry for one another.'

Now, since loving Philip with a passionate, physical love, she had indeed learned the difference between the loves in her life. Danny would always be her first love, an innocent and pure emotion that would never die, never be replaced, maybe, in some ways, never be equalled. But it was true what Beth had tried to tell her; there were many kinds of love and now she had experienced quite another with Philip. Her longing for him, for his arms about her, was a physical ache, a passionate, bodily longing, so strong at times she almost blushed. Now Philip Trent was gone from her life, without knowing he had fathered her child. And at this moment, it would be grossly unfair of her to add to his burdens by telling him.

As they neared Suddaby, Kate said, 'You don't need to go through the village Grandad, if you take the next right turn . . .'

'There's summat I want to show you. Ya don't think I've come all this way just for the good of me health, do ya?'

Puzzled, Kate said, 'Well, I just thought you wanted to bring me back to camp . . .'

He sniffed. 'Well, I did, of course, but I wanted to talk to you and tell you summat it's high time ya knew. Something mebbe you should have been told years ago . . .'

'I don't understand. What's all the mystery? What is it I don't know?'

'All in good time, Katie, all in good time.'

He guided the trap through the village. 'That's where I used to live.' He pointed with the whip to the middle cottage of a row of six. 'That's where you came when you ran away from school. D'ya remember?'

Kate shook her head. 'Not really. I mean, I remember running away and being given a lift by a carrier, and some woman looking after me.'

'Aye, that was Minnie Raby. Dead and gone now, she is, God rest her.'

'She wasn't that old, was she?'

'No, younger than me.' He laughed wheezily. 'I'm a stubborn old bugger. Ya mam's allus reckoning she'll have to knock me on the head to mek me lie down.'

400

He did not stop the trap near his former home but carried on along the village street towards the church, where he pulled the trap to a halt and climbed down stiffly. 'Come on, lass,' he ordered, holding out his gnarled hand to help her down.

The iron gate to the churchyard squeaked as he pushed it open. Will sniffed. ''Spect this'll be disappearing soon – for the war effort,' he remarked to no one in particular.

Kate followed her grandfather's bent form as he walked up the path towards the church porch. But instead of going into the building he moved on and turned on to the grass between the gravestones. He came to a place and stopped. Kate moved to stand beside him and saw in front of her two white headstones, identical in size and shape but with an unmarked plot between the two.

'That's where I'm to be buried when I go, Kate. Ya mam's promised me to see to it.'

Kate read the inscriptions on the two headstones. One was Will's wife, Rebecca Benson, who had died in 1919.

But Will was pointing to the companion headstone. 'That's ya grandmother, Kate.'

Kate gave a startled gasp and stared at him. Slowly she turned her gaze back to the graves. She bent closer and read. 'In loving memory of Constance Everatt who fell asleep 9th June 1893, aged nineteen years. The Lord giveth and the Lord taketh away.'

'Ya mam was born . . .' Will's voice shook a little, 'out of wedlock.' He couldn't bring himself to use the name her mother used so scathingly. Of herself, it seemed, Kate realized with a sudden shock.

Esther Everatt had been born a bastard.

Suddenly – everything fell into place.

'I loved Connie,' Will was saying simply and he drew the back of his hand, now thin and bony, the skin paper-thin, across his eyes which suddenly watered. It was difficult to imagine this bent old man standing in the draughty church-yard being young and virile; virile enough to sire a bastard on a younger girl.

'Rebecca were a good wife and I didn't mean to hurt her. We never had any children, Rebecca an' me, and then after a few years she didn't like that side of married life . . .' He ran the back of his hand across his mouth. 'Connie were a young lass in the village. I – couldn't help mesen, Kate. I just couldn't help mesen . . .' His voice faded away and he was lost, looking back down the years to a time when he had known a brief time of passionate happiness. 'She were a lovely girl, a lovely girl.'

'What happened?' It was Kate now whose voice was a husky whisper.

'She – died giving birth to Esther.'

'And then?' she prompted gently. She wanted to know it all. It was important that she knew everything.

He sighed heavily. 'Poor little lass. She was brought up by Connie's older sister, Hannah. She was married to George. A nice chap, but slow. They had seven bairns of their own. But she was a shrew of a woman and only took Esther in out of duty to her dead sister. She never showed young Esther a shred of affection and never let her forget the facts of her birth. So ya see, ya mam does understand, knows only too well, but from the other side, lass, from the other side of things. She knows what it's like to *be* the bastard. That's why she fought like a she-cat for her own place, that's why she married Matthew Hilton when he offered. And he did ask her, Kate.' Will's voice was firm now. 'Whatever anyone tries to tell you different, Matthew did want to marry her. He was mad to have her, 'cos she wouldn't give hersen to him without a wedding band, see? It was only when he found out afterwards that he'd left

Beth Hanley pregnant with Danny that he was resentful towards ya mam and tried to put the blame on her. And her only fault was that she wanted to be respectable and have a home she could call her own. That was her only fault, Kate, her *only* fault.'

'And that's why she's so mad at me,' Kate murmured, her gaze still on her grandmother's headstone, 'for bringing another bastard into the world.'

They were silent, then Kate put her hand through the crook of his arm again. Hugging him to her, she said, 'I'm so glad you've told me everything, Grandad. It helps me understand things a lot better. And why my mother's – well, like she is.'

'We don't realize,' he murmured, 'when we're young and foolish how the mistakes we make are going to affect those who come after us . . .'

'But you don't regret having loved Connie, do you?'

He pursed his frail mouth and shook his head. 'Never, I'll never regret that.'

'Or having Esther?' she asked, suddenly feeling the wiser one of the two.

Again he shook his head. 'I'm proud to be her father.'

'Well, then,' Kate said rationally. 'I'm going to be proud to have my child. I'll look after it, love it and never regret having it.'

'What about the father, lass, can he really not marry you?'

Kate looked down again at Connie's grave, sharing for a moment the same feelings she must have known so long ago. 'No, Grandad, he can't,' she told Will simply. 'There are other – complications.'

'Does he know about . . .?'

'I can't tell him, Grandad. It – wouldn't be fair.'

'So, ya've to bear it on ya own then?' He looked back

down at the gravestone and his whispered words were more of an apology to the love of his youth than sympathy with Kate in her present similar, predicament. 'Aw, lass, I'm sorry, so sorry.'

Thirty-Eight

Kate missed Philip more than she would have believed possible. She longed to have his arms about her, to rest her head against his shoulder and to be able to tell him about the child. She needed his reassuring strength, too, to cope with her fears for Danny. But Philip had burdens enough of his own.

It seemed particularly cruel that she should lose both the men in her life so suddenly – and when she needed them most. She felt a young girl again; alone and lost, with no one to turn to for help.

The man who took his place as Station Commander was older than Philip. Thin, with a balding head and wearing steel-rimmed spectacles, he was tall, but stooped slightly and was very round-shouldered. He was also thin-lipped and humourless, so that the pleasure Kate had enjoyed as Philip's driver – quite apart from her more personal relationship with him – was gone. This man showed no concern for her as a human being and he extended that lack of concern to all the personnel on the station.

If he had shown a caring attitude towards his aircrews then Kate could have forgiven his brusque treatment of her. As it was, his indifference was universal.

'He'll not last,' Mavis said. 'You can't have the man at the top as cold as ice. He's not human.'

'Well, for the first time, I'm quite pleased I'll be leaving before long,' Kate said feelingly. 'I hate the job now.'

405

'You wouldn't have liked whoever came in *his* place, now would you?' Isobel said reasonably. 'Mind you, I have to agree – this one's a bastard.'

Hearing her friend use the word as an insult made Kate shudder inwardly. Instinctively she put her hands protectively over her stomach, feeling the growing roundness. It was what her mother was and it was what her mother called the child she was carrying.

'When are you planning to leave?' Mavis asked.

Kate's two friends had been as good as their promise; even Isobel had relented and they helped her whenever they could. Although her driving work was not heavy, if she was suddenly asked to do something that might be harmful for her or the child, one of them would step in immediately and cover for her.

Kate smiled thinly. 'I'll have to see Ma'am soon. My skirt's getting too tight for me now. I'll be showing before long.'

'Are you going home?' Isobel asked.

'I—' Kate hesitated. 'I'm not sure. Me mam's mad as hell. I've got a seventy-two-hour pass this weekend. I'm going home to see – well – how the land lies.'

And, she thought to herself, this time I'll have to tell Rosie and Danny's mam.

Kate entered through the back door and put her bag down in the scullery. As she stepped into the kitchen, her mother looked up from where she was rolling out pastry on the kitchen table. Lilian sat at one end, her school books open on the scrubbed surface.

'Oh, it's you, is it?' Esther said, and banged the rolling pin down hard upon the pastry.

Lilian's glance went immediately to Kate's stomach. With a mumbled 'Hello', the girl lowered her eyes, her face red with embarrassment, and concentrated on the exercise book lying open in front of her. Her pen moved swiftly across the page as she wrote.

'Hello, Mam – Lilian,' Kate said brightly and moved round the table to kiss her mother's cheek.

But Esther leaned away. 'Dun't you "mam" me, me girl, coming in here all brazen and bold as ya like. You're no daughter of mine. Thought I made that clear last time you come.'

Kate gasped. She had known her mother was furious but she hadn't realized just how deep her outrage was. Like Jonathan, Kate had believed that given time her mother would at least stand by her.

She made to move towards the door leading into the hall and to her grandfather's room.

'And dun't go whining to him. I've telled 'em both, I ain't having you back home. Ya've made ya bed, ya can lie on it!'

Kate swung round. 'Is that what you'd have wanted folks to say to your mother – if she'd lived?'

Esther's mouth pursed and she rolled the pastry viciously until it was too thin and tore. She gave a click of exasperation and bundled it up into a ball again to begin rolling it out once more. 'So I was right. That's where he took you that last time, did he? Meant you knowing all about my shame. As if that excuses you.'

More gently now, Kate said, shaking her head in disbelief, 'I'd have thought you'd be more understanding, that's all.'

'Understanding? Expect me to understand when me mother died and left me to the mercy of me Aunt Hannah all me young life till I was old enough to get out and come here? Aye, an' me troubles didn't end there, did they? I got mesen a whole lot more with Matthew Hilton and Beth – and Danny.'

'Your mother couldn't help dying, Mam,' Kate said

quietly. 'She'd have loved you and looked after you if she'd lived.'

'Aye, well, mebbe so . . .' for a moment there was a fleeting uncertainty about Esther, as if she would dearly like to believe what Kate was saying, and yet the resentment surrounding the circumstances of her own birth was too deep-rooted to forgive the years of hardship it had caused.

'And *him*,' she flung out her hand towards the direction of Will Benson's room, 'even he didn't acknowledge me as his daughter till after his wife 'ad died.'

'Well, he couldn't really, could he? But he's always cared about you, always been on your side. He explained more about – well, how things happened here. It made me see things . . .'

'I dun't need no one to mek excuses for me. I dun't need no one on my side, 'cept p'raps yar dad . . .' She paused and then added pointedly, 'Yar *step*dad.'

Kate came back and stood on the opposite side of the table, leaning across it. 'Mam, why are you still so bitter?'

'I wasn't – at least, I thought I wasn't. But you – this—' She jabbed a floury finger towards Kate's stomach. 'It's brought it all back. Everything I've tried to live down, everything I've tried to do to make sure you never made the same mistake. All for nothing! It's in the blood. It must be.' She nodded her head towards Lilian. ''Spect she'll do the same, an' all.'

Lilian's head snapped up, goaded at last. 'Oh no, I won't, Mam. I've got more sense than that. Besides, I'm staying on at school, going to better myself and get an education. Go to university, if I can. I'm not going to wreck my life . . .' She stopped short of actually voicing the words, but they hung in the air between them, ' . . . like Kate!'

'There you are, see?' Esther said triumphantly. 'At least

one of me daughters 'as got a bit of sense, a bit of my ambition.'

Kate looked at Lilian; at the short-cropped mousy hair, the owlish spectacles she wore, the smug expression on her plain face. Rather than feeling resentful towards her younger sister, Kate pitied her. She could visualize Lilian, with that attitude, being lonely all her life.

Kate sighed and turned away. There was no point in continuing to argue. She walked out of the house and stood in the yard. She pulled her coat closely around her and her collar up against the blustery wind which swept in from the sea, even today when it was supposed to be summer. She looked around, but could not see her stepfather. She pushed her hands deep into her pockets and felt the whelk shell. Since the night Danny had gone missing, she had carried it everywhere with her.

She sighed again. She'd better get it over; she would go and see Beth – and Rosie.

'Why, lovey, how grand it is to see you.'

The greeting was the same as ever from Danny's mother. Rosie hugged her warmly and smiled brightly, though the worry never quite left her eyes. Kate was saddened to see that Rosie was no longer the bouncy chatterbox; Danny's disappearance had caused that.

They can't know about me, Kate thought, as she allowed herself to be ushered into the kitchen and pressed into the chair near the range. Kate looked around. 'Where's – the baby?'

'Robbie's asleep in the back garden,' Rosie said. 'Me Uncle Georgie brought one of those big baby cars home. He's buried in it, poor little mite.' She held back the curtain at the kitchen window and Kate looked out to see a black perambulator in the middle of the strip of grass outside the window. It was so deep that only the covers were visible. From here she could see no sign of the baby in its depths.

'He'll wake up soon. Always hungry, he is. I'll fetch him in then for you to see him. He's growing so fast, ain't he, Nan? We call her Nan now. She loves being a grandma, don't you?'

Beth smiled gently, her brown eyes soft with love for her grandson. Then, in her quiet, concerned way, she asked Kate, 'How've you been then, lovey?'

Kate glanced from one to the other of them. Did they know? They were looking at her, but their expressions gave nothing away.

'Er – well . . .' She hesitated, twisting her hands together in her lap.

Beth touched her hand lightly. 'It's all right, Katie, we know about the bairn.'

The gentleness in her tone touched Kate more deeply than her own mother's wrath. Tears sprang into her eyes and there was such a lump in her throat that for a moment she couldn't speak.

She brushed the tears away from her eyes with the back of her hand, like a child. 'I'm sorry. It's just that – me mam's that mad . . .'

'Oh, we know all about yar mam being mad,' Beth said grimly. 'I've heard her.'

'She's told you?'

Beth shook her head. 'Oh, no. She's not speaking to me again now. I heard her through the wall when she comes to see Grannie Harris next door. Ranting and raving, she was, one day. I could hear ev'ry word.'

Kate sighed with resignation. 'I might have known you two wouldn't be speaking again by now! I really thought it might be different – I mean, after the bomb, and then how she came at once to Rosie when Robbie was born. Didn't need asking twice . . .'

Beth nodded. 'She's a strange woman, ya mother. She was kindness itself when Robert was killed, I can't deny that. But – well – we've had this all our lives. There's that much between us. We can't be friends – not ever – but, whenever there's trouble, we can't be enemies either.' She smiled a little self-consciously and added, 'I s'pose I'm as much to blame as she is. In the early years, it was me who was bitter towards her.' She shrugged, but the years could not be shrugged off so easily. 'Never mind about that now, lass. What about you?'

'I – I don't know. I'll have to leave the WAAFs soon, and me mam, it seems, doesn't want me to come home.'

The two women gasped, their eyes wide. 'Not want you to come home?' they chorused in surprise.

'Oh, she's going too far this time,' Beth muttered, at once like a mother hen with ruffled feathers. 'I'll go and tell her what I think . . .'

'No – no, don't,' Kate said swiftly. 'I've caused enough trouble. Besides,' she added, and although she spoke bravely, she couldn't keep the doubt from her tone, 'I'm hoping Dad will be able to bring her round in time.'

Her feathers smoothed a little, Beth said, 'Well, if anyone can make her see sense, it's Jonathan . . .'

From the garden came a wail and Rosie rushed out to bring in her son. 'Here you are.' She came back in and placed the baby in Kate's arms. 'Here's ya Auntie Kate to see you.' And Kate found herself looking down into the solemn brown gaze of Danny's son.

The baby gazed back at her and then a broad smile stretched across his chubby face and his fat little hands wavered towards her face.

'Oh, Rosie, he's lovely!' she exclaimed, and the little fellow's mother and grandmother stood watching, beaming proudly.

'I won't have her here and that's an end to it.'

'Very well,' Jonathan said, his mouth tight and a deep frown on his forehead. 'If that's your final word, Esther, so be it. But I think you're wrong – and I think you'll regret it.'

'Where would you've been if ya Aunt Hannah had said the same all them years back?' Will Benson raged. 'Answer me that!'

'A lot better off, probably,' Esther retorted, unrelenting.

'Don't talk daft, girl,' her father snapped back.

Despite the family quarrel Kate had caused, she almost laughed to hear her mother addressed as 'girl'. But then, she supposed, to a parent their child is always a child.

'Ya'd have been in the workhouse but for her,' Will went on.

'It weren't no better than the workhouse. I might have fared better there.'

'Oh, Esther, that's not fair . . .' Jonathan began.

'What do you know about it?' She rounded on him. 'You've always had a loving, close family. A mother, a father *and* a sister. You're spoilt with family! I was nothing but a skivvy to the lot of them and never allowed to forget the circumstances of my birth. Never! "Me sister's bastard!" – that's what me aunt used to call me.' She turned then on Kate. 'That's why I'm bitter. I'm bitter for what you're doing to an unborn mite with no choice in the matter. It's not the poor bairn I'm against, it's you for causing it. You should have known better.'

Jonathan was staring at Esther.

'And what's up with you?' She rounded on him.

'Nothing. Nothing at all. You've just given me what could be a very good idea,' he said thoughtfully.

'What?'

'Ah – now that, for the moment, is my secret.'

He got up from the kitchen table and went through into the living room. They heard him open his bureau in the corner of the room, heard the rustle of paper and the scrape of a chair, and then there was silence. Intrigued, Kate peeped through the doorway into the room.

His head bent, her stepfather was seated at the table, busily writing a letter.

Thirty-Nine

A week after her return to camp, during which she had expected that each day she might be summonsed to Ma'am's office to be confronted with the words, 'You're pregnant, Hilton, aren't you?', Kate received a letter from her stepfather, containing one from his sister Peggy, in Lincoln.

In his letter, Jonathan merely said, '*I think, my dear, that the enclosed letter will be the answer for you, at least for the time being . . .*'

Kate unfolded it and began to read.

'*My dear Jonathan, Of course Kate can come back to us. We should love to have her – it will be like old times – and she would be company for mother, who although still lively in her mind, is increasingly confined to the house and, indeed, to her sofa.*' Did Peggy really understand what she was offering, Kate wondered. Would Mrs Godfrey be so happy to have her if she knew she was going to be an unmarried mother? But as she read on it became clear that Peggy and her mother understood the situation exactly.

'*As you know, since Father died, Mother has slept downstairs in the living room, and so Kate, and her little one when it arrives, could have Mother's bedroom upstairs. I'm still in my own room anyway, so it won't be putting us about at all! And there's still the tiny bedroom Kate had before, when the little one gets older . . .*' Peggy, bless her, seemed to be offering Kate a long-term home, not just a temporary stop-gap. '*Besides,*' she went on, '*it will be lovely for Mother to have more company in the day when I have to be at work – she gets very lonely. Do give Kate our best love and tell her to come and see us as soon as she can and we can talk everything over . . .'*

The words blurred now for tears were coursing down her cheeks. How kind they were, even making it sound as if she, Kate, would be doing them a favour.

Mavis came thundering down the hut. 'Kate – what's up? Is it bad news . . .?' The wooden slats creaked as she dropped her weight on to the bed at the side of Kate.

Kate shook her head. 'No – no,' she sobbed. 'Just the opposite.'

Then she told Mavis what had happened when she had gone home and then about the letter she had just received.

'Well, that's all right, then,' Mavis said in her matter-of-fact manner. 'I thought there was something wrong – all that blubbering.'

Kate smiled and wiped away her tears. Dear friend though Mavis was, she could not be expected to understand the relief that Jonathan's letter had brought to her. Her mother's initial reaction had been expected, but Kate had not believed that Esther Godfrey would turn her face away from her own daughter quite so heartlessly and so completely. Kate had suddenly felt very alone; the only people who were on her side were powerless to help her – her grandad, old and increasingly infirm and dependent upon Esther, Beth Eland and Rosie and even, she had thought, her stepfather. But Jonathan Godfrey was nothing if not resourceful, and for once he had acted without reference to Esther.

Whether her mother approved or disapproved, she had no way of knowing for neither Jonathan nor Peggy mentioned Esther in their letters.

Two days later, Kate was able to hitch a lift into Lincoln and go to see Peggy and Mrs Godfrey.

'It really is so kind of you,' she began hesitantly, after the first flurries of welcome were over and she had been seated near the fire opposite Mrs Godfrey, a cup of tea balanced on her lap. 'Are you sure you really don't mind? I mean, the neighbours . . .'

Mrs Godfrey laughed. 'There's a lot worse goes on down this street behind the lace curtains than you bringing a baby into the world, my dear. But if it troubles you, you can always wear a wedding ring and call yourself Mrs Hilton. There's lots of women on their own now with this war on, and no one bothers to ask questions any more. But we're not worried one way or the other, are we, Peggy love?'

Peggy was standing beside Kate, looking down at her thoughtfully. 'No, Mother, we're not,' she said absently.

Suddenly she sat down beside Kate and looked her full in the face. 'Kate, you're obviously still troubled as to what we think of you and how it will reflect upon us, aren't you?'

Kate glanced down at the liquid in her cup. 'Well, yes, you see, me mam . . .'

'We know about your mother – Jonathan told us just enough to enable us to put two and two together . . .'

' . . . And make five,' put in Mrs Godfrey.

Kate smiled wanly. 'She – she was so upset. It's always been so important to her, you see. In her eyes, I've done just about the worst thing I could have done.'

For a moment there was silence in the room. Peggy was still watching Kate then she took a deep breath and seemed to come to a decision. Kate saw her glance at her mother and raise her eyebrows as if seeking approval for something she was about to do.

'It's up to you, love,' the older woman said quietly, obviously understanding her daughter's meaning.

Peggy turned back to Kate and smiled gently. 'You won't remember much about the last war, you'd only be little. I

416

was a young girl of eighteen when I met Michael. He worked with Jonathan and they volunteered together. We – fell very much in love, and we knew that any day he might be sent to France. So, we were going to get married – with the blessing of both our parents, even though we'd only known each other three months. The date was set and everything arranged and then his unit was posted overseas at short notice and all leave cancelled. He begged and pleaded with the authorities to allow him just a few days to get back here so that we could get married by special licence before he went. But he couldn't get leave. He had to – to go without even seeing me again.' Peggy's hands were twisting in her lap now, but her voice remained strong and there was a tender smile on her lips as though her story brought back happy memories as well as the sad times. 'A few weeks after he'd gone, I – I found I was carrying his child.'

Kate gasped. 'Oh Peggy . . .'

'I got three letters from him before he was killed on the Somme and I never got the chance to tell him he was to be a father. Maybe it was for the best in a way, because I was dreadfully ill after we'd heard he'd been killed and I – I lost the baby.' There was a haunted look in her eyes now.

'Did – did me dad know?'

'Not at the time,' Mrs Godfrey put in. 'When Jonathan came home wounded, Peg was over the worst, except that she was thin and dreadfully unhappy. He was worried enough about her, as it was. But after the war, when he was home for good, well, we told him then.'

'So you see, Kate,' Peggy said softly, 'we do understand. I would have given anything – anything – if I could have kept that baby and brought it up – wedding ring or no wedding ring. I would have had something left of Michael.'

Kate eyes went to Mrs Godfrey. As if reading her unspoken question, the woman nodded. 'Yes, her father and

I stood by her,' she said softly. 'We'd have brought the little one up, if it had lived.'

The lump in Kate's throat was so large, she found it impossible to speak.

'So,' Peggy said gently, 'we feel – Mother and me – that it's as if we've been given a second chance. Do you see?'

Kate nodded. 'Yes,' she whispered. 'And I'm so very grateful.'

Mrs Godfrey suddenly slapped her hand on to her lap, rattling the cup in the saucer.

'Careful, Mother, you'll spill that.' Peggy jumped up to rescue the wobbling cup.

'I've just had a wonderful idea.' Mrs Godfrey beamed at the other two. 'When you leave the WAAFs, Kate, why don't you start dressmaking again?'

'Oh, but I couldn't expect you to look after the baby all day while I go out to work . . .'

'I don't mean that. I mean here, in the front room, just like I used to do. There's folks crying out for it now, wanting their old clothes made over because of the rationing. They still knock on my door even now, at my age, asking if I "couldn't just sew this seam up, Mrs Godfrey . . ." You know they do, Peg.'

'Well, it's whether Kate wants to . . .'

As Peggy turned back to look at her, Kate knew the answer was plainly written in her shining eyes and her wide smile. 'Want to! Oh, I'd love it. It was the sight of your room when I visited from school that made me take up sewing and dressmaking in the first place.'

'Was it really?' Mrs Godfrey laughed aloud. 'Well, who would have thought it, all my clutter inspiring you like that!'

Peggy was smiling too. 'Well, that's settled then.'

Indeed, everything seemed to be settled very satisfactorily, Kate thought as she waited for the transport back to camp.

For the first time in months, she dared to feel a tinge of hope. Suddenly, she felt a flutter beneath her ribs and, smiling, she put her hand over the place. Her child had moved for the first time.

She would see Ma'am first thing in the morning, she decided.

'Well, you're not the first and I don't expect you'll be the last!' Ma'am was tight-lipped and disapproving, but had become resigned to the fact that in her position in charge of a clutch of women, this kind of interview was bound to happen. 'But I must say, I am surprised at you, Hilton. You had a wonderful job as personal driver to the CO, one which you've kept despite a change at the top.' The shrewd eyes were regarding her keenly.

Kate made no comment but kept rigidly to attention, her gaze unflinchingly on the top button on Ma'am's jacket.

The officer sighed. 'Very well, dismissed.'

Outside, the air cooling her hot cheeks, Kate let out a sigh. Now the only thing she had to face was the gossip spreading round the camp . . .

'Think you can run the gauntlet of the pub tonight, Kate?' Mavis asked cheerily. 'Me and Isobel have actually got a night off together. Thought we'd take you out for a farewell drink . . .' She grinned. 'Well, in your case, orange juice.'

Kate threw her shoe at Mavis, who ducked smartly. The shoe sailed across two beds, landed on the floor and skidded under the third. Kate padded across the floor after it and, panting against her tight waistband, bent to retrieve the shoe. 'Yes, I suppose so. Does everyone know now?'

Mavis shrugged. 'Shouldn't let it worry you – 'sides, me and Isobel will be there.'

'Oh well, then. I'll have no trouble,' Kate laughed.

She needn't have worried; everyone was far more wrapped up in their own worries or bent on having a good time before tomorrow's op than worrying if a silly little WAAF was pregnant.

Kate was sorry to say goodbye to Mavis and Isobel, but apart from that, leaving was easy. There had been no word from Philip; in one way she was disappointed and hurt, yet in another, it was a relief. Since making her decision not to tell him about the child, she had been worried what she would do if he wrote to her. But with every day that passed without a letter, her decision not only seemed right, but also easier to carry through. And with Philip gone, she really had no reason to regret leaving the WAAFs.

'You won't get rid of us as easy as this though, will she, Iso? We'll come and visit you.'

'Even if it's only to bring those ghastly bootees you're trying to knit, Mave,' Isobel drawled. 'Poor child!' she added, but now there was no malicious bite to Isobel's teasing.

Mavis laughed good-humouredly. 'You're right there, Iso. I'll never win prizes for knitting and that's a fact!'

They walked with her to the gate and helped her into the back of the lorry which was taking her into Lincoln. Kate waved as the lorry drew away, but then her glance went beyond them, taking a last look at the station that had been her home for over eighteen months. So much had happened here and she had made so many friends, she mused, as she watched the two waving figures grow smaller and smaller. She had fallen in love with Philip and known a very different kind of love that had obliterated the unhappy childhood romance, so cruelly shattered.

Danny . . . Her mind shied away from thinking about him. But she couldn't – not for ever. Where was he, her beloved brother? Was he alive? He must be. Surely she'd know – she would feel it – if he wasn't? What was it he had said all those years ago? 'What would I do if you were no longer in the same world as me?'

She thought of Rosie waiting in the tiny cottage at Fleethaven Point with the son Danny had never seen.

Kate ran her hand over her stomach.

Oh Danny, her heart cried silently. I wish you were here for me to tell you about this.

How am I going to get through it without you?

Kate was surprised how quickly she settled in the terraced house with Mrs Godfrey and Peggy. For appearances she wore a ring on the third finger of her left hand and when giving her name she just said Kate Hilton and left it to others to add the 'Mrs' themselves.

Soon several ladies were coming to Mrs Godfrey's front parlour with their sewing or dressmaking demands. All were Mrs Godfrey's former clients and word soon spread that there was a very clever little dressmaker back in business at number eight. Kate enjoyed the work, even though as the months passed she found it increasingly difficult to bend over her bulge to operate the sewing machine.

'You've done Mother a power of good,' Peggy told her.

'Have I? How?' Kate asked, surprised.

'Now she can't get about, while I was at work she used to get so lonely before you came. Oh, she'd have a few visitors, but not like now when your clients pop through for a bit of a chat about the old days. She's loving every minute of it.'

Kate pulled a face. 'She might not when there's a squalling infant keeping her awake half the night.'

Peggy's expression softened. 'You'll see – she'll make the world's best doting grandmother – oh no, wait a bit, *great-*grandmother.'

How kind they were to her, Kate thought, she was very lucky, but she was saddened by the thought that the coming child's true grandmother wanted nothing to do with it.

'Peggy! Peggy!'

Kate knocked on the bedroom door. From inside she heard the squeak of bedsprings and the door opened.

'What is it?'

'Pains. I've got pains, Peg. Here . . .' Kate clutched her groin and gasped, doubling over as another spasm gripped her.

'How often are they coming?'

'I – don't know.'

'Right – back to bed and I'll . . .'

At that moment the siren began to wail.

Forty

'I'll phone for the midwife from next door. Joe's an ARP Warden so they've got a telephone.' As she spoke, Peggy was already stripping off her nightdress and struggling back into her clothes.

'What about getting your mother into the shelter?' Kate shouted above the noise.

Peggy laughed. 'If I were to get her in, Kate, it would be the first time. She never goes.'

'Oooh—' Kate let out a yowl and thought, now I know why Rosie was squealing so much.

'Is it bad? They're coming a bit close together for my liking.'

'No – no – not that bad,' Kate lied bravely. 'I just squeaked because they take you by surprise a bit.'

Peggy ran lightly downstairs while Kate staggered back to the big bedroom and heaved herself back on to the bed. She lay there propped up against the pillows, her knees drawn up, her legs apart, trying to remember all the things her mother had instructed Rosie to do.

And all the while the siren wailed.

By the time Peggy's footsteps came pounding back up the stairs, Kate's pains had increased in intensity and frequency.

'About every three and a half minutes,' Kate told her calmly.

'Oh dear.' Peggy ran her hand distractedly through her hair. 'Kate – I can't get through. The lines must be down and Joe's out because of the raid . . . '

'Don't worry,' Kate said. Despite the pain, a strange calm seemed to spread through her. 'It can't be very different to calves and piglets being born and I've seen enough of those.'

'But I haven't,' Peggy wailed. 'I don't know what to do . . . '

'I was there when Rosie had . . . ' Kate gasped as another pain clenched her abdomen, 'her – her son. I think I can remember what me mam did.' For a moment a feeling of intense longing swept over her; oh, how she would love it to be Esther standing beside the bed at this very moment! Dearly as she loved Peggy, she was not at this moment inspiring Kate with confidence and composure. Indeed, it was the patient who was having to calm the nurse.

As the wave of pain subsided, trying to lighten the situation, Kate smiled and said, 'Shouldn't you be boiling water or something, Peg?'

Peggy stood at the end of her bed, her eyes wild, wringing her hands. 'Oh Kate . . .'

'Peg – Peg! What's happening?' Mrs Godfrey's anxious voice drifted up from the room below.

Peggy hurried to the door and shouted down the stairs. 'It's coming – and I don't know what to do, Mother . . . '

Kate heard the older woman's voice. 'Just calm down, Peg. Rita's here, she's coming up . . . '

Footsteps sounded on the stairs and as Rita, their next-door neighbour, came into the bedroom, Kate panted hard as a spasm of pain began and swelled, until she was gripping the mattress beneath her.

'Well, you're well on, by the look of you,' Rita smiled down at Kate. 'I'm just off on me bike to find our Joe. He'll get the midwife for you.' She turned to Peggy. 'Don't worry,

Peg, just keep mopping her brow and try to get her to relax when the pains come. And pant hard, Kate, don't push yet, else you might tear yourself.'

'Oh, Rita,' Peg began again. 'Can't you stay? I'll go and find Joe.'

'No, Peg. I know all the places he might be better'n you.'

'Do be quick, won't you?'

Rita laughed as she left the room and ran lightly down the stairs. 'I'll do me best, if Hitler'll let me . . .'

'I wish I could get you to the Maternity Home, but I don't know anyone with any petrol.'

'It's not fair to – to ask anyone – in an air raid, Peg.' Kate panted.

'Oh, they wouldn't mind that . . .'

As if to refute Peggy's statement about the generosity of their neighbours and their brave disregard for safety if called upon, they heard the whine of a bomb and then there was a terrific blast. The house shuddered and the windows rattled.

'I think,' Kate said with wry humour, 'I'd rather stay here, if you don't mind, Peg.'

'What's happening?' came Mrs Godfrey's voice from below. 'Is she all right?'

'Tell her I'm fine. I think the pains are not as bad at the moment.'

Peggy relayed the message and then came back to stand nervously at the side of the bed. 'I am sorry I'm not being much use, Kate,' she said. Kate reached out and clasped Peggy's hand. 'Of course you are, Peg . . . We – we'll do it together. We'll manage – bombs or no bombs.'

For a while Kate's labour eased. 'I think it's taking a rest before the final push,' she joked, and Peggy smiled thinly.

When the pains began again, strongly and more frequently, Peggy seemed calmer, although she kept casting anxious glances towards the open bedroom door and straining to hear the sound of footsteps above the noise of the raid going on all over the city.

'They're here,' came Mrs Godfrey's voice at last. 'Rita's found the midwife.'

Tears of relief streamed down Peggy's face. 'Oh, thank goodness – we'll be all right now, Kate.'

Kate did not reply. For the moment, her eyes screwed up with effort and her face growing redder by the second, she was too busy . . .

Peggy, happy now under the midwife's guidance, bustled up and downstairs, fetching and carrying whatever was needed. Rita was dispatched to the kitchen to make a cup of tea and Mrs Godfrey sat on her sofa downstairs, her hands folded placidly in her lap, waiting to hear the first cry of the newborn baby from the bedroom above her.

Outside the bombs continued to whistle down. They heard another one quite close and as it landed the ground shook and the glass in the bedroom window cracked. But the midwife just stood at the side of the bed, her hand resting lightly on Kate's stomach. She didn't even flinch.

Fancy bringing a child into a world like this, Kate thought. I should have been more careful, I should have . . . 'Aaah . . .'

'You're doing fine. Not much longer now,' came the soothing voice.

Kate's daughter was born just as the all-clear sounded. It seemed like a good omen.

'Oh, she's lovely, Mrs Hilton – just perfect,' said the midwife as she laid the child in Kate's arms.

Kate's eyes roamed over the tiny form, counting fingers and toes and drinking in the look of her child.

'What's that mark on her left cheek?'

'Oh, just a little birth-pressure mark – it will soon fade,' the nurse said casually, used to reassuring worried mothers.

Kate wasn't so sure.

On the left side of the baby's face, just on the line of the jaw, were marks in the shape of two tiny fingers.

Remembering, Kate could almost feel again the stinging slap Esther had dealt her on the side of her face in exactly the same place as the marks on her baby's.

'Oh, she's beautiful,' Peggy cooed as she bent over the cradle the following day. 'Isn't she good? I quite expected her to be bawling loudly.'

Kate lay back against the pillows. The first euphoria of the birth had deserted her and now she felt rather tired and strangely lonely, even though Peggy and Mrs Godfrey were ecstatic in their delight in the newest member of their household.

'What are you going to call her?'

Kate hesitated and then she began to laugh, a little hysterically, so that Peggy patted her hand in alarm. 'Don't, Kate, don't,' she beseeched.

Tears poured down Kate's face. 'I'm sorry, I'm not usually so emotional. I don't know what's the matter with me.'

'It's just all the excitement,' Peggy soothed.

Calmer now, Kate watched the baby sleeping placidly in the cradle. If only Peggy knew how she had agonized over the naming of her baby.

Peggy, misreading Kate's silence, said, 'Well, you'll have to think of one now. You have to register her soon, you know.'

'Yes,' Kate whispered, still staring at her daughter. She would love to call her daughter Philippa, but how could she? So far she had managed to keep the father's identity secret, although she felt that Isobel and Mavis had guessed the

427

truth. But she knew her two loyal friends would keep silent, and that was the way she wanted it. She loved Philip enough to want to protect him and spare him any further distress.

And if she could not call her daughter after him, then there was really only one other name she would consider.

The interview with the Registrar was a little embarrassing, as he went through the questions.

' . . . And what is the surname by which the child is to be known?' the man asked, writing with meticulous care as Kate answered each question.

'Hilton.'

'Name and surname of mother?'

'Katharine Hilton.'

'No, Mrs Hilton, I need your maiden name.'

When she did not answer immediately, he looked up over his steel-rimmed spectacles.

She returned his gaze steadfastly and said quietly, 'Hilton is my only name. I'm not married, Mr Forbes.'

'Ah – I see,' he said evenly, giving no indication in his tone as to his feelings on such a matter. 'Then I presume we cannot fill in the father's name on the certificate. In these circumstances,' he went on to inform her, 'it is necessary for the father to be present at the time of registration to give his consent for his name to be on the certificate.'

Kate nodded. 'I understand,' she said huskily. Clearing her throat nervously, she said, more strongly, 'I'm afraid it's – not possible.'

He said no more but filled in the other details, and a few moments later, Kate left the room with her daughter's birth certificate in her hand.

Born on the sixteenth day of January, 1943
Danielle Hilton.

Forty-One

Kate could imagine the furore her choice of name would cause at Fleethaven Point. She didn't care. She wanted to call her baby after Danny and she would not apologize to anyone for having done so. How she wished with all her heart that Danny could see the little girl she had named after him. Mindful, however, of the feelings of others, Kate decided that the little girl would be known as Ella.

At home in the little terraced house, Mrs Godfrey fussed over the infant. 'Leave her with me, Kate. She'll be right as ninepence here in her crib. Go and have a lie down, dear. You look exhausted. You really didn't ought to be sewing again yet.'

'Oh, I'm fine really. I didn't sleep too well last night.'

'Really? I didn't hear her crying.'

'Oh no, she only woke the once to be fed. She's a good little thing. No – it was just that – well, after I fed her I couldn't get off again.'

Mrs Godfrey eyed her sympathetically. Kate knew the older woman understood some of the thoughts going through Kate's mind. 'Peg's written last weekend to tell Jonathan, so – your mother will know.'

Kate nodded, biting her lip. She forced a smile. 'I didn't expect to hear anything.'

She bent over the baby, asleep in the cradle. The child was a sweet little thing, with tiny features and downy fair hair. The birthmark along her jawline was fading a little and only deepened in colour when the child screwed up her face and cried. It seemed a cruel twist of fate, Kate thought, that the innocent child should bear the mark of Esther's wrath.

Mrs Godfrey sniffed disapprovingly and rocked the cradle with her hand as it stood at the side of her sofa. 'Well, I'd have expected better from our Jonathan.'

Mavis and Isobel arrived on the doorstep bearing gifts for the baby.

'Sorry we haven't been before,' they explained. 'We wanted to come together and couldn't seem to organize leave at the same time.'

'They can't manange without us, you know,' Mavis joked.

While Isobel sat and chatted to Mrs Godfrey and nursed Ella, Mavis drew Kate into the front room. She fished a letter out of her bag.

'This arrived for you at camp last week. I – didn't want to post it on to you. I wanted to make sure you got it.'

Kate took the letter as Mavis said, 'It arrived in the mail from a station up north – in Yorkshire.' When Kate did not answer, Mavis persisted, 'The CO went up to Yorkshire, didn't he?'

'So he did, Mave,' Kate murmured, and composing her face, she looked up again and smiled. 'I expect it's just a friendly letter.'

'Oh, most probably,' Mavis said, with more than a hint of sarcasm. Kate felt her friend's shrewd gaze upon her face. ''Spect he doesn't know you've left, does he?' she remarked pointedly.

Slipping the letter into the pocket of her wrap-around apron, Kate said firmly, 'No, and I don't want him to know either.' She saw Mavis open her mouth to say something more, but before she could do so, Kate linked her arm through hers and pulled her back into the living room. 'Come on, Auntie Mavis, it's time you nursed your god-daughter.'

Mavis's eyes widened. 'God-daughter? You mean – you mean you want *me* to be her godmother?' Her face was growing pink with pleasure.

Kate smiled at her. 'Yes, you and Iso, if you will. And Peggy too.'

'Oh, I'd love it. I've never been a godmother.' She paused, then asked, 'Er, aren't you supposed to have two godmothers and one god*father* for a girl?'

The smile faded from Kate's face. 'Yes,' she nodded, 'but there's only one person I would want as her godfather – and – and he's not here just now.'

'You – you mean – Danny?'

Kate's voice was a whisper, 'Yes.'

'Oh. Oh, I see,' Mavis murmured. It was obvious that her friend did not see at all. In fact she was more perplexed than ever. Kate watched Mavis looking down at the child in Isobel's arms, her forehead creased and chewing the side of her thumb. Kate could almost read the thoughts running through Mavis's mind. Kate had been in love with Danny Eland, but he had married someone else. They believed Kate and Philip Trent had been lovers, yet when her child was born, Kate had called her Danielle and now she was admitting that the only man she would want as a godfather was Danny Eland. It was all too much for Mavis to take in.

It was exactly what Kate wanted, although she felt a little guilty at deliberately trying to turn away suspicion from Philip and back on to Danny.

Later, in the privacy of her bedroom, Kate read Philip's letter. It was carefully worded so that to the uninformed eye, it would be a friendly letter from a superior officer to his one-time driver for whom he had an affectionate regard. But to Kate there were hidden references that told her his feelings had not changed.

'... *I expect Lincolnshire is looking a little wintry at the moment – no fields of rippling ripe corn ... My current driver is not nearly so efficient at changing a wheel in the dark ...*'

He remembered everything that had happened and between the lines, Kate could detect his longing for her. There was a paragraph in which there was more than a hint of anxiety. '*I have written twice before, but have not had a reply from you. Perhaps you did not get the letters?*' No, she had not received his letters and had begun to think his silence meant the end of their affair. And then came his final words.

'... *Kate, we must meet. I shall be attending a big meeting in Grantham the week after next. If you're still the new CO's driver, you should be bringing him ...*'

Kate closed her eyes and groaned. She had dreaded something like this happening. Now he was going to find out she had left the WAAFs and, most probably, why! But if he had to know, then he should hear it from her, and not from any other garbled source.

'... *We could meet on the Wednesday about four, at the station, if you could manage it,*' Philip suggested.

'Heavens!' Kate murmured, as she turned over his letter and re-read the date. 'That's only the day after tomorrow.'

Her mind worked feverishly. She'd have to find a way to go and meet him. Now she knew he wanted to see her again, she would have to tell him about his baby daughter. 'Oh dear,' she agonized. 'I hope I'm doing the right thing.'

Luckily for Kate, Wednesday was the day when Peggy, on her half-day off from work, took complete charge of Ella. 'Much as you love her,' Peggy had told Kate from the very first week, 'you need a break. Besides,' she had smiled down tenderly at the infant, 'I want her to myself for just a few hours . . .'

So on Wednesdays, Kate was free to wander into town, to shop, to go to the cinema, or even to go home to Fleethaven Point if she had wanted. Thank goodness Philip had suggested a Wednesday, she thought; she didn't even need to tell Mrs Godfrey or Peggy where she was going . . .

The biting February wind whipped along the platform as she waited for him, pulling her coat around her. Then suddenly there he was, striding towards her, and she felt tears prickle her eyes at the sight of his tall, lean figure. He grasped her hands in his, enveloping her cold hands in his huge warm grasp. 'Kate . . .' he whispered. 'Oh my dear, don't cry.'

She tried to laugh through the tears she could no longer hide. How could she explain, so quickly, that she was still a little emotional after the birth of her daughter? *Their* daughter.

Philip tucked her hand through his arm. 'Come on – let's see if we can find the famous British Restaurant,' he said, trying to make her laugh. 'How have you been? How are things at the station? I want to hear everything that's been going on since I left.'

Kate swallowed nervously, realizing what a shock for him her news was going to be. As they walked, she glanced up at him. His face seemed thinner and there were dark shadows beneath his eyes. He looks desperately tired, she thought. Even his voice sounded weary as if he were having to force himself to speak cheerfully. 'I've only just realized what's different about you,' he said as he sat down opposite her in a secluded corner of the restaurant. 'You're not in uniform.'

Kate drew in a deep breath. 'Oh – er – no. I'll explain –

in a minute . . .' She bit her lip. Before she told him anything, there was something she must know first. Leaning forward across the table, she said softly, 'Philip, how are things with you? I mean – with Lizzie?'

The look of pain that was suddenly in his eyes shocked her in its intensity. 'Oh, Kate. That's partly why I asked you to meet me. I wanted to see you, of course. You'll never know how desperately I've missed you all these weeks and months . . .'

And I you, she thought, but for the moment she remained silent.

'But . . .' He was strangely, unnervingly hesitant now, and Kate found she was holding her breath. Intuitively, she knew suddenly that she did not really want to hear what Philip was about to say.

He reached across the table and took her hands in his. 'My daughter died three weeks ago. She suffered greatly during the final weeks and it has been a dreadful time for the whole family. Grace is distraught and needs me to be with her . . .'

How cruel it was, Kate thought, that Philip believed he had lost his only child, when in truth, he now had another. But she could not tell him now. Enough time when he had grieved for Lizzie and his wife was strong again. Oh yes, Kate promised him silently. One day you'll know you have an adorable, perfect daughter. One day, when the time is right and you can rejoice whole-heartedly, I will tell you.

'Poor Grace,' she heard him saying, dragging her wandering thoughts back to the present, 'after being so strong all these years while caring for Lizzie, she's gone to pieces now.'

Now Kate knew what it felt like to be a mother, she

spared a compassionate thought for the unknown woman who was Philip's wife.

She squeezed his hands and whispered, 'Philip – I'm so sorry.'

'You do understand.' His blue eyes, clouded with misery, searched her face. 'I can't bear the thought that I might lose you, but I must stay with Grace for a while.'

'Of course I understand. I told you when you left, I would be waiting. It's just going to be a little longer, that's all.' Her words were brave, but inside her something died. Would he ever come back to her?

As if reading her thoughts, he said urgently, 'One day, we'll be together. I promise you, Kate.'

He was a man of honour who was compelled, at this moment, to put duty before his own happiness; yet she knew he would not make such a promise lightly. She knew he truly believed he would be able to keep his pledge.

As they walked back towards the station, he said again, 'You never did say why you're not in uniform.'

Kate's heart hammered. 'Oh, I – er – thought it might be less conspicuous for you. Me being', her voice broke a little, 'a lowly corporal meeting a Group Captain.' And when he said, 'That was thoughtful of you, darling,' she hated her lie all the more.

'I'll write to you,' he said suddenly.

'Oh er, yes, c-could you send the letters to my relatives in Lincoln? I'll give you their address.' She felt her cheeks grow hot as he glanced down at her.

'Of course, if you'd rather.'

'Only your letter took several days to reach me and – and I never did get the other two you mentioned. Besides . . .' I might as well make it convincing now I've started, she told herself. 'There are too many prying eyes at the camp . . .'

'That's true. You can write to me, though, at my new station. There's no problem my end.'

When they parted two hours later on the platform, he said, 'We'll try to meet again . . .'

For a moment she clung to him and then, tears blinding her, she turned away and stumbled on to the train. As it pulled away, Kate sat huddled in the corner of the carriage, unable to bring herself to wave goodbye to him.

Forty-Two

Every day, Kate watched for the postman until even Mrs Godfrey remarked upon it. 'Are you expecting a letter, dear?'

'No . . . yes . . .' Kate sighed. 'Not really.'

'Still hoping to hear from your mam?' Mrs Godfrey asked gently.

Kate sighed heavily and forced a wry smile.

Mrs Godfrey shook her head. 'I really don't know what the woman can be thinking of. I'm sorry, Kate. I know she's your mother, but honestly . . .'

Kate shrugged her shoulders in sad agreement. She could not tell even the kindly Mrs Godfrey everything that was locked away in her heart. She seemed to have lost everyone; Danny, Philip, and even her family at Fleethaven Point. If asked, she would have been hard-pressed to say which loss hurt the most.

The following day, they heard footsteps coming down the passage at the side of the house to the back door.

'Now, who can that be, just as we're sitting down to dinner?' Mrs Godfrey grumbled, but without real rancour as she, more than anyone else in the house, loved visitors to call and relieve the monotony of her day.

The latch on the back gate clicked and through the living-room window which looked out over the back yard, they saw Jonathan and Rosie appear.

Kate gave a squeal of delight and rushed to open the door. 'Dad – and Rosie!'

There was much hugging and kissing and cooing over the baby before Kate could bring herself to ask the two questions uppermost in her mind. 'How's me mam?' and 'Is there any news of Danny?'

In answer to the first question, Jonathan pursed his mouth and shook his head, apology in his eyes. 'Kate dear, I've tried everything I can think of, but she won't budge. I begged her to come today but she refused. Your grandfather would have come, but he's chesty this winter and travelling is so uncertain just now.'

Kate nodded. 'I understand. I've taken some photographs of Ella with the camera he gave me. I'll sort out one or two for you to take back.'

'He'd like that, and maybe if your mother sees a picture of her grand-daughter . . .'

Kate forced a smile. 'Maybe, Dad, maybe,' but her tone did not hold much hope.

It was then she asked, 'And Danny? Have you heard anything?'

Rosie's mouth quivered and her eyes filled with easy tears. 'Not a word, Kate. He must – be . . .'

'No!' The rebuttal came out sharper than she intended. 'No, Rosie, don't say that. Don't even think it!'

Kate picked up the baby. 'Come upstairs with us, Rosie, while I change her.'

Leaving Jonathan chatting to his mother, Kate and Rosie went upstairs to the large bedroom which Kate shared with her child.

'Are you really happy here, Kate?'

'As happy as I can be, Rosie,' Kate said honestly, 'in the

circumstances. The Godfreys have been wonderful. I don't know what I'd have done without them.'

Rosie bit her lip. 'We all feel bad about ya mam's attitude.' She giggled. 'Did ya know Danny's mam went and had a big row with her? You should have seen 'em, standing toe to toe in the yard of Brumbys' Farm going at each other hammer and tongs. Just words, like, I don't mean it got to fisticuffs.'

'Thank goodness for that,' Kate said, feeling once more the stinging slap on her cheek. 'Even so, I'm sorry they had a quarrel over me. I didn't want to be the cause of more resentment between them. There's enough already!'

Rosie shrugged. 'I reckon they both enjoyed it really. Danny's mam came back her eyes sparkling and her cheeks red. I think they both got a lot of things off their chests they've been harbouring for years. Mebbe they'll start speaking to each other now.'

Kate laughed and said wryly, 'I shouldn't hold your breath waiting for that to happen, Rosie!'

Rosie smiled. 'No, mebbe you're right.' Then her smile faded. 'I seem to spend me life waiting.'

'I know, love, I know.'

Rosie sat down on Kate's bed watching the baby kicking in her high-sided cot. 'Poor Danny. He's got a son he's never seen and now a niece he doesn't even know about.'

Kate sat beside her, putting her arm around the girl. Rosie leaned her head against Kate's shoulder, drawing strength. Her action reminded Kate sharply of their childhood.

'You must believe he's still alive, Rosie. I do,' she said firmly.

'I'll try, Kate. But if he isn't – I really don't know how I'm going to live out the rest of my life without him.'

Silently, Kate thought, 'I know just how you feel, Rosie.'

*

The weeks of winter turned into spring. Despite the deprivations of war, Ella thrived and the little terraced house was a haven for Kate. She received letters frequently from her stepfather with loving messages from her grandfather. But no word came from her mother or from her sister, Lilian.

There was still no news of Danny, and no more letters from Philip either.

Then suddenly, one morning while she was busy sewing, she heard Mrs Godfrey's voice raised in alarm. 'Kate, Kate, come quick . . .'

Fearful that something was wrong with either the old lady or Ella, Kate hurried through to the back room to find Mrs Godfrey waving a yellow envelope at her. 'It's one of those dreadful telegrams. It's addressed to you and the lad's waiting for a reply.'

With trembling fingers, Kate tore open the thin envelope and unfolded the single sheet of paper. There was no name or address of the sender and the message just said, '*Meet me Grantham station. Thursday the twenty-fifth.*'

Kate gasped. Philip. It must be from Philip. He wanted to see her again. He was trying to keep the promise he had made to her.

'Well, what is it?' Mrs Godfrey asked.

'It's nothing – I mean, it's not bad news . . .' She went to the back door to tell the boy that there was no reply. Closing the back door, her eyes still on the piece of paper in her hand she walked back into the room to stand uncertainly beside Mrs Godfrey's sofa.

'Who's it from, then?'

'I – it doesn't say . . .' Kate hesitated. This time she had no choice but to take Mrs Godfrey partially into her confidence. 'I – I think it's from Ella's father.'

'Oh!'

'He – wants me to meet him – in Grantham, the day after tomorrow.'

'Do you want to go?'

Kate met the older woman's gaze and nodded, knowing her eyes were shining her answer.

'Then go, my dear. I can mind Ella until Peg gets home from work. She can put her to bed.'

'Are you sure?' Kate asked diffidently.

'Of course I am. The little one's taken well to the bottle and it's time you had a day out and I'm sure ...' the older woman wriggled her shoulders as if she too shared Kate's excitement, ' ... you'd like to see your young man again.'

Deeply moved by the woman's understanding, Kate bent and kissed the wrinkled cheek. 'Oh, you're so good to me!'

The old lady flapped her hand and shooed Kate back to her sewing, but the pink tinge on her face told Kate she was touched by the younger woman's display of affection.

She was standing, huddled into her thick coat, on the draughty station at Grantham staring up the track – just waiting.

'Wouldn't you be better in the waiting room, Miss?' a porter – only a young boy – asked.

'What? Oh, no – no thanks. His ... The train should be here in a minute. I don't want to miss it.'

The young boy nodded knowingly. 'Your feller coming home on leave, is he, Miss?'

She nodded. She didn't want to go into explanations.

'We get a lot of reunions and partin's on this station. Breaks ya heart sometimes, miss. Specially when they're leavin'. Might never come back again, see.'

Kate swallowed the lump in her throat as she remembered the last time she had seen Danny; she had not thought then that it might be the last time she would see him. Yet when she had left Philip on this very platform only a few weeks ago, she had been only too aware that they could be parting for ever. She should have trusted him, she castigated herself, she should have had more faith in his love for her.

'When's the next train due in from the north?' she asked.

The boy shrugged his shoulders. 'Difficult to say. There should be one in about an hour. Why don't you wait in the waiting room, Miss. It'd be warmer in there.'

'I'm fine – really. To tell you the truth, I can't settle to sit down.'

A train came drew in from the south and passengers spilled on to the opposite platform. Kate hardly glanced across the tracks, her gaze intent on the empty track curving northwards out of the station. Behind her there came the clatter of footsteps as passengers from the train made their way over the tracks and on to the platform where she was waiting and towards the main exit. There was laughter and chatter as people greeted each other. Then, with a great deal of hissing and puthering smoke, the train pulled out of the station again to continue its journey. The noises faded and there was silence once more.

She heard her name spoken softly. 'Kate?' and again, 'Katie.'

For a fleeting moment, she felt devastated; that was not Philip's voice. He had not come.

But in the next instant her heart soared. She knew that voice – oh, how well she knew that voice! Hardly daring to believe it, she turned around slowly to stare at the man limping towards her, muffled in an RAF greatcoat; a short, stocky man, his black hair ruffled by the breeze . . .

As tears filled her eyes, his image blurred and wavered like a mirage so that for a moment she didn't know if what she was seeing was real. She reached out and felt him grasp her hands in his and then – she knew he was real.

'Danny!' she gasped, and the tears spilled down her cheeks. 'Oh, thank God you're safe!'

Their questions were tumbling over each other until he said, 'Come on, let's find somewhere warm and a cup o' tea.'

Once in the tea-room, sitting opposite each other over the small table, cocooned from the other travellers in their own little space, they began to talk.

'Are you really all right? Why are you limping? What happened?' her questions came again.

Danny winked at her and grinned widely. 'I'm fine, honest. Oh, me leg's bad though, but that's all. That's why I've been repatriated.'

'Repatriated? Were – were you captured then?'

'We'd reached the target, dropped our bombs and were banking away when we were hit. The pilot nursed the kite for several miles but I think we all knew we couldn't make it back home. Anyway, he was doin' his best to get as near to the coast as he could when one of the engines caught fire. He kept flying to give us all time to bale out, but I couldn't get to me 'chute . . .'

Kate felt herself going hot at the thought; she well knew that the rear-gunner could not wear his parachute in the confines of his turret.

'Well, there I was swivelling the turret so I could get out and take me chances by jumping just before the 'plane crashed. And do you know what happened? The whole rear turret fell off! And guess what?'

Wordlessly, Kate shook her head.

'It landed in a tree! I smashed me leg up badly, and because I tried to evade capture for two days, I didn't get proper medical attention. It'll never be right again.'

'But you're alive,' Kate said.

Danny pulled a face. 'If that tree hadn't been there, I wouldn't be.'

'Then thank goodness it was.'

They sat in silence for a moment, then she asked, 'How come they've let you go?'

'The leg won't mend properly. They know I'll be no good for any more fighting so . . . here I am. Mind you, I made 'em think me leg was a lot worse than it is. Reckon I deserve a medal for me acting!'

'Oh Danny.' She laughed and then wanted to know, 'How did you get back?'

'Through Sweden.'

There was another pause while they just sat looking at each other across the table, drinking in the sight of each other.

Then he asked gently. 'How've you been, Kate? Why aren't you in uniform? Aren't you in the WAAFs any more?'

She circled the cup with her hands and glanced down at it. She shook her head. 'No. I – had to leave.'

'*Had* to leave? Why?'

'I – got pregnant.'

'Pregnant!' he burst out, so loudly that one or two people nearby looked across. Some smiled, thinking that a young husband was hearing the joyous news for the first time; others curious in case there was a shotgun wedding about to be arranged.

'Sssh,' she hissed.

'Shush be damned! Who is it? I'll bloody kill him!'

'Danny – don't. It's not like that. Just calm down – and listen.'

'Well,' he said, but his tone was not encouraging, 'I'm listening.'

'I've grown up a lot since – well – since I last saw you . . .'

His mouth was tight as if he would like to refute that

444

particular statement, but he held back any retort and let her continue. 'There was someone on our station – don't ask me who 'cos I'm not going to tell you. We had an affair. I loved him, Danny. Not in the same way I once loved you, but . . .'

She saw his eyes soften as if the memory of their young, innocent love still hurt him too.

' . . . but I did love him – I still do.'

'Why don't you get married then?'

'He – he'd already gone when I found I was pregnant.'

'Gone? Do you mean – he was killed?' Danny asked gently now and reached across the table to take her hand.

Kate shook her head. 'No – no, he's already married.'

'Oh, Kate.' There was reproach and yet sympathy too in his tone.

Her head jerked up. 'I know you must think badly of me. But I'm not sorry. I have a beautiful baby girl whom I love dearly and things – well – they're working out.'

'But you're not living at home, are you?'

'No – and that reminds me; was it you sent that telegram?'

''Course it was. Who did you think it was from?'

She smiled. 'I – I thought it was from – Ella's father. You didn't put a name on it.'

Now he looked suddenly boyishly self-conscious. 'I thought you'd know who it was from. 'Course I didn't know about the other bloke in your life, now did I?' He was teasing her now and the brief anger had gone. 'I sent one to – to Rosie too, so they'll know I'm on me way home.' His embarrassment deepened. 'But I wanted to see you first. After all, Rosie's got me for the rest of me life . . .' His voice was a hoarse whisper and Kate knew then that deep down, he still felt about her as he always had, but knew also that life had to go on. They could not cling morbidly to the past and their smashed childhood dreams. He squeezed her hand tightly and she returned the gesture. They sat holding hands across the table.

'So – how did you find out where I was?' she prompted.

'Mavis. As soon as I landed in England, I rang Suddaby. Some stuck-up woman on the switchboard said you weren't there anymore, but that's all she would say. So I rang back again a bit later and got hold of Mavis. She told me you were staying with the Godfreys.' He grinned. 'But that's all *she* would tell me. You've got some very loyal friends.'

'Good old Mavis,' Kate murmured and inside she was bubbling with laughter to think just how confused Mavis would be feeling now.

'Why aren't you at home, then?'

'Me mam won't have anything to do with me now – because of the baby.'

'Huh!' Danny grunted expressively. 'I might have known.'

Kate sighed. 'Oh, it's not that simple. Me grandad explained a lot of things to me. I'll tell you all about it sometime. Not now, but sometime.'

'But you're all right with the Godfreys? You're happy there?' She nodded, but he was not convinced. 'You sure? I can't imagine you living in a city for ever.'

'Oh, I'm getting more used to it. I take the baby out in the pram to the Arboretum and up the hill to the cathedral.' She smiled. 'I love that cathedral – I really do. And sometimes we get right out of the city into the countryside. Besides, I'm so lucky to be able to work from Mrs Godfrey's front room. What I'd have done without her and Peg, I don't know.'

He nodded and was thoughtful for a moment. Then he looked up. 'What do you call her?'

'Who?'

'Ya baby?'

'Oh,' Now it was Kate's turn to be embarrassed. 'I hope you don't mind – I called her Danielle.'

He stared at her for a moment and then threw back his head and laughed. 'You little devil! That'll set the tongues wagging again.'

'You're not angry, are you?'

'No, 'course I'm not. I'm tickled pink. I'll come over and see her as soon as I can . . .' He seemed reluctant to speak of his home, of Rosie and their child. But then she realized, he would think they were still enemies.

People were beginning to leave the tea-room and Danny glanced up at the clock. 'Me train'll be leaving in a minute. Come to the platform with me, will ya? How are you getting back to Lincoln?'

'I can get a train in about half an hour, I think.'

On the platform, he kissed her cheek. 'Thanks for coming – even if you did think it was some other feller!'

'I'm so very thankful it was you.' If fate could only allow one of the men in her life to come back, she thought, then it had to be Danny. She touched his face gently with her fingertips. 'Go home, Danny. Go home to Rosie – and your son.'

The astonished look on his face was almost comical. She nodded in answer to his unspoken question. 'When you were missing – we helped each other, supported each other. I was there when Robbie was born. Rosie and I, we – got close again.'

He put his arms around her, pulling her close and resting his cheek against her hair. 'Thank you,' he said simply.

They stood, just holding each other, then he asked softly, 'What's he like, this son of mine?'

'He's got brown eyes and black hair, just like his father.' Her voice broke a little as she added, 'He'll break a few hearts too . . .'

His arms tightened about her momentarily and then a whistle sounded shrilly, reverberating down the platform. There was a sudden flurry of activity all around them. Last-minute travellers dashed on to the platform and jumped aboard. Lovers tore themselves apart, reaching out with extended fingers, touching until the very last moment.

Reluctantly, Danny drew back and held her from him at arm's length. For a long moment he looked deep into her eyes. 'Take care of yourself, Katie Hilton. And your little lass. If you ever – ever need me, you know where I am.'

She nodded, not trusting herself to speak. His words from their childhood echoed down the years: 'I'll always care for you, Katie Hilton, dun't ever forget that'.

His arms came fiercely around her once more and for a timeless moment, she clung to him. Then he turned away and climbed aboard the train, pulling the door to behind him with a thud. He pushed down the window and leaned out. As the train pulled away, he was still waving.

'God bless and keep you,' she whispered, as his face became smaller and smaller until she could no longer see it through the blur of her tears. She watched until the train was out of sight and then turned and walked across the empty platform, her footsteps echoing eerily in the stillness.

Hunching her shoulders and hugging her coat around her, she plunged her hands deep into her pockets and, once more, she felt the wrinkled surface of the whelk shell.

And remembering, she smiled.

Plough the Furrow

The first book in the
Lincolnshire Fleethaven trilogy

Lincolnshire, 1910. Shunned by her own family, Esther Everatt walks through the night to Sam Brumby's farm, seeking the chance to earn her keep. Reluctantly, the old man takes her on.

Able to work alongside any man, Esther soon earns Sam's grudging respect and affection, and at last feels she has found a home she can call her own. But her peace and security are cruelly shattered when old Sam dies. As a woman, she has no right to inherit the lease on the farm.

Believing her passion lies solely with the land, Esther prepares to risk everything to secure her future, seeking marriage with a local farmhand. But as the First World War arrives to dash the hopes of a generation, Esther begins to discover that it is only the truest love that can survive the passing of the seasons . . .

Reap the Harvest

The third book in the
Lincolnshire Fleethaven trilogy

Following the disastrous floods of 1953, Ella Hilton finds
herself living at Brumbys' Farm with her grandmother Esther
and is soon made acutely aware of the mysteries surrounding
her family's past.

As Ella grows up and falls in love, the story of three generations of women – Esther, Kate and Ella – comes full circle and
history seems destined to repeat itself.

In the concluding part of this glorious Lincolnshire trilogy,
Margaret Dickinson brings the 1950s vividly to life in a story
of secrets and love, buried under years of pride and misunderstanding.

Bello:
hidden talent
rediscovered

Bello is a digital-only imprint of
Pan Macmillan, established to breathe new
life into previously published, classic books.

At Bello we believe in the timeless power
of the imagination, of a good story, narrative
and entertainment and we want to use digital
technology to ensure that many more readers
can enjoy these books into the future.

Our available books include
Brenda Jagger's *Barforth Family* saga; and
Janet Tanner's *Hillsbridge Trilogy*.

For more information,
and to sign up for regular updates visit:
www.panmacmillan.com/bellonews

FOR MORE ON

MARGARET DICKINSON

sign up to receive our

SAGA NEWSLETTER

Packed with **features, competitions, authors'
and readers' letters** and **news of exclusive events**,
it's a 'must-read' for every Margaret Dickinson fan!

Simply fill in your details below and tick to confirm that you would
like to receive saga-related news and promotions and return to us at
Pan Macmillan, Saga Newsletter, 20 New Wharf Road, London, NI 9RR.

NAME _____

ADDRESS _____

_____

_____ POSTCODE _____

EMAIL _____

☐ *I would like to receive saga-related news and promotions (please tick)*

*You can unsubscribe at any time in writing or through our website where you can also see
our privacy policy which explains how we will store and use your data.*